The Unexplained Mysteries of The World

By David Pietras

1 2 3 4 5 6 7 8 9 10 13

ISBN-13:
978-1511405867

ISBN-10:
1511405864

Part I
Cryptozoology

The Beast of Gevaudan Caused Panic and Controversy
The Mothman Mysteries
Legends of Spring Heeled Jack
Bigfoot
Loch Ness Monster Mysteries
Mysteries of Chupacabra
The Grinning Man
Have the Earliest Animal Footprints Been Discovered?
Phoenix from the Ashes
Giant Skeletons

Part II
Mysterious Places

Stonehenge
Mexico's Zone of Silence
The Legend of Morrow Road
Skinwalker Ranch
The Kensington Runestone
A Terrifying Legend is real?
The Cursed Rocks of Hawaii
The Legendary Land of Lyonesse
Parallel Universes — Thoughts to Ponder
The Mysteries of The Bermuda Triangle
Did the Garden of Eden Really Exist?

Part III
Ancient Mysteries

Alien Artifacts ~ Writings
Aotearoa Mythology: The Maui Cycle
The Unexplained Mysteries of the Baghdad Battery

Part IV
Ghosts and Hauntings

Part V
Psychics and Mediums

Part VI
UFOs and ALIENS

Part VII
MYSTERIOUS EVENTS

Mysteries of the Sliding Rocks
Marfa Lights
Mysteries of Cannibalism
The Little Ice Age and the Year without summer
What happened at Hanging Rock?
The Unexplained Mysteries of Dark Matter
The Knights Templar Curse and Friday the 13th
Is Planet X Really on Its Way Here?
The Unexplained Mysteries of Cattle Mutilations
Astronomers vs. Astrologers
The Unexplained Mysteries of the Miracles of Lourdes
The Unsolved Mystery of Jeannie Saffin
The Shroud of Turin

Prologue

What *is* paranormal?

We are often asked, "What exactly does paranormal mean?" The term paranormal is used to describe a wide variety of activity and phenomena. According to the Journal of Parapsychology (a quarterly publication devoted primarily to the original publication of experimental results and other research findings as published by the Parapsychological Association), the term paranormal describes "any phenomenon that in one or more respects exceeds the limits of what is deemed physically possible according to current scientific assumptions." The actual word is derived from the Latin use of the prefix Para meaning "outside or beyond" what is considered normal.

Many people associate the term paranormal as only dealing with hauntings and ghosts. However, the paranormal also includes subjects considered to be outside the scope of parapsychology including UFOs, cryptozoology, telepathy, ESP, faith healing, clairvoyance, and many other subjects.

An anomalous phenomenon is an observed incident or experience for which there seems to be no agreeable scientific explanation. Because such observations do not easily fit into how many view our reality, these instances can be (and usually are) the subject of controversy.

Since paranormal phenomena is not generally accepted as real by traditional scientists, most of these ideas and theories about hard-to-reproduce anomalies are considered pseudoscientific (not a real science), partly because science needs evidence to be reproducible in a controlled environment.

Some anomalies eventually get a scientific explanation, losing their status as unexplained phenomena. For example, while the idea of stones falling from the sky was once considered anomalous, meteorites are now acknowledged and generally well understood.

Ghosts

So what exactly is a ghost? Ghosts are phenomena which have several possible definitions:

*The spirit or soul of a person who has died, which haunts a place which was of emotional significance to that person when living.

*The personality of a person after his or her own death which is not directly tied to the soul or spirit. A type of psychic memory imprint.

*The character or memory of some being or thing which has died or, if it was never alive, has been somehow destroyed or dissembled, which nevertheless remains existent (and sometimes detectable) in a semi-corporeal form.

*An overlapping of parallel worlds into our own in which we can see, hear, feel, or occasionally interact with a person or thing that lives or exists in that parallel.

While some individuals accept ghosts as a reality, many others are skeptical of the existence of such. Much of the scientific community believes that ghosts, as well as other supernatural and paranormal entities, do not exist. Skeptics often explain ghost sightings with the principle of Occam's razor which basically states that the explanation of any phenomenon should make as few assumptions as possible. In short, when given two equally valid explanations for a phenomenon, one should embrace the less complicated formulation. Some examples of such would be:

*Ghosts are often associated with a chilling sensation, but a natural response to fear is hair rising, which can be mistaken for a chill.

*Peripheral vision is very sensitive to motion, but does not contain much color or the ability to sharply distinguish shapes. Any random motion outside the focused view can create a strong illusion of an eerie figure.

*Sound waves with frequencies lower than 20 hertz are called infrasound and are normally inaudible, but British scientists Richard Lord and Richard Wiseman have concluded that infrasound can cause humans to feel a "presence" in the room, or unexplained feelings of anxiety or dread.

Psychological factors may also relate to ghost sightings. Many people exaggerate their own perceptions, either when visiting a place they believe to be haunted, or when visiting a site which they know unpleasant historical events have occurred. Certain images such as paintings and movies might "program" a person to automatically associate a certain structure or area with ghosts. Also, the psychological phenomenon of pareidolia (seeing recognizable shapes and patterns in everyday objects i.e.: face of Mars, Rorschach inkblots) may cause people to perceive human-like faces or figures in the otherwise mundane surroundings of their environments, particularly in conditions where vision is partly obscured, as in a dark corridor or at night. Skeptics also apply this theory to EVP's (when anomalous voices, often purported to be of supernatural origin, are reportedly heard on audio recordings.)

Cryptozoology
Cryptozoology is the study of animals that are rumored to exist, but for which conclusive proof is still missing. Scientists have demonstrated that some creatures of mythology, legend or local folklore were rooted in real animals or phenomena. Thus, cryptozoologists hold that people should be open to the possibility that many more such animals exist. In the early days of western exploration of the world, many native tales of unknown animals were initially dismissed as superstition by western scientists, but were later proven to have a real basis in biological fact. Cryptozoological supporters have noted that many unfamiliar animals, when first reported, were considered hoaxes, delusions, or

misidentifications. The Platypus, Giant Squid, Mountain Gorilla, Grizzly-polar bear hybrid, and Komodo dragon are a few such creatures.

Paranormal phenomena

A Paranormal phenomenon is a term that has been used to describe previously unknown forces which at first appeared to be paranormal and were later verified scientifically. The name is derived from the Greek peri, meaning "in the vicinity of". While paranormal phenomena remains scientifically questionable ("beyond the range of normal experience or scientific explanation"), paranormal phenomena can eventually be shown to be "skeptic-approved".

One significant modern example of a paranormal phenomenon is electromagnetic fields (EMFs). At one time EMFs were debatable from a scientific perspective but later were proven to be real and is currently accepted by scientific and medical communities.

PLACE MEMORIES

Some hauntings have an eerie resemblance to life, where apparitions are observed performing activities that are common to living people such as walking around a home or grocery store, or even working. Some people describe these hauntings in several ways. The first is that the entity is simply doing something that he/she did frequently in life. The second assumes that the concept of time-space continuum is real and that sometimes two time frames overlap. The third explanation is referred to as a "place memory", which is like a recording of a past event that has imprinted itself on the environment. These are also called residual hauntings and recordings. Images and sounds are impressed upon a place and later replayed in a phenomenon that is similar to watching a loop of a movie film. And despite what you may think, these experiences are not acted out by just the departed. It is very possible to experience witnessing yourself in one of these "memories." This is known as the doppelganger effect.

Part I
Cryptozoology

The Beast of Gevaudan

France experienced a panic in the 1760s when there were a numerous deaths associated to animal attacks credited to a mythical creature known as the Beast of Gevaudan.

Folklore has distorted the facts so much that what the animal really looked like is not determinable. Some locals of the former Gevaudan area think that it was a type of werewolf or shape shifting sorcerer that became the creature so he could eat flesh.

Researchers of the beast of Gevaudan believe that there were a minimum of two creatures which can be credited to the wide variations of descriptions. That is providing that the people were not so panicked that they incorporated figments of their imagination into the descriptions. Things such as the fur coloration and size of the Beast varied greatly.

The beast was said to have patches that were white and black in color without any red and at other times it did not have any of these colors in its fur. There are numerous variations of what the creature looked like although the consistent descriptions can be used to gain an idea of what the Gevaudan beast looked like.

The beast of Gevaudan that was reported by several witnesses in France was supposedly four times larger than a horse resembling a panther, wolf, bear and hyena combination. Large teeth lined the animal's snout that resembled a pig or wolf depending on who provided the description. The beast had a strong, long neck and a tail that was described as long, thick and strong that it utilized like a weapon to knock down victims. People reported that the tail of the beast hit them with incredible force. The feet were either claws, hoof tipped digits or cloven hooves depending on the witness.

Witness reported that the Beast of Gevaudan tore the throat out of its victims to kill them.
There were several people that formed a group and went out to hunt the animal which was usually solitary or roamed with a smaller female creature that did not attack.

The beast of Gevaudan was witnessed performing its first attack on the 1st of June during 1764 when a woman spotted a large creature charge at her only to be scared off by bulls. 14-year old Jeanne Boulet was the first actual victim when she was killed on the 30th of June close to the Les Hubacs village close to Langogne where the first would be victim had escaped. Reportedly the beast preferred to attack people instead of animals since it reportedly attacked people in the same field as cattle on numerous occasions.

The sightings of the beast of Gevaudan have been credited to wolf attacks being exaggerated and God's punishment. Other explanations are that domestic dogs breed with wild wolfs because of the coloration and size. Crypto zoologists are having trouble coming up with an answer that satisfies curiosity of what the beast was or if there was an actual beast of Gevaudan due to the folklore that had added to its incredible legend.

The Mothman Mysteries

It's hard to pin down exactly when the legend of Mothman begins.

Every part of the U.S. has its local monster. The Pacific Northwest has its famous Bigfoot. The Jersey Devil prowls the New Jersey Pine Barrens. In the depths of Vermont's Lake Champlain lurks a serpentine creature called Champ. And West Virginia is stalked by a creature known only as Mothman.

The best documented sighting was on November 15, 1966, but there were several alleged sightings before that going back to the early 1960s, with West Virginians claiming to have seen something that resembled "an angel," or at least a winged human being. On November 12, 1966, five gravediggers working near Clendenin, West Virginia, said they had seen "a brown human being" flying above the trees for over a minute before it went out of sight.

A few days later, on November 15, two couples, Roger and Linda Scarberry and Steve and Mary Mallette, were driving past an abandoned World War II explosives plant just north of Point Pleasant, West Virginia, when they noticed two red lights in the shadows of the buildings.

Approaching, they discovered that the lights were the eyes, "like automobile reflectors" as Linda Scarberry later described them, of a huge creature. Roger Scarberry said that it was "shaped like a man, but bigger.... maybe six and a half or seven feet tall. And it had big wings folded against its back." Roger Scarberry, who was driving, panicked and drove away at "over 100 miles an hour," but the creature unfolded its wings and flew after them, matching their speed without apparent effort, making a squeaking sound "like a big mouse," according to Mary Mallette. However, it finally abandoned the chase, and the couples drove into town and told their story to deputy sheriff Millard Halstead, who returned with them to the site but found nothing.

They did notice that a dead dog by the side of the road, which they had noticed during the escape, had disappeared by the time of their return.

The next night, several townspeople searched the area around the plant for signs of the creature, which had been dubbed "Mothman" by the local press, but found nothing. However, the same night, Ralph Thomas and his wife, who lived near the explosives plant, were entertaining guests when they saw a "big gray thing" with "terrible, glowing red eyes" rise up from the ground. Raymond Wamsley, one of the guests, called the police while the creature walked onto the porch of the Thomas home and peered through the window. Mrs. Marcella Bennett, another one of the visitors, said it made a sound like "a woman screaming."

After that, sightings came frequently through the rest of 1966 into 1967. Mothman was seen standing, taking off, or flying. It occasionally was reported to chase cars. Accounts regularly mentioned its glowing red eyes and the high-pitched noises it made. A rash of paranormal phenomena was also reported in the area, including UFO sightings, mysteriously mutilated animals, "Men in Black," and poltergeist activity. Mothman's appearances came less and less often as 1967 went on.

On December 15, 1967, the Silver Bridge, which crossed the Ohio River, collapsed during rush hour, killing 46. After that, Mothman was seen only rarely, although sightings are still occasionally reported in the area. Naturally, there are rumors that Mothman had something to do with the collapse, but these have never been substantiated.

The mystery of who, or what, Mothman is has never been solved. John A. Keel, a paranormal investigator, wrote the best-known book on the subject, The Mothman Prophecies, in which he argued for a supernatural explanation, connecting Mothman with other unexplained events in the area. Others dismiss Mothman as a hoax, or a misidentified large bird, or a case of mass hysteria. Whatever it really is, a statue of Mothman now stands in Point Pleasant, and the area hosts a Mothman Festival every September.

Legends of Spring Heeled Jack

Reports of his existence date back to the 19th century.

One very creepy criminal case that has never been solved concerns Spring Heeled Jack. For at least 150 years, there were many alleged, frightening experiences with this strange creature, and to this day, no one knows just who—or what—he was exactly. Of course most would write him off as being nothing more than a folktale, but people have been frightened of him nonetheless.

So what do the legends say about Spring Heeled Jack? For starters, it's said that he was "capable of leaping very high, as if he were bouncing on springs." He allegedly wore a helmet and very tight clothing. He also apparently had claws, and his skin was described as being "oily" and his eyes were red, and some witnesses claimed to have seen him "exhale blue flame." At least two witnesses claim that he could speak in clear English. He also had a very strange laugh.

While this sounds nothing more than a myth or an urban legend, there was a dark, disturbing side to this story as well—he apparently was capable of sexual assaulting young girls. His first sighting was around London in October of 1837, when he attacked a servant girl named Mary

Stevens. Thankfully, her screams were overheard by others nearby, and they managed to save her. The creature then fled and "disappeared". Assuming that this incident was only a myth, it was strange coming from the Victorian period. Tales and folklore those days usually aren't so dark and sexual.

Shortly after this alleged incident, many more girls claimed to have been attacked by Spring Heeled Jack. Some girls only claimed that he "hit" them. Men claimed to have seen him too.
 Mass hysteria formed throughout England, and most were certain that Spring Heeled jack was an incarnation of the Devil, if not the Devil himself.

In 1870, he was spotted by a group of soldiers. They shot at him, but he "disappeared" for a second and then zoomed right in front of one of the soldiers, whom he then slapped. He then bounced off and was not seen again until later in the year when a mob spotted him and shot him. Apparently, the bullets only "bounced off" of him, and he leapt away once again.

In 1953, 120 years after he was first spotted in London, he somehow managed to make it to Texas. If not him, it was at least another creature resembling him. Three witnesses near an apartment complex described seeing a creature wearing "a long black cape," "tight pants," and "boots." Could he have "leapt" all the way to Texas? Or were there more Spring Heeled Jacks out there?

The last known Spring Heeled Jack sighting was back in England 31 years later. In 1985, a salesman in England claimed to have seen him leaping around as usual, while wearing his tight clothing. The creature, of course, stopped and slapped the man, as it was his custom.

Spring Heeled Jack has not been seen since, and if he has, witnesses are probably too weirded out to say anything. Whoever he was/is, he's one truly odd creature. Some say he could've been a crazy, but otherwise ordinary, human man. Perhaps mass hysteria caused witnesses to see things that didn't really happen (such as his unnatural leaping).

Bigfoot

Bigfoot has been sighted throughout the United States, from the 16th Century to present. The first reported sightings were by Native Americans. He was called numerous names by different Indian tribes, "sasquatch" was only one of over 50 different Indian names given to the creature. This creature looks more like a hairy man than an ape or monkey. It is mostly reported as being between 6 - 8 feet tall, but has been sighted with a smaller female and even offspring, as small as human children. The larger, adult male of the species is rugged, and built very muscular. Its shoulders are wide, and it has very little neck area. It has short brown to black hair covering its body, with longer hair on the head. Most reports have the creature's eyes glowing or shining red in the dark when reflected by a flashlight or some other light source.

Most folks report no odor when they have encountered Bigfoot, but the others that do, have started showing a pattern of a strange anomaly, the creature can project or discharge a scent, at will, not like a skunk, by spraying, but by some other means.

People have reported one smell, then suddenly it changes into an entirely different odor. Odors have been described as: rotten flesh, poop, old vomit, out-houses, rotted fish, rotten eggs, or foul and just sickening. Bigfoot seems to make Ape-like grunts and growls, to almost a scream like sound, and others have heard whistles and strange calls.

Indians almost all believe Bigfoot is a non-physical creature. Some Indian tribes mention that they have seen the creature transform into a wolf. Others think that these creatures live in another dimension from the physical plane, but can come here as they desire.

Indians also believe Bigfoot has great psychic abilities, reports of sightings show the creature can be visible to some people, while at the same time remain invisible to others in the same group. There are many reports from non-Indians who saw the creature after a UFO sighting. And others that have searched for, and researched Bigfoot for years are coming to the conclusion that the creature is a spiritual being, because he can appear or disappear at will.

Great Lakes Indians mention that if one is walking in the woods and you hear the sound of a stick being hit against a hollow log or tree, beware, for this area is Sasquatch territory. This seems to be an interesting thing to note, because other non-Indians have even reported this. People have reported that sometimes the stick hitting is loud or thud like, like a large log is being hit against a tree, while at other times it is more like a small stick is being used. Some Bigfoot researchers have reported sightings right after hearing these strange sounds. Besides, the stick hitting, another well documented fact many Bigfoot researchers report is rock throwing. Researchers have had stones thrown at them, and at their vehicles, and there have also been reports from people living in Bigfoot hot spots, of having stones thrown on their roofs and against their homes and cabins.

The creature's episodes of hitting sticks and rock throwing may be the best evidence we have to show that they are spiritual beings. If you research paranormal cases involving 'poltergeist' incidents, you will soon realize that many of the cases involve the throwing or dropping of stones against houses, and on the roofs of the homes where the poltergeist attacks are occurring. In many of the poltergeist cases, the stones being dropped and thrown were the beginning of the infestation, or encounter, just like in the Bigfoot cases.

When it comes to the sticks being hit against logs or trees we have yet another connection to the spiritual world. When I was very young, I remember reading an advertisement in the back of a magazine. The ad was titled something like this: 'Talk to the Spirits with amazing Juju Sticks'. The Juju sticks were cut from some sacred wood and were blessed by a voodoo practitioner. The sticks were hit against a table or some other wooden item, and one could supposedly hear taps or other communication back, from the spirit world.

Loch Ness Monster

The first recorded stories of a water dwelling beast in this region comes from the tales of the "Life of Saint Columbia" by the 7th century writer, Adomnan.

Of all the cryptozoological creatures reported around the world, the lake monster of Loch Ness, Scotland is surely the most well-known and beloved of them all. That a possible prehistoric creature still shares our world in the deep, murky waters of this long lake fuels not only our imaginations but also a vast tourist industry.

The first recorded stories of a water dwelling beast in this region comes from the tales of the "Life of Saint Columbia" by the 7th century writer, Adomnan. The holy man reportedly saved the life of a swimmer from the attack of a "water beast" in the River Ness in the 6th century. Nothing more was heard officially about such a creature again until the early 20th century.

On June 5th of 1933, Margaret Munro said she watched a beast on the shore of the lake for over twenty minutes. She said it had elephant-like skin, a long thin neck with a small head and two short fore-flippers. In late July of 1933 Mr. and Mrs. George Spicer reported a large, unknown creature running across the road in front of them. They said the creature was perhaps 4 feet high and about 25 feet long. It had a long, sinuous neck and disappeared into the Loch that was about 20 feet from the road. The next month, August, and Author Grant claims to have almost collided with the beast with his motorcycle before it ran back into the lake.

After that, reports of sightings of the Loch Ness monster came in sporadically from a multitude of people. Occasional photographs and grainy film of something unusual in the waters of the Loch began to materialize. Probably the most famous, the "Surgeon's Photograph", taken in 1934 endured much publicity both good and bad until a deathbed confession by Christian Spurling debunked it as a model built onto a toy submarine.

Less easily ignored though are some of the sonar readings that have been taken in the lake by modern scientists. Robert Rines managed to take a few underwater photos of what appeared to be a large flipper at the same time as sonar recordings were registering movement by something between 20 and 30 feet in length. Other sonar searches of Loch Ness by different expeditions also recorded various anomalous sonar readings. In 1987 the director of "Operation Deepscan", Darrell Lowrance recorded an echogram of a large object moving near Urquhart Bay at a depth of 600 feet. In conclusion he is quoted as saying, "There's something here that we don't understand, and there's something here that's larger than a fish, maybe some species that hasn't been detected before. I don't know."

Skeptics insist that the causes of all the Loch Ness monster sightings are either, hoaxes and lies, the misidentification of sturgeon, eels, seals, deer, moose, floating logs, or temperature differentials in the water itself. No one has yet to present a body or a live, captured beast and biologists say the lake is incapable of supporting a creature or creatures of the size reported for the Loch Ness monster. They say that even were the ancient dinosaur, plesiosaur, of which descriptions fit the closest, it would take a minimum of ten creatures to maintain a viable community and that the lake could not support or likely hide that many such beasts.

Barring further data to conclusively prove or disprove the existence of the Loch Ness monster, we are left with a continuing mystery and the hope that even in this mundane world, such wonders as "Nessie" can survive in more than just our imaginations.

The Chupacabra

The late 20th century saw the first reports of what has become known as the Chupacabra.

While the legends of some cryptids extend back centuries, others are relative newcomers to human experience and sightings. The first officially reported sighting of this strange beast was in Puerto Rico in 1995. In the midst of a rash of animal deaths to small livestock, Madeleine Tolentino and some friends saw what they described as a being about four feet tall with a large head that had a lipless mouth, fangs and large red eyes. They said the beast had kangaroo-like hind legs, short clawed arms and webbed wings like a bat.

Just a few weeks before this, a number of sheep had been found with only a few puncture wounds to their necks but totally drained of blood. The multitude of animal deaths in the town of Canovanas also displayed small wounds and an absence of blood in the bodies. These deaths, usually occurring among chickens, dogs, pigs, sheep, goats and other small animals was very similar to a number of events that took place around the city of Moca twenty years earlier. At the time it was blamed on a vampire but the sightings of the creature responsible had the beast confirmed and named "El Chupacabra" the goatsucker.

Soon reports of blood-drained animal deaths spread to Mexico and then south from Central to South America and up into the United States, especially the southern regions. Along with the increased numbers of exsanguinated farm animals, fear of this strange and ghastly looking creature spread among the population, especially among rural farm communities.

New witnesses added to the general look of the bipedal, lizard like creature reported from Puerto Rico.

A line of sharp quills down the back of the beast was reported. Others said that Chupacabra had a forked tongue. Finally there were reports of a more dog-like looking creature being seen running from the area of blood-drained corpses. The only good news was that Chupacabra confined its depredations to farm animals. There are no reports of the beast attacking or killing humans.

There have been several bodies brought in for scientists to examine. Several of these bodies were discovered in Texas. DNA analysis has stated the beasts in question were mange ridden grey foxes and mutated coyotes. One body, provided by Reggie Lagow of Coleman, Texas, was described by him as being a mix of hairless dog, rat and kangaroo. He gave the body to Texas Parks and Wildlife officers for identification but it swiftly disappeared without a further trace.

Speculations on the actuality and origins of Chupacabra are many. There are those who insist this blood drinking creature is an extraterrestrial beast that has been let loose on our planet. Some conspiracy theorists claim it must be the result of genetic experiments gone wrong and escaped from secret government labs. Whatever the truth behind the legend of the Chupacabra, none seem to have ever been photographed alive.

For the most part the bodies that have been found have been identified as mundane, if abnormal, creatures. As a contemporary legend, the belief in Chupacabra has grown to worldwide proportions and is not slowing down for lack of proof.

The Grinning Man

The Grinning Man is a name given to a mysterious creature that has been reported in various areas over the last century. He usually appears around the time of UFO sightings.

He is believed to either be an alien or some other type of unknown creature. If nothing else, he is very creepy and all the witness accounts describe him as being very strange. Everyone who has seen him will never forget him or what he looks like. Nobody knows if there is just one Grinning Man or many, or if the whole thing is just an urban legend.

One account of the Grinning Man happened in October 1966. Two boys in NJ were walking along Fourth Street, and when they reached a corner parallel to the NJ Turnpike, one of the boys, James Yanchitis, could see a strange figure standing on the other side of a fence. He nudged his friend, Marvin Munoz, who then noticed the man too. They both describe the man as being "a really big man with a big old grin". Allegedly, another resident in the neighborhood claimed to have been "chased by a tall green man" down that very same street.

John A. Keel, a well-known paranormal investigator and author of "The Mothman Prophecies", visited the boys a few days later to speak to them about their incident. He interviewed each boy separately and they both gave the same exact story. The man, they claimed was more than six feet tall and was dressed in a green coverall costume. The costume even appeared to be shimmering in the street lights. There was a black belt around his waist. Neither boy noticed any hair, nose, nor ears on the man, just two, beady eyes and a really big grin.

There were other, similar reports of such a strange man in other parts of the country, including on in Parkersburg, WV, which is about 40 miles away from where the Mothman sightings took place. In Nov. 1966, Woodrow Derenberger was driving home in his truck when he heard a crash.

  Out of nowhere, a vehicle came zooming up behind him and quickly passed him up. After passing him up, the vehicle slowed down and stopped, blocking the road. The witness noticed that it was the strangest vehicle he had ever seen, and described it as looking like a "kerosene lamp chimney". It apparently was flaring at each end, and the ends were narrow. The vehicle had a large bulge in the center.

All of a sudden, a strange, tall man stepped out. He was described as being "really tall and tanned". Derenberger claimed that the man had a "gleaming green" outfit on, similar to what the boys in NJ noted. The Grinning Man alleged communicated with Derenberger telepathically and asked him strange questions about UFO sightings in the area. The entity then, telepathically, revealed his name to be "Indrid Cold".

There have been other reports of a strange, grinning man, including on in Point Pleasant, WV, where the Mothman sightings took place. Nobody knows for sure who---or what---this strange man was, or why he was here. Of course, he could just be an urban legend. Or, he could've just been an ordinary, albeit strange man. There haven't been any more reported sightings of him as of late. Whenever he had been around in the past, there were usually UFO sightings or crypto sightings such as Mothman.

He couldn't be associated with the Men in Black, since he supposedly wears a shimmering green outfit.

Have the Earliest Animal Footprints Been Discovered?

Archaeologists have just recently discovered evidence that an aquatic animal with legs may have walked this earth at least 30 million years earlier than what has been believed. Professor Babcock discovered the mysterious tracks in 2000 in the mountains near Goldfield, Nevada.

Tracks were found that appear to consist of two parallel rows of small (2 millimeters in diameter) dots. It obviously wasn't very big, but this find is still fascinating. Evidence suggests that these tracks date back to approximately 570 million years ago to the Ediacaran Period! It's normally thought that most groups of land animals with legs didn't begin evolving until the Cambrian period, millions of years later.

Loren Babcock, Earth Science Professor at Ohio State University, explains: "This was truly an accidental discovery. We came on an outcrop that looked like it crossed the Precambrian-Cambrian boundary, so we stopped to take a look at it. We just sat down and started flipping rocks over. We were there less than an hour when I saw it."

Professor Babcock discovered the mysterious tracks in 2000 in the mountains near Goldfield, Nevada. Of course Nevada was covered by the sea 570 million years ago, which makes the sediment surface a good place for excellent preservation.

Other tracks have been found around the world dating back around 520 - 540 million years ago. One fossil trail was discovered in Canada in 2002, and another was found in South China.

Since this one found in Nevada is believed to be approximately 570 million years old, it helps prove that complex animals lived on earth long before other creatures, including the dinosaurs.

Babcock explains that there "will be a lot of skepticism" about his discovery. "There should be. But I think it will cause some excitement. And it will probably cause some people to look harder at the rocks they already have. Sometimes it's just a matter of thinking differently about the same specimen."

We can only hope that his hypothesis turns out to be true. It would be very fascinating if complex species truly existed on this planet a longer than we originally expected. It will hopefully open the doors for more discoveries to be made.

Phoenix from the Ashes

Phoenix, in my opinion, can be a lot. First of all, in ancient times he was used as a sign or omen in many cultures and countries, e.g. Greece, Egypt, Ancient Rome, China, Theban, the Hebrews, Mexico, and the Orient and as well in Christianity. For some of them the Phoenix even was a god.

The Phoenix is a symbol of immortality and of resurrection. The origin of its name comes from a Greek word which refers to the color of fire: red. According to legend, the Phoenix died and resuscitated in the purifying fire.

According to the belief of different countries the Phoenix shows the appearance of different birds. In Greek and Egyptian mythology it was a heron. In Christianity it was a pelican. In China it had similarity with the peacock. In the Orient it symbolized the mythological bird "Simorgh", in Mexico the "Quetzal" and in Hebrew tradition the bird "Milcham".
In Ancient Rome it was just a multi-colored bird with mighty feathers, and there it symbolized the vital energy.

After the Phoenix has lived for hundreds of years and when thousand years had passed, a fire starts in its nest and burns everything entirely. It only remains an egg that transforms into a chick. The bird continues to live. It renews its feathers and flies for the first time. He has never been prey to the death.

In general, the fire is an element that is associated with the vital energy, the heart, spiritual enlightenment, creation and the sun. The Phoenix has nearly the same associations. In some sacrificing rituals the fire is used because of its purification factor.
Because it represents the power of the spirit and the light, the fire becomes the main sign of enlightenment which is looked for by mystics and yogis.

Giant Skeletons

Giant skeletons have remained a mystery since the early days in the 1800's. One particular finding was in 1965, where an eight foot nine inch skeleton was found in Kentucky under a rock ledge by Holy Creek.

Giant skeletons have remained a mystery since the early days in the 1800's. One particular finding was in 1965, where an eight foot nine inch skeleton was found in Kentucky under a rock ledge by Holy Creek.

Although, many of the stories surrounding the giant people are just that, stories, one has to wonder what about the stories that tell of people finding such skeletons. Although the man that found the skeleton in Kentucky reburied the skeleton without showing anyone, we must think for a moment, why are there so many stories where people claim to have found giant skeletons?

The man that claimed to have found the Kentucky skeleton has since died and along with him, the exact location of the giant skeleton. It is not unusual for people to be six or seven feet tall, but eight feet some inches is huge. One can only wonder if people did exist that were considered giant people. If there were giant people, why is it that we do not see anyone of such height today? One has to think about all the mysteries of the world before saying that these skeletons never existed. One has to question the evolution of man and apes before anyone can rule out the possibly of giant people walking the earth so many years ago.

In 1947, a newspaper account of someone finding thirty-two caves with remains of what appeared to be eight to nine feet skeletons resembling a humans remains were found. These caves bordered Arizona, California and Nevada. The skeletons were still wearing what appeared to be skins from some type of animal. The clothes resembled that of pre-historic times.
This find was first discovered years earlier by a man who then reported the find to the Smithsonian. The remains were stolen after that conversation and a cover up seem evident.

The Smithsonian was also named for other cover-ups through the years when others reported their own findings. Was it possible that these findings were scooped up by the Smithsonian or did they report the findings to another organization that wanted to keep this information secret? Were there giant people walking the earth many years ago? If so, what made them so big? Why did the giant population disappear from the earth? Why are the accounts of giant people kept relatively quiet? Why is there no word from anyone about the possibly of giant people that once may have walked the earth?

One can only read about the possible findings of the giant people. Someone or some organization has to have the information regarding the findings. They must know what happen to the skeletons that were found so many years ago. If the human race was once giant in size, what happen over the years to cause us to be shorter in size? Is there a connection to human beings today and the giant people from centuries ago? This is one mystery that may never have an answer since the skeletons seem too unavailable for viewing.

Part II
Mysterious Places

Stonehenge

Stonehenge is a prehistoric, mysterious circle of upright stones in southern England. Construction on the great monument began 5,000 years ago; the famous stones that still stand today were put in place about 4,000 years ago.

The great age, massive scale and mysterious purpose of Stonehenge draw over 800,000 visitors per year, and several thousand gather on the summer solstice to watch the sunrise at this ancient and mystical site.

The stones are aligned almost perfectly with the sunrise on the summer solstice, and it is almost unquestioned that Stonehenge was built as a spectacular place of worship.

Although the faith of the Stonehenge builders predates any known religion, the site has become a place of pilgrimage and worship for Neopagans who identify themselves with the Druids or other forms of Celtic paganism. It is also popular with New Age devotees, who report powerful energies at the site.

The current site, awe-inspiring as it is, is only part of the original Stonehenge. The original construction has suffered a great deal from both weather damage and human pillage of its rock over the millennia.

Stonehenge has been the subject of much archaeological and scientific inquiry and research, especially in the last century. The modern account of the construction of Stonehenge is based primarily on excavations done since 1919 and especially since 1950.

Archaeologists believe the construction of the site was carried out in three main stages, which have been labeled Stonehenge I, Stonehenge II and Stonehenge III. The native Neolithic people of England began construction of Stonehenge I by digging a circular ditch using deer antlers as picks. The circle is 320 feet in diameter, and the ditch itself was 20 feet wide and 7 feet deep.

Next, they used the chalky rubble taken from the ditch to build a steep bank circle just inside the outer circle. Inside the bank circle, they dug 56 shallow holes known as the Aubrey holes (named after their discoverer, 17th century scholar John Aubrey).

Finally, two parallel stones were erected at the entrance to the circle, one of which, the Slaughter Stone, still survives. Also surviving are two Station Stones, positioned across from each other on opposite sides of the circle, which may also have been erected during this time. Stonehenge I seems to have been used for about 500 years and then abandoned. Construction of Stonehenge II began around 2100 BC.

 In this phase, a semicircle of granite stones known as bluestones (from their original coloring) was assembled within the original bank and ditch circles. Several aspects of this phase are intriguing.

First, the bluestones come from the Preseli Mountains in South Wales, nearly 250 miles away. There were about 80 of them, weighing up to 4 tons each. How they were transported is not known, although scholars don't regard the feat as impossible and various theories have been presented.

It is intriguing to wonder, however, what makes the Stonehenge site so special that so much effort would be expended to drag the giant stones 250 miles instead of constructing the monument near the quarry.

Second, the entranceway to the semicircle of bluestones is aligned with the midsummer sunrise. The alignment was continued by the clearing of a new approach to the site, "The Avenue," which has ditches and banks on either side like the original outer circle. Two Heel Stones (so-named from the shape of the one that remains) were placed on the Avenue a short distance from the circle (and, today, very close to Highway A344).

Stonehenge III is the stone circle that is still visible today. During this phase, which was started in about 2000 BC, the builders constructed a circle of upright sarsen stones, each pair of which was topped with a stone lintel (horizontal capstone). The lintels are curved to create a complete circle on top.

There were originally 30 upright stones; 17 of these still stand. These stones came from the Marlborough Downs, 20 miles to the north, are 7 feet tall and weigh 50 tons each. The outside surfaces of all these stones were pounded smooth with hammers, and dovetail joints fasten the lintels to their uprights.

Within this stone ring was erected a horseshoe formation of the same construction, using 10 upright stones. Here the trilithons (set of two uprights plus the lintel) stand separated from one another, in 5 pairs. Eight of the original ten stones remain. The horseshoe shape opens directly towards the Slaughter Stone and down the Avenue, aligned with the summer solstice sunrise.

About a century later, about 20 bluestones gathered from Stonehenge II were placed in a horseshoe shape inside the sarsen horseshoe. Less than half of these remain. Some shuffling around of the bluestones and digging of holes (probably in preparation for placing the bluestones, which was not completed) occurred around 1500 BC.

The Altar Stone is the biggest of these newly-arranged bluestones that remains. Around 1100 BC, the Avenue was extended all the way to the River Avon (over 9,000 feet from Stonehenge), indicating that the site was still in use at that time.

Mexico's Zone of Silence

Deep in an arid desert region of Mexico lies a little known area that seemingly defies the physics of sound. Known as the Zone of Silence and locally as the Vertice de Trino, it is a place where radio waves barely permeate the air. Located between the states of Chihuahua, Coahuila and Durango and only 400 miles from the U.S. Border, something in the area makes it almost impossible to receive radio, television, cell phones or any other sound related transmissions.

 While the exact cause of this phenomenon has not been fully explained to date, there are many theories abounding that the area has been heavily influenced by past extra-terrestrial and other paranormal activities. Regardless of the cause, the Zone of Silence continues to be a fascinating study into the unknown.

The unique qualities of the region were first discovered when Mexican aviator Francisco Sarabia reported radio trouble while flying over the area in the 1930s. This phenomenon was then later confirmed in 1966 when an organic chemist could not contact fellow team workers on his hand-held radio while conducting a field study. However, full awareness of the unique sound anomalies within the zone did not arise until July 11, 1970. On that date, a faulty U.S. Air Force rocket launched from the

White Sands Missile Base in New Mexico went suddenly off course and crashed into the remote desert region. Because the rocket was carrying two containers of radioactive elements, an Air Force recovery team was immediately dispatched to the area where it was once again confirmed that all types of radio signals failed to travel through the air. As a result, research headed by the Mexican government was established to study the unique plant, animal and mineral components of the area in an effort to determine the cause of the drop in signals.

The most commonly held position among scientists for the sudden disappearance of radio waves is the high amounts of mineral deposits in the region. Very high levels of both magnetite and uranium are present, which could create enough electromagnetic pulses to interfere with radio signals. In addition, the region has also received an unusually high level of meteorite activity over thousands of years. This has given rise to speculations that there may be some unusual magnetic properties in the soil arising from the breakdown of meteorite fragments.

The high level of meteorite activity has generated many theories that the region is a vortex where an extraordinary amount of earth energy is concentrated, leading it to be a hot spot for paranormal activities. Numerous reports by local residents of UFO sightings and contact with extra-terrestrial beings have been documented on a regular basis since 1910. Some people have claimed to be witness to "large disks" landing on area hills, while many others describe a regular occurrence of mysterious lights and fireballs in the night skies. Backing the theory of spaceships landing in the area are reports of contacts with alien beings. In all cases, these beings have been described as strange looking blond people wearing long raincoats and ball caps. When asked by a rancher where they came from, their response was "from above".

How the Zone of Silence disrupts radio signals and seems to attract extra-terrestrial activity has yet to be fully explained. But there is little question that the area contains many phenomenon that continue to defy logical explanations.

The Legend of Morrow Road

Located in Clay Township, Michigan, old Morrow Road is famous for a horrifying reason.

The story goes that a mother and child went missing from their home on this road sometime in the late 1800's. The little boy disappeared into thin air and shortly after, the mother also vanished. It is believed she died a terrifying death while searching for her son. Locals say the ghostly figure of a mother can still be seen wandering old Morrow Road to this day.

The rural road spans 2.5 miles and, until recently, was all dirt until half of it was paved over as citizens relocated to the area. In the last 200 years that this legend has survived, several different versions have come together to create one startling likeness between them. Each version differs only slightly:

- A kidnapper was involved, ripping the young boy from his mother's arms.

- A momentarily distracted mother makes the realization that her son has drowned and upon finding his lifeless body, she becomes distraught and takes her own life.

- A home invasion -- their old farm house was robbed and they were the only two victims.

- A fire, maybe an out-of-control bonfire took hold of the boy and claimed his life. The mother last saw him near the fire and came to this conclusion. She herself succumbing to the flames after making this terrible realization.

- A freezing, stormy night may have captured the boy as he wandered away from home. As the mother searches, she also succumbs to the blistering cold.

- A murderer on the loose takes hold of the boy, ending his life. The mother meets the same demise while searching for her lost son.

- The mother gives birth out of wedlock and due to the shame she felt (in the late 1800's), she abandons her child outdoors. However, her guilt overcomes her and when she returns to fetch her child, he is gone and her endless search begins.

As locals and tourists alike drive up and down the old rural road they have reported actually hearing the mother screaming out for help in the fruitless search for her child. Many of these people independently report the ghostly woman to be wearing the same blue nightgown. Orbs have been spotted floating in the woods nearby; many people believe this type of phenomenon to be the energy of a spirit.

One must wonder how this legend has survived generation after generation, all the while gaining so much popularity that it has captured the attention of people across the country. Something is acting to perpetuate the life of the legend and it doesn't seem to be slowing as time goes on. Could it be the repeated sightings or audible recognitions of a ghostly mother crying out in pain? How is it that complete strangers have recognized this woman always wearing and shouting the same things? Some may say it is coincidence or possibly bored teenagers on a Friday night; the thing to consider is the length of time this legend has continued to scare young and old alike. Over two centuries of torturing those who dare to take a drive on old Morrow Road, just to see what they can find.

Skinwalker Ranch

Skinwalker Ranch, also known as Sherman Ranch, has been the sight of many paranormal experiences that have been reported by people who have both lived and visited this Utah based property.

The name Skinwalker comes from local folklore, which is the tale of a supernatural creature who can take the shape of both a man and an animal. Some of the strange occurrences at this location include crop circles, glowing orbs, bigfoot-type creatures, poltergeist activity, and even UFO's. This ranch, located on the border of the Ute Indian Reservation in west Uintah County, has been popularly known as "UFO Ranch" due to the odd events that have reportedly taken place here for more than half a century.

Some of the disturbing things that have been said to occur here are the mutilation and vanishing of cattle, animals that have piercing yellow eyes that don't seem to be harmed by guns, and unidentified orbs and flying objects. The most reported type of anomaly seen at the ranch is something described as "The Spotlight". This is a beam of light that reportedly hovers around 8 feet above the ground and is similar to a motorcycle headlight. It usually lasts anywhere from 10 seconds to 15 minutes, and at times has been seen with a red tail light in the background. It sometimes beams right on a witness, and at other times seems to ignore them. It has also been reported to be interactive at times.

Another mystery of the ranch includes what is known as a "mini stealth". This appears to be a mini version of a stealth fighter, reported to be about six feet wide with a length of about eight feet. It has been reported by witnesses to fly around 500 feet overhead and usually is moving across the ranch from south to north. It is a black aircraft that can only be seen for about 5 to 10 seconds due to the high rate of speed it is traveling at Sightings of the "bullet-proof wolf" have also been reported not only by witnesses, but also two researchers who were working on the ranch as well.

The researchers reported that the wolf actually manifested itself from another anomaly associated with the ranch, the "Flash Drones", which are pulsating, spherical balls of light that hover in silence.
The wolf does not exude the personality of a normal wolf, as it is known to approach to within ten feet of the witness. It also is said to have yellow eyes and an abnormally long and bushy tail.

There are also reports about an "orange football". This approximately 15x10 orange glowing plasma ball is said to have the shape of a football with red tendrils around the edges. It usually hangs around for about 5 minutes and seems curious about those that have witnessed it. Several past investigators have also reported hearing the voice of a little girl around the ranch. The voice is reported to be so low that witnesses cannot figure out if the girl is speaking English or some other language.

Other reported anomalies include the "Invisible Chopper", which can only be heard but not seen, and what are known as "The Controllers", which is the voice of two men speaking in an unknown language that is usually heard by witnesses after hearing the chopper fly over. There have also been reports of what is known as "The Portal", which is a very bright flash of light that is rumored to emit creatures and beings from other dimensions, as well as act as a portal for vehicles to pass through.

The Kensington Runestone

The history of the Kensington Runestone, which is 16 inches wide and 31 inches high weighs 202 pounds and is six inches thick, fascinates historians and caught the attention of a Wisconsin university student Hjalmer Holand. He deciphered the writing on the stone, which reads:

We were and fished one day. After we came home, 10 men red with blood and tortured. Hail Virgin Mary, save from evil. Have 10 men by the sea to look after our ship, 14-day journeys from this island year 1362.

The stone was unearthed in 1898 by Olof Ohman, whose ten year old son Edward found the rock slab as his father was clearing land to make level ground on a hill top two and half miles from Kensington. The Historical Society of Minnesota had the stone authenticated by five scholars.

Other evidence found were the triangular holes in rock ledges where boats were anchored with pins, which is conclusive with how the

Vikings secured their boats and is still practiced in Norway. Early settlers and the Indians of Minnesota didn't use these types of holes for securing boat. Norse instruments from 1362 were found and said to be identical to the tools used by the Norwegians.

Another stone that was found in 1783 by the North Dakota city of Minot may have been another message from the Vikings. The Verendrye Runestone was taken to Canada, then to France where it disappeared. The Historical Society of Minnesota offered a reward of $1,000 for its return, without any success. Many believe that this may have been another message from the Vikings that also carved the Kensington Runestone.

Those that study the Vikings and their exploration of the Minnesota area, feel that the Vikings taught the Mandan blued-eyed Indians about Christianity. The Indians lived in buildings of Norwegian design. It is said that the Vikings for some reason, may have had problems returning to the boat to travel back to Europe and settled in with the Mandan Indians.

Controversy over the authenticity of the Kensington Runestone that would predate the arrival of Columbus leaves people wondering about the stone. The controversy is warranted as some say, but those that have studied the stone and the instruments from around the same area suggest that it was indeed the Vikings, not Columbus that took their first steps on the soils of Minnesota.

The Kensington Runestone changes history as it is taught in schools. It may be that the Vikings that discovered America and not Columbus. Until the Verendrye Runestone is found, no one may ever know for sure.

Since no can explain how the blue-eyed Mandan Indians learned about Christianity before the arrival of Columbus, the logical conclusion would be that they learned from the Vikings. Their way of building must have come the Vikings as well. How else could they have built buildings of Norwegian design?

A Terrifying Legend is Real?

The high rolling hills and deep valleys of the forested places of Kentucky are serenely beautiful, but these hills have long been rumored to be the dwelling of spirits and strange terrifying beasts.

The state gets its name from the Cherokee, Shawnee, Pawnee, and the other Native American dialect word of the tribes that lived in what would become the surrounding areas of what would become the states of Tennessee, Ohio, Missouri, and Virginia and West Virginia. Can-tuck or Kain-tuk-ke, means "Dark and Bloody Ground". It was considered to be sacred ground. This was the land of restless spirits and strange creatures. One such creature was feared more than most by the native tribes, and the legends and tales of encounters with this terrifying beast still continue to this day.

The first close encounter with this creature was during a camping trip about 10 years ago. We were wakened by our two friends who had pitched their tent several yards away from our van. They had been awakened by a terrifying, unearthly sounding howling that neither could really describe. They also heard the sounds of a great deal of snapping of what sounded like branches and other sounds of destruction. (My mate and I had not heard anything but we are very sound sleepers.) We all remained awake the rest of the night sitting in our van talking about this incident, waiting for morning to break. As soon as it got light enough to see by we went looking to see what we could find. We found an area of ground torn up and very large tree branches snapped from fairly high up on several trees. We also found what looked like really large foot prints of a bi-pedal creature that had some rather large claws extending from the toes. We all decided to make a quick breakfast and pack up. No one really wanted to stay another night in the area.

A few weeks later my mate and I were at another camping area and there was a large creek between us and a large expanse of forest when we had a more personal encounter with that horrible screaming howl. Fortunately we were in our van and that gave us some sense of protection, (but this thing sounded as though none of that would have really mattered if it really wanted to get at us.) The sound this creature made is very hard to describe. Over the years both of us have heard panther, bobcat, bear, deer, and a host of other indigenous creatures, but NEVER anything like this! This was like a howl, moan, and screech and scream all rolled together. Nothing in nature should be able to sound like that.

The next day we crossed the foot bridge over the creek and saw an amazing amount of destruction. Trees up to 5 inches in diameter had been snapped off about 2-3 feet up the trunk and the picnic table in the area had been smashed in to bits. There were some very deeply scored claw marks on the trunks of some of the trees. Something sure seemed to have been angry.

Over the years other people we have met and known have come forward with tales and descriptions of encounters with a creature that left them utterly terrified. The old legends of the native tribes have of this creature say that it is a demon of sort.

The descriptions in the old legends, and more recent encounters, says that this beast walks on two legs like a man and stands around 7 feet tall. It is covered in shaggy grey-white fur and has large, dead black eyes, sometimes also described has having a red glow. It has long vicious looking claws on the ends of very long fingered hands and a mouth full of teeth that look quite capable of rending flesh. One of the names given by the Cherokee people for this thing was the Ewah, or "Soul Stealer".

Whatever this thing is, one thing is for certain, and something dark and truly terrifying roams the Appalachian hills of Eastern Kentucky.

The Cursed Rocks of Hawaii

Hawaii is one of the top vacation spots in the world, but tourists need to be careful with the souvenirs they want to bring home.

According to superstition, those who take lava rocks home with them meet with bad luck and horrible misfortune. There have been a large number of reports over the years of tourists picking up rocks near the Hawaiian volcanoes and taking them home, only to be "cursed" by Pele afterwards.

So who is Pele? She is the mythological volcano goddess, and the volcanoes in Hawaii are said to be her domain. She apparently isn't too happy with tourists "stealing" her rocks as she sends a curse to follow all of them home. It's believed that each rock in the Hawaii Volcanoes National Park has its own energy and that when they're all together, the volcanoes are in "harmony", just as the goddess made them.

Every year, the Hawaii Volcanoes National Park receives hundreds of packages from tourists sending their rocks back. The packages come from all around the world, and many of them are addressed to "Queen Pele" herself. Letters of apology are also sent with the rocks.
Even tourists who are usually skeptic against superstition admit that they made a mistake by taking off with the volcanic rocks. Hawaiians believe

that the rocks, sand, and shells should always be kept right where Pele put them. Is this legend true? Or do people just have overactive imaginations? Could this urban legend have become so widespread that people now believe in it? Whether there's any truth to the myths and superstition or not, it is against the law to take anything out of the Hawaii Volcanoes National Park.

The Legendary Land of Lyonesse

The lost land of Lyonesse is often mentioned in British and Cornish folklore. It joins other mysterious places such as Camelot and Avalon in King Arthur legends.

According to legend, Lyonesse once existed between the coasts of Cornwall and the Scillies. During the 16th century, an antiquarian named William Camden interviewed many Cornwall locals about their folklore beliefs. They often mentioned the "City of Lions", and how they could sometimes hear the "ghostly bells" ringing out. It was said that only a man named Trevelyan escaped the sinking of Lyonesse by riding away on a white horse.

The legends say that Lyonesse sank to the bottom of the sea, just as Atlantis did. There have been field remains showing up at low tides along the Sampson Flats sands, which is between the islands of the Scillies. Could these alleged field remains be the lost land of Lyonesse? According to ancient Roman maps, the Isles of Sicily were all once linked together as a single island. Seven Stones Reef, which is located in the Sicily Isles, is said to have once been the capital of Lyonesse.

Lyonesse has been linked with Lothian, Scotland, as well as Leonais in

Brittany, although neither of these places has ever "been lost to the sea". According to the ancient Saxon Chronicle, Lyonesse was destroyed on November 11, 1099. The tale explains how the people, towns, and animals were taken by the sea. This date shouldn't be taken too seriously though, as other versions of the tale date back to the 6th century.

Lyonesse plays a large part in many Arthurian legends. In some versions of the legend, King Arthur was born at Tintagel castle in Cornwall; in other tales, he was born in Lyonesse. In some tales, it was the ghost of Merlin who flooded Lyonesse. King Arthur and his fabled knights fled to Lyonesse to get away from the evil Mordred. They climbed to the highest peaks of the Sicily Isles while Merlin brought the tides in to sweep Mordred's army away. It's also been said that Sir Tristran's uncle, King Mark, ruled over Lyonesse.

If the Isles of Sicily are all that remains of the Great Land of Lyonesse, can't researchers search the waters surrounding The Scillies? Legends describe Lyonesse as being a "densely populated" area, containing many villages and churches. To this day some still claim to hear those church bells ringing from beneath the sea. So why then have no physical remains of the villages or churches ever been found?

Sometimes fishermen claim to pick up "old pieces of buildings" with their fishing nets, but unfortunately there's no real, conclusive, scientific evidence. Despite that, people will continue being fascinated by tales of long, lost lands. We'll perhaps never learn the truth of Atlantis, either, yet many people still believe in some of those legends.

Parallel Universes — Thoughts to Ponder

A lot of research has been done over the last few years over parallel universes. Do alternative dimensions really exist? Are we living in a "universe" or a "multiverse"? Is it possible that the Confederacy won the Civil War in another universe or dimension?

Are Marilyn Monroe and Elvis still alive in an alternate reality? Could the "ghosts" or "spirits" that we see in this world actually be living, breathing people in another dimension? Are other dimensions getting close to ours when we see this phenomenon? Is it possible that there is a version of "you" and "me" both in another dimension? What happens when we die in that dimension?

These are only a few questions that we'd all like to know the answer too. Physicists have been studying dark matter, hyperspace, and the "string theory for some time now. Recent studies have led them to believe that there might just be more than just three dimensions. There may be more to time and space than originally thought. It appears that the universe may be one bubble floating around an infinite space with many other bubbles.

Whenever two or more bubbles "run into" each other, strange phenomenon can appear. This could also create a "big bang" that results in a new universe being formed! Will we even *know* when our universe crashes into another one? Will there be physical catastrophes or only subtle clues such as an increase in strange activity?

If there is a version of each of us in different universes, what happens when a copy of ourselves dies? Whenever we have dreams that we're dying, could it mean that we really *are* dying, only in a parallel universe? And as we wake up, does that "copy" of ourselves join us in this world? It also begs the question, what happens when we die in THIS world? "Do we just go on living in another dimension or plane of existence, as if nothing ever happened? These are very strange questions, but they are nice to ponder about.

Even if there is a great multiverse out there, filled with an infinite amount of "bubble" dimensions, does any of it really matter? We don't have any machines or equipment to allow us to visit other dimensions, and even if we did, how would we travel to them? Would it ever be possible to have real life star gates to take us from dimension to dimension? Or will such things always be out of our realm of possibilities? Perhaps someday we'll have more answers, but for now, we only have our imaginations.

The Mysteries of The Bermuda Triangle

The Bermuda Triangle sometimes referred to as the Devils Triangle has been a mystery for centuries. It was once thought that traveling in the Bermuda Triangle was deadly because of the strange and mysterious things that happen.

Many ships have reported navigation equipment going haywire while some have reported having an eerie feeling. The Bermuda Triangle did not become well known until 1945 when the Navy Avenger bombers disappear.

Then a rescue plane vanished when trying to find the missing five aircrafts. Altogether, there were twenty-seven men missing along with six planes. The story about the Bermuda Triangle and the missing five bombers was explained away by military personal. They said that the planes flew in the wrong direction because of bad equipment. They speculated that the planes flew deeper out into the Atlantic Ocean and eventually disappear from earth so to speak. They believe that they flew as far as the Puerto Rico Trench in the Bermuda Triangle, which is said to be at least thirty-thousand down below the surface. They then claimed that the search craft blew up shortly after takeoff, although no wreckage in either disappearance has ever been found.

The stories that have come from the Bermuda Triangle may be explained for some instances, but not all mysterious happenings can be explained that easy. Is there really something mystical about the Devils Triangle or are these just stories being told. The truth is that no one has ever been found to explain what happened to them. They have vanished, never to be heard from again. Is it really just faulty equipment that causes navigation systems to malfunction when ships or aircrafts get near the Triangle? What really causes the navigation equipment to stop working or go haywire? Is there a mysterious force taking control of the ships and aircrafts?

If you ask the Navy, they will tell you that the commander in charge of the five bombers was hung over, the equipment malfunctioned, and he was fighting by landmarks. What caused the equipment to malfunction you might wonder. Why did they let him fly if he was hung-over? Why did the others follow if they thought he was going the wrong way? There are too many answers and not enough truth about the Bermuda Triangle. One can only believe that, yes, there is something strange happening in the Devils Triangle and no one has ever lived to tell the story. That alone tells a different story.

If the Navy feels that the planes flew into the depths of the Atlantic Ocean all those years ago, then why have they not used the newest technology we have today to go find those aircrafts and prove to everyone that there are no mystical powers in the Bermuda Triangle? Surely, someone could invent something that crawl the depths of the Bermuda Triangle to see what is down there or are they afraid of what might happen or what might not be found? Only those who disappeared in the Bermuda Triangle know for sure what happen and they cannot tell us.

Did the Garden of Eden Really Exist?

Everyone who is the least bit familiar with the biblical story of the creation is aware of the idyllic setting in which the first man and woman found themselves. By all accounts the Garden of Eden must have been a wonderful place filled with beauty and lush vegetation.

If the Garden of Eden ever existed trying to find its actual location has been no easy feat. According to the Bible a river flowed out of the garden and branched into four rivers. Those four rivers were named as the Pishon, Gihon, Tigris and Euphrates. The location of the Pishon and Gihon have been a problem in determining the location of the Garden of Eden. The flood of Noah's time changed the geography of the world making it very difficult to pinpoint the location of the garden. Some speculate that the river referred to as the Pishon may have been the Nile. There are numerous theories as to the location of the Garden of Eden.

There are many locations that have been considered for such a coveted spot as the Garden of Eden. Egypt, Iran, Iraq, Turkey, Saudi Arabia and Israel are among those locations thought to be the original home of the garden. Some believe that the Garden of Eden was located in Turkey because the Euphrates and Tigris rivers originate there. Others believe Saudi Arabia to be the actual location since it has been associated with the biblical land referred to as Havilah. Then there are those who believe that the Garden of Eden lies beneath the waters of the Persian Gulf. The Garden of Eden has even been believed to be the lost continent of Atlantis. There are also people who believe that the Garden of Eden never had an earthly existence at all and was simply viewed as an earthly reference to a heavenly paradise.

The word Eden seems to have its roots in a Sumerian word meaning plains. According to the Talmud, Eden refers to the territory where the garden was located rather than the garden itself. In the late 1990's an archaeologist named David Rohl claimed to find the Garden of Eden 10 miles from the Iranian city of Tabriz in a valley walled by towering mountains. He identified the Gihon and Pishon rivers as the Araxes and Uizhun. He was also supposed to have located the biblical Land of Nod and Cush.

Is this the actual location of the Garden of Eden? Did it really exist there at one time? One thing is certain, deep down inside somewhere within the collective conscious of humanity there is a desire to return to the idyllic state of existence as it was before Adam and Eve fell from grace. The Garden of Eden will always represent that desire for such an existence

Part III
Ancient Mysteries

Alien Artifacts ~ Writings

Although it was a fictional television show, a line delivered by one of the characters from "The X-Files", when asked if there really were aliens among us, stated "Oh, they've been here for a long time".

While strange flying craft have been witnessed for millennium, these are still just sightings; they offer no concrete proof or even an artifact to speculate upon. But have there been objects found on our planet that could possibly be identified as being of an extraterrestrial nature?
In the early 1920's a copper coin-like artifact was dredged up from a well digging at Lawn Ridge, Illinois. The strata this object came from were about 114 feet underground and the Illinois State Geological Survey confirmed that the surrounding deposits were from between 200,000 to 400,000 years old. A drawing of the "coin" was made before the actual artifact was sent to the Smithsonian Institute for safekeeping. Regrettably this object, as well as many other objects that do not fit the "official" version of history, has since vanished from the Smithsonian's care and all that is left is the drawing made of it.

Depicted on the coin was the design of a large two legged figure with what appears to be a feathered headdress like attachment on its head holding a club of some sort over a prostrate figure at its feet. Around the edges were a number of markings that might pass for an alphabet of sorts. It is this "lettering" we wish to pay attention to.

Now we look at an incident from November of 1967 in which around 11:30 p.m. a pulsing light was seen to descend onto the Riverside Municipal Golf Course of Edmonton, Alberta, Canada. The witness to the event stated that he saw this from his residence about 1,500 feet from the golf course. He watched as the light descended and resolved itself into a "squashed globe". The object at first radiated a reddish light but that the lights changed to a soft violet color and he heard it giving off a buzzing sound like an electrical transformer. He witnessed the craft fly over the Saskatchewan River and land.

Then the lights from the craft went out and he saw that it shone a silver color in the moonlight. After about five minutes the lights came back on and the craft leapt into the sky and was gone.

The next day, the gentleman went over to the course to see if he could find where the craft had landed. After a brief search he discovered a circle of mashed down grass in a circle about fifteen foot across. About 6 foot out from the circle of mashed grass were a number of holes about 4 inches in diameter each. As he was looking over the area he caught a glint of light off an object that, when he picked it up, was a piece of copper colored metal about 7 inches by 5 inches along the sides and about 1 millimeter thick.

On one side of this metallic plate were etched a number of lines of unidentifiable characters and a drawing that could be interpreted as possibly a small topographical map. A number of the symbols on this copper plate match some of the symbols on the coin unearthed in Illinois.

The third piece of this written puzzle comes from recent sightings of some extraordinarily bizarre shaped craft that have been spotted over the Appalachian hills.

While there are not a lot of the characters that show in the photographs of this floating anomaly that are large enough to make out, all those that do show in this photograph of one of the "wings" can be identified as matching characters found on the ancient coin and the mysterious metal plate as well.

If this truly is the same script, written by the same beings in the same language, then these "extraterrestrials" have most definitely been here for a long, long time.

Aotearoa Mythology: The Maui Cycle

The demigod Maui is undoubted the most famous character in the mythology of the Maoris and as hero and "trickster" he reflects and shapes value conception of the culture of his people.
An analysis dedicated to a "name relative of a kiwi singer"

The demigod Maui is undoubted the most famous character in the mythology of the Maoris and as hero and "trickster" he reflects and shapes value conception of the culture of his people. In a society that grants the highest rank in the family to the first-born as well as the succession to the father, he assumes as the youngest of the family (potiki) a certain exceptional position – similar to the "nestling" in our society. He is spoilt and meets with more indulgence than his elder siblings.

It is interesting to state that the majority of the male heroes in the Maori mythology are eldest sons or chiefs. But also a lot of Potikis cause a stir. They are outsiders like Maui. At the beginning they are discriminated but later on they leave the "natural" heroes far behind because of their cunning and their very great particular daring.

They are the ones who violate all rules. Maui proves that orders are not irrefutable and that cunning and a good portion of having no scruples form a promising combination. His story shows also that man has certain limits and it can end bitterly for him when he does not recognize those limits or is not ready to accept them: Mauis End is Hine-nui-te-po's bosom points that out.

Mauis Birth and Return to his Family: A child that was born before its time and died shortly afterwards was buried in a particular ceremony. Non-observance of the ceremonial rules and otherwise removal of the corpse made an evil spirit of the child that was malicious to the men. All malevolent gods originated from this mode.

Maui spy on his Mother: Illegitimate births were not unusual in a society that granted visiting chiefs the sexual services of local women. The assembly house (whare hui) is a central element of each settlement. Mostly it is named after a significant forefather and symbolizes the body of this ancestor. The ridge is symbol for this ancestor's spine, other parts of the building stand for the arms, eyes, ribs etc. Activities that take place in the assembly house are dance, music and poetry which demonstrate an inseparable unity.

Maui finds his Parents: Mauis encounter with the parents in the underworld (paerau) points to an important convention: It is a violation of the good tone to ask someone directly who she/he is. It is accepted to ask for the religion. This rule is still manifested today when Maoris of different tribes meet each other in the towns of New Zealand.
The Tohi ceremony is the purification ceremony for the new-born and at the same time the new member of the tribe will be welcomed.

A priest purifies the child by speckling the new-born with water. Sons of aristocrats have been either consecrated to Tu, the god of the war or to

Rongo, the good of the peace. The according gods were asked to provide the sons with the corresponding features.

Maui and the Magical Jaw-Bone: The jaw-bone symbolizes knowledge. Kauwae runga, the upper jaw- bone, stands for the knowledge of celestial and divine things that cannot be shared with mortals. This knowledge was passed on to a few chosen people of male gender in the whare wananga – the houses of learning. Kauwae raro, the lower jaw-bone, symbolizes the knowledge of worldly things. Both types of knowledge are highly respected. It is interesting that Maui obtains the jaw-bone (it is not known if it is the upper or lower jaw-bone) of Muriranga-whenua, one of the relatively few female characters in the mythology of the Maoris. Muris jaw-bone becomes a weapon that defeats the sun and from its bone Maui manufactures the fishing-hook with which he finally fishes for land.

Maui fishes for Land: After the violent separation from the parents in the creation mythology, the division of Maui's fish without compliance with the necessary rituals is the second great sin in Maori mythology. It is absolutely necessary to thank the gods for the gifts of nature. Non-observance of this rule has negative consequences.

Maui and the Goddess of Fire: The elder not always pass on their knowledge with ease and often the young only succeed in obtaining it after conquest of several resistances. In the Maori mythology the names of the trees in which Mahuika throws her sparks are as follows: Kaikomako, Pukatea, Porokaiwhiri, Mahoe and Taraire. All this trees are indigenous to New Zealand and their wood has been used by the Maoris to make fire.

Maui transforms his Brother-in-Law into a Dog: The dog – kuri – is the only domestic animal of the Maori and has been imported from Hawaiki to Aotearoa. The Kuri of the Maori has been used as hound. His flesh was eaten and from his coat warm capes have been produced.

How the Death came into the World: Hine-titama became Hine-nui-te-po, the great goddess of the night and guardian of the underworld. To obtain the eternal life for mankind, Maui penetrates in form of a lizard into Hine. Besides Papa, Hine is one of the most prominent female characters in Maori mythology and like her she influences the history of mankind to a decisive degree.

The Unexplained Mysteries of the Baghdad Battery

In 1936, archaeologists discovered a strange object while excavating the ruins of a 2,000 year old village around Baghdad. At first glance, the object appeared to be a clay pot. But when a German archaeologist named Wilheim Konig took a good look at it, he concluded that it was actually an ancient electric battery! It sounds strange, doesn't it? But upon close study, it doesn't appear that there's much to it.

It's simply a pot or bucket that contains metal, and if it's filled up with acid or alkali, a chemical reaction takes place which creates electricity. It is no more or less the first "modern battery", and it doesn't necessarily mean anything out of the ordinary, nor does it mean the ancients were even USING it as a battery. How could they have? Ancient civilizations didn't even know what batteries were, right?

There are some who do believe that it was something special though, and that modern mainstream science isn't looking into it as much as they should be. They believe that ANY type of battery—including a simple one, dating back to 250 B.C. is evidence of something extraordinary. The only explanations could be that either aliens walked this Earth thousands of years ago, or that ancient civilizations were much more advanced than we now give them credit for.

Konig himself speculated that the Baghdad battery could have been used for electroplating gold onto silver objects.
Of course there's no real evidence for this, and most modern mainstream scientists are skeptical toward that idea. They don't see any reason(s) to believe that the Baghdad battery had any electrical use, and that its existence may have been for more simple purposes such as storing important papyrus scrolls. If this is true, the scrolls would have obviously rotted away since then, leaving behind a bit of acidic residue. This explanation is more likely than most others---and while there are many "archaeological anomalies" from the past, this one doesn't appear to be one of them.

King Solomon, the Wise

Solomon, the sage king of the Israelites, was particularly known for his "judgment" that permitted the rendering of a child to his veritable mother. Two prostitutes disputed about to whom of the both that child belonged. Solomon decided to sacrifice the child.

Solomon, the sage king of the Israelites, was particularly known for his "judgment" that permitted the rendering of a child to his veritable mother. Two prostitutes disputed about to whom of the both that child belonged. Solomon decided to sacrifice the child. He proposed to cut it in two with his sword; afterwards each of the women should get one half. The king recognized the real mother because she wanted to give the child to the other to prevent it from being killed.

Solomon was the son of King David and Bathsheba. He pacified the tumultuous relations between Egypt and Phoenicia; developed the commercial exchange; renewed the organization of the army; simplified the administration and re-established the prosperity of his kingdom. The construction of the Temple in Jerusalem - which was ordered by him - marked afterwards the total history of Israel.

The Temple of Solomon occupied an essential place. It is still - and particularly at the epoch of the conquest of Palestine by the Crusaders - a symbolic challenge of the first order. At the same time, it is a permanent reference for the constructors of occidental churches and cathedrals. The Temple became one of the central symbols which presided over the birth of the different orders of Freemasonry. Since the construction of the Temple of Solomon, God decided for himself for a permanent residence in Jerusalem.

In the Bible, Solomon was traditionally the author of Proverbs, a part of the "Book of Wisdom" and especially the "Song of Songs". The Christian interpretation of this text is a link of love which unites Christ to his Church or the mystical re-union of the soul with the fundamental divine principle. "The hexagram"; the six-pointed star, is considered either as the Shield of David, or as the Seal of Solomon. This seal is sometimes in the interior of a circle. It is one of the major symbols of traditional esoterism since its geometric balance gives the image of a perfect world. The Seal of Solomon can be observed in the star-shaped roses with six petals in gothic cathedrals. This radiating figure is also called "Star of the Magi" which has shone over the crib where Jesus, the Child King, was resting.

King Arthur and his Knights

Sovereign of the Knights of the Round Table, Arthur was the adulterous son of Uther Pendragon and the beautiful Ygerne whom Pendragon induced by mistake by taking the traits of her husband.

Historically he was inspired by a real Gallic king who lived at the turning of the V (fifth) and VI (sixth) century. He took the lead of the resistance against the conquest of Great Britain by the Angles and Saxons. This king became a national hero because the remembrance was immediately transmitted from generation to generation. King Arthur was quickly taken into a mythological movement which amounted to what is called the "British material" and the cycle of the Grail.

Brought up away from the court and from men but placed under the protection of Merlin who had already intrigued for his conception, Arthur acceded to the royalty. Arthur drew out the sword Excalibur from a rock, forged in Avalon – the land of the apples, also called the other world. He married Queen Guinevere and founded the "brotherhood" of the round table where no knight took precedence of the other. When some of the knights (Perceval and Gawain) left for the quest of the Grail, Arthur discovered that his wife cheated him with Lancelot, one of the bravest heroes of the round table. Subject to the usage of that time like all human institutions – even if it is from a spiritual inspiration and marks the supernatural manifestation in the order of terrestrial affaires – Arthur's kingdom exhausted bit by bit.

When in the quest of the Grail the young Galahad, son of Lancelot, took the place of Perceval; when Lancelot himself violated all the virtues of the "worldly chivalry" in his love for Guinevere; when the quest of the Grail finally came to its end, Arthur's kingdom was subject to declination. It was a real end of the universe that happened at the moment when the king died, succumbed in the battle where he affronted the arms of his incestuous son Mordred whom he had with his half-sister Morgan. Because of this incest the whole society was messed up; dusk has fallen upon humanity.

The cycle of the Grail and the history that began with the passion of the Christ closed with this death: while Arthur was interred at "Black Chapel", someone threw his sword in the neighboring lake where a hand grasped it and carried the sword with it to the bottom of the lake. In an evident relation with this hand, that has then thrown the sword into the air, the Grail could be seized. Some versions reported as well that after his death, Arthur went on a voyage towards the isle of Avalon where Morgan came to pick him up in a bark, accompanied by his servants.

Nyx, the Greek Goddess of Night

The night is not only the absence of sunlight. It symbolizes as well the obscurity filled with mysteries and the protective mother's breast. In Greek mythology the night represents a conception where it signifies the great goddess Nyx who is wearing a black dress ornated with stars. The night dispenses the sleep and allows to forget the pains. It is the mother of the sleep, the dream, the love-pleasure and also the death. Because of its disquiet aspect the night is sometimes considered as mother of corruption and vengeance.

In many different cultures the rituals dedicated to the earth and to the dead were celebrated during the night just as in primitive Christianity where the reunions of the faithful and interments took place in the night. Later on, it was associated with witches who celebrated nocturnal orgies likewise the Night of Walpurgis.

Concerning a second signification the night becomes a true mystical symbol. That is the reason why the night is to be found often in the three monotheistic religions: Judaism, Christianity and Islam. In the immediate sense, the night provides the levels of examinations and tests the soul have to pass on its way to the union with God. When there will be an obscure night, when sometimes exist as well an illuminated night: This is the night when to discover the pilgrimage of the soul and the "midnight sun".

 After this illuminated night can exist a new black night again that symbolizes God's most guarded truth: The light of the lights and the shadows are balanced in opposite conjunctions. It's in the silence where the secrets of this divine shadow can be learned that shines in the brightest lights at bosom of the blackest obscurity.

As black forms a couple of opposition with white, it forms as well another one with its proper significations. It also refers to the chaos and the death up to the unity where the whole life is issued. All ambivalence of the notion of obscurity can be found which can likewise represent the absence of all light. It remains only one light that is too pure that it blinds the people and seems to them being a shadow.

In the Apocalypse the shadows announce the imminence of the World's end. The Masonic Mystery Circle lights up the most painful enigma of life: The light and the shadows are one. Life is likewise death, the shadows are also light.

The Great Pyramids and Other Structures

The pyramids are right on center for the diagonal line that encases the Delta Nile. Some have often said that there was no way that man could have built the Great Pyramids or other rock structures because it is physically impossible for men. Some believe that aliens built the pyramids. This piece of information comes about because of the diagonals lines. The pyramids are right on center for the diagonal line that encases the Delta Nile. This is harder to understand and that is why most people do not give it a second thought.

Another reason it is believed that man did not create the pyramid is because that the pyramid is facing the magnetic North Pole. It is lined up exactly. How could Egyptians with no means of geography reading possibly do this? Now comes the theory that something or someone with all the technology could have been the only one to make this possible. That would have to mean that aliens or beings from outer space are more sophisticated than we are. They had this knowledge thousands of years ago.

Another mystery is that the sun sets right in the center of the two pyramids, the Great Pyramid of Giza and the neighboring pyramid. Some believe that the Egyptians could not have determined the summer solstice or known about how many days are in a year to do this. The days in a year did not evolve until much later. So, how did the Egyptians build the pyramids to be so precise? Many believe that they did not have anything to do with building the pyramids or any other of the structures around the world. One would have to believe then, that there are life forms more advanced than we are.

The mystery behind the pyramids must be recognized. The fascination of the pyramids may be something that was not made by man at all. Another form of live that we once only wondered about or may not have believed might have made them.

Are the Carnac Stones Part of Atlantis?

Drive to the northwest part of France and you'll run into a region called Brittany. A small village, Carnac, is in this peaceful region. It's very quaint and different from Paris, consisting of livestock, beautiful green fields, and quiet French life. However, something is different about this village.

Look closely. Carnac isn't only the home of livestock and quiet French life. It is also the home of the infamous Carnac stones. These ominous stones stand in Carnac's landscape, dotting fields with rows of gray, thick rocks. Some resemble prehistoric cemeteries, although no one is buried here. These rows of rocks engulf northwestern France, edging off into the ocean.

Some researchers think these stones are part of the lost city of Atlantis, perhaps they are.

What are the Carnac Stones?
The Carnac stones are a collection of monoliths (usually called megaliths) in northwestern France, surrounding the village of Carnac.

These stones range in size and thickness, from small, scattered, round rocks to massive, pointed rocks that tower over 6.5 meters. From 4500 B.C. to 2000 B.C., people places these rocks all over northwestern France.

These rocks are crudely constructed. These are normal rocks mined from different areas within northern Europe, with little modifications. They are unlike the rock statues of Easter Island in that regard. These people merely rolled it to its location, set it up, and left it for eternity (or in this case, over 5,000 years).

The Carnac stones are assembled differently from area to area. This might be the time gap (the stones' construction is over a period of 2,500 years) or just a pace in direction. These stones had different purposes varying from area to area. Some Carnac stones are aligned like desolate graves; some Carnac stones are actually stone forts.

What's more interesting is these stones trail off the French shores into the ocean. These stones existed on solid ground -- at least that's what researchers believe. If that is the case, then a dramatic change in sea level brought these stones to its watery graves. The sea level dramatically changed around 12,000 years ago. It's very possible that these stones were constructed well over 4500 BC. But who? Even the Celts didn't exist at this time. Was it the Celts' ancestors?

These ancestors could also come from the lost city of Atlantis.

Carnac Stones Built By Atlanteans?

It is believed Atlantis disappeared in 10,000 B.C. This coincides with the time the sea levels rose around Carnac. There is a time gap between the time these rocks were built and when they were closely built around Carnac. Coincidence? Some researchers think these prehistoric Celts could be the people of Atlantis, disappearing when the sea levels rose in 12,000 B.C. It's very possible that today's Celts -- the people of France and England -- are the descendants of Atlantis.

Could it be? No one can deny the proof that the half-emerged rocks off Carnac's shores are much older than the ones immediately surrounding Carnac. They might date back to 12,000 B.C. When the ice caps melted, Atlantis disappeared, creating the Atlantic Ocean -- hence the name "Atlantic".

We might already have evidence of the lost Atlantis and not even know it.

The 13 Crystal Skulls'
Connection with Armageddon

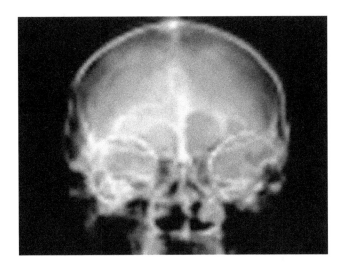

Mayans are revered as an incredibly intelligent people. They predicted their demise, and they also predicted the demise of our world -- 2012. Although no one knows that as fact, they accurately predicted many things in their time.

One thing they prophesied was the legend of the 13 Crystal Skulls. The legend goes as so: skulls gathered in a tight circle, mysteriously scattered about the earth for thousands of years. One day these skulls will reunite at the Ark -- the circle, the center of the earth. Once they realign, they will trigger a worldwide rise of consciousness. Earth shall be transformed anew.

This sounds eerily familiar to the Age of Aquarius, a period when a new form of consciousness is reborn from the ashes. It's thought this rejuvenation will occur on December 12, 2012. The coincidences don't end here. It's also eerily similar to an event prophesied in the Bible. That event is Armageddon.

Is it true? Do these skulls symbolize the end of the world?

Beware. The prophecies of the Mayans never faltered. They even predicted the demise of their own people.

Similarities between Armageddon and the Crystal Skulls
There are striking similarities between the Biblical Armageddon and the legend of the 13 Crystal Skulls.

1. Israel originally had 13 ancient tribes. In the legend, 13 skulls exist in the world.

2. Just like the skulls, Israel's tribes are scattered also.

3. Just like the skulls also, Israel's tribes will gather when the world ends. A true prophetic vision.

4. When the tribes gather, a new consciousness forms. Just like the crystal skulls. Perhaps the crystal skulls are symbolic of the deceased ancestors of these tribes?

5. The ark is the 13th skull. It's unlike the other skulls. It is the leader. Conversely, the 13th tribe is unlike the other tribes. It is the leader.

These skulls could symbolize the 13 tribes of Israel. In the legend, Mayans talk of an 'ark', the stronghold for all skulls. This ark could symbolize Israel.

If these magical crystal skulls meet in the center of the earth -- Israel, in this case -- then a new wave of consciousness would sweep over the earth. The earth is reborn. The earth is renewed. This doesn't match up with the biblical Armageddon, however. Armageddon is the coming of God's son, Jesus.

Armageddon is the battle between good and evil, and good wins. Unfortunately, life is eradicated and life is wiped out. Christians rise to heaven; sinners fall towards Hell.

At least that was the story.

Think about it. Is Armageddon the violent end of the world, or is it the rebirth?

How Did Mayans Know About This?
Knowing about an event a whole continent away is no small feat. How did the Mayans predict this?

The Mayans are an ancient race. They figured out everything, using astronomy to tell their tales. It was their form of astrology.

Scientists have proposed one solution to this. The Mayans are one of the ancient races from Israel. The crystal skulls are those tribes. They are part of those tribes. In the bible, the tribes spread across the earth, creating the population that we know today.

Will the crystal skulls gather in 2012 to equal our demise? Only time will tell

Origins of Easter Island

Easter Island is a small, volcanic island located between Chile and Tahiti, surrounded by clear water and volcanic rock. Easter Island itself is a mass of volcanic ash and rock, dotted with a sparse coastline and dry plains scattering the landscape.

Easter Island's iconic Moui statues guard the edges of this island. Although most are broken or worn, they still stand stoic, centuries after its erection. Easter Island's population has been extinct for centuries, so outsiders have little clues about these origins and their purpose. Some believe it exists for supernatural, mystical reasons, and they're right.

Recently, DNA evidence proved that Easter Island\'s inhabitants were Polynesian settlers. Researchers believe they came from the neighboring island of Marquesas. Around 320 A.D., Polynesians settled this isolated island, only 100 people in existence. At its height, it grew up to 11,000 people. It was during their height that they constructed Moui statues.

Stoic in breadth, these stone-faced creatures dotted the shores of Easter Island, with dark, elongated faces and pronounced noses. Construction of these statues stopped in the late 1600s. Famine spread across Easter

Island, and without food, people resorted to cannibalism. The population eventually died out in the 1800s.

With the extinction of these people comes the extinction of why these statues existed. Why do these statues exist?

There are many theories on why the Moui statues existed. The most common belief is for religious purposes. Dutch commander Jacob Roggeveen (who visited Easter Island in the 1700s) noted the discovery of 'lighter-skinned' people, disputing the Polynesian theory that worshiped these giant statues. Covered in tattoos and extended earlobes, they held rituals and ceremonies before these stoic statues, holding some sort of spiritual or religious significance. Other archaeologists dispute this claim, claiming Roggeveen made it up. There is evidence of lighter-skinned people living on Easter Island, however.

Another common theory was to honor the chiefs and religious leaders that led the island. They believed that these statues held manna, their version of magical energy. It contained the manna of the chiefs, protecting the island from disaster. They also believed it brought good fortune and luck. Unfortunately the manna didn't protect them from killing each other.

There is evidence these Moui statues served as sacrificial or spiritual sites. Ahu Akivi, one Moui site on Easter Island, is surrounded by cremation pits filled with bones and shells. At other sites, scientists discovered skeletons at the base of the statues.

Also, the Moui statues are interestingly aligned with certain astronomical points in the galaxy. Did they gain manna from the astronomical alignments in the sky? Did the Moui statues have a different spiritual purpose?

Scientists will never know the true purpose of these Moui statues, but just like the people of Easter Island, these statues will remain a supernatural memory in the past lives of this small, uninhabited island. Only science will uncover the many secrets of this crematory island.

Part IV
Ghosts and Hauntings

The United States of America is a country often associated with all kinds of scary ghosts and reported real haunted houses and haunted mansions, and Plantations.

Quite often a few have made the claim of being "The scariest" and of course "The Most Haunted House in America". And there's quite a bit of anecdotal real haunted history evidence to support those most famous haunted House ghost filled claims.

Much of all haunted house lore is often vague, and riddled with urban legends and embellishments. Records exist always of terrible events occurring, but over the decades and even centuries, details are forgotten...new generations are born... and much is lost to time. And so to often the truth is never quite told.

"All houses wherein men have lived and died are haunted houses."
...Henry Wadsworth Longfellow

Ghosts of West Point

The United States Military Academy at West Point is an old but still functional military post plagued by a history of paranormal darkness.

Though it's been in official operation only since 1802, the whole area, which sits atop the approaches of the Hudson River, has been in use for as long back as 1778. It's a national landmark brimming with historical buildings, monuments, and ghosts & hauntings galore.

A lot has occurred at the grounds of West Point. It was used as a fortress during the American Revolution.

Later it was used to teach by generals such as Grant, Lee, MacArthur, Patton, and Pershing. Nowadays it still functions as a military school, but not necessarily one you would want to attend. According to many current and former students, sinister forces haunt its halls.

Take for instance room 4714 in the 47th Division Barracks. In 1972, two freshmen cadets reported seeing the apparition of an 18th-century Revolutionary soldier materialize from the wall. They first tried ignoring it, but it soon began tampering with their belongings, e.g., ruffling their bathrobes, turning the lights on and off, and even breaking plates and cups.

After several days, the cadets then reported the event to their superior, Cadet Captain Keith B. He attempted to investigate by spending an evening in the room, only to be awakened in the middle of the night by an "unnaturally cold" force. A subsequent investigation performed via the use of a thermocouple revealed that a significant decrease in temperature was indeed occurring in the room—though only at certain times of the day.

No other significant paranormal events have been 'reported' from Room 4714 since 1972, but many current and former cadets who are or were living in it claim having had strange experiences.

Some merely experienced abnormally cold temperatures, while one even swore he once woke up and felt someone standing on his chest.

Room 4714 isn't the only haunted room at West Point. There's also talk of a female, Irish cook who can be seen and heard making bread in the Superintendent's Mansion. Some cadets speculate that she is the ghost of "Miss Molly," a long-deceased maid who used to work for Brigadier General Sylvanus Thayer in the 1800s.

There's also the tale of Pershing Barracks, though it is one of the few unconfirmed instances of paranormal activity. Legend has it that a cadet was walking home to his room, when his roommate suddenly yelled a greeting at him from their window. The cadet turned toward his roomie, but he didn't just see one person at the window—he saw two. Beside his roommate was a fully armed cadet dressed as if he was about to go off to a Civil War reenactment. This wasn't strange, so the cadet continued on his way. Upon arriving at his room, he asked his roomie who had been with him. His roomie replied, "Nobody."

Perhaps the most disturbing event to ever occur at West Point was when a priest was summoned for an exorcism on Professor's Row. Newspaper clippings from the time speak of a possessed servant girl who began running around naked at night, screaming from the top of her lungs. A priest was subsequently brought in to cure her. There is no mention of what happened to her or the priest.

Despite West Point's sinister history, many cadets manage to make it through there without ever laying eyes on a single ghost, or experiencing anything paranormal whatsoever. However, even they are quick to assert that West Point is indeed haunted. It's not just ghosts and apparitions that have made West Point into what it is today. It's the overall atmosphere—one of a long, tumultuous history marred by the violence of war.

Fühlingen House in Cologne's Quarter Fühlingen (Haunted Locations in Germany)

During the years 1884 until 1888 the ground was built on with a stud, stables and as well the manor "House Fühlingen". The purchaser of the ground was Eduard Baron of Oppenheim. Firstly, he bought a part of the area and later on the entire territory of the so-called "Fühlinger Moor".

Any investment in the construction of House Fühlingen failed and cause ruin and bad luck for its occupants.

Oppenheim was the first victim. The stud was a bad investment and he resold it in 1907. Then a gravel works arose on the ground. From this has been existing the "Fühlinger Lake" even till today, but it was also a bad investment. Hard labourers were stationed there during the Second World War. One of them is said to have been executed. After the war, a "Nazi" lived there under a false name. When he was caught and saw no way out, he shot himself. In the years 50, the construction of a railway test track began but turned out to be a bad investment again.

Three years ago, a new building permission was submitted for a private investor. But the sanitation and reorganisation of Fühlingen House was delayed. The investor had to change the ground-plans for some apartments because no purchasers were found for the bigger ones of the apartments that measured up to 171 square meters.

Originally 21 apartments were scheduled. But as a condition requested by the town, 33 dwellings had to be constructed on the former monument-protected riding court. The already approved building permission expired because of re-scheduling. For the revised version a new approval had to be obtained. The authority for monument-protection had already approved the new plans. Since autumn 2007, the place has been again "under construction".

Also a lot of suicides took place on the site. Probably that refers to people who saw no way out of their financial ruin. There also exists a tombstone of a teacher situated behind the house, nearby in the forest.

But right there on this spot never existed a cemetery neither was one of the owners/occupants of Fühlingen House a teacher. So, from where originates the teacher respectively the tombstone? Perhaps there exists no relation between him and Fühlingen House? It is left open for any speculations.

Ghosts and spirits might be active on this ground considering the mischief and bad luck that ails/ailed the owners/occupants. In fact, there is something wrong about it. The ground is very historic. The entire territory is called – as already mentioned above – "Fühlinger Moor".

 In the year 1288, the Battle of Worringen took place on the Fühlinger Moor which cost thousands of people their lives. It is said to have been very bloody and mad.

The dead of this battle could be reason for so many things which have been taken their course not before the last 150 years. Probably the haunting was aggravated by additional dead of latter times like the hard labourers, the suicides, the Nazi? There is also everything open to any speculations.

Perhaps someday the truth/solution of the haunting will be found.

The Hauntings of The Hot Lake Hotel

The red brick building with its stately white columns echoes back to an earlier time, when healing waters were all the rage and ladies carrying parasols strolled the grounds. But lurking beneath the serene exterior is a history colored by elements of supernatural and strange.

Once known as "the Mayo Clinic of the West," Hot Lake Hotel was constructed in 1907 and purchased in 1917 by Dr. W.T. Phy, who added modern medical facilities, including a hospital, surgery, and X-ray room, to the hotel and created a popular resting spot renowned for the supposed medicinal properties of the spring's thermal waters. People came from throughout the country to partake of the spring's purported healing properties, and patient ailments ranged from rheumatoid arthritis to fatal cases of syphilis and tuberculosis.

After Dr. Phy's death in 1931, the hotel fell into decline, and in 1934 the wooden structures of the building burnt down, leaving only the red brick exterior. Although rumors that the hotel served as an insane asylum after 1934 are unsubstantiated, that it was used as a nursing home in the 1950s is well documented. It was ultimately abandoned in the 1970s, until it was purchased privately in 2003. Following substantial restoration work, and the collapse of the entire west wing in 2008, the hotel finally reopened in 2010 and is listed on the National Register of Historic Places.

Among the most commonly reported supernatural phenomenon are numerous reports of unearthly piano music. In its early days, the hotel acquired a piano owned by Robert E. Lee's wife—a piano which was already reputed to play by itself before the hotel's acquisition of it. In the early days, guests would report hearing the eerie music, and though the piano was later removed by a former owner (who committed suicide), the music can still be heard.

Another popular story involves a gardener who committed suicide on the grounds. It is said that he hung himself behind the hotel, and to this day reports circulate that he wanders the grounds.

A gazebo located near one of Hot Lake Spring's many lakes is frequently the subject of reports of voices whispering—perhaps the voices of long-ago lovers finding a stolen moment alone? Along the lakes' shores, many people report seeing the shadowy figures of long ago guests strolling.

Along the highway leading to the hotel, a thick fog oftentimes appears, and stories abound of ghostly apparitions emerging from the mist. Prior to the highway, the hotel was connected to the town of Richmond by a four-mile rail line built by Chinese workers who may still lurk along its path.

In the hotel, doors open and close by themselves, footsteps pound across the upper floors, and strange voices echo down the halls.

 Stories to explain these ghostly occurrences range from claims of vacationers who passed away to patients who were the victims of horrendous experiments to the departed spirits of the building's former nursing home residents.

Although the current owners of Hot Lake Hotel eschew all mention of the hotel's supernatural reputation, many residents of La Grande have their own anecdotal evidence to add to the more infamous stories of the hotel's ghostly denizens. A visit to the site is sure to leave the guest with the unearthly impression of sulfur-laden hot springs, swirling mists, and the sense that the door between the past and the present swings open at Hot Lake Hotel with unnerving frequency.

The Ghosts and Hauntings of Fort Mifflin

There were unsuccessful attempts by the British army to overtake the fort, and after serving its purpose as a means of defense, it was later used as a prison for soldiers from both the North and the South. The fort had served other miscellaneous purposes as well until it was finally closed in the 1960's. Since then it has been restored to resemble the original structure of the building, and was used as a historical site which featured tours for visitors, though it seemed these visitors were not the only ones that had a presence within its walls.

Fort Mifflin has also gone by other names, including Fort Island Battery and Mud Island Fort, but no matter how it was known by name, it was also known by many as a place where spiritual encounters and paranormal events would take place, leading to many stories of basic hauntings and unexplainable events.

One of the most talked about hauntings of Fort Mifflin is that of the "Screaming Woman". This is said to take place in an area known as the Officer's Quarters, where Elizabeth Pratt was said to have hung herself in regret for not making amends with her daughter over a love interest of her daughter before she succumbed to death from "yellow fever". Her spirit still seems to be present within the room, and people have talked about hearing a woman's scream coming from this room. Police have actually been called to this location numerous times by people hearing the scream, fearing that someone may be getting murdered, but the police have never found anyone present upon their arrival.

There are also rumors of a friendly tour guide in the Power Magazine area dressed in Revolutionary War attire who enjoys socializing, joking, and answering questions for people who are touring the fort. However, the officials that handle the visitors and tours for the fort say that they do not have any employee who dresses in this manner, nor gives the same tour that has been given by this "special" tour guide.

Another popular haunting of Fort Mifflin is the story of what is known as "The Blacksmith". The blacksmith's shop is located in the middle of the fort, where a blacksmith named Jacob would frequently get in trouble by his commander for wanting to leave the door to the shop open while he was working. There have been numerous accounts of problems in keeping the door shut in this area to this day.

Another location that has given rise to stories of paranormal activity is Casemate 5. It is believed that the spirit of William Howe is the one haunting this location. Howe was a deserter of the Civil War and also a convicted murderer, and was the only person who was sentenced to hanging at Fort Mifflin. An underground casemate was discovered which resembled a jail cell, and Howe's signature was found here scrawled on the wall.

It is said that many who have entered this room have felt a presence and even seen what they call "a faceless man", and those who have blond hair seem to have more experiences here than others. This is one area of the fort that many voices have been heard along with stories of other apparitions.

While these are some of the most famous hauntings of Fort Mifflin, the bloody battles that took place here along with the rest of its history has led to many stories of ghostly encounters and unexplained occurrences. If you are not a believer in the paranormal, a trip to haunted Fort Mifflin just might enough to change your mind.

Ghost Flight 401

Eastern Air Lines Flight 401 was one of the deadliest plane crashes in the history of the United States. Of the 163 passengers and 13 crew members, 101 died when the plane crashed in the Florida Everglades on December 22, 1972.

The flight had left John F. Kennedy International Airport and was nearly at its destination of Miami International Airport when things started to go wrong. As the aircraft approached the airport, the landing gear was lowered, however, the landing gear indicator, which lets the crew know that the gear is properly locked in the "down" position, did not light up.

As the Pilot circled the area and the crew tried to determine why there was no confirmation light indicating the gear was down, the plane somehow got switched to autopilot. The plane began to descend, but the distracted crew did not notice. The final report on the crash stated it was completely due to pilot error.

For some time following the crash, employees of the airline reported seeing the ghosts of dead crew members on other planes. Many believed this was due to the fact that parts from the Flight 401 plane were salvaged and refitted on similar models of plane. The employees specifically spoke of seeing the spirits of Captain Bob Loft and Second Officer Don Repo.

One story claims that on a 1973 flight, a Flight Attendant saw Captain Loft on her flight and questioned him as to who he was since she had not seen him board. He did not reply, so she went and got the captain to accompany her to talk to him. The captain immediately recognized Captain Loft. When the flight captain called out Loft's name in shock, Loft immediately disappeared, apparently in front of dozens of passengers.

On a 1974 flight, the Pilot claims to have seen Don Repo sitting in the Flight Engineer's seat. The pilot said that Repo told him that he and Loft would not allow another crash like Flight 401, and then he vanished into thin air. A crew member of another flight said that Repo appeared to him and said he had completed the pre-flight check.

Another time, a Flight Attendant saw a Flight Engineer fixing the plane's microwave oven. While speaking to the Flight Engineer later, she asked what was wrong with the microwave. He replied that had no idea what she was talking about, and he had not known anything to be wrong with it. Repo also appeared several times in the electronics room beneath the cockpit. Usually it was to crew members who went to investigate knocking sounds they heard coming from the room.

The stories were so common and spreading so fast that the management of Eastern Air Lines warned its employees that spreading these stories could result in their dismissal. In 1976, a few years after the ghost sightings stopped, John G. Fuller published a book titled The Ghost of Flight 401, which detailed the events leading up to the crash and the stories of ghosts told later. Much of the information in the book came from his wife, Elizabeth, who had been an Eastern Air Lines Flight Attendant.

Phantom Phone Calls

Is it possible for those who have passed from this mortal coil to make contact from the spirit world through electronic media? Can a loved one make contact through the humble telephone to say one last good-bye or even give warning of impending disaster?

As odd as it may seem, this phenomenon is not an unusual one and occurs quite frequently, usually with in the first 24 to 48 hours after someone has died. However, many people have reported getting phone calls from deceased loved ones years after they have passed on. These calls are nearly always filled with heavy static and the caller's voice sounds faint, as if it is coming from a great distance.

Countless people have reported receiving telephone calls that seem to have come from a deceased relative or friend. These strange calls usually happen not more than once or twice and are nearly always brief messages.

For some, these phone calls can be frightening, but for others they are a source of comfort and help grieving loved ones move on with their lives.

Often when a person receives such a phone call he or she may not realize, at first, that the person that they are talking to is someone who has passed on from this world and thinks that he or she is talking to corporeal person.

Man people have reported receiving phone calls from a person that they never knew directly in life, but receive an urgent message to relay to another person he or she and the deceased both know/knew. These types of phantom phone calls are rarer. Often, the recipients of such calls say that the voice sounds odd, almost mechanical or unreal in some way.

In most of these phantom phone call cases, people reported that the ring sounded different than it usually did.

The tone would be different and the rings would come in shorter than usual bursts. Considering that paranormal investigators use all sorts of electronic equipment to detect spirit activity due to the fact that spirits do indeed seem to be able to communicate through electronic means; then it is not at all farfetched to think that the spirits of departed friends or loved ones could conceivable use the telephone as a medium to make contact between this world and theirs.

If this is indeed the case, then it is quite possible that one day we may find a way to develop such a device that is specifically designed to be able to allow direct interaction with the spirit world using the basic telephone technologies and developing them to a whole new level. Not only would this enable people to talk to their loved ones, but it would invariable prove that we continue to live on even after physical death. Perhaps we could gain new insights as to what happens after we die and remove the fear and uncertainty from this seemingly inevitable process.

Until such a time comes, the mystery of these phantom phone calls will continue to be just that, a mystery.

Roadside Ghosts

All across America and in many other parts of the world, there are haunted highways and back roads and many people report encounters with the spirits and ghosts who roam these often lonely roads.

Seemingly seeking a way home, or trying to hitch a ride to the destination they were heading for when death severed them from their mortal bodies. Still, other people report seeing phantom cars that disappear as they reach a certain curve or area of a road, or even ghostly wagons being pulled by wispy horses and driven by spirits dressed in period clothing. Many folks have reported picking up a hitchhiker only to have the shock of witnessing the seemingly solid, living person transfigure into the image of a rotting corpse before completely fading away.

One such place is in Tompkinsville, Kentucky. Tompkinsville is located in the south central part of Kentucky, about twenty miles southeast of Glasgow, Kentucky. There is an old road outside of Tompkinsville that is called the Meshack Road. Tompkinsville is a small town itself is located just a few miles north of the Tennessee border.

For many years, people who have lived in the area, and even tourists who know nothing of the area's history, have been reporting encounters with a ghostly young girl associated with this road. One of the many similar reports tells of two young men were on their way to a local weekend dance that was always held in town on the weekends back during the 1950s. One Friday evening while they were on their way to the dance they saw an attractive young woman walking along Meshack Road. They offered her a ride into town and she accepted.

She looked like she was dressed for a night out on the town, although the dress looked somewhat old-fashioned, and they decided to invite her to go along to the dance with them. Reportedly, she danced with both of the young men that evening and there were witnesses who remembered seeing the woman, noting that she was a stranger to the area.

As the dance ended, the young woman agreed to let the boys drive her home, but only if they would let her out at a certain area. It was pouring the rain when they left the dance hall and one of the boys offered her his coat. He told her that he would pick it up later.

The two young men dropped the strange girl off at a small, somewhat run down house along Meshack Road and a few days later, the young man went back to pick up his coat. He walked up on the porch and asked the middle-aged woman for the girl he had dropped off a few nights earlier. The woman told him that while she had once had a daughter, she had died in an accident on the road a few years earlier. She told the confused young man where her daughter's body was buried and he went to the churchyard. There he found his coat draped over the gravestone. There is another strange phantom that is also reported to haunt Meshack road.

For many years, people who have traveled along this road have reported that they have felt an unseen presence holding tightly to the waist of a person riding a horse or riding a motorcycle. This unseen entity holds onto the rider's waist for about a mile and then disappears. No one seems to know who or what could be behind this strange occurrence.

There are many other such tales all across America and such places always seem to have been the site for traumatic and/or violent, unexpected deaths. Perhaps, one day, these poor lost souls may find their way to their destinations, or perhaps, they will forever walk the lonely roads and byways where they met their end, forever reliving their last moments. Perhaps, one day you will meet one of the roadside ghosts of America.

The Curse of the Hexham Heads

The discovery of two hewn stone heads in a garden in Hexham seemed to worth no particular attention at the beginning. But then a nightmare began because the heads were probably the reason for paranormal phenomena and caused the frightful appearance of a werewolf-man.

Hexham is a borough in the valley of the Tyne, 32 kilometres far from Newcastle-upon-Tyne. Here, one afternoon in February 1972, the 11 year old Colin Robson weeded the garden behind the house of his parents. In doing so, he found a round stone in the size of a tennis ball with a mysterious lead on one side. When he removed the earth, he discovered rough carven human traits on the stone; the lead was actually the throat.

Full of joy he called his younger brother Leslie to come. Together, the both boys continued to search and soon Leslie found a second head.

The stones, which were called the Hexham-heads, represent two different types. The first was similar to a skull and seemed to bear male traits; it was called "boy". The stone was of a greenish grey and glittered with quartz crystals. It was very heavy, heavier than cement or concrete. The hair seemed to run in stripes from front to back. The other head, the "girl" was similar to a witch. It had wild pop-eyes and the hair was tied back to some knot. In the hair, traces of yellow and red colour could be found.

After they have dug up the heads, the boys took them into the house. Thereby, the whole disaster commenced.

The heads turned round without reason, objects broke to pieces without evident cause. When the mattress of one of the two daughters of the Robson's was dotted with broken glass, the girls moved out of the room. In the meantime, a mysterious flower bloomed at Christmas exactly on that spot, where the heads were found. Besides, a strange light was glowing there.

It could be stated that the events at the Robson's have nothing to do with the appearance of the heads but deals with poltergeist-phenomena, which has been evoked by the adolescent children of the Robson's. Nevertheless, the neighbour of the Robson's, Ellen Dodd, had such a frightful experience, that cannot be explained easily.

Later on, Mrs Dodd said a being on all fours had carefully touched her at the legs. It has been half man, half sheep. Mrs Robson remembered that in the same night she has heard a cracking sound and screams next door. Her neighbours told her that those sounds derived from a being that looked like a werewolf.

Dr Anne Ross, a significant expert of the Celtic culture, stated that the heads would be approximately 1800 years old and were originally used during Celtic head-rituals. The apparitions stopped after the heads has left the house.

In 1972, the story took a new turn, when truck driver Desmond Craigie stated that the "Celtic" heads were only 16 years old and that he has manufactured them as toys for his daughter Nancy. Astonishingly, the age of the heads could not be determined even with the help of a scientific analysis.

When the heads really stem from the Celtic epoch, it can be easily imagined that an ancient curse weighs on them. But when they are not old, how can it be explained that they evoke paranormal phenomena? It exists a theory that mineral art products can store visual pictures of humans from which they have been created. It is supposed that localities and objects can take up information that can cause particular phenomena.

The scientist Dr. Robins was also interested in the reports about the sounds that are said to have been occurred in connection with the heads. He pointed to a parallel of a being from the ancient Nordic mythology, the "Wulver". He was powerful and dangerous but benevolent towards human people as long as they did not provoke him. Dr. Robins was so fascinated by the heads that he intended to take them home with him. When he laid them in his car to drive home and turned the ignition key, all electrical appliances on the dashboard failed. He took a look at the heads and commanded them: "Stop with that!" – And the car started.

The present whereabouts of the Hexham-heads are not known. But it cannot be doubted that they really caused the phenomena which are similar to those that are usually attributed to poltergeists. They functioned in some form as a trigger. But why? This leads to the question of their age. Are they of Celtic origin as Dr. Ross has stated or have they been recently manufactured in 1956 by a Hexham-inhabitant for his daughter? The theory of Dr. Robins says: When an object is in the position to cause poltergeist-phenomena, so it does not depend on who has manufactured it but "where" it had been manufactured.

Bachelor's Grove Cemetery Hauntings

Close to the southwestern suburb of Midlothian is Rubio Woods Forest Preserve. This little secluded area of trees sits in the very urbanized sprawl of Chicago.

This quiet little wooded sanctuary gives one the illusion that they are far away from the hustle and bustle of the crowded city; far away from the rat race of everyday life. However, right on the edge of the diminutive forest is a small graveyard that many people believe is the most haunted place in all of the Chicago area. The name given to this cemetery is Bachelor's Grove and this once long forgotten graveyard seems to be teeming with ghosts. Over the years, numerous people have report many cases of paranormal phenomena, everything from full bodied apparitions to glowing balls of light. There have been no new burials in Bachelor's Grove for many a long year, and up until the last 15 to 20 years had been almost completely forgotten. In recent years, though, it has become a favorite place for ghost hunters to carry out their investigations.

The history of Bachelor's Grove is a bit sketchy, but all of the local historians agree that this enigmatic burial ground was started in the very early part of the 1800s. One of the local legends says the cemetery got its name because only single men were buried here, but Bachelor's Grove got it's name from the family who settled in the area during the latter part of the 1700s and early 1800s. A nearby town dating back to the 1820s was settled mainly by German immigrants from New York, Vermont and Connecticut.

One of the families that moved into the area had the surname of "Batchelder" and it was their name was given to the land where they settled.

The small settlement continued to be known as Batchelder's Grove, until 1850, when postmaster Samuel Everden changed it to 'Bremen', which is where the new post office was built. In 1855, it was changed once again to "Batchelder's Grove" by the new postmaster Robert Patrick, but the post office was shut down three years later and the settlement, officially, ceased to exist and, in time, was reclaimed by the forest.

The cemetery itself continued to be used up until 1989, then it too was forgotten by all but a very few. The land was set aside by Samuel Everden to be used as a burial ground in 1844, when one of the first of the locals passed on, Mrs. Eliza Scott. The land had been donated by Mr. Everden and it was named "Everden" in his honor. The last burials to take place in Everden Cemetery were that of Laura M. McGhee in 1965 and Robert Shields, who was cremated and then buried in 1989.

The last caretaker of the cemetery was Clarence Fulton, whose ancestors were some of the early settlers in the old township. Mr. Fulton reportedly said that Bachelor's Grove was a sort of park for many years and people would go there to fish and swim in the pond. He also said that families would come on weekends to care for the graves of the deceased and to have nice picnics in the cool shade under the trees. However, as often happens, people eventually stopped coming to the quiet little cemetery to pay their respects and care for the graves of those who had passed on.

Vandals and grave robbers found Bachelor's Grove sometime during the 1960s and began to trash the lovely little cemetery. Gravestones were pushed over, broken and destroyed and even stolen. Graves were dug up and opened. Bones of the deceased were sometimes found to be strewn all over the grounds of the cemetery.

It is these disturbances, many people believe, that started the haunting of the cemetery. However, others say that there is another reason for the activity. Forest rangers, and other people who have been visitors to the cemetery, have reported that they found the mutilated bodies of chickens and other small animals that had been killed in a sort of ritualistic fashion near the small pond on the edge of the cemetery. Police officers that have been on patrol around the woods during the night have often reported seeing evidence of occult rituals in and around the graveyard. Strange inscriptions and odd sigils have been carved or painted on trees, the grave stones and on the cemetery grounds as well. This, of course, has led many of the locals to believe that the cemetery has been, and is still being used for occult activities.

Finally, authorities closed down the road ways leading to the cemetery and it became hardly more than a memory. For those curious folks who decide they want to check out Bachelor's Grove for ghosts, it can be found by leaving the Midlothian roadway and taking a short walk up an overgrown gravel path that is surrounded on both sides by the forest. The old road is blocked with chains and large concrete blocks, as well as a "No Trespassing" sign, near the head of the old trail. The burial ground lies about a half-mile beyond it in the woods.

Today, the cemetery is choked with weeds and is surrounded by a tall, rusting, chain-link fence, but it's easy enough to gain access through the holes that vandals and trespassers have cut into the fence. The cemetery sign has long since rotted away. The grave stones are scattered about, no longer marking the resting places of the folks whose names are cut into them. Many of the stones are missing, probably lost forever to vandals and time. The most shocking thing to the people who see them is the graves that have been violated due to grave robbers attempting to make off with skulls or any valuables from those whose rest they disturbed.

One night during the late 1970s, a couple of Cook County Forest Preserve officers were on their usual night patrol around the cemetery and swore that they both saw the apparition of a horse pulling a plow behind it that was steered by the ghost of an old man rising up out of the waters of the pond. The creepy apparition crossed the road in front of the ranger's vehicle and then vanished into the forest. The men later reported the incident and they have not been the only people reporting to have seen the ghosts of the old man and the horse.

What gives more credence to the ranger's story is that in the 1870s, a farmer was plowing a nearby field when something startled his horse and the old farmer became tangled in the reins. He was dragged behind the horse and it plunged into the small pond. The farmer was pulled down into the dark and murky water by the weight of the horse and the plow they drowned. Neither of the officers were aware of this little piece of the area's history.

It is also along this piece of deserted road where other odd occurrences have been reported. One such tale is of the "phantom farm house". Scores of people have reported seeing this strange apparition appearing and disappearing along the trail for many decades now. What makes these reports so credible is that they come from people who had no idea that the house doesn't actually exist.

The house has been reported to be seen during all types of weather, as well as during both the day and at night. While there is no historical record of any house existing in that particular location, the descriptions do not vary. Each person who has seen the house describes an old, two-story farm house that is white washed, a large front porch with post to either side of the porch entrance, a porch swing and a light that cheerily burns in the front window. As people approach the old house, usually to seek directions to the cemetery, it is reported that it seems to shrink until it finally just fades away. No one has ever claimed to have actually set foot on the front porch of the house and local legend says that if a person does enter the house they will never return.

There are also reports of the spooky orbs or "ghost lights" being seen on a regular basis floating around the cemetery as well as numerous apparitions of the ghost of a woman walking aimlessly around the cemetery with a baby wrapped in a blanket and held in her arms. In 2006 Ken Melvoin-Berg, one of the most well-known of the local psychic detectives, went with a reporter from the Chicago Tribune to the old graveyard and there Mr. Melvoin-Berg encountered the spirit of a young boy.

Ken heard the child crying and telling him that he had lost some money. The reporter stated that Ken got a very odd look on his face and seemed "to lose it himself".

Ken then staggered out of the cemetery toward the pond. Wading into the dark and scummy water, Ken stopped, bent over and stuck his hands into the muck, and found a 1942 Walking Liberty half-dollar coin. It was just where the little ghost boy said it would be.

It would seem that the spirits of the Bachelor's Grove cemetery do not rest in peace, forever wandering this lonely little patch of ground that seems to be a shadow's thickness and a age away from our modern world and big cities.

Poltergeists and PK energy

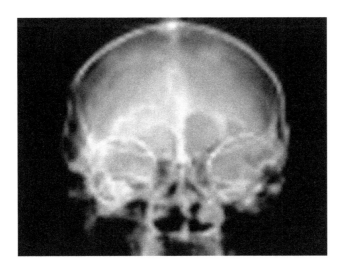

Written reports of poltergeist activity go as far back as ancient Rome, medieval China and Germany, but one can well imagine that such things have probably been going on since humans arrived on the planet.

A Poltergeist, from the Germany words Polter, meaning noisy, and Geist, which is ghost, is used to refer to a malevolent spirit or a form of energy which generally manifests as strange noises, knocking, disappearing objects or objects flying across a room, door opening and closing by themselves, and strange, or foul, unexplainable odors.

The ancient written reports tell of dirt being thrown by something unseen, objects hurtling across a room all by themselves, loud noises, unexplained lights and horrible stenches, as well as ghostly apparitions. All of these reports from ancient times sound nearly identical to modern reports of poltergeist activity.

Study after on-going study has been done to try and seek out the cause of this phenomenon. The phenomenon seems to be linked to a type of subconscious psychokinesis (PK), and generally such activity seems to center around a specific person, also called an 'agent', and seems to usually be focused around a pre-pubescent or pubescent girl. Sometimes, such activity only lasts a short period of time; while in other cases it may go on for years.

Some scientists believe that poltergeist/PK activity may stem from emotional problems associated with anxiety, anger, over-stress, or mental disorders such as obsessions, phobias and schizophrenia. In many cases when the particular person/agent got treatment for their emotional or mental issues the poltergeist activity disappeared completely.

However, not all poltergeist cases are associated with a person. In these cases the entity seems to be separate from any influence other than it's own. Many experts on the paranormal/supernatural world believe these cases are the result of demonic activity, or some other sort of non-human spirit entity. In these types of poltergeist activity such entities can become violent and actually physically attack anyone around it causing injury, or even in some cases, death.

If you believe that you, or you and your family, are experiencing poltergeist activity then get help. You should be able to go online and find a priest or even a paranormal research group that specializes in such things. Taking care of this type a problem before it gets too out of hand can help reduce the risk of the situation turning violent and prevent anyone from being hurt.

If ANYONE tries to charge you money for getting rid of something like this then look elsewhere for help. More than likely such persons are of no real use and are just trying to scam people out of their money.

Do not try to get rid of a poltergeist by leaving or running from your home, as this rarely works. Most people find that the poltergeist merely follows them and continues to make life even more difficult.

In some cases, these types of spirits are linked to an object. If think this may be the case, then get rid of that particular object either by returning it to where you found it, or by simply just getting out of your house and on its way to the local landfill.

A look into the Black Hope Curse

Just outside of Houston, Texas, is a subdivision called Newport; an upper-middle class neighborhood with neat lawns and very nice houses--a normal looking place; however, the land on which this neighborhood was built is anything but normal.

In early part of the decade of the 80's, a couple named Sam and Judith Haney decided to buy one of the lovely houses in the new housing development of Newport Subdivision--they would soon wish they had not.

What the developers had not disclosed about the land they chose to turn into this upscale subdivision was a dark and morbid secret that would turn their lives, and the lives of some of their neighbors, into a nightmare. Sam Haney said it all started when a strange, old man showed up at their door with an eerie tale that would soon prove to be true.

The old man told them that their house, and the entire subdivision, was built on an old burial ground called Black Hope...a potter's field where the majority of its inhabitants were once black slaves. The last burial in the potter's field cemetery was back during the Depression Era of the 1930's.

He also told them that many of these graves were in their backyard and the developers had only moved the grave markers, not the bodies.

This bit of creepy news alarmed the Haney's, and since they had decided to add an in-ground swimming pool in their backyard, Sam and Judith, his wife, would soon find out if the old man's claims were true.

Sam Haney rented a small back hoe and started digging, and it wasn't long before the Haney's found something that would mortify them. Mr. Haney found a pine coffin and realized that the old man was telling the truth.

Mr. Haney immediately called the local Sheriff as well as the county coroner, and they conducted an official exhumation of the remains. They also found another coffin that was right next to the first one that had been uncovered. Inside the second coffin they found two thin wedding bands on the brittle finger bone of the skeleton and then handed them to Judith. She and her husband was horrified to realize that they had desecrated the graves of two people.

The Haney's decided they would try to find out whose remains had been buried on the property and they finally found an old man by the name of Jasper Norton who could give them information about the land and the property their house was built on. Many years ago, Mr. Norton had been employed as a gravedigger, and had been the person to inter as many as 60 people in the area during the late 20's and during 30's. He said that the Haney's house and a quite a few of the other houses had been built on top of an old cemetery called Black Hope. Many of the deceased were former slaves who had settled, died, and been buried in the area during the 1800s.

Norton identified the remains of the two people found buried in the Haney's backyard as an old couple by the names of Betty and Charlie Thomas, who had been former slaves and died during the early thirties. When Sam and Judith Haney were unable to locate any living relatives of the Thomas', the Haney's decided to rebury the remains back where

127

they found them and live happily knowing they had restored the Thomas' to the rightful resting place. Unfortunately, things did not remain peaceful or happy.

Not long after they reburied Charlie and Betty's remains, the Haney's started having weird and unexplainable occurrences happen in their home. They would hear eerie voices talking while they were trying to sleep, and one night Judith was startled awake when a clock in the bedroom, that was unplugged, began giving off sparks and an eerie glow. One night after her husband had left for work, and Judith was alone in the house, a disembodied voice asked Judith "What are you doing?" Spooked by the unfamiliar voice, she checked for intruders, but there was nobody there and the door was locked. The next morning, while getting dressed to go out, Judith couldn't find her favorite red shoes. When she finally found them, they were outside, sitting on top of Betty Thomas' grave. It was also the date of Betty Thomas' birthday.

Another couple by the name of Ben and Jean Williams were also having some serious trouble with unexplainable and creepy occurrences.

They lived just across the street from the Haney's with their granddaughter, Carli. They had been having problems from almost the moment their house was finished and they moved in. The house was always cold and felt clammy and icky all the time, no matter how hot the weather was, and Jean and Carli couldn't shake the feeling they were always being watched. The toilets were always flushing by themselves and doors were being open and shut by unseen hands. Household appliances seemed to operate on their own. Perfectly rectangular sinkholes would opened up in the yard, and no matter how well, or how often, the Williams would fill them in, the sinkholes would show right back up in just a matter of days. Any new plants, trees, or anything else the William's would plant would die no matter what they would do. The Williams noticed some rather odd markings on an old oak tree that stood by the sinkholes, an arrow carved into the tree that pointed downward with two horizontal slash marks beneath it. Finally, a longtime resident of the area told them he had made the marks on the old tree as a way to be able to identify where his two sisters had been buried. This shocked and disturbed the Williams.

Not only were the Williams being plagued by apparitions, voices, and unseen footsteps, but 6 members of their family were stricken with rare types of cancer and 3 of them died, all within 6 months.

The Haney's were also being plagued with strange health problems and terrified of staying in their house, Sam and Judith decided to fight back and sue the developer for not disclosing that the houses had been built over a cemetery. At first they were awarded $142,000 by a jury, but a judge decided that the developers were not liable nor required to pay the Haney's anything, and reversed the decision, ordering the Haney's to pay $50,000 in court costs. Beaten, broken, and financially ruined, the Haney's filed bankruptcy and abandoned their home.

The Williams' decided to also take legal action, but were told that unless they had proof of a cemetery on their property, then there was nothing they could do. So, Jean made a decision she regrets to this day. Out of desperation, and to prove their home was built on a cemetery, Jean started digging up the sinkholes beneath the oak tree, positive she would find the proof they needed. Jean started feeling ill and couldn't dig any longer, so her daughter, Tina, picked up where her mother left off and kept digging. After digging for about a half-hour, Tina collapsed, and knowing something seriously was wrong, her last words to her parents were for them to take care of her baby.

Two days later she died, at the age of thirty, of a massive heart attack. She had no prior heart disease or any other health conditions that would have caused her collapse and death. Grieving terribly, the William's fled their house, leaving everything behind.

Apparitions

The term 'apparition' is defined simply as a supernatural manifestation, or in more common terms, the appearance of a ghost or spirit of a human or an animal.

These strange, and often frightening, manifestations have been reported for as long as mankind has walked the earth, and are as variable and different as the people who witness them. Let's look at some of the various types of this particular phenomenon.

One type of apparition is called an 'atmospheric apparition'. These types of manifestations are not usually considered to be what experts in the paranormal would call an 'intelligent haunting', but a haunting that is more like a tape recording. Most of the time these types of apparitions stem from very violent and tragic events. The energies released from the individuals involved in these events seem to become imprinted upon the very fabric of time and space, what is known as the Akashaic record in Hindu beliefs. These events, like fierce battles that took place on a particular piece of ground, such as Gettysburg, may leave a sort of recording that replays itself over and over for a period of time. One of the interesting things about such manifestations is that they do fade over a period of time; much like a video tape will eventually wear out after much usage.

Another type of apparition are called 'historical apparitions.' These apparitions generally consist of seeing people from another time period of a certain house or area that has a particular sort of history. These apparitions are always dressed in period clothing and never seem to be aware of the witnesses or other people who may live in the residence in the present time.

One of the most common forms of this phenomenon is called 'Recurring apparitions'. These are ghosts or spirits that occur in regularly at a specific time each year. The manifestation usually occurs on the specific date or anniversary of the event which caused this sort of haunting to transpire.

Such reports of recurring apparitions often include murder victims, people who have committed suicide, quite often people have reported seeing ghostly armies or soldiers marching and running across battlefields to the sounds of cannon and gun fire.

Crisis or Death Bed Apparitions are spirits of the dying or deceased individual that appear to loved ones or close friends shortly before or just after their physical death. These are probably the most common types of apparitions. These types of apparitions rarely go on for more than 3-5 days after a person's body expires. This type of apparition seems to be most common during times of war. During all the wars of the last 200 or so years, there were hundreds of reported cases of the appearances of dying or dead service men to family members even though they were thousands of miles apart. The most common ideology with this particular type of apparition is that the spirit of the departed appears one last time to take care of some unfinished business, to say a final goodbye, or let their loved ones know they are at peace.

Benevolent and Malevolent Fairies

Are they the so-called Irish "Tuatha De Danan", who when no longer worshipped und fed with offerings, dwindled away in the popular imagination, and now are only a few spans high?

Who and what are fairies? Are they fallen angels who were not good enough to be saved, nor bad enough to be lost? Are they the gods of the earth or of pagan history? Are they the so-called Irish "Tuatha De Danan", who when no longer worshipped und fed with offerings, dwindled away in the popular imagination, and now are only a few spans high?

There is much evidence to prove them fallen angels. Witness the nature of the creatures, their caprice, their way of being good to the good and evil to the evil, having every charm but conscience – consistency. Beings so quickly offended that you must not speak much about them at all, and never call them anything but the "good people". So easily pleased, they will do their best to keep misfortune away from you, if you leave a little milk for them on the window-sill overnight. On the whole, the popular belief tells us most about them, telling us how they fell, and yet were not lost because their evil was wholly without malice.

Are they the "gods of the earth"? Perhaps! Occultists, from Paracelsus to Elephas Levi, divide the nature spirits into gnomes, sylphs, salamanders, undines; or earth, air, fire and water spirits. The gnomes are covetous and of melancholic temperament.

Their usual height is but two spans, though they can elongate themselves into giants. The sylphs are capricious and of bilious temperament. They are in size and strength much greater than men, as becomes the people of the winds. The salamanders are wrathful and in temperament sanguine. In appearance they are long, lean and dry. The undines are soft, cold, fickle and phlegmatic. In appearance they are like man. The salamanders and sylphs have no fixed dwellings. Many mystic writers – in all ages and countries – have declared that behind the visible are chains on chains of conscious beings, which are not of heaven but of the earth, who have no inherent form but change according to their whim or the mind that sees them. You cannot lift your hand without influencing and being influenced by hoards. The visible world is merely their skin. In dreams men go amongst them, play with them and combat with them.

Fairies are not always little. They seem to take what size or shape pleases them. Their chief occupations are feasting, fighting, making love and playing the most beautiful music. They have only one industrious person amongst them, the leprechaun, and the shoemaker.

They have three great festivals in the year: May Eve, Midsummer Eve, November Eve.

On May Eve, every seventh year, they fight all round for the harvest, for the best ears of grain belong to them. On Midsummer Eve, when the bonfires are lighted, the fairies are at their gayest and sometimes steal away beautiful mortals to be their brides. On November Eve they are at their gloomiest, for this is the first night of winter. This night they dance with the ghosts, and the Pooka is abroad, and witches make their spells.

After November Eve the blackberries are no longer wholesome, for the Pooka has spoiled them.

When they are angry they paralyse men and animals, when they are gay they sing.

Do they die? No, they are said to be immortal....if not their shapes, so their souls.

Some famous representatives of the "good people":

The name "Leprechaun" is from the Irish "leith brog", i.e. the One-shoemaker, since he is generally seen working at a single shoe. He is withered, old and solitary and dressed with all non-fairy homeliness. He belongs to the mischievous phantoms and is a great practical joker among the good people. The leprechaun makes shoes continually and has grown very rich.

The Pooka seems essentially an animal spirit. Some derive his name from "poc", a he-goat.
He lives on solitary mountains and among old ruins – grown monstrous with much solitude – and is of the race of the nightmare. November-day is sacred to the Pooka because he is a November spirit. It is hard to realize that wild, staring phantom grown sleek and civil. He has many shapes – is now a horse, now a donkey, now a bull, now a goat, now an eagle. Like all spirits, he is only half in the world of form.

The Banshee is an attendant fairy that follows the old families, and none but them, and wails before a death. Many have seen her as she goes wailing and clapping her hands. The keen, the funeral cry of the peasantry, is said to be an imitation of her cry. When more than one Banshee is present, and they wail and sing in chorus, it is for the death of some holy or great one. An omen that sometimes accompanies the Banshee is an immense black coach, mounted by a coffin, and drawn by headless horses. It will go rumbling to your front door, and if you open it a basin of blood will be thrown in your face.

Demons of the Night

By that time when people only had candles to keep the darkness away, a frightful horde of spirits awoke during the long hours between dusk and dawn. They appeared as bodiless shadows or transitory shapes which had been a patchwork of motley parts – goat hooves and cat paws, dog-teeth and human faces.

By that time when people only had candles to keep the darkness away, a frightful horde of spirits awoke during the long hours between dusk and dawn. They appeared as bodiless shadows or transitory shapes which had been a patchwork of motley parts – goat hooves and cat paws, dog-teeth and human faces. Evil to the backbone, they cowered in hedges or scraped at doors and window shutters, always ready to pinch and to scratch, to seduce, to paralyse and to kill.

Common people spoke about goblins, ghosts or gnomes, and they were afraid of them. Even scholars and sorcerers feared those creatures, but they tried to master and to command these supernatural beings to render them serviceable to human purposes. Learned sorcerers called them demons, sometimes also scions. The signification of this word - that originally designated the scions for grafting the trees – turned into "offspring". When sorcerers used it, they expressed that the demons were offspring's of Satan, the Foe.

The exact determination of the demons' powers was a step to dominate them and the scholars went astonishing far in doing so. The most industrious among them asserted for example, that the different spirits which haunted the world constituted an infernal hierarchy with Satan as their leader and those they were classified into six legions.

Each legion consisted of 66 cohorts or divisions, each cohort had 666 companies and each company comprised of 6666 soldiers.

This nocturnal army indulged only in the fancies of the scholars: The total number of demons in the system would have exceeded one billion – that would have been more demons existing on the earth than humans at that time. Most scholars were not so much interested in such calculations but more in the denomination and characterization of certain demonic spirits.

The description of powerful demons had been rendered more difficult because they were masters of transformation. A spirit was in the position to assume a harmless shape to attend to his hellish business in the mortal world. He could appear as domestic animal, for example as dog, as fly, toad or mouse to execute his work unnoticed.

His real shape was a hideous reflection of his malignity, a scorn of all natural living beings and shapes. There was for example Eurynome. He devoured corpses, had an ugly, wrinkled skin, sharp teeth and claws at hands and feet. He was said to be Satan's Prince of Death und his services were useful for those who were up to murder.

The demon Ronwe – clumsy, heavy with giant ears and long tail – imparted to the knowledge of all languages – a dangerous weapon for all who worked with magic spells. Xaphan on the other hand, who always carry along with him bellows, was only an ugly curiosity; he was occupied with – so it was said – fanning the eternal fire in hell. Orobas held a high rank in the infernal realm. When he was summoned, he sometimes appeared as a human and another time again as a horse. He could report the truth of all historical events or predict the course of history. Astaroth, the Grand Duke of Hell, appeared on some occasions as man in many colours and on others as fallen angel – what he really was. His once beautiful angelic traits were distorted and his gorgeous wings were lustreless. He was spreading such a terrible stench around him that the sorcerers who summoned him wore a silver ring that should protect them against the demonic evaporation. Like Orobas, Astaroth could also predict the future and reveal the lost past and he possessed of the complete knowledge of all skills that a man or sorcerer could master.

Sorcerers could evoke a lot of other Satan's servants – Abracax and Flauros, Behemoth and Belial, Buer and Asmodeus – and about their powers had been kept book thoroughly. Of course, the masters of magic knew that they once would have to pay dearly for their servants, but often they made the experience that the price was very high indeed.

Haunted Eastern State Penitentiary

Eastern State Penitentiary was opened in 1829 in Philadelphia, Pennsylvania with a new idea for the rehabilitation of those unlucky enough to find themselves incarcerated inside this daunting structure.

This "new" approach placed the inmates into constant solitary confinement and hard labor. Cloth hoods were placed over the heads and faces of each inmate when they were removed from their cells to make sure there was absolutely no interaction between any of them nor could there be any chance of them learning how the prison was actually laid out.

This method of "rehabilitation" came from strict Quaker ideology-- meaning the idea was that if you isolated the inmates from each other, the guards or any other human contact, then they would have to face up to the crime(s) they had committed and as a result become repentant and remorseful for the actions that had landed them in prison in the first place. During their confinement, the prisoners were not allowed any contact with their family or friends; nor were they allowed any news from the outside world.

John Haviland, an architect from Great Britain, was hired to design the new prison. He was told it had to have seven different cell blocks that were to connect in the middle of the prison to a central surveillance area. The cells were to be designed to hold only one person and to be centrally heated and equipped with a toilet, sink, and a private, outdoor exercise yard that was surrounded by a ten-foot high wall.

Each cell had a single skylight to provide some natural light to the inmates and in keeping with the ideology; the sky lights were given the name, "the eye(s) of God".

The prison remained in operation until the 1970s. Unfortunately, as the years went by, Eastern State Penitentiary developed the same problem as most prisons, the issue of over-crowding. Overcrowding forced the prison officials to start housing two or three inmates in these small, cramped, single person cells and forced the state to add new cell blocks. When Cell block 15, also known as Death Row, was added in 1956, the prison had finally abandoned the original Quaker ideology. Cell block 15 would be the last cell block added to the building. Finally, as the years took their toll and the repair costs became too much, Eastern state penitentiary officially closed down in 1971.

However, long before the prison shut down, tales of paranormal activity and experiences were being reported by inmates and guards in the 1940s.

One of the most famous of the spooky tales of Eastern State came from the infamous Al Capone. Many of the other prisoners said they could hear Capone incessantly screaming and begging for someone named "Jimmy" to leave him alone. Capone stated many times that this "Jimmy" was a man by the name of James Clark.

James Clark was one of the men who were viciously murdered in the infamous St. Valentine's Day Massacre that authorities believed that Capone was responsible for. Many people reported that the spirit of "Jimmy" haunted Al 'Scarface' Capone even after he left Eastern State Penitentiary--and until Capone's death in 1947.

Jimmy wasn't the only ghost to haunt Eastern State Penitentiary. To this day many of the caretakers and tourists report hearing screams, creepy footsteps, disembodied voices talking, whispering, laughing and crying. There are also reports of seeing dark, shadowy figures darting from cell to cell and walking up and down the hallways. The most active areas seem to be Cell block 12, Cell block Six, Death Row, and the Infirmary.

Shadow Creatures

Tales of these creatures have been around for almost as long as humanity has dwelt upon the planet. They always appear as a dark shadowy form, often in the peripheries of people's vision, as well appearing in full view. If they become aware of being noticed they will simply disappear, or fade away into the dark and shadowy corners of rooms and closets.

Many times my mate and I have these shadow beings outside on dark, rainy, overcast days darting through the shadows of the surrounding trees, or in the shadows and the alleyways between buildings. They seem to be drawn to places where violence has been perpetrated, or is immanent. Many theories abound as to what these creatures are and why these things are drawn to violence, sorrow, and other forms of suffering, but none have been proven to be fact. Most of the time we see them on those nights when, in spite of there being an almost full moon and plenty of security lights burning, the night is unusually dark and feeling extremely tense and creepy. They will dart through the shadows of the trees and have even rise right up in front of us...seemingly from the very ground itself.

Reports of shadow creatures are very common. People sensitive to the supernatural world seem to see these creatures on a pretty routine basis, but even folks who have never seen a U.F.O or have not so much as a hint of psychic ability about them report seeing these bizarre beings. The reports about these shadow beings differ in one respect from the usual spirit or ghost sightings in that these creatures have no human features like spirits or ghosts.

Shadow creatures are never reported wearing either modern or period clothing, nor do they make any attempt to communicate with the observer.

There have been a few reports of people being chased by shadow creatures, and even more rarely, of people being attacked by shadow beings. There have been numerous reports of shadow creatures just popping right into being in front of witnesses, linger for a few seconds, and then disappear just as fast. Most people report that these encounters almost always leave them with feelings of a heavy sadness and dread. Indeed, my mate and I have felt on those nights when these creatures are swarming thicker than fleas that it is always a creepy and foreboding night that gives us the chills and a bit of dread.

The numerous accounts given by countless witnesses about these shadow beings usually describe them as being a dark, solid black, humanoid shape having little or no facial characteristics. There are also several reports of these beings appearing to be child-sized, or shapeless, dark, black or gray mass that will often shift to a more human like form. Sometimes these creatures are reported as having glowing red eyes.

Some other, much more frightening accounts are given by people describing what appears to be a dark, humanoid shaped phantom with the outline of a cloak, and the outline of a flat wide-brimmed hat.

This last type is sometimes called the "hat-man" and is often a terrifying and malevolent apparition that is accompanied by paralysis, bone-chilling coldness, and a feeling of fear for one's life.

The Battlefield Apparitions of Gettysburg

On one warm, humid morning in July 1863 two armies met around the small town of Gettysburg, Pennsylvania, a crucial meeting point between the North and South during the Civil War.

Three days later, 7,000 soldiers surrounded the Pennsylvanian landscape, pools of blood flowing down Gettysburg's Cemetery and Culps hills. Months after the fabled Battle of Gettysburg, confederate soldiers rotted in mass graves as the townspeople struggled to heal the 30,000 wounded soldiers, some on the brink of death. Over 140 years later, the souls of these soldiers still linger around Gettysburg, making Gettysburg the most haunted battlefield in the entire world.

After the bloody battle of Gettysburg ended in July 1863, the people of Gettysburg, around 3,000 strong, struggled to find a way to treat the injured soldiers. The number of those injured soldiers was ten times the size of their entire town. As the people of Gettysburg treated the injured, the dead rotted in the hot, July sun. The smell was horrific; people could not leave their houses without scented handkerchiefs. Without the handkerchiefs, people vomited upon smelling the appalling stench.

When people die without proper, dignified burials, such as the soldiers of Gettysburg, ghosts appear. The ghosts haunt their grounds as a way of seeking redemption after death. All 7,000 of Gettysburg's soldiers never received this dignified burial, some rotting in mass graves for months after the battle itself. Over 5,000 ghosts haunt Gettysburg now, seeking that unclaimed redemption.

The poor residents of Gettysburg first piled these dead, decaying bodies in the streets of Gettysburg. They took the wounded inside houses, setting up makeshift medical centers.

 A lot of these wounded soldiers died, soaking up these houses with thick, dark blood. During the couple of weeks that followed the battle, the North attempted to properly bury the Union soldiers. The confederate soldiers continued to rot in makeshift mass graves until they were properly dispersed and buried months later.

Years after this battle, people would begin to report ghostly sightings on Gettysburg's Cemetery and Culps Hills.

The Battlefield Apparitions of Cemetery and Culps Hills
Now over a century and a half since Gettysburg's end, ghosts still haunt their final resting place.

Cemetery Hill and Culps Hill, two hills outside of Gettysburg, is where most of the soldiers met their end. During the first night of Gettysburg, soldiers retreated to the safety of Cemetery Hill, only to be killed by opposing troops. Both Cemetery and Culps Hill saw the deaths of thousands of soldiers, both from the North and the South. Cemetery Hill sees more ghosts, however.

People frequently report smelling faint peppermint or vanilla. This smell comes from the scented handkerchiefs the people of Gettysburg used while they took care of the wounded -- and the dead.

Disturbed apparitions also haunt the living that continually visits Cemetery and Culps Hill. People report seeing ghosts walking around these hills, along with other angry ghosts touching them and warning others to leave.

The two most haunted places in Gettysburg are not Cemetery Hill and Culps Hill -- in fact, the concentration of these hauntings occur on Rose Farm and the neighboring Devil's Den.

Rose Farm, located outside of Gettysburg, worked as a makeshift hospital after the battle. Rose Farm took on a huge number of injured and dead soldiers, most of the dead buried outside in rows. To this day, the dead still scare others and cause ghostly visions inside the house, including blood-stained walls. Residents warn others from visiting Rose Farm and the nearby Devil's Den.

Devil's Den, where most of the battle took place on day two, was also the sight of strange apparitions before the battle took place. Native Americans say that another huge battle took place here, earning the name Devil's Den. With the death of additional soldiers in 1863, it added to the story, making this the most haunted place in Gettysburg. One woman reported being approached by a dirty, shoeless man while taking pictures of Devil's Den. When she turned around to thank him, he was gone.

 Many people have reported the same sighting as well. In the nearby Triangular field, electrical equipment refuses to work -- even cameras. It is the US's modern version of the Bermuda Triangle and is extremely haunted.

Are all of these places really haunted? The locals swear it is, and visitors have as well. Gettysburg still lives on through its haunted apparitions -- but only you can find out by checking it out for yourself.

Visitors often report ghostly encounters, many of whom initially believe they've seen Civil War re-enactors, only to find out later that no such groups are at the park. There are allegedly a number of ghosts that lurk within the park, especially at a place called Devil's Den where hundreds of men lost their lives. Many have also reported hearing disembodied screams and numerous others report malfunctioning cameras
Many believe they met Civil War re-enactors, only to find out later that no such groups were at the park.

Soaked in the blood of both Confederate and Union soldiers, Gettysburg is prime ghost-hunting location.

Civil War battles have been the subject of many motion pictures, but one of the best and most moving was 1993's *Gettysburg*. During the filming of that movie, much of which was done right on location at the actual battlefields, some of the participants had an unexplained encounter. Because the film required so many extras to serve as soldiers, the production hired re-enactors who regularly portray the Union and Confederate armies.

During a break in filming one day, several of the extras were resting at Little Round Top and admiring the setting sun. They were approached by grizzled old man, who they described as wearing a ragged and scorched Union uniform and smelling of sulfur gunpowder. He talked to them about how furious the battle was as he passed around spare rounds of ammunition, then went on his way.

At first, the extras assumed he was part of the production company, but their minds changed when they looked closely at the ammunition he gave them. They took the rounds to the man in charge of giving out such props for the movie, and he said they did not come from him. It turns out the ammunition from the strange old man were genuine musket rounds from that period.

The Tie between Kids and Ghosts

There is a tie between kids and ghost because kids are innocents and do not have a fear of things they do not understand.

Their innocent is why ghosts seek out the children. They have no fear and show no signs of threat towards a ghost. Many will say that this is untrue, but the facts are true. A ghost is more apt to visit a child than an adult. The adult will display fear and act upon it, where a child will be relaxed and not have any animosity towards the ghost.

People have thought this way for years. Many people question whether a child can actually see ghosts or rather are they making it up, like an imaginary friend. This has been challenged for years. However, many kids and ghosts have communicated and the kids know things that no one else can possibly know. This makes everything more challenging. How could these kids know the things they do if it was not told to them by the ghost in question. Yes, kids can see ghosts that many adults cannot. One has to believe this if they have no other logical explanation as to why kids know things that only a ghost could tell them.

You have heard about ghosts that play with kids when the parents are out of the room. One such case was a ghost that was in a home lived in by a family of two adults and two children. The children would wake up at night because someone was tickling their feet. Since no one was in the room but the kids who were asleep when it happened, who could it of been. The only logical reason is a ghost was doing it. It happened to both of the kids. People find this hard to believe, but kids are innocents and do not threaten or feel threatened by the unknown.

There are ghosts it seen everywhere. Kids and ghosts are a combination that should not be dismissed for any reason. If a child says that they see something or feel someone touching them, you need to investigate.

You need to know if it is a friendly ghost or a ghost that could cause harm. Yes, ghosts are a reality and adults do have to listen to what children are telling them. For those who think ghosts do not exist, how can you explain some imaginary friends that actually play with your kids and keep them occupied? Is it really just the imagination or is your child seeing a spirit that has adopted them as a friend or even a foe.

The ghosts may be kids from the past. These ghosts may not be harmful ghosts, but rather playmates. Not all ghost watchers believe in bad child ghosts, but then again, can you afford not to find out who your child is playing with and what their names are for reference.

Paranormal Happenings or Not?

In Missouri, Pikes Lodge is a place where paranormal happenings occur. It is said that a woman spirit usually only shows herself to small groups of people.

The Iowa Villisca House was the scene of ax murders and is said to have unexplained happenings occurring within the walls. The Iowa Villisca House was the scene of ax murders and is said to have unexplained happenings occurring within the walls. What happen in this house is documented as the worst murder that the community has ever seen or heard about and they now know that some of the spirits of the victims have remained in the home. The victims were the Moore family and two visiting children from the Stillinger family. An ax murderer had killed the family. Although police had their suspects, no one was ever convicted of the crimes.

The Linns purchased the home in 1994, just before it was to be razed. The intention was to restore the house back to its original state when the murders occurred. The home was then entered into the National Register of Historical Places. It is said that many strange things happen to people who are in the house. Although nothing was ever officially documented, it is possible that the Moore's or some of them still live in the house waiting for justice.

In Missouri, Pikes Lodge is a place where paranormal happenings occur. It is said that a woman spirit usually only shows herself to small groups of people. However, at a large gathering, the music sound stop, the light were turned off and the guests were left with an eerie feeling. Many neighbors report hearing unexplained noises coming from the lodge when no one is around. A little girl plays in the halls at night. There was a little girl killed when the building was school. Their neighbors hear laughing, doors slamming and windows appear to be shaking.

In Hall of Waters in Excelsior Springs, Missouri, people have reported seeing a boy by a pool area. In Odell Sports Center, some have heard a door slam in the locker room, a man laugh and have seen a man in the shower. Many of these paranormal happening have some history behind them, as to why it is happening. Many are not investigated because it has become a way of life for people that work or live in the buildings. Ghostly sounds have been recorded in many areas as well.

The Battleship North Carolina has a recording of an unidentified voice. In Raleigh, a voice recording captures a baby crying. It is said that a baby did die in the Mordecai home long ago. On time, a camera operator was making a joke, when the video was replayed, an unidentified voice was heard mimicking the camera operator. With all the new technology that helps investigators learn about the unexplained, it is only a matter of time before someone finds answers to why spirits remain on earth.

There are many such reports throughout the United States and other countries. Many are unexplained, but some are believed to be that of someone that died in that particular location. The unexplained and paranormal happenings will continue throughout the years. There are always going to be new reports and new encounters.

The world of the unknown is a mystery to many, but many investigators and physics believe that they are lost souls who want to remain on earth or want justice for any wrong doings against them. This may be the case in many unexplained occurrences. However, many ghostly happenings are related to years past and may never find a happy ending, leaving the ghost to move around the buildings they haunt forever. Some spirit however are ghosts that do not want to leave a place that made them happy. For the most part, ghosts are friendly, but can be harsh if they feel threatened.

The Tower of London Ghosts

The Tower of London is known to be one of the most haunted places in the world. The Tower has an extensive history that's filled with horror and blood. There have been hundreds of brutal executions held at the Tower of London during its 900 years of existence, including the gruesome beheadings of prominent political figures and noble ladies. Countless prisoners were also held inside the Bloody Tower and suffered from horrific torture and "unspeakable acts".

Even children were killed in the Bloody Tower. In 1483, Edward IV died unexpectedly, and his young, twelve year old son, Edward V was set to inherit the throne. Unfortunately, his uncle, the Duke of Gloucester received permission from Parliament to ascend the throne himself. Edward V and his younger brother, Richard, mysteriously disappeared shortly after and were never heard from again. All though child mortality at the time was high, the young princes both disappeared at the same time. It was rumored that their uncle had them killed (or killed them himself) in order to secure his spot on the throne. In 1674, small skeletal remains were found, and recent testing has found them to be the remains of both humans and animals. Were the young princes held prisoner with their pets? Or perhaps buried along with dead animals? We may never know.

Nevertheless, there have been sightings of two ghostly boys over the centuries. Later in the fifteenth century, after they [the princes] disappeared, guards reportedly saw the ghosts of two boys in the Bloody Tower. The boys appeared to be wearing white nightgowns and they were moving down the stairs with "frightened" looks on their faces. They were holding on to each other and eventually faded away.

Other sightings of the two ghostly princes have been reported over the centuries, and they're all similar — the boys appear frightened and saddened, and when the observer tries to comfort them, they fade away.

Another popular ghost that haunts the Tower of London is that of Anne Boleyn. She was accused of "infidelity", and there were also rumors of her being a "witch". Her husband, King Henry VIII had a bad habit of either divorcing his wives or killing them, ordered her to be beheaded. She was beheaded on May 19, 1536, and to this day she can still be spotted gliding through the Tower with her head tucked under her arm. There are also reports of her leading a ghostly procession of other noble Ladies and Lords down the Chapel Royal aisle.

Catherine Howard was another one of King Henry VIII's wives that was beheaded. She was supposedly in love with a man named Thomas Culpepper, who was also executed right before she was. Her last words were allegedly, "I die a queen, but would rather die the wife of Culpepper." She was only around 18-21 when she was killed, and it's said that she lives on still in the Tower of London. Unlike Anne Boleyn, Catherine Howard's ghost appears in the likeness of her human form — the head is where it's supposed to be.

Many other nobles were tortured and executed in the Tower of London over the last several centuries. The Tower is one of the hot spots for tourists visiting London. Everyone loves a good ghost story, and every year people flock to the Tower hoping to get a glimpse of a famous ghost or two. Paranormal and psychic investigations have also been undertaken at the Tower of London. Hopefully someday these restless spirits can finally find some peace.

Waverly Hills Sanitarium

Waverly Hills Sanitarium is considered to be one of the most haunted locations in North America. The Waverly Hills Sanitarium, which is located in Louisville, KY, once held thousands of patients. It was built as a hospital in the early 20th century, and its original purpose was to keep and quarantine tuberculosis patients.

Tuberculosis was a very horrible and widespread disease in the early part of the 20th century, and doctors didn't know how to treat it properly. During the time of Waverly Hills Sanitarium's construction, Louisville, KY had the highest number of people suffering with tuberculosis.

Since there was no cure for tuberculosis, most of the patients went to Waverly Hills Sanitarium and never came back out again. Not only did patients go there to die, but legends say there were horrific "experiments" done on them as well. It's estimated that thousands upon thousands of people died within the walls of Waverly Hills Sanitarium, but there is no official count. It's rumored, though, that the number could be as high as 63,000! If that is true, then it's no wonder that the place is haunted.

Not only did tuberculosis patients die there, but some of the staff did as well. According to legends, in 1928, one of the nurses supposedly hanged herself in "Room 502". The nurse was Mary Hillenburg, and she allegedly killed herself for being unwed and pregnant. Another nurse was said to have thrown herself out of the window in "Room 502" a few years later. Some also speculate that she was pushed.

In 1961, shortly after advanced treatment was found for tuberculosis, Waverly Hills Sanitarium was finally shut down.

It reopened two years later as the Woodhaven Geriatrics Center. It also became a rest home for the elderly, and remained open until 1981 when it was closed down for good. Local churches did plan on turning it into a chapel and a theater, but their funding fell through. It has since then deteriorated.

All that remains of Waverly Hills Sanitarium is an old, run down building. The only "patients" left inside are ones that have already died, and unfortunately haven't moved on. Sometimes ghost hunters and other curious folks will go there looking for ghosts. Room 502, "THE Room", is said to be a hotspot for paranormal activity. Some claim to have seen strange things in Room 502. Others claim to have heard voices, including one telling them to "get out!" It's also reported that a strange "figure" can be seen on the fourth floor, and that lights will sometimes come on when they shouldn't be, and so forth.

Skeptics, of course, believe that the strange activity only comes from people's overactive imaginations, and that people only "see" and "hear" what they want to see and hear. Whether Waverly Hills Sanitarium truly is haunted or not, it still remains one of the creepiest buildings in North America. Skepticism can't erase the history of the harsh, brutal, and sad events that took place at Waverly Hills Sanitarium.

The Waverly Hills Sanatorium opened in 1910 as a two-story hospital to accommodate 40 to 50 tuberculosis patients. Though considered the best site at the time for treating the disease, the procedures were primitive; doctors experimented, and used illegal drugs. Tuberculosis sometimes ravaged the mind, causing patients to go insane. More than 6,000 patients died during the time that the Sanatorium was open. It closed in 1962.

Tuberculosis swept across America in the 1800s and early 1900s, filling hospitals and necessitating the construction of brand new hospitals dedicated to caring for patients with TB. The Waverly Hills Sanatorium was one such structure. Completed in 1926, Waverly Hills was considered far more advanced than most of the other facilities used to treat TB in the United States. Despite its rather distinguished reputation, the facility was still a failure in terms of its mission. While many of the patients taken to Waverly Hills for treatment recovered from their illness and were able to leave, there were also many who weren't as lucky and often times, even those who survived wouldn't necessarily call themselves lucky.

The treatments for tuberculosis in Waverly Hills were oftentimes as bad as, or worse than, the symptoms of the disease itself. Little was understood about TB in those days and there was no medication to offer patients that could effectively combat the symptoms patients suffered through. Because so little was known about the disease, treating it involved a lot of experimentation. Some of the experiments were valuable and helped make important advances in how TB was treated. Others were far more barbaric. Even seemingly innocent treatments look a little harsher when you really think about how they were done. Fresh air, rest and nutritious foods were all factors thought to be important to recovering from TB.

For that reason, Waverly Hills featured sun rooms used to treat patients. In some of these rooms, patients were exposed to ultraviolet light meant to mimic the sun. The theory was that this light would help slow the spread of bacteria. Sun rooms that used ultraviolet light via an artificial light source were sometimes unpleasant but they pale in comparison to the porches or open windows patients were sometimes set in front of. While during warmer months, this treatment would probably work wonders, this treatment wasn't just offered in warmer months. Photos exist of patients sitting on the porches or in front of the windows at Waverly Hills Sanatorium in the midst of winter; snow seen clearly *on* the patients.

Of course, the treatments at Waverly Hills Sanatorium went far beyond the sun rooms and porches. Some of the more brutal treatments included the surgical insertion of balloons into a patient's lungs. The balloons would then be filled with air, expanding the balloons inside the patient's body. The result of this one was almost always devastating. Of course, it doesn't compare to the treatment referred to as "the last resort". For this procedure, doctors would remove muscles and ribs from the patient's abdomen. The theory was that by doing this, the doctors were allowing the lungs more room to expand. Patients who underwent this treatment rarely survived.

Waverly Hills did not have the abysmal success rate some would like to claim. Many patients did recover from the disease and were able to leave on their own accord. There were, however, many who didn't. Survivors left Waverly Hills through the front door. Those that died inside Waverly Hills left via the body chute. The body chute is just as macabre as it sounds. Because doctors at Waverly Hills felt it was important to care for patients mentally as well as physically they decided it wouldn't be good for anyone if patients saw how many of their fellow sufferers didn't make it.

To attempt to hide the mortality rate from patients – and possibly from outsiders as well – a secret tunnel was constructed that connected the hospital to the train tracks that were conveniently located at the bottom of the hill the hospital had been constructed on. Bodies would be moved through this tunnel to trains waiting below. The trains would then take the bodies away from the hospital. No one knows for sure how many bodies made this sad journey.

The discovery of new medications more or less eradicated TB in the US, meaning there was little need for Waverly Hills to remain open. It closed its doors in 1962. That is not the end of the Waverly Hills story though – just the end of the story under that name. A year after closing, the Sanatorium reopened once again; this time under the name "Woodhaven Geriatrics Sanitarium". Woodhaven was plagued by rumors of mistreatment and abuse by staff but many of those rumors were later proven false. Even so, electroshock therapy was used to treat a wide variety of ailments – something not terribly uncommon in those days.

When budget cuts in the 1960s and 1970s struck Woodhaven, conditions inside the facility deteriorated rapidly. Woodhaven eventually closed its doors in 1982, bringing to an end its legacy of abuse.

Today, Waverly Hills Sanatorium/Woodhaven Geriatrics Sanitarium continues to draw thrill seekers and ghost hunters, eager to experience a real life sighting or some other kind of paranormal activity. Many skeptics have become believers thanks to Waverly Hills which isn't all that surprising considering its history. Described by its current owners as "the most spiritually active place in the world," sightings have been reported of the apparition of a nurse who committed suicide in Room 502 during the 1930s. Currently, there are plans to turn the historic building into a hotel even though it is said to be one of the most haunted hospitals in the United States. Visitors experience cold spots, disembodied voices, and ghosts roaming the halls. The spirit of a little girl has been seen on the third floor solarium playing hide and seek with visitors, a small boy has been spied playing with a ball, and an old woman has shown herself running from the front door with her wrists bleeding screaming: "Help me. Somebody save me!"

Other phenomenon includes rooms lighting up when there is no power in the building, doors slamming of their own accord, cries and screams, and at least one report of a ghostly hearse driving up to drop off coffins.

At least 6,000 deaths occurred there, and some residents still haven't left! A woman with slashed wrists has appeared to visitors, screaming and begging for help, and yet others have reported spotting moving shadows and hearing screams of pain.

One of the more famous spirits is that of a little boy who often shows up in both pictures and video. Still open to visitors and paranormal teams alike, would you be brave enough to communicate with the poor souls who still haunt Waverly?

Some claim a resemblance to one of the most famous "inhabitant" Mary
Lee

Theories about Shadow People

The shadow people mystery has been a hot paranormal topic for a while now. There are many theories as to what exactly shadow people may be.

Shadow people are strange, shadowy "beings" that sometimes appear to us. These beings are shaped like humans, but they have no real body. They are merely dark shadows lurking in various places. They are simply dark silhouettes that are shaped like humans, but they're obviously not human at all. If you've ever noticed a strange shadow that seemed out of place, it's possible you were witnessing a shadow person. Whenever a living person sees a glimpse of a shadow person, it will usually disappear. Shadow people don't usually stick around for very long.

But why are shadow people here in the first place? Do they want anything? Where do they come from? There are just as many theories as there are questions. While for the most part they don't appear "threatening", some witnesses feel a sense of foreboding when one is around. Perhaps it's simply because those people have a subconscious fear of the darkness, and are overreacting to something they don't understand. Or perhaps shadow people can represent something sinister, something that truly should be feared. Could it be that shadow people are evil spirits of some sort, and are here to cause trouble?

While that is a tempting thought, there really isn't much evidence of anyone coming to harm after coming across one. If they truly do wish to cause mischief, they apparently only do it in subtle ways. Or perhaps they aren't evil at all; perhaps they're simply spirits or ghosts that, for whatever reason, haven't moved on to the next world.

Another theory suggests that shadow people are time travelers or visitors from another world/universe. Do they come here to check on us for some reason? Are they simply curious about us? They apparently do spend a lot of time here. Why? Maybe they're not even here at all. Is it possible that they're simply "people" that live on another plane of existence? Could we be getting a glimpse into that parallel dimension? Perhaps we also appear as shadow people to them.

Whoever shadow people are, and wherever their origins are, we'll most likely never know. We can have our ideas and theories, but we'll never have all the answers. If you've ever witnessed a shadow person before, you can only use your imagination as to what it was and why you saw it. Unless shadow people actually take the time to "talk" to us, their mystery will always remain unexplained.

Shadow Ghosts

Appearance of Shadow Ghosts Shadow ghosts (also known as shadow men, shadow folk, or shadow beings) are gray-black in color and often resemble human silhouettes with no discernible features.

Have you ever been quietly reading a book, or simply sitting daydreaming, when you noticed a flicker of movement in your peripheral vision? Was it like a shadow or haze, passing briefly by your side – but when you looked around there was nothing there? If so, you may have encountered a shadow ghost.

Appearance of Shadow Ghosts Shadow ghosts (also known as shadow men, shadow folk, or shadow beings) are gray-black in color and often resemble human silhouettes with no discernible features. They are mist-like with no real mass, and can appear as a dark cloud between two and eight feet in length, or as a human figure wearing an old-fashioned hat or hood. These shadow beings can appear in flat 2D forms, or even as vaporous 3D forms as if made from smoke. Most are thought to be adults – but even shadow children have appeared from time to time.

Shadow ghosts are known to be evasive, often darting about in dark corners and raising suspicion, but never quite confirming their presence.

In fact, most people who report seeing shadow ghosts say that they either pass between walls or disintegrate completely when noticed. They are most frequently spotted in the home, although some sightings put them outdoors as seen from a distance.

It is intriguing that reports of shadow ghosts make them out to be playful, cheeky and elusive – as if they are playing a game with us. Others have reported more threatening encounters, where the "hat man" (as he is known) stands menacingly in the doorway and looks down at the floor.

But more commonly, shadow ghosts dance about on the walls, first moving slowly as if passing through mud, then quickly hopping about the room, as if in fast-forward mode. This makes them extremely difficult to catch on camera – although such photos do exist. The difference between shadow ghosts and regular ghosts is that shadow folk don't wear clothing (except for the hat or hood) and they don't attempt to communicate. However, their presence is often accompanied by a feeling of fear or dread, and sensitive individuals feel the air go temporarily cold.

There are many theories about where shadow ghosts come from. The most common belief is that shadow people are the unattended remnants of ghosts; persisting in our reality even though the spirit has moved on to the next plane of existence. They may also arise due to a buildup of negative energy, where extreme emotional or physical trauma has occurred, or even where occult practices have taken place.

Some people believe they are demons. In fact, if the eyes are seen, they are only ever reported as being red and glowing. This also supports the feeling of fear reported when a shadow man is present. Another explanation is that they are entities from an alternate dimension that only show through into our reality when the realities occasionally overlap. If so, they might only catch glimpses of us, the way we only partially see them. Some people believe they are demons. In fact, if the eyes are seen, they are only ever reported as being red and glowing. This also supports the feeling of fear reported when a shadow man is present.

Do Ghosts Only Haunt Houses?

It's believed that ghosts only haunt houses and cemeteries, but that wasn't the case in South Korea. In 2005, an unnamed woman boarded a flight from Sydney, Australia to Incheon, South Korea.

It seems that she chose this airplane for her final resting place. After the flight took off, she quickly excused herself to a small bathroom stall in back of the airplane. It was there that she attached a rope to the bathroom ceiling, fastening it around her neck. She jumped. When airplane attendants noticed she hadn't left the bathroom, they opened it to find her dangling from the ceiling, rope taut around her limp neck. She had hung herself in this bathroom, seemingly losing the battle with her depression. To avoid any commotion, they quietly removed her lifeless body, storing it in a secure place. They quietly removed her body at the end of the flight. They thought this would be the last of their worries, but that wasn't the case.

The Dead Housewife Begins to haunt

a couple of months after her death, the dead housewife returned from her grave. Flight attendants reported odd sightings in the airplane. Some attendants refused to fly on the plane, ordering to be switched to another plane. These are some of those sightings first reported by them:

After a long shift, one flight attendant went to his bunker to sleep. After a restful sleep, he started to feel cold. He felt someone lay a blanket over his body. Startled, he awoke. A mysterious voice told him to go back to sleep, and he did – but not before looking around for the mysterious voice. He then saw a disambiguated hand sticking out from the wall. He never went back to sleep.

A smoke detector went off in one of the airplane bathrooms. When personnel opened the door, they found nothing except for an empty stall. Upon inspection, the smoke detector was working perfectly fine. It was then that they realized that it was the stall where the housewife had hung herself. Housewife haunting or malfunctioning smoke detector? They believe it's the housewife.

On the same airplane, an airplane attendant and a monk were alone in one section of the airplane. The monk began chanting to himself. When the flight attendant asked why, the monk looked up. He said that he saw dead people in all of the unoccupied seats. The work of the housewife? The monk denies fabrication of this story to this day.

Do Ghosts Only Haunt Houses?

Do ghosts really only haunt houses and cemeteries? According to the flight attendants on board this mystery airplane, not necessarily so. Some of them have switched airplanes just to avoid seeing this mystery housewife. Airplane officials laugh at their tales, calling it the work of their imagination. For the flight attendants, however, this is no work of the imagination.

Is this the work of the housewife or their imagination? It's up to you to be the judge of it.

Black Eyed Kids - Unexplained Mystery/Urban Legend

The mystery of the black-eyed kids started growing strong back in 1998 when a journalist, Brain Bethel, reported an incident he had with two black-eyed kids. They were young, not teenagers, but a bit younger.

The story starts with Bethel sitting in a parking lot when the two male children approached his car and asked for a ride. He claimed that they were dress in style and were normal looking accept for the eyes. He became overwhelmed with a feeling of danger. The boys had needed a ride home. He said that the two boys were insistent and annoyed when he would not let them into the car.

Bethel stated that the two boys became annoyed and repeatedly asked for ride home to get movie money. Bethel stated that he felt something come over him and he wanted to open the door. However, once he looked at their eyes, they were black with no irises or pupils and he felt paralyzed with fear. Bethel said he was somehow able to get over his fear long enough to leave the parking lot and the two boys behind.

This not the only story told about black-eyed children. Many people have reported that a black-eyed kid has appeared at their doors asking to be let in because of one reason or another. The male is said to be about twelve to seventeen. People have reported a fear that comes over them when the boy talks to them. The eyes are black with no irises or pupils, but the boy is dressed according to the style for that year. Is this an unexplained mystery or an urban legend?

People have tried to rationalize these cases and reports by saying they boy could be wearing black contact lenses or that people have an over active imagination. Unfortunately, the people that have told the story are so passionate about their fear that one has to wonder if it can be true. Do black-eyed kids exist and if so, what or who are they?

Although people have rational explanations, there are also the facts that cannot be ignored. People sense a fear when they are in the company of the black-eyed kids. Many people have said that the eyes could have something to do with how they feel as well as the overwhelming feeling to do as the boy asks. Could the eyes be used to post a hypnotic suggestion? It is possible, but people do overcome the feeling to allow them into their homes or like Bethel, into his car.

We know they cannot be an evil spirit because they would not just give up when some refuses them entry into their homes. However, no one has ever let them in or have they? Maybe they are not here to tell the story about what happens if you let the black-eyed kids into your home.

The story about black-eyed kids might not be very much of an urban legend, but a true unexplained mystery. If you have ever heard the story about the Hotel San Carlos in Phoenix, Arizona, you would have to wonder if black-eyed kids do exist and just what can they do to you. The story is about a picture in a hotel room, of a black-eyed girl. Guests who have stayed in the room have reportedly checked out of the hotel because they felt the black eyes following them. They were frightened and needed to get out of the hotel.

This was not a personal sighting, but it was a picture of a girl with black eyes. If no one has put the two things together, how can one say for sure that there are no black-eyed kids? If you think about the picture in this

180

hotel room and guests seeing the black eyes following them, how can anyone explain this happening? The only way to explain this is by agreeing that there may be black-eyed kids living amongst us and we do not even know who they are or where they are. Before any one can say if the black eyed kids are a urban legend or an unexplained mystery, more information is going to be needed. It might be wise for someone to study other paranormal happenings to see if any other kids, alive or otherwise have had black eyes.

The Ghost of Edgar Allan Poe

Edgar Allan Poe's life is marked by tragedy and suffering, his death marked by an equal amount of confusion. Regarded as simply 'a mediocre poet' during the 1800s, Poe grew up orphaned, living with the Allan family until he attended college in 1826. He only stayed for a year before leaving for the army because of severe gambling debts.

His life from there is marked with tragedy, marrying his 13-year-old cousin Virginia in 1835, losing her to sickness in 1847. He never held a steady job, fired from numerous jobs mostly due to a severe drinking addiction. Although he could never hold a job, editors held him in high regard with his ingenious poetry and short stories, including The Raven and The Tell-Tale Heart. Nevertheless, his drinking and depression took hold of his life. He died two years after his wife, passed out in a street in Baltimore. He died hours later in the hospital, crying manically about someone called Reynolds. Although he was dead physically, his spirit lived on in his residences and final resting place.

Edgar Allan Poe's Hauntings at His Grave Decades after his untimely death, people began reporting sightings of his ghost appearing at his grave site. On his birthday, January 19, people say they have seen a man shrewdly covered in black, walking towards the grave of Edgar Allan

Poe. His face is unrecognizable because of the black scarf that disguises his face from view. Nevertheless, the black-coated man walks towards Edgar Allan Poe's on his birthday, leaving a bottle of cognac and three roses. The black-coated man then disappears in the night, slowly meandering through the graveyard with a walking stick. People speculate that this is the ghost of Edgar Allen Poe, honoring himself with the ceremonial bottle of cognac and three roses. People are discouraged from approaching the ghost and not to disturb the spirit.

In 1990, the curator of the Edgar Allan Poe house, Jeff Jerome, permitted photographers to shoot Poe's grave site on his birthday for any evidence of this mystery ghost. Sure enough, the ghost walked towards his grave, kneeling down. In the picture the ghost is clearly seen with his trademark black clothing and black fedora, scarf covering his face. The ghost then disappeared into the night.

Hauntings in Edgar Allan Poe's House His grave isn't the only place that is haunted by ghosts. During his marriage to Virginia Clemm, they lived in a small, understated house on North Amity Street, located in Baltimore, Maryland. It is believed this house is haunted as well. People have reported seeing a gray-haired woman wearing early-1800s clothing, reportedly overweight. Some people believe this in the ghost of Poe's aunt, Maria Clemm. People have also reported feeling 'cold spots' (things mostly associated with the presence of ghosts), hearing voices, and seeing windows and door open without help from outside sources. No explanation is offered for these incidences.

Is Poe's spirit alive where he once dwelled? It might his tortured spirit, seeking redemption from beyond the grave. Others say its mere fantasy, just like Poe's stories. Although no one will know the true origins of these incidences, Poe will continue to live on through his stories and poetry.

The Haunting Of The Lizzie Borden House

The Lizzie Borden house is always going to be any historical place to visit because no one knows for sure what exactly happened in the house that day.

Is the Lizzie Borden house haunted? All findings in the house conclude that spirits visit the house. You can participate in one of the séances that are held, but if you want to conduct your own test, you will find that Mr. and Mrs. Borden do frequently walk the rooms of the Lizzie Borden house. A couple that was staying there had their own equipment to see just what was going on in the house. They took a camcorder and the EMF sensor headed for the cellar. This is where they started having a communication with a man.

People have said that they have seen the spirit of what could possibly be the housekeeper. Her name was Bridget Sullivan. This female figure attached herself to the man that was investigating the house. He had the feeling that somebody was always right next to him and continually followed him around the house. He actually felt as though someone had touched him. Once he saw a picture of the housekeeper he realized it was not the housekeeper that was following him, it was Emma. There is also a spirit of a black cat. Abby Borden loved cats and had a favorite cat that was black. The story surrounding the cat is that Lizzie killed Abby Borden's cat in the basement of the house.

There are two other spirits in the house, a boy and a girl. The ages of the children were about five to eight years old. It is said that a family that lived next door to the Lizzie Borden house had children and that Mrs. Kelly was actually mentally disturbed and had drowned both of her children before Abby and Andrew were murdered. The Kelly home and the Lizzie Borden home are the only two regional houses on the street. There is however two other children that play in the house with the Kelly children, but no one knows who they are or where they came from.

Abby Borden is seen in the house from time to time, but Andrew makes his presence known all the time. It is said that Andrew does not appreciate how people come into his home and mock him. The couple staying in the John Morse room that were doing the investigation were the only ones in the house, but heard footsteps coming up the stairs. Upon investigating, they found that there was nobody there. It was probably Andrew Borden walking the steps as he did many times.

The Lizzie Borden house has many paranormal happenings inside. One can only go to the Lizzie Borden Bed and Breakfast, spend the night and experience the happenings. It is truly amazing to know that you are living with the spirits of Abby, Andrew, the kids and the black cat. It is said that the presence of Lizzie Borden is felt from time to time, but no one has actual proof that it is her. She is usually only seen for a split second.

Most people that have stayed in the Lizzie Borden house does agree that it is haunted. The one thing that everyone can agree on is that there are four children and not just the two next-door neighbor children. Where the other two children come from nobody knows. Further investigation of the surroundings and the neighborhood may prove where the other two children come from, but until then nobody will ever know for sure who the two unidentified children are or why they are at the house.

Lalaurie House, New Orleans, Louisiana

The three-story building at the southeast corner of Royal and Governor Nichols street, to some the most famous private residence in old New Orleans, gained its eerie title, 'The Haunted House,' from an oft-repeated tale in which spirits of tortured slaves clank their chains during the midnight hours in remembrance of awful punishment meted out to them by their mistress – a high-bred lady of old New Orleans who had been charged with finding an uncanny delight in dealing inhumanly with her slaves.

Like all such tales, the story has grown in ferocity through its countless retellings and the probabilities are that even the original story of over a century ago was a gross exaggeration. It now appears that the mistress of this home was the first victim of yellow journalism in this country and that she was far from being the 'fiend' tradition has labeled, or should we say, libeled her. The facts of this 'strange true story' are as follows:

The traditional tales of the Vieux Carre have it that this house was built in 1780 by two brothers, Jean and Henri de Remarie, and those guests as Marshal Michel Ney, Napoleon's famous commander; the duc d'Orleans, later, Louis Philippe, king of France; and the Marquis de Lafayette have slept in this mansion. But we are compelled to make the pertinent observations that Marshal Ney never came to Louisiana, that Louis Philippe was here in 1798, and that Lafayette visited New Orleans in 1825 – yet the 'Haunted House' was not built until 1832!

There are those who denounce historical accuracy when it destroys fallacious tradition … those who claim that a good story must never be sacrificed and crucified on the cross of truth. Much as one admires the colorful tradition of old New Orleans, our mission is to give a factual history of the landmarks of the Vieux Carre. So, to stick to fact, we must point out that the lots upon which the 'Haunted House' stands were purchased by Madame Louis Lalaurie, September 12, 1831, from Edmond Soniat du Fossat, and the house then built was not ready for occupancy until the spring of 1832. As it was part of the tract given the Ursuline nuns, this was the first, and only, house built on this particular site.

Madame Lalaurie was one of five children born to Louis Barthelemy Chevalier de Macarty and Marie Jeanne Lovable, two who stood high in the social life of old New Orleans. One of their daughters was christened Marie Delphine Macarty. She first married, on June 11, 1800, Don Ramon de Lopez y Angula, the ceremony being performed at the St. Louis Cathedral by Luis de Penalvery Cardenas, the first bishop of the diocese of Louisiana, and the marriage certificate was signed by the celebrated Fray Antonio de Sedella. The husband was described in this document as Caballero de la Royal de Carlos, Intendant of the Provinces, a native of the community of Regno, Galicia, Spain, and the legitimate son of his Lordship Don Jose Antonio de Lopez y Angula and Dona Ana Fernande de Angule, daughter of Dona Francisca Borja Endecis.

Shortly after the Louisiana Purchase, on March 26, 1804, Delphine Macarty's husband was recalled to the court of Spain, the letter carrying this royal command stating that the young Spanish officer was 'to take his place at court as befitting his new position.' At this time Don Ramon was consul general for Spain in this new American territory. While in Havana, en route to Madrid, Don Ramon suddenly died and a few days later his daughter was born in the Cuban city. This infant was baptized Marie Delphine Borja Lopez y Angula de Candelaria, but she became best known in later years as 'Borquita,' meaning 'little Borja,' from the fact that she was named after her father's grandmother.

Left a widow, Delphine Macarty and her baby daughter returned to New Orleans. Four years later, in 1808, she again married, choosing for her husband a prominent banker, merchant, lawyer, and legislator named Jean Blanque, a native of Bearn who had come to Louisiana with Prefect Laussat in 1803. At the time of his marriage, June 16, 1808, Blanque purchased the residence at 409 Royal Street and in this home Delphine became the mother of four other children: Marie Louise Pauline, Louise Marie Laure, Marie Louise Jeanne, and Jean Pierre Paulin Blanque. In that stylish Royal Street home or in the 'Villa Blanque,' a charming country place fronting the Mississippi River just below the city limits, Delphine Macarty Blanque divided her time, both places frequented by the socially elect.

Jean Blanque died in 1816, and Delphine Macarty remained a widow until June 12, 1825, when she again married. Her third husband was Dr. Leonard Louis Nicolas Lalaurie, a native of Villeneuse-sur-Lot, France, who came to New Orleans to establish a practice. Borquita, the daughter by her mother's first marriage, became the wife of Placide Forstall, member of a distinguished Louisiana family, and Jeanne Blanque married Charles Auguste de Lassus, only child of Don Carle de Lassus, former governor of Upper Louisiana, and later governor of the Baton Rouge post of West Florida when they were under Spanish rule.

The Lalaurie mansion was erected in 1832 and for the next two years was the scene of many fashionable affairs, for the Lalauries entertained on an elaborate plan. On the afternoon of April 10, 1834, an aged cook set fire to the house during the absence of her mistress. When neighbors rushed into the mansion to fight the fire and try to save the furniture and other valuables, slaves were found chained in their quarters. The fire had started in the kitchen and upon entering the home, police found an elderly woman, the cook, chained to the stove from the ankle.

According to the New Orleans Bee of April 11, 1834, bystanders found 'seven slaves, more or less horribly mutilated ... suspended by the neck, with their limbs apparently stretched and torn from one extremity to the other', who claimed to have been imprisoned there for some months. Upon hearing this and once the fire was out, an angry mob descended upon the house and all-but completely destroyed it.

Although the fire was extinguished, the indignation of those who found the helpless slaves blazed high and a newspaper editor, Jerome Bayon of the Bee, published a heated account of the happening and quoted those who had investigated the Lalaurie slave quarters. This newspaper account roused public indignation to such a pitch that on April 15 a mob, led by irresponsibles, charged the house and began to wreck it. The rowdies were finally dispersed by a company of United States regulars who had been called out by a helpless sheriff.

During the excitement Madame Lalaurie and her husband took to their carriage and, with their faithful Creole black coachman Bastien on the box, swept through the howling, cursing rabble and, with the horses lashed to a the full gallop, made her way out of the city. It is supposed the carriage reached Bayou St. John where a lake craft was secured, for on April 21, 1834, the Lalauries were in Mandeville, across Lake Pontchartrain, at the home of Louis Coquillon.

There Madame Lalaurie signed a power-of-attorney placing her son-in-law Placide Forstall in charge of her affairs, while her husband signed a similar document in favor of his wife's other son-in-law, Auguste de Lassus. From Mandeville the Lalauries made their way to Mobile, where a ship took them to France.

Neither Delphine nor her husband ever returned to New Orleans. She remained in Paris, living there honored and respected in spite of the lurid tales that lived after her in New Orleans. Following her death on December 7, 1842, her body was secretly returned to New Orleans and buried in St. Louis No. 1 Cemetery.

The Lalaurie mansion was sold to various owners but the tale that it was 'haunted' and the midnight rendezvous for ghosts grew in the telling as only such stories can grow. The principal 'ghost' is, according to the most frequently quoted tale, that of a little girl slave who, to escape the whip of her mistress, climbed to the roof and jumped to her death into the courtyard below. Another tale, equally untrue, was that the mistress of the mansion buried all her victims in the courtyard well. The general impression that the place was haunted was sufficient to keep superstitious blacks from passing the house after nightfall.

In the days of Reconstruction following the Civil War, the old Lalaurie mansion became the Lower Girls' School. During the government of the carpetbaggers, whites and blacks were taught in the same rooms until the formation of 'The White League' in 1874, when the white element marched on the house and expelled the black pupils. In the 1880's the mansion became a conservatory of music. No matter who has lived in it since, or the manner of business that was carried on in the ground-floor stores, the name 'haunted' has clung to it in spite of the testimony of those inhabiting the place that ghosts have never disturbed their slumbers.

Tradition has it that the handsome entrance door 'was hammered out of iron by the slaves Madame Lalaurie kept shackled to the anvil.' This must be taken with several generous pinches of salt, for the doors is not of iron but wood and the decorations on it were not cared but put on by appliqué, a sort of plastic wood applied and formed as a sculptor would lay on modeling clay. These ornamentations show, in the lower oblong panel, Phoebus in his chariot, lashing his griffins. Scattered over the door are urns, flowers, trumpet-blowing angels, a beribboned lyre, an American eagle bearing on its breast the shield of the Union, leaves, scrolls, and whatnots – a marvelous example of some unknown craftsman's art. To save the door from the knives of souvenir-hunters, one owner painted it a dingy brown-black.

George W. Cable's Strange Stories of Louisiana, and Judge Henry C. Castellanos' New Orleans as It Was, contain full accounts of the Lalaurie episode. My account, differing in many respects from those of these earlier writers, is based on recently found documents, notarial acts, and family documents."

Delphine LaLaurie and her third husband, Leonard LaLaurie, took up residence in the house at 1140 Royal Street sometime in the 1830's. The pair immediately became the darlings of the gay New Orleans social scene that at the time was experiencing the birth of ragtime, the slave dances and rituals of Congo Square, the reign of the Mighty Marie Laveau, and the advent of the bittersweet Creole Balls. Madame LaLaurie hosted fantastic events in her beautiful home that were talked about months afterward. She was described as sweet and endearing in her ways, and her husband was nothing if not highly respected within the community.

At the same time, it is said, Madame's friendship with infamous Voodoo Queen, Marie Laveau, began to grow. Laveau lived not far from LaLaurie's Royal Street home and the two women became acquainted when Laveau did Madame's hair occasionally. It is said that under Laveau's tutelage, Madame LaLaurie began to act upon her latent interest in the occult, learning the secrets of voodoo and witchcraft at the hands of a might mistress of the craft.

There are reported incidents of people seeing, feeling and hearing the ghosts of tormented slaves in the LaLaurie home, and there are even reports of the Madame herself being seen there. The docile house servants who entreated the assistance of outsiders when the house was about to burn to the ground are said to often return to their task - running and slamming doors and shouts are heard repeatedly. Nor are the spirits of the restless dead quiet: the reports of moans and weeping outnumber all others. Furniture moves about by itself, people feel the touch of unseen hands, and there are several who have seen the ghostly faces of the dead peering from the upper windows and the chamber of horrors that became the crucible of their miserable lives.

New Orleans is one of the oldest and most multi-faceted cities in the United States, and there are other tales, similar to those of the LaLaurie home that, sadly, have made their way into our history. But the gruesome horror of this particular event was so ghastly that it stains the city's memory to this very day.

At one point actor Nicolas Cage owned the home, and while he said he never saw any ghosts, he wasn't immune to the home's sinister vibes; he lost the property to foreclosure in 2009.

The Stanley Hotel, Estes Park, Colorado

Famous for being the place where Jack Nicholson went crazy in 'The Shining,' this hotel is a hot spot for paranormal activity.

Their famous spooks include a young boy who makes his presence known in room 1211 and a young man who likes to hang out in closets and bedrooms. The hotel's owner, Mr. Stanley, also makes his presence known by appearing to visitors in the lobby and billiards room, while his wife Flora entertains guests by playing a piano. The hotel offers ghost tours, so next time you're there, bring a camera. Who knows? Perhaps a friendly spirit will appear for a picture!

The Stanley Hotel was the inspiration for Stephen King's book *The Shining*, but director Stanley Kubrick used the Timberline Lodge in Mount Hood, Ore. for exterior shots in the movie.

In addition to its regular guests, the hotel is also said to play host to a number of other worldly visitors. The most notable is F.O. Stanley himself who is most often seen in the lobby and the Billiard Room, which was his favorite room when he was still alive. On one such occasion, he was said to have appeared during a tour group's visit to the Billiard Room, materializing behind a member of the tour. Bartenders at the old hotel also report having seen F.O. stroll through the bar, disappearing when they try to cut him off at the kitchen.

Not to be left out, Flora Stanley also haunts the hotel, continuing to entertain guests with her piano playing in the ballroom. Employees and guests have reported hearing music coming from the room, and when they take a peek in there, they can see the piano keys moving. However, as soon as someone walks across the thresh-hold to investigate further, the music stops and no more movement can be seen upon the keys of the piano.

There are several rooms in the hotel that seem to be particularly haunted. One is Room 407, which is said to sometimes be occupied by Lord Dunraven, who owned the land prior to F.O. Stanley. Reportedly, he likes to stand in the corner of the room near the bathroom door. On one such account, witnesses reported that a light in that corner kept turning on and off. While the light was off, they told the ghost that they knew that he was there, they would only be staying two nights, and would he please turn the light back on. The light turned back on. However, later when the lights were turned off and they were trying to sleep, noises were constantly heard from the nearby elevator during a time when the elevator was not in use. At other times, a ghostly face has been reported to be looking out the window of Room 407, when the room is not booked.

Room 418 gets the most reports of haunting activity apparently from children's spirits. Cleaning crews report having heard many strange noises from the room, as well as seeing impressions on the bed when the room has been empty. When guests stay in the room, they often report that they hear children playing in the hallway at night. One couple reportedly checked out of the hotel very early in the morning, complaining that the children in the hallway kept them up all night. However, there were no children booked in the hotel at the time.

There have also been many reports by guests of haunting activities in Rooms 217 and 401.

Tour guides tell a story of the ghost of a small child who has been seen by many of the staff in various areas of the old hotel. Reportedly, Stephen King also saw the child, who was calling out to his nanny on the second floor. Other past employees report footsteps and apparitions seen throughout the building.

The Whaley House, San Diego, California

Located in San Diego, California, the Whaley House has earned the title of "the most haunted house in the U.S. Built in 1857 by Thomas Whaley on land that was partially once a cemetery, the house has since been the locus of dozens of ghost sightings.

Author deTraci Regula relates her experiences with the house: "Over the years, while dining across the street at the Old Town Mexican Cafe, I became accustomed to noticing that the shutters of the second-story windows [of the Whaley House] would sometimes open while we ate dinner, long after the house was closed for the day.

On a recent visit, I could feel the energy in several spots in the house, particularly in the courtroom, where I also smelled the faint scent of a cigar, supposedly Whaley's calling-card. In the hallway, I smelled perfume, initially attributing that to the young woman acting as docent, but some later surreptitious sniffing in her direction as I talked to her about the house revealed her to be scent-free."

The Whaley House is a two-story Greek revival style brick residence in San Diego's Old Town, was designed by Thomas Whaley and completed in 1857. The home, acclaimed as the "finest new brick block in Southern

California" by the San Diego Herald, contained mahogany and rosewood furniture, damask drapes, and Brussels carpets. Whaley established his general store in this residence, and solicited cash customers only. The site of the house is also where gallows once stood and where "Yankee Jim" Robinson (photo) was hanged for attempted grand larceny.

Whaley reportedly witnessed the hanging, but was not fazed by it, since he bought the property a few years later, removed the gallows, and built the Whaley family home on the site. Shortly after moving in, heavy footsteps could he heard throughout the house "by the boots of a large man." Whaley concluded it was Yankee Jim, whose spirit is alive and well two centuries later. Two later tragedies occurred in the house: the Whaleys' second child, Thomas, Jr, died at 18 months of scarlet fever and their fifth child, Violet, committed suicide in 1885. The home was designated a California State Historic Landmark in 1932 and is open to public tours.

The Whaleys moved to San Francisco but returned to San Diego in 1868. Whaley family members would live in the house for nearly a century.

Side note: Thomas Whaley had some prominent family history: His grandfather, Alexander Whaley, supplied George Washington with badly needed muskets during the American Revolution's Battle of White Plains and his mother, Rachel, made some shrewd real estate deals including buying "Sheeps Meadows," which was used as grazing land in New York City. It is now known as Central Park.

"Yankee Jim" Robinson

From October 1868 to January 1869, the Tanner Troupe Theatre operated out of the front upstairs bedroom. The San Diego County Courthouse utilized the former granary in August 1869 and rented three upstairs rooms for records storage. After the establishment of New Town San Diego by Alonzo Horton in 1868, the town focus changed to present day downtown San Diego.

During a March 1871 raid, courthouse documents were removed from the Whaley House and taken to Horton's Hall on 6th and F in San Diego. After the County's exit, Whaley connected the former granary and courtroom to the residence, changed windows and doors, and altered the front portico.

On October 31, 1956, the County of San Diego purchased the historic Whaley House, and undertook a major renovation of the property, which is still evident today. In September of 2000 Save Our Heritage Organization assumed the stewardship of the property for the County of San Diego and is in the progress of restoring the house to its original appearance.

Some of the other ghostly encounters include: the spirit of a young girl who was accidentally hanged on the property; the ghost of Yankee Jim Robinson, a thief who was clubbed to death and who can be heard on the house's stairway where he died, and has sometimes been seen during tours of the old house; the red-haired daughter of the Whaley's sometimes appears in such a realistic form, she is sometimes mistaken for a live child. Famed psychic Sybil Leek claimed to have sensed several spirits there, and renowned ghost hunter Hanz Holzer considered the Whaley to be one of the most reliably haunted structures in the United States.

The Winchester House, San Jose, California

There have been a number of strange events reported at the totally unique Winchester House for many years and they still continue to be reported today. This Haunting makes the top ten in the USA, Number 4 Haunted House in America.

In 1884, a wealthy widow named Sarah L. Winchester began a construction project of such magnitude that it was to occupy the lives of carpenters and craftsmen until her death thirty-eight years later. The Victorian mansion, designed and built by the Winchester Rifle heiress, is filled with so many unexplained oddities, that it has come to be known as the Winchester Mystery House.

Sarah Winchester built a home that is an architectural marvel. Unlike most homes of its era, this 160-room Victorian mansion had modern heating and sewer systems, gas lights that operated by pressing a button, three working elevators, and 47 fireplaces. From rambling roofs and exquisite hand inlaid parquet floors to the gold and silver chandeliers and Tiffany art glass windows, you will be impressed by the staggering amount of creativity, energy, and expense poured into each and every detail.

Many psychics have visited the Haunted house, most have come away actually convinced, that Sarah Winchester and many other tormented spirits still wander the Great maze of rooms.
Sarah reportedly held nightly séances to gain guidance from spirits and her dead husband for the home's design. What resulted was a maze-like residence full of twisting and turning hallways, dead-ends, secret panels, a window built into a floor, staircases leading to nowhere, doors that open to walls, upside-down columns, and rooms built, then intentionally closed off — all to ward off and confuse evil spirits.

In the years that the house has been open to the public, employees and visitors alike have had one to many unusual encounters with ghost. There have been the sounds of haunted footsteps; music and many a banging doors; too often one hears mysterious echoing ghostly voices; several unexplainable cold spots; strange moving lights and orbs in ghost photos; witnesses have seen doorknobs that turn by themselves... and don't forget the scores of people who have their own claims of phenomena to report but just are too afraid to do it.

Tour through 110 of the 160 rooms and look for the bizarre phenomena that gave the mansion its name; a window built into the floor, staircases leading to nowhere, a chimney that rises four floors, doors that open onto blank walls, and upside down posts! No one has been able to explain the mysteries that exist within the Winchester Mansion, or why Sarah Winchester kept the carpenters' hammers pounding 24 hours a day for 38 years. It is believed that after the untimely deaths of her baby daughter and husband, son of the Winchester Rifle manufacturer, Mrs. Winchester was convinced by a medium that continuous building would appease the evil spirits of those killed by the famous "Gun that Won the West" and help her attain eternal life. Certainly her $20,000,000 inheritance was sufficient to support her obsession until her death at 82!

The Behind-the-Scenes Tour is a guided tour which takes guests into areas which had been unexplored for over 75 years. On tour you will learn how Mrs. Winchester's 160-acre estate functioned. You will go into the stables, dehydrator, Plumber's workshop, the unfinished Ballroom, and one of the basements.

You will also learn about Victorian architecture as your guide points out the many features used in the building of the Winchester mansion. Safety hats will be worn on the tour. The Behind-the-Scenes Tour is limited to those 10 and older. Sorry, due to safety concerns, children 9 and under and babies are not permitted.

The Winchester Firearms Museum

The "Gun that Won the West" is the main attraction in the Firearms Museum, one of the largest Winchester Rifle collections on the West Coast. See the collection of guns that preceded the famous Winchester Rifle, including B. Tyler Henry's 1860 repeating rifle that Oliver

Winchester adapted and improved upon to produce his first repeating rifle, the Winchester Model 1866. Learn about the Model 1873 which came to be called the "Gun that Won the West." See a collection of the Limited Edition Winchester Commemorative Rifles including the Centennial '66, the Theodore Roosevelt, and the renowned John Wayne.

The Winchester Antique Products Museum

This museum contains a rare collection of antique products once manufactured by the Winchester Products Company, a subsidiary of the Winchester Repeating Arms Company. In the years following World War I, the parent company launched a Post-war Program, aimed at expanding the manufacture of new products in order to fill the factory space previously used for military production. At one time there were 6,300 individually owned Winchester stores carrying these products, which made it the largest hardware chain store organization in the world! The museum now displays items produced in the 1920's ranging from Winchester cutlery, flashlights, lawn-mowers, boy's wagons, fishing tackle and roller skates, to food choppers, electric irons, and farm and garden tools.

The White House, Washington D.C.

1600 Pennsylvania Avenue in Washington, D.C. is not only home to the current President of the United States, it also is home of several former presidents who occasionally decide to make their presences known there, despite the fact that they are dead.

Americans have long enjoyed telling scary ghost stories. From the ghost of Abigail Adams doing her laundry in the East Room to the spirit of Dolley Madison overlooking the Rose Garden, the White House has its own legend of ghost stories that have been passed down over the years.

There is a story of a British soldier who died on the White House grounds during the war of 1812 in 1814. The British came through Washington in 1814 during the war of 1812 and burned all of the federal buildings in Washington, including the White House. A number of years ago, when a restoration project of the exterior stone walls of the residence, restores found scorch marks around the windows and doors that were deep into the stone and were obviously part of the damage from this fire in 1814. It is said that some people have seen a ghost of a British soldier with a torch in his hand.

Members of the staff, who have worked in the White House for many years, recently shared some of their stories of strange noises in the White House, sightings of President Abraham Lincoln's ghost and many, many more.

After Lincoln's assassination in April 1865, Mary Todd Lincoln attempted to stay in contact with her dead husband through private readings and séances. Whether she achieved genuine communication with the late president will never be known. Mary also visited the studio of William Mumler, a Boston engraver who claimed to photograph the dead.

This photo of Mary with the ghostly Lincoln was the result of her sitting with Mumler.

In 1869, Mumler was arrested for public fraud, larceny, and obtaining money under false pretenses. The highly-publicized trial ended in dismissal for lack of evidence. Was Mumler a fraud? Probably, although many of his sitters claimed to recognize loved ones in Mumler's photos who had never been photographed in life. Others claimed that some of the "spirits" in his pictures had been identified as living models.

Another popular legend is that of Dolley Madison coming back during the Wilson Administration when Mrs. Wilson wanted the rose garden dug up. Dolley's ghost arrived, supposedly, and told them not to disturb her garden.

President Harrisons' ghost is said to be heard rummaging around in the attic of the White House, looking for who knows what.

President Andrew Jackson's' ghost is thought to haunt his White House bedroom. And the ghost of First Lady Abigail Adams was seen floating through one of the White House hallways, as if carrying something in her hands.

Mrs. Mary Todd Lincoln held real séances in the White House, it was said she would try and recall the spirit of their dead son Willie who died in the White House during his father's Presidency. After Willie's death, Mrs. Lincoln was seated at a table and held the séance in the green room to try and contact Willie's spirit.

Legend has it that Mary Lincoln reported hearing Andrew Jacksons' ghost walk around the halls of the White House and supposedly swearing up a storm.

The most frequently sighted presidential ghost has been that of Abraham Lincoln. Eleanor Roosevelt once stated she believed she felt the presence of Lincoln watching her as she worked in the Lincoln bedroom. Also during the Roosevelt administration, a young clerk claimed to have actually seen the ghost of Lincoln sitting on a bed pulling off his boots.

On another occasion, while spending a night at the White House during the Roosevelt presidency, Queen Wilhelmina of the Netherlands was awakened by a knock on the bedroom door. Answering it, she was confronted with the ghost of Abe Lincoln staring at her from the hallway. Calvin Coolidge's wife reported seeing on several occasions the ghost of Lincoln standing with his hands clasped behind his back, at a window in the Oval Office, staring out in deep contemplation toward the bloody battlefields across the Potomac.

President Harry Truman's White House Renovation Era

On the right hand side of this photo you can make out a figure standing

On the left hand side of this photo you can make out a figure standing

The next picture was taken inside the White house during the renovations. Note the figure standing in the center of the photo.

The apparent apparition is clear and startling. Compared to the other men in the photo, its size scale is accurate. And if this were due to some motion or long exposure effect, the rest of the photo should be affected, as well.

Here's a closer look at the area containing the figure:

Here's a close-up of the figure:

It makes sense that a home this old and with so much history has a lot of ghosts. Abigail Adams, wife of second president John Adams, is considered to be the "oldest" ghost in the White House since she and John were the first to live in the big, drafty home that was still unfinished when they moved in on Nov. 1, 1800. She was known to hang her laundry in the East Room and is still "spotted" there to this day. But perhaps the most notable ghost is 16th president Abraham Lincoln who reportedly had psychic powers and even anticipated his assassination days before.

Many former presidents, residents and heads of state have seen Lincoln or felt his presence throughout the White House, including British Prime Minister Winston Churchill and Queen Wilhelmina of the Netherlands, who fainted at the sight of him.

Other famous ghosts include Dolley Madison who stands watch over her Rose Garden; 7th president Andrew Jackson has been heard laughing in the Rose Bedroom; 3rd president Thomas Jefferson plays his violin in the Yellow Oval Room; and British soldiers are seen walking the hallways.

The most famous Abraham Lincoln story is from Winston Churchill, who was staying at the residence after World War II, the British leader had just emerged from a bath, wearing nothing and smoking a cigar. He reportedly met the late president. "Good evening, Mr. President. You seem to have me at a disadvantage," Churchill allegedly said. He also refused to stay in the room after the encounter.

Ronald Reagan's White House Ghost Story

According to the President, Rex, the King Charles Cavalier spaniel who had recently replaced Lucky as First Dog, had twice barked frantically in the Lincoln Bedroom and then backed out and refused to set foot over the threshold. And another evening, while the Reagans were watching TV in their room, Rex stood up on his hind legs, pointed his nose at the ceiling and began barking at something invisible overhead. To their amazement, the dog walked around the room, barking at the ceiling.

'I started thinking about it,' the President continued, 'And I began to wonder if the dog was responding to an electric signal too high-pitched for human ears, perhaps beamed toward the White House by a foreign embassy. I asked my staff to look into it.'

The President laughed and said, 'I might as well tell you the rest. A member of our family [he meant his daughter Maureen] and her husband always stay in the Lincoln Bedroom when they visit the White House. Some time ago the husband woke up and saw a transparent figure standing at the bedroom window looking out. Then it turned and disappeared. His wife teased him mercilessly about it for a month. Then, when they were here recently, she woke up one morning and saw the same figure standing at the window looking out. She could see the trees right through it. Again it turned and disappeared.'

Lincoln's Ghost

There have been several stories about ghosts of former Presidents revisiting the White House. However, the most common and popular is that of Abraham Lincoln. Lincoln's Ghost, otherwise known as The White House Ghost, is said to have haunted the White House since his death. It is widely believed that when he was president, Lincoln might have known of his assassination before he died.

According to Ward Hill Lamon, Lincoln's friend and biographer, three days before his assassination Lincoln discussed with Lamon and others a dream he had, saying:
Lincoln had a dream in April 1865, the month that he was assassinated. As he recounted to friends the day he died:

214

"About ten days ago," said he, "I retired very late. I had been up waiting for important dispatches from the front. I could not have been long in bed when I fell into a slumber, for I was weary. I soon began to dream. There seemed to be a death-like stillness about me. Then I heard subdued sobs, as if a number of people were weeping. I thought I left my bed and wandered downstairs. There the silence was broken by the same pitiful sobbing, but the mourners were invisible.

I went from room to room; no living person was in sight, but the same mournful sounds of distress met me as I passed along. It was light in all the rooms; every object was familiar to me; but where were all the people who were grieving as if their hearts would break? I was puzzled and alarmed. What could be the meaning of all this? Determined to find the cause of a state of things so mysterious and so shocking, I kept on until I arrived at the East Room, which I entered. There I met with a sickening surprise. Before me was a catafalque, on which rested a corpse wrapped in funeral vestments. Around it were stationed soldiers who were acting as guards; and there was a throng of people, some gazing mournfully upon the corpse, whose face was covered, others weeping pitifully. 'Who is dead in the White House?' I demanded of one of the soldiers. 'The President,' was his answer; 'he was killed by an assassin!' Then came a loud burst of grief from the crowd, which awoke me from my dream. I slept no more that night; and although it was only a dream, I have been strangely annoyed by it ever since."

The White House's most famous alleged apparition is that of Abraham Lincoln. Eleanor Roosevelt never admitted to having seen Lincoln's ghost, but did say that she felt his presence repeatedly throughout the White House.

Mrs. Roosevelt also said that the family dog, Fala, would sometimes bark for no reason at what she felt was Lincoln's ghost.

President Dwight Eisenhower's press secretary, James Hagerty, and Liz Carpenter, press secretary to First Lady Lady Bird Johnson, both said they felt Lincoln's presence many times.

The former president's footsteps are also said to be heard in the hall outside the Lincoln Bedroom.

As reputable an eyewitness as Lillian Rogers Parks admitted in her 1961 autobiography *My Thirty Years Backstairs at the White House* that she had heard them.

Margaret Truman, daughter of President Harry S. Truman, said she heard a specter rapping at the door of the Lincoln Bedroom when she stayed there, and believed it was Lincoln.

President Truman himself was once wakened by raps at the door while spending a night in the Lincoln Bedroom.

Others have actually seen an apparition of the former president. The first person reported to have actually seen Lincoln's spirit was First Lady Grace Coolidge, who said she saw the ghost of Lincoln standing at a window in the Yellow Oval Room staring out at the Potomac. Winston Churchill, Theodore Roosevelt and Maureen Reagan and her husband have all claimed to have seen a spectral Lincoln in the White House. A number of staff members of the Franklin D. Roosevelt administration claimed to have seen Lincoln's spirit, and on one occasion Roosevelt's personal valet ran screaming from the White House claiming he had seen Lincoln's ghost.

Perhaps the most famous incident was in 1942 when Wilhelmina of the Netherlands heard footsteps outside her White House bedroom and answered a knock on the door, only to see Lincoln in frock coat and top hat standing in front of her (she promptly fainted).

One of the most recent sightings came in the early 1980s, when Tony Savoy, White House operations foreman, came into the White House and saw Lincoln sitting in a chair at the top of some stairs.

Several unnamed eyewitnesses have claimed to have seen the shade of Abraham Lincoln actually lying down on the bed in the Lincoln Bedroom (which was used as a meeting room at the time of his administration), and while others have seen Lincoln sit on the edge of the bed and put his boots on. The most famous eyewitness to the latter was Mary Eben, Eleanor Roosevelt's secretary, who saw Lincoln pulling on his boots (after which she ran screaming from the room).

Abraham Lincoln is not the only Lincoln ghost witnesses claim to have seen in the White House. Willie Lincoln, Abraham Lincoln's 11-year-old son, died in the White House of typhoid on February 20, 1862.

Willie Lincoln's ghost was first seen in the White House by staff members of the Grant administration in the 1870s, but has appeared as recently as the 1960s (President Lyndon B. Johnson's college-age daughter, Lynda Bird Johnson Robb, saw the ghost and claims to have talked to him).

The Myrtles Plantation, St. Francisville, Louisiana

Saint Francisville is located in West Feliciana Parish Louisiana. A small town on the Mississippi River. Once the Capital of the Republic of West Florida, it is here that John James Audubon (Birds of America Collection) created over 80 of his beautiful watercolors. There are seven Magnificent Plantation homes opened for public tours. And The Myrtles Plantation is the one you would not want to miss. And with all the recent investigations by TAPS is now fast becoming the most famous ghost filled haunted house in America.

Exploring the myrtles you will see grand fine antiques and architectural treasures of the old South and you personally might discover why The Myrtles has been called "America's Most Haunted Homes".

"The actual haunting hour at the Myrtles Plantation is said to be at three AM. At that exact hour each dark night, Chloe's restless ghost roams the great dark haunted plantation. The Myrtles isn't an ordinary plantation. It's supposed to be one of the most haunted houses in America. "

"Whiskey Dave" Bradford--former leader of the whiskey rebellion--built the great haunted house on a Tunica Indian burial ground in 1794. He was actually the very first to see a ghost at the Myrtles Plantation, a naked Indian girl wandering lost on the grounds is what he is said to have observed. But Many of the locals state it is Bradford's' many ghostly children and grandchildren that haunt the Myrtles today.

Sara Matilda, Bradford's' daughter, married Judge Woodruff. Woodruff was said to have kept a slave mistress named Chloe or so the haunted tale goes....

When Woodruff grew tired of Chloe, and she was afraid she would be sent to the fields she is said to have started eavesdropping on him to learn of her future fate.

When Woodruff caught her, he cut off her left ear and sent her to work in the kitchen. From then on, Chloe wore a green turban to hide her disfigurement. She devised a plan to regain the affection of him and the family. She boiled poisonous oleander leaves and baked them into a cake.

Chloe believed the children would become ill and need her to nurse them back to health. But she used too much. Sara Matilda and two of the children died that night from the poison.

When the other slaves heard about Chloe's actions, they hung her from a tree. They then weighted her body with stones and threw her into the Mississippi river.

Chloe still wanders the house and grounds of the Myrtles Plantation. She sometimes shows up in photos. The Woodruff children are also heard playing and laughing on the veranda on rainy nights.

The Chloe story is the most popular haunting tale at the Myrtles, but many more people met their untimely demise on the premises and can be seen and heard wandering.

A Civil War soldier died on the floor near the front door from battle wounds. He was an avid cigar smoker who stayed at the house before his death. The smell of cigars sometimes fills his room. (And smoking isn't allowed at the Myrtles...)

William Winter was said to have died on the 17th step of the staircase after a mysterious man shot him through the study window in 1871.

The steps heard on the stairs in the middle of the night are attributed to him. Those who count claim the footsteps stop at the seventeenth step.

Another young girl died of yellow fever in one of the upstairs bedrooms. Her parents called on a voodoo priestess to help her, after all traditional medicines had failed. When the little girl died, the parents hung the priestess from the chandelier.

In 1927, the caretaker was murdered during a robbery attempt. The owners claim that he can sometimes be seen at the plantation gates telling people to leave.

The Myrtles is now a bed and breakfast, so guests can stay in these rooms and see if the ghosts come out and play. The proprietors, John and Teeta Moss, claim that the Best Western loves the Myrtles, because so many guests get spooked in the middle of the night and run to the other hotel.

Whether you believe in ghosts or not, it's fun to be scared. This house has a creepy vibe. Bursts of cold air come from nowhere. Former owners have had church stained glass installed in the front doors to keep out the evil spirits. Also, the keyholes of every door have a small cover over them. In the nineteenth century, people thought ghosts came into a house through its keyholes, and these covers were designed to keep them out.

People also believed that the ghosts would hide in the corners until nighttime, when they would come out to pester the living. The Myrtles contains custom plaster work nun and cherub charms specially designed to keep the spirits away from the corners. Every resident has painstakingly tried to protect himself from wandering spirits.

Ghosts or not, everyone who has owned the property has either seen ghosts, has turned into a ghost, or tried to keep the ghosts away. Mysterious figures and spheres often show up in ghost photos.

The Myrtles has been featured in New York Times, Forbes, Gourmet, Veranda, Travel and Leisure, Country Inns, Colonial Homes, Delta SKY, and on the Oprah Show, A & E, The History Channel, The Travel Channel, The Learning Channel, National Geographic Explorer, and GOOD MORNING AMERICA. It was also featured in The Hauntings of Louisiana.

Relax in the giant rockers on the 120-foot verandah or stroll through the lush ten acres filled with majestic live oaks. The 5000 square foot old brick courtyard is the perfect place to unwind before enjoying a delicious candlelight dinner at our Carriage House Restaurant.

Hull House, Chicago, Illinois

THE LEGEND OF HULL HOUSE LIVES TO THIS VERY DAY

Hull House was constructed by Charles J. Hull at Halsted and Polk Streets in 1856 at a time when this was one of the most fashionable sections of the city. After the Chicago Fire of 1871. In the 1880's, Hull House was surrounded by factories and tenement houses and soon after, became one of the most famous places in Chicago.

A black and white infrared picture taken at Hull House in downtown Chicago, Illinois by Dale Kaczmarek in November of 1980. This is enlarged blowup of the interior staircase of this most haunted house in Chicago.

There was nothing visible to the naked eye when the photograph was taken but what appears are four distinct shadowy monk-like figures standing on the bottom four or five steps. The one directly in the middle appears to be dressed in monk's habit with his two hands together in prayer. There are two other figures to the left of the center monk and one to the right superimposed on the banister which apparently has no head!

Although it was never originally to be known as a "haunted house"... it would not be unscathed by stories of ghosts and the supernatural.

Jane Addams died in 1935 but the Hull House Association continued her work at the settlement house until the 1960's. At that time, the property was purchased by the University of Illinois, bringing an end to one of Chicago's greatest achievements in social reform.

In 1889, Jane Addams and another social worker took over the Hull mansion at 800 South Halsted and turned it into a community center. The house, now part of the Chicago campus of the University of Illinois, is currently a museum dedicated to Addams and her work.

Mrs. Hull's bedroom was first occupied by Jane Addams herself, who was awakened one night by loud footsteps in the otherwise empty room. After a few nights of this, she confided her story to Ellen, who also admitted to experiencing the same sounds. Jane later moved to another room.

But she would not be alone in noticing the unusual happenings. Helen Campbell, the author of the book PRISONERS OF POVERTY, reported seeing an apparition standing next to her bed (she took Jane up on the offer of staying in the "haunted room"). When she lit the gas jet, the figure vanished. The same peculiar sounds and figures were also observed by Mrs. Louise Bowen, a lifelong friend of Jane's, Jane and Mary Smith, and even Canon Barnett of Toynbee Hall, who visited the settlement house during the Columbian Exposition in 1893.

According to Jane Addams' book, TWENTY YEARS AT HULL HOUSE, earlier tenants of the house, which included the Little Sisters of the Poor and a second-hand furniture store, believed the upstairs of the house was haunted as well. They had always kept a bucket of water on the stairs, believing that the ghost was unable to cross over it.

Regardless, the ghost was always considered to be rather sad, but harmless, and residents and guests learned to live with its presence. Unfortunately, it was not the only "supernatural" legend connected to Hull House!

THE DEVIL BABY OF HULL HOUSE

Hull House received its greatest notoriety when it was alleged to be the refuge of the Chicago "devil baby". This child was supposedly born to a devout Catholic woman and her atheist husband and was said to have pointed ears, horns, scale-covered skin and a tail. According to the story, the young woman had attempted to display a picture of the Virgin Mary in the house but her husband had torn it down. He stated that he would rather have the Devil himself in the house that the picture. When the woman had become pregnant, the Devil Baby had been their curse. After enduring numerous indignities because of the child, the father allegedly took it to Hull House.

After being taken in by Jane Addams, staff members of the house reportedly took the baby to be baptized. During the ceremony, the baby supposedly escaped from the priest and began dancing and laughing. Not knowing what else to do with the child, Jane kept it locked in the attic of the house, where it later died.

Rumors spread quickly about the baby and within a few weeks, hundreds of people came to the house to get a glimpse of it. How the story had gotten started, no one knew, but it spread throughout the west side neighborhood and was reported by famous Chicago reporter Ben Hecht. He claimed that every time he tried to run down the story, he was directed to find the child at Hull House. Many people came to the door and demanded to see the child, while others quietly offered to pay an admission. They believed the wild story to be absolutely true!

Each day, Jane turned people away and tried to convince them that the story was fabricated. She even devoted 40 pages of her autobiography to dispelling the stories. Even though most of the poorly educated immigrants left the house still believing the tales of the Devil Baby, the stream of callers eventually died out and the story became a barely remembered side note in the history of Hull House.

As the years have passed, some people still maintain the story of the Devil Baby is true... or at least contains some elements of the truth. Some have speculated that perhaps the child was actually a badly deformed infant that had been brought to Hull House by a young immigrant woman that could not care for it. Perhaps the monstrous appearance of the child had started the rumors in the neighborhood and eventually led to Hull House.

Regardless, local legend insists that at some point, there was a disfigured boy that was hidden away on the upper floors of the house. The stories also go on to say that on certain nights, the image of a deformed face could be seen peering out of the attic window.... and that a ghostly version of that face is still seen by visitors today!

Lemp Mansion, St. Louis, Missouri

Said to be one of the ten most haunted places in America, the Lemp Mansion in St. Louis, Missouri, continues to play host to the tragic Lemp family. Over the years, the mansion was transformed from the stately home of millionaires, to office space, decaying into a run-down boarding house, and finally restored to its current state as a fine dinner theatre, restaurant and bed and breakfast.

The Lemp Family began with Johann Adam Lemp who arrived in St Louis from Eschwege, Germany in 1838. Building a small grocery store at what is now Delmar and 6th Streets, he sold common household items, groceries, and homemade beer. The light golden lager was a welcome change from the darker beers that were sold at the time. The recipe, handed down by his father, was so popular that just two years later, he gave up the grocery store and built a small brewery in 1840 at a point close to where the Gateway Arch stands today.

Lemp first sold his beer in a pub attached to the brewery, introducing St. Louis to its first lager. Before long, Lemp found that the brewery was too small to handle both production and storage and found a limestone cave south of the city limits. The cave, which was located at the present-day corner of Cherokee and De Menil Place, could be kept cool by chopping ice from the nearby Mississippi River and depositing it inside, providing perfect conditions for the lagering process to run its course. Lemp's Western Brewing Co. continued to prosper and by the 1850s was one of the largest in the city. In 1858, the beer captured first place at the annual St. Louis fair.

A millionaire by the time of his death, Adam Lemp died on August 25, 1862 and his son, William, began a major expansion of the brewery. He purchased a five-block area around the storage house on Cherokee, above the lagering caves. In 1864, a new plant was complete at Cherokee Street and Carondolet Avenue. Continually expanding to meet the product demand, the brewery eventually covered five city blocks.

By the 1870s the Lemp family symbolized both wealth and power, as the Lemp Brewery controlled the St. Louis beer market, a position it maintained until prohibition.

In 1868, Jacob Feickert, William Lemp's father-in-law, built a house a short distance from the Lemp Brewery. In 1876 William Lemp purchased it for his family, utilizing it as both a residence and an auxiliary office. While the home was already impressive, Lemp immediately began renovating and expanding the thirty-three room house into a Victorian showplace.

From the mansion, a tunnel was built from the basement through the caves to the brewery. When mechanical refrigeration became available, parts of the cave were converted for other purposes, including a natural auditorium and a theatre. This underground oasis would later spawn a large concrete swimming pool, with hot water piped in from the brewery boiling house, and a bowling alley. At one time, the theatre was accessible by way of a spiral staircase from Cherokee Street.

By the middle 1890s, the Lemp Brewery gained a national presence after introducing the popular "Falstaff" beer, which is still brewed today by another company. The Lemp Western Brewery was the first brewer to establish coast-to-coast distribution of its beer.
At the same time he was building his own business empire, William, Sr. also helped Pabst, Anheuser and Busch get started.

William Lemp

In the midst of this success, the Lemp family experienced the first of many tragedies when Frederick Lemp, William Sr's favorite son and heir apparent died in 1901 at the age of 28. Frederick, who had never been in extremely good health, died of heart failure. The devastated William Lemp was never the same, beginning a slow withdrawal; he was rarely seen in public after his son's death. On January 1, 1904, William's closest friend, Frederick Pabst, also died, leaving William indifferent to the details of running the brewery. Though he still arrived at the office each day, he was nervous and unsettled. His physical and mental health began to decline and on February 13, 1904, he shot himself in the head with a .38 caliber Smith & Wesson.

It was in this corner that William Lemp's desk, where he shot himself, once sat. Notice the streak across the top of the mirror. Similar streaks showed up in many pictures that included mirrors.

In November 1904, William Lemp Jr. took over as the new president of the William J. Lemp Brewing Company. Inheriting the family business and a vast fortune, he and his wife, Lillian, began to spend the inheritance. Filling the house with servants, the pair spent huge amounts on carriages, clothing and art.

Lillian was a beautiful woman who came from a wealthy family herself. She and William Lemp, Jr had married in 1899 and William J. Lemp, III was born on September 26, 1900. Before long Lillian became known as the "Lavender Lady" because of her fondness for the color. In addition to her lavender attire and accessories, she went so far as to have her carriage horses harnesses died lavender. In the beginning, Will enjoyed showing off his "trophy wife" but Will was a "player." Born with a "silver spoon in his mouth," he was used to doing and acting as he pleased.

When William began to tire of his beautiful wife, he demanded that she *must* spend her time shopping. Allotting her $1,000 a day, he gave her an ultimatum that if she didn't spend it, she would get no more.

In the meantime, Will was busy running the brewery during the day and pursuing all manner of decadent activities during the night. Holding lavish parties in the caves below the mansion, he would bring in numerous prostitutes for the "entertainment" of his friends. Enjoying the swimming pool, the bowling alley, and the free flowing beer, his friends who attended these lavish events were known to enjoy a high time in the earth below.

Will's shenanigans caught up with him when he sired a son with a woman other than his wife. Today, there is no official documentation that this boy existed. However, the rumors that this boy was hidden in the mansion attic for his entire lifetime have been prevalent over the years. According to St Louis historian, Joe Gibbons, when he interviewed a former nanny and a chauffeur who worked at the mansion long ago, both of them verified that the boy *did* exist and was housed in the attic quarters that also housed the servant's rooms. Spawned from Will's philandering with either one of the many prostitutes or a mansion servant, the boy was born with Down's syndrome. A total embarrassment to the family, the boy was hidden away from the world in order to cloak the Lemp's "shame." Known today as the "Monkey Face Boy," this unfortunate soul continues to show his presence at the Lemp Mansion.

Finally, William, Jr. tired of his "trophy wife" and filed for divorce in 1908. Why she didn't make this step with all of his goings-on, could be nothing more than a sign of the times. The court proceedings surrounding the divorce became a major St. Louis scandal with all four St. Louis newspapers devoting extensive front page coverage to the messy affair. The trial opened in February, 1909 to crowds that flocked to the courthouse each day to witness the drama of tales of violence, drunkenness, atheism and cruelty.

Virtually ignoring William's decadent activities, Lillian almost lost custody of William Lemp, III because of a photograph that was presented at the trial that showed her smoking a cigarette. In the end, she retained custody of their son but soon retired from public eye. The only time that she was ever seen wearing anything other than lavender was on the final day of her divorce proceedings, when she appeared entirely in black before the judge.

With the divorce, Will's troubles had only just begun. In 1906, nine of the large breweries in the St. Louis area had combined to form the Independent Breweries Company, creating fierce competition that the Lemp Brewery had never faced. In the same year, Will's mother died by cancer on April 16th.

Though the brewery's fortunes were continually declining, the Lemp Mansion was entirely remodeled in 1911 and partially converted into offices for the brewery. At this same time, William allowed the company's equipment to deteriorate, without keeping abreast of industry innovations. By World War I, the brewery was just barely limping along.

William soon built a country home on the Meramec River, to which he increasingly retreated and in 1915 he married for a second time to Ellie Limberg, widowed daughter of the late St. Louis brewer Casper Koehler.

Then Prohibition came along in 1919. The individual family members were already wealthy so there was little incentive to keep the brewery afloat. For a time, Will hoped that Congress would repeal Prohibition but finally gave up and closed the Lemp plant down without notice. The workers learned of the closing when they came to work one day and found the doors shut and the gates locked.

On March 20, 1920, Elsa Lemp Wright, William's sister, the wealthiest heiress in St Louis, shot herself just like her father had years before. Elsa was said to have been despondent over her rocky marriage.

Liquidating the assets of the plant and auctioning the buildings, William, Jr. sold the famous Lemp "Falstaff" logo to brewer Joseph Griesedieck for $25,000 in 1922. The brewery buildings were sold to the International Shoe Co. for $588,000, a fraction of its estimated worth of $7 million in the years before Prohibition.

After the end of the Lemp's brewing dynasty, William, Jr. slipped into a depression. Acting much like his father, he became increasingly nervous and erratic, shunning public life and often complaining of ill health. On December 29, 1922, William shot himself, in the heart with a .38 caliber revolver, in the very same building where his father had died eighteen years before.

William, II took his life on the main level of the mansion, just inside the entrance to the left. At the time of his death, this room served as his office. He was interred in the family mausoleum at Bellefontaine Cemetery, in the crypt just above his sister Elsa.

William's brothers, Charles and Edwin had long ago left the family business, so with William Jr. gone, it seemed that the Lemp empire had finally ended. Edwin had entered into a life of seclusion at his estate in Kirkwood, Missouri in 1911. Charles had never been involved in the brewery and had chosen to work in the banking and real estate fields instead.

In 1943, yet another tragedy occurred when William Lemp III died of a heart attack at the age of forty-two.

Brother Charles eventually remodeled the mansion back into a residence and lived in the house along with two servants and the illegitimate child of his brother William. Charles, too, became an odd figure, as he grew older. Developing a morbid fear of germs, his obsessive compulsive behavior included wearing gloves at all times to avoid bacteria and constantly washing his hands. It was during this time that William's illegitimate child, now in his 30s, died at the mansion. He was buried on the Lemp Cemetery plot with only a small flat marker, with the word "Lemp."

Shortly after the "Monkey Face Boy's" death, Charles became the fourth member of the Lemp family to commit suicide. First, he shot his beloved Doberman pinscher in the basement of the mansion. Then, climbing the staircase to his room on the second floor, he shot himself. Charles was discovered on May 10, 1949 by one of his staff, still holding a .38 caliber Army Colt revolver in his right hand. Though the dog was shot in the basement, he was found half way up the stairs.

Of the Lemps, only Edwin Lemp, who had long avoided the life that had turned so tragic for the rest of his family, remained. He was known as a quiet, reclusive man who had walked away from the Lemp Brewery in 1913 to live a peaceful life on a secluded estate in Kirkwood, Missouri. Edwin passed away quietly of natural causes at age 90 in 1970.

According to Edwin's last wishes, his butler burned all of the paintings that the Lemps had collected throughout his life, as well as priceless Lemp family documents and artifacts. These irreplaceable pieces of history vanished in the smoke of a blazing bonfire.

The Lemp family line died out with him and the family's resting place can now be found in beautiful Bellefontaine Cemetery.
After the death of Charles Lemp, the mansion was sold and turned into a boarding house. Along with the nearby neighborhood, the building began to deteriorate, and the haunting tales began. Residents complained of ghostly knocks and phantom footsteps being heard throughout the house. As these stories spread, tenants were hard to find for the boarding house and it continued to decline to a near flophouse status.

However, in 1975, the old mansion was saved when Dick Pointer and his family purchased it. Immediately they began to renovate the building, turning it into a restaurant and inn. Workers within the house often told stories of apparitions, strange sounds, vanishing tools, and a feeling of being watched. Frightened by the hauntings, many would leave the job site never to return.

Since the restaurant opened, staff members have reported several strange experiences. Again, apparitions appear and then quickly vanish, voices and sounds come from nowhere, and glasses will often lift off the bar flying through the air by themselves. On other occasions, doors are said to lock and unlock by themselves, lights inexplicably turn on and off of their own free will, and the piano bar often plays when no one is near.

Said to be haunted by several members of the Lemp family, there are three areas of the old mansion that have the most activity -- the stairway, the attic, and what the staff refers to as, the "Gates of Hell" in the basement. It is this area of the basement that used to be the entrance to the caves running below the mansion and the brewery.

The attic is said to be haunted by William, Jr's illegitimate son, referred to only as the "Monkey Face Boy." This poor soul, born with Down's syndrome, spent his entire life locked in the attic of the Lemp Mansion.

Strange occurrences are often witnessed on this third floor level of the mansion. The face of the boy has regularly been seen from the street peeking from the small windows of the mansion.

Ghost investigators have often left toys in the middle of his room, drawing a circle around them to see if the objects have been moved. Consistently, when they return the next day, the toys are found in another location.

In the downstairs women's bathroom, which was once William, Jr's personal domain and held the first free standing shower in St. Louis, many women have reported a man peeking over the stall. On one such occasion, a woman emerged from the bathroom, returning to the bar and and stated to the two men she was there with: "I hope you got an eyeful!" However, the two men quickly denied ever having left the bar, for which the bartender verified. This ghost is said to be that of the womanizing William Jr.

In William Lemp, Sr's room, guests have often reported hearing someone running up the stairs and kicking at the door. When William killed himself, William Jr was known to have ran up the stairs to his father's room and finding it locked began to kick the door in to get to his father.
Several years ago a part time tour guide reported hearing the sounds of horses outside the the room where William Lemp, Sr had kept his office. However, when the tour guide looked through the window, nothing was there. This area, north of the mansion and now used as a parking lot, was once utilized as a tethering lot for horses.

The mansion has been featured in a number of magazine articles and newspapers and now attracts ghost hunters from around the country. Today it features a bed and breakfast with rooms restored in period style, a restaurant featuring fine dining, and a mystery dinner theater. Tours are also available at the mansion.

The Lemp Mansion is located at 3322 De Menil Place, a short distance from the Mississippi River. To get there Take Broadway from Interstate 55 and follow that to Cherokee Street. Go west on Cherokee and turn right onto De Menil Place.

Part V
Psychics and Mediums

What is Parapsychology?

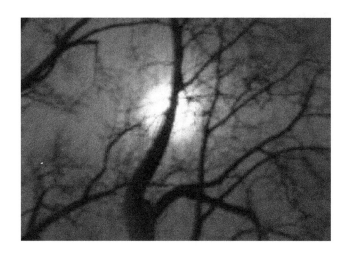

Paranormal phenomenon remains of intense interest to the general public. There is a fascination with what might be possible.

The term "parapsychology" is said to have been invented by psychologist Max Dessoir around the time of 1889 if not before and it emerged as a field of interest in the late 19th century. It was then called psychical research.

Parapsychology today is described as the scientific study and search for confirmation of paranormal phenomena such as ESP, telepathy or clairvoyance. Paranormal means "beside" or "beyond" normal and it refers to strange or odd experiences which do not seem to have an explanation for occurring.

Parapsychology is the study of perceptions, events and behaviors which do not fall into the category of what most people would consider a human can. Special abilities such as ESP and telepathy are called psi or paranormal abilities. Parapsychology is an attempt to find and describe things that are unusual and outside the realm of traditional experience

Paranormal occurrences almost always appear to be bizarre mysterious or unusual. In general they are quite rare but there are some who claim to have frequent paranormal experiences.

Para psychological phenomena can generally be broken down into three general categories:

• Telepathy which is the ability to communicate with another by only the power of the mind

• Clairvoyance or precognition which involves the ability to learn or have knowledge of events which have not yet happened
• Telekinesis which is the ability to move objects by the power of the mind

Spiritualism involves the ability to commutate with spirits of the dead and it is closely related to telepathy, clairvoyance and telekinesis because it often involves the moving of objects and predictions of the future.

A common misconception is that a parapsychology is of a psychic nature. This is far from the truth. Parapsychology is a scientist or scholar who is seriously interested in the "paranormal."

Parapsychology is the study of phenomena suggesting that the assumption of a strict separation between subjective and objective may be wrong.

What do parapsychologists study?

The basic parapsychology phenomena are classified as follows:

Psi: is a term used for parapsychology phenomena. Psi, psychic, and psychical are other terms used.
Telepathy: is communication between two or more people without

speaking a word. Communication can take place between people or between a living person and a spirit.

Precognition: is also called premonition which involves knowing about future events without prior knowledge of them

Clairvoyance: is a French word that means "clear seeing." Clairvoyance is described as the ability of a person to see present or future events without prior knowledge of them.

ESP: Extra-sensory perception
Psycho kinesis: is direct mental interaction with animate or inanimate objects.

Bio-PK: are direct mental interactions with living systems.

NDE: is near death experience.

OBE: Out-of-body experience.

Reincarnation: is the belief that we live successive lives.

Haunting: pertains to particular locations that include lingering apparitions, sounds, movement of objects, and other effects.

Poltergeist: often attributed to spirits, but which are now thought to be due to a living person, frequently an adolescent.

Déjà vu: is very common. Almost everyone has said they have experienced being in a place they have never seen or know anything about. The words are French and mean "already seen."

When it comes to opinion about and discussing parapsychology people tend to fall into two opposite-thinking groups. One group is dedicated believers who accept all aspects of the paranormal and who will not listen to any arguments that dispute the existence of the paranormal. The other group is strict skeptics who reject any and all evidence that the paranormal exists.

Many scientists have also viewed parapsychology with such skepticism because parapsychology is often inappropriately linked with a variety of "psychic" entertainers, magicians, and so-called "paranormal investigators." But this is far from what parapsychologists study. For them the study of paranormal phenomena is real and viable.

The paranormal has occurred in all cultures throughout history, and they still do today. Paranormal phenomenon remains of intense interest to the general public. There is a fascination with what might be possible.

For decades there have been numerous books, movies and television programs that have explored various aspects of the paranormal and the current trends seem to suggest that there will be many more such books, movies and television shows which will explore the fascination with the paranormal.

HSP (Highly Sensitive People)

A lot of HSPs are strongly empathetic. They strongly get into the spirit of their fellow-men, thus share their feelings and obtain on this way understanding for the action of the others. Empathy is a gift that makes it possible to have a close link to the psyche of other people.

Highly Sensitive People have according to a psychological disposition an increased susceptibility for stimulations. This increased receptivity for outer (e.g. noises, odours, contacts) und inner stimulations (e.g. reminiscences, ideas, thoughts) leads to the fact that Highly Sensitive's perceive more information. In addition, they process these vastly deeper and profounder than non-Highly Sensitive People.

The term "Highly Sensitive Person" (in short: HSP) had been raised in 1996 by the American psychologist Elaine Aron in her bestseller: "The Highly Sensitive Person: How To Thrive When The World Overwhelms You".

Studies proved that Highly Sensitive's – as far as they are not under acute pressure – are healthier and happier than Non-HSPs. Healthier because their marked early warning system informs them in time of sanitary and other dangers. And happier because HSPs perceive all emotions more intensive. Predominate positive emotions significantly, HSPs live deeper and more intensive moments of happiness.

A negative side-effect of the high sensitivity is the early reach of feelings like flood of stimulation or over taxation. So, vapours or dust in the air can influence a Highly Sensitive as strong as loud music, glaring light, tight clothes or the noises of computers or other machinery. Hunger can bring a Highly Sensitive so out of control that he cannot concentrate any longer even with great efforts. Lack of sleep reduces the efficiency of HSPs massively, mutual tensions or conflicts upset them completely and in situations of competition or under observation it is more difficult for them to obtain good results. Often there will be found a strong appeal of Highly Sensitive's to fears, sorrows and needs of their fellow-men or other creatures in general. A lot of difficulties go along with the fact that a Highly Sensitive Person expects unconsciously the same sensitiveness from his fellows. This can easily lead to be misunderstood or to feel being treated unjust. Often the Highly Sensitive's are those who risk their lives in times of terror and absurdity to help other or to honour the truth.

Typical mostly positive lived aspects of high sensitiveness are:

- marked intuition and the ability to read between the lines
- strong sense of justice and idealism
- sensitiveness
- intensive feeling, perception and living
- perfectionism und reliability
- very good perception of details
- being strongly attracted by the beauty of nature and art
- thinking in wider connections, deep reflexion
- strong sympathy for the sorrow but also for the happiness of other people
- susceptibility for mysticism and symbolism
- creativity

Typical mostly negative lived aspects of high sensitiveness are:

- support stress and hectic only with difficulty
- inclination to diverse over sensitiveness's (allergies, food incompatibilities etc.)
- have difficulties in demarcation
- being startled easily
- the feeling to be less able to stress
- inclination to overreaction
- inclination to pondering
- the frequent need to withdraw

A lot of HSPs are strongly empathetic. They strongly get into the spirit of their fellow-men, thus share their feelings and obtain on this way understanding for the action of the others. Empathy is a gift that makes it possible to have a close link to the psyche of other people. People who project themselves too much into other peoples' mind are endangered to put their own wishes and feeling so far in the background that they forget to perceive them not at all.

Further typical abilities and talents of Highly Sensitive People are:

- great potential in recognizing of avoiding of mistakes or errors
- conscientiousness and ethics
- above-average ability to concentrate
- marked ability to recognize little differences
- Reflectiveness, thorough procession of the perceived
- being very critical and perfectionist
- lifelong ability to learn and curiosity
- strong influence by stimulations and emotions of others (positive as well as negative)
- good listener, patient
- rather "right brain half" thinker, that means less straight but instead of creative and synthesizing.

The first human job sharing might have been into shaman and non-shaman, with other words: HSP and non-HSP. The earliest task of a

245

shaman or High Sensitive were probably the observation, interpretation and influencing of nature. It was HSPs who recognized the relations between man and nature, observed the weather cycles and interpreted the most favourable time for cultivation, harvesting or chasing. They were mediators between mankind and the non-human or godly world and thus some kind of a primeval priest. The conjuration of natural demons by self-created images with the help of rhythms and plastic models and the creation of communication with the higher powers could be considered as beginnings of ceremony and art.

Besides the priesthood, HSPs also dominated the domain of art and science. Further traditional responsibilities of High Sensitive's were the tradition and archives. In addition, HSPs often were competent in healing and health, the wholeness and life-help. Another resort was that of a consultant who cared for the maintenance of social stability by forming the voice of reason and deliberateness on the side of ruling people. Thus HSPs had a firm place in the middle of society where their far-sightedness and complex perception was highly appreciated.

However, in our modern Western civilisation HSPs are rather pushed to the edge. They mostly do not place them into the foreground, feel not well in situation of competition and thus are mostly those in professional life who obtain no promotion. They do not put themselves on the stage or sell themselves noisy. Besides that, the professions which former were typical for Highly Sensitive People changed in recent time's und now they are too profile-oriented and nerve-racking. Professional refuges for Highly Sensitives are still therapist, psychologist, helping professions but also programmer and other resorts where consequent logic is asked as well as recesses in teaching. Also scientists, artists and archivists of knowledge and art are still in the hands of High Sensitives.

But all societies and life-forms sooner or later pay their price for the non-integrity and non-consideration of the valuable and particular abilities of their highly sensitive representatives. A society without a sensitive consultant will come sometime into difficulties because it is lacking the necessary balance against the cult of the stronger and the chase for short-term success. These difficulties can already be seen and felt and it is hopefully only a question of time until it will be acted correspondingly.

What are Telekinesis and Psychokinesis?

Telekinesis, or Psychokinesis, describes the ability to move objects from one place to another.

It basically means mind over matter, in the sense that it can reshape objects using the energies of the mind.

The word "Psychokinesis" means "psyche", which is derived from Ancient Greece and means "life", and "kinesis", of course, means "to move". There have been many books written about the subject, both fictional and non-fictional. Many people are familiar with the term "telekinesis" from the Stephen King book and film *Carrie*.

According to believers, it really is possible to move or change objects without having any physical contact with them, although it takes a lot of practice and training. It's done by manipulating chi, which is universal life force---or psychic energy. Some individuals believe that telekinesis and psi energy are actually the cause of poltergeist-like activities. It's believed that some people can influence objects when under emotional stress without even realizing it.

Indeed, some researchers seem to agree that the most common form of telekinesis is one that's not realized consciously, and occurs unintentionally. Sometimes people become so angry or upset that they cause strange things to happen without even knowing what they're doing. These things can include: causing objects to break, unexplainable noises, ceiling fans to move by themselves, or even levitation.

Many paranormal experts and exorcists have gone to homes to investigate "hauntings", and discovered that there was unrest at the home by the families themselves. There was usually at least one person in the home who experienced most of the unexplained events, and that person, the experts concluded, was going through a hard time in his or her life. Normally, teenagers are emotional enough to cause strange occurrences usually associated with poltergeists.

Whether or not any of this is true is often debated. It does make sense though, in theory. But, if it's possible to cause such things to happen unintentionally, wouldn't it make sense that such things could be caused intentionally? Is it really possible for humans to control things with their minds? Some people seem to think so. There are many studies currently being conducted over the phenomenon. There are tips and guides available that provide exercises that allegedly help individuals develop and enhance psi abilities.

Kombucha Fungus - Healing with Tea

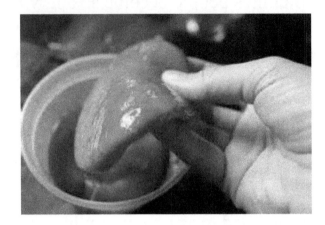

A guide how to preserve, conserve and to use it - Kombucha tea can be applied/drunk in case of gastric complaints, indigestion and constipation or simply as a precaution, because it does not harm your body. Moreover it has a purifying effect and supports liver function.

The Kombucha tea-culture is very often called a mushroom, but it is more a fungus, some sort of steadily growing bacteria.

Kombucha tea can be applied/drunk in case of gastric complaints, indigestion and constipation or simply as a precaution, because it does not harm your body. Moreover it has a purifying effect and supports liver function.

How to prepare, conserve and remove old cultures

It was fifteen years ago, when I got a "new skin" piece of that fungus from my colleague. The fungus has already been attacked by heat, worms, rottenness but it survived all this. It is a strong fungus which is continually creating "new skin" which you can use as branch.

To prepare the tea, you have to boil 4 liters of water. After boiling you put in 10 tea bags black or green tea. Do not use flavored teas as a basis, the fungus will not forgive!!

When you have left those 10 bags in the water for about 10 minutes, you put them out. Afterwards you have to add sugar. 100 gram sugar for each liter would say 400 gr. sugar. Then stir the pot contents thoroughly.

Now leave the tea to get cold. You have not to put the fungus in anything hot or even warm. Leave cooling for about 4 to 5 hours. Then put in the fungus.

To keep the mixture free of germs, just lay a cotton towel across the pot overture instead of a cover. The tea should not be firmly covered! The fungus have somewhat to breathe!

You leave that fungus mixture in a dark, dry place, not too warm nor too cold (15 degrees Celsius would be fine). 8 days later you should have a glass bowl and 4 glass bottles ready. The fungus does not like any plastics or high-grade steel. Use as cooking pot enamel, if you have.

Fill the tea extract by means of a filter into the glass bottles. The filter retains pieces of the fungus. You should leave a little rest of the tea. Put the fungus into the glass bowl and cover it with the rest of the tea. The fungus must always be entirely covered with the fluid. Then put the towel across the bowl to avoid germs.

Now store the fungus at the same warm, dry and dark place as the tea. After 7 days you have to repeat the procedure.

Even if you do not drink the tea or so much of it or you are fed up for the moment, continue procedure. That will keep the fungus living for ages.

After the 7 days of rest, the fungus will have created a new branch. You can remove the old piece and only keep the new one.

But be very careful!!! This is a fungus, a bacteria and it will grow new cultures wherever you leave it. So do not throw it away without thinking. Nobody wants to have a fungus culture in the dustbin or in the garden. So the best way would be to put it into a plastic bag and then in the dustbin or thrusting it in the WC with long water flush.

Street Light Interference Syndrome

Have you ever noticed that whenever a certain person is near electronic devices, that they seem to go out or malfunction?

Or perhaps you have this problem with electronics yourself. Even streetlights seem to go out whenever a certain person is around them, especially when they're giving off a lot of psychic energy. Why?

This phenomenon is called street light interference — SLI. Street lights, televisions, computers, cell phones, watches, etc. seem to have problems whenever a SLIder is near. Allegedly, this is some type of electromagnetic disturbance that their subconscious gives off. Those who have this ability seem to be unable to control it. They're not like Carrie White, who can telepathically destroy everything in her path. No, street light interference and electro-interference appear to be triggered subconsciously by certain individuals.

Of course you won't read about this in scientific journals, as there haven't been any scientific studies concerning this phenomenon. Since it's something that can't be purposely triggered, it usually happens sporadically. SLIders can't seem to control when they trigger street lights or electronics. There are plenty of subjective reporting though, as well as anecdotal experiences. More and more people are taking notice of SLI syndrome every day.

SLI affects women and men of all ages and from all backgrounds. For the most part, they appear to trigger the psychic interference when they are giving off a lot of psychic energy. It can be when they're extremely angry or stressed, or even very happy. During times of extreme emotions, they are more likely to trigger street lights to go out, or electronics to act up. While this does sound like a neat thing, it can obviously cost a SLIder a lot of money. Think of all the electronics they go through.

You yourself may even have this SLIder ability if you seem to have "bad luck" with electronics. Or, if you've ever walked home during a time when you felt extreme anger, stress, or happiness, and the street lights seemed to blow out every time you walked by them, you just may be a SLIder. You're not alone. There are plenty of others out there who have this same ability.

The Mysteries of Crystals

It is said that crystals can help bring balance to our chakras and restore the energy within us.

Crystals have always been used to heal the mind, body, and soul. Ancient civilizations used crystal healing all the time, and many alternative healers are using them now.

Crystals all carry a certain vibration that can align with our own systems in a positive way. Crystals come in all shapes, colors, and sizes, and they each have their own usefulness and purpose. They can be used to help in any situation, including emotional, mental, spiritual, or physical problems. Some crystals can even be used to attract good luck and financial well-being!

Here is a list of some popular crystals and gemstones and their supposed uses:

· Amber: Amber is used to help relieve depression. It clears out emotional blockages and helps bring wisdom.
· Aquamarine: Aquamarine is a stone that helps us understand wisdom, and gives us the ability to communicate better.
· Amethyst: Amethyst is said to help activate psychic abilities. It is also used to calm the mind, especially when we're feeling overwhelmed. It

gives us mental clarity.

· Bloodstone: Bloodstone also helps calm the mind and eases tension. It is also said to help physically detoxify the blood.

· Carnelian: Carnelian helps us to manifest our own personal power(s). It also helps us with making important decisions.

· Cintrine: Cintrine is also said to help us manifest personal power. It helps make us stronger and pushes away obstacles that are hindering our progress.

· Hematite: Hematite helps us keep our emotions in check. It brings us emotional clarity. It is also used for grounding.

· Labradorite: Labradorite helps us discover our psychic powers. It gives the appropriate wisdom where intuition is concerned.

· Malachite. Malachite helps with cleansing negative emotions. It brings balance to us mentally. It can also be used to help with creativity.

· Moonstone: Moonstone is not only very beautiful, it's also very helpful. It can be used to help calm down our emotions, and helps us to create emotional balance. It is used for self awareness.

· Obsidian: Obsidian is used to guide us into taking appropriate responsibility. It helps us realize the truth(s) that we normally wouldn't want to hear.

· Pyrite: Pyrite is known as "fool's gold", so obviously it used to help us find solutions for financial problems. It helps open our mind's eye so to speak, so that we can think of new ways to fulfill our dreams.

· Rhodochrosite: Rhodochrosite can be placed on the solar plexus chakra to aid in breathing. It assists with relieving anxiety.

The healing powers of the crystal, the colours and their effects and the 7 chakras in combination with crystals, elements and astrology (for more practical knowledge)

Gentle, healing powers

Crystals can harmonize and increase well-being

Anxiety in general: citrine, amethyst, ruby, golden topaz

Emotional blockades: fire opal, obsidian, tiger's eye

Depression: lapislazuli, garnet, chalcedon, citrine, pink and dark red coral, jade, aquamarine, golden topaz, malachite

Colds: green turmalin, emerald, tiger's eye

Unfeelingness: moonstone, rose quartz

Throat Inflammation: amber, light blue turmalin, chalcedon, blue topaz

Lacking Intuition: turquoise, sapphire, lapislazuli, amethyst, aquamarine

Headache: green clear and white turmalin, amethyst, lapislazuli, agate, golden topaz, emerald

Lover's Grief: malachite, rose quartz

Despondency: garnet (polished), diamond

Negative Thoughts: turmalin, lapislazuli, white coral, citrine

Unimaginativeness: rose quartz, garnet, coral

Restlessness: amethyst, jade

Stress: amethyst, dolomite

Sadness: hyazinth, ruby, orange sapphire

Emotional Unbalance: malachite, emerald, jade, aventurin, agate

Lacking Will-Power: black obsidian, ruby, red coral, garnet

Lacking Affection: rose quartz, red-purple jadeite

A crystal was hanging around the neck of our father Abraham and every patient who saw it recovered immediately. (Talmud)

The colors of the crystal already reveal a lot of their effects

Red symbolize vitality and energy. It activates and vitalizes, gives warmth, power and courage.

Pink is the color of gentleness and tenderness, it spreads beauty and harmony.

Orange takes an effect of revival and stimulation and wakes the pleasure in sensual enjoyment.

Yellow conveys easiness and gaiety, advances mental activity and communication.

Gold gives a feeling of fullness, brilliancy and light-full warmth.

Green calms, harmonizes and advances regeneration.

Light blue gives inspiration and the feeling of inner freedom.

Dark blue gives peace and concentration.

Purple is the color of transformation, spirituality and meditation.

Colorless **White** symbolizes purity and perfection.

Black opens the inner eye for the depths of the soul.

Brown conveys the feeling of being deeply rooted and grants steadfastness.

The 7 Chakras and their associations with crystals, elements and astrology

Chakra 1 (root chakra):

associated zodiacs: Aries, Taurus, Scorpio and Capricorn
associated planets: Mars, Venus, Pluto and Saturn
associated crystals: agate, blood jasper, garnet, red coral and ruby
associated element: earth

Chakra 2 (sacral chakra):

associated zodiacs: Cancer, Libra and Scorpio
associated planets: Moon, Venus, Pluto
associated crystals: carneol, moonstone
associated element: water

Chakra 3 (solar plexus chakra):

associated zodiacs: Leo, Sagittarius and Virgo

associated planets: Sun, Jupiter, Mercury and Mars
associated crystals: tiger's eye, amber, topaz (golden yellow) and citrine
associated element: fire

Chakra 4 (heart chakra):

associated zodiacs: Leo and Libra
associated planets: Sun, Venus and Saturn
associated crystals: emerald, jade (green), rose quartz and turmalin (pink)
associated element: air

Chakra 5 (throat chakra):

associated zodiacs: Gemini, Taurus and Aquarius
associated planets: Mercury, Mars, Venus and Uranus
associated crystals: Aquamarine, turquoise and chalcedon
associated element: void (Akasha)

Chakra 6 (third eye chakra):

associated zodiacs: Sagittarius, Aquarius and Pisces
associated planets: Jupiter, Uranus and Neptune
associated crystal: Lapislazuli, indigo blue sapphire, sodalite
associated element: none

Chakra 7 (crown chakra):

associated zodiacs: Capricorn and Pisces
associated planets: Saturn and Neptune

associated crystals: amethyst and rock crystal
associated element: none

The Essence of Crystal Knowledge

Crystals - gentle power, inspiring beauty, healing vibration... When we look at crystals and their beauty, brilliancy and their pure color or clarity takes an effect on us, we cannot only resist the fascination and attractive power that crystals have exercised on people at all times, but as well divine something of their mysterious effects.

When we look at crystals and their beauty, brilliancy and their pure color or clarity takes an effect on us, we cannot only resist the fascination and attractive power that crystals have exercised on people at all times, but as well divine something of their mysterious effects.

The knowledge of the signification and powers of crystals was mostly lost in course of time, but today their original place they held in old times is restored gradually: to be helpful companions on the way to more happiness, love and fulfillment.

In former times, people have been satisfied with the intuitive grasp of these powers. Today, logical explanations are demanded like those that are offered by the quantum physics and the law of the resonance of vibrations. Meanwhile it belongs already to general education that everything is vibration. The vibrations of the green color effects calming and red has an activating influence – accordingly a red ruby and a green emerald take effect.

For millions of years the crystals have grown to their perfect form in the bosom of the earth. Moreover, their light and pure colors are carrier of cosmic energies.
When we wear or lay on crystals, they cause a fine resonance in our own vibration. Powers, that are corresponding with the crystals and which are also part of our own original essence, are once more stimulated.
Blockades which prevent the expression of these powers disintegrate step by step. We can be led to the experience of inner oneness, joy of life

and creativity: the natural characteristic of someone who lives in harmony with his innermost essence.

In all known ancient civilizations crystals had not only been appreciated because of their beauty but as well because of their mysterious effects. People loved and adored them as messengers of godly powers, they saw in them an effective protection against mischief and illness, they used them to fill heart and mind with power, love and wisdom. Healing priests in Egypt were surrounded by crystals to connect themselves with the power of the gods and to give their words and deeds a greater effectiveness. Indian Shamans wore a little bag with crystals and other objects with them which should connect their mind and soul with the powers of heaven and earth. The custom to wear crystals as head-jewels or in crowns was known to almost all civilizations. In this way, the stones should grant universal powers to their carrier.

Nowadays, this knowledge experiences a remarkable renaissance in the conscious using of the crystals for healing purposes, as meditation help and for harmonization of body, soul and mind. Thereby exists no simpler means of application for crystals as to wear them as jewels – their vibrations take effect on us and support the self-healing powers of the body.

When we wear or lay on crystals for the support of self-healing powers or for the general harmonization of body, soul and mind, it is wise to pay attention to good quality. The clearer the stone and the purer the structure, the clearer and purer is as well their power which they radiate and activate in us.

Crystals, these wonderful fascinating gifts of planet earth, can become protectors in daily life.

Numerology

Can figures tell something about the future? Or reveal hidden character traits of a person? The followers of the ancient art of number science affirm this.

Number science is a process, in which certain figures are attached to names, time and events. In general, these are the numbers 1 to 9, although sometimes 11 and 22 are included. Each figure has a specific meaning: William Shakespeare is assigned to the five which stands for versatility and ingenuity.

The connection is created that the letter of the alphabet is attached to the figures of the "Hebrew system" according to the table below:

1 = a, i, q, j, y
2 = b, k, r
3 = c, g, l, s
4 = d, m, t
5 = e, h, n
6 = u, v, w, x
7 = o, z
8 = f, p

To find out your personal number just write down to each letter of your name the corresponding figure and then add them. If the result is greater than 9, add the numbers showing the number, and go on until the result is less than 10. The letters of the name Charlotte Bronte reveal 5 (Charlotte = 3 +5 +1 +2 +3 + 7 + 4 + 4 + 5 = 34; Bronte = 2 +2 +7 +5 +4 +5 = 25, 34 + 25 = 59; 5 +9 = 14, 1 +4 = 5).

If the numbers of your name are 1, you are likely to be a dominant type, a leading personality. The Ones are regarded as researchers, inventors, designers - but they often put their ideas into practice without worrying about how people concerned can cope with. They want to dominate all, have rarely close friends and are sometimes, despite their confident appearance, very lonely people.

The 2 is defined as the number of passive, only receiving people. The Twos are quiet, without ambition, friendly and nice, orderly and responsibly. They can still often achieve their target, but not through violence but through gentle persuasion. They are often timid, postpone their decisions, what sometimes brings them into difficult situations.

The 3 is the most extroverted number and belongs to the intelligent, creative and witty people who are easy to find new friends, and apparently always succeed. They are proud, ambitious and gay. Their weakness lies in their inability to take anything seriously - ideas or people - over a long time.

The 4 is like the two the number of reliable, practical people, born organizers. Although they lack the mobility of one and three, but therefore they are fairly and thoroughly also in detail. Sometimes they may be surprised by an irrational anger or depression, although they are otherwise an example for prudence. The Four has always been seen as an unlucky number. Often people whose number is four have hard to pay for every success in life.

The 5 is the number of alert, fast, smart and impatient people. They are extravagant, sociable and curious, often beautiful, but they are extremely reluctant to engage in something. The five embodies the sex. People to whom the five is assigned, often have a busy and exciting love life, sometimes full of tragedies. It also happened that they tend to perversions and excesses in the sexual field.

People, who are assigned to the 6, are among the happiest of the whole number system. They master happy, peaceful, balanced and domestic life, are tenderly, loyal, honest and conscientious. They are not lacking of creativity. Many of them are successful artists. A negative trait of their character is the tendency to narrow-mindedness, arrogance and complacency.

7 is the number of outsiders, self-observing scholars, philosophers, mystics or occultists. Frequently on the edge of life, they are satisfied with observing it. They are dignified, reserved and controlled. Temporal wealth is often indifferent to them. Although they often seem aloof and arrogant, they prove themselves as loyal friends. Despite their strong intellectual skills, they are often poorly in wording their thoughts. Also they are reluctant to argue when they feel that their ideas are criticized.

The 8 embodies the worldly success. People, to whom this number is assigned, are often businessmen, politicians or lawyers. Their success depends to a large extent on hard work, what often happens at the expense of their warm, human qualities. They often seem to be hard, egocentric and greedy. But behind these uncongenial traits often hides a charming character.

The 9 stands for the highest intellectual and spiritual empowerment. Idealists, romantics, poets, priests, teachers and scientists belong to nine. Their features are selflessness, self-discipline and decisiveness. Their idealism covers the whole person. In everyday life, they want to stand in the limelight. However, as friends or lovers, they are volatile.

11 is the number of people who experience revelations and die as a martyr. They feel very often convoked to their work like preachers, doctors, nurses or teachers, and often prefer the ideas to real people.

22 is the master: people whose name is 22, unite in them the best qualities of all the other figures.

The sum of the number of vowels in your name results in your heart figure. It reveals your inner character. The sum of consonants is your personal number. It says what effect you have on your environment. Check it and try out what numbers you are! Your name/character number, heart figure and personal number!

It is not so good to reveal my real name in public, so simply telling you that I am a 9 (name), 7 (heart) and 11 (personal number).

Dowsing with the Divining Rod

Construction of a divining-rod

To get the traditional divining-rod you cut a branch fork or have to connect two bent branches at one end together. The tradition showed that hazelnut and elm deliver the best wood for divining-rods. In any event, the branches should be fairly thin and flexible. Those two sides should have a fork length of 30 cm and the connecting piece should be 5 cm long. At the end, everyone prefers his own format. There are also other materials in question, such as bamboo or metal.

How to hold a diving-rod

You hold the rod with the palms up, so you can stretch it between the thumb and the other fingers. The arms are stretched to the front, while the elbows cling fairly close to your body. The divining-rod is held horizontal to the ground with the top forward. It must rotate. The signals that we receive from the outset, can vary. You can adhere to the old dicing-rod traditions, which provide the three typical movements: 1.) The rod spins in an angle of 90 degrees above (positive response) 2.) The rod spins in an angle of 90 degrees below (negative response) 3.) The rod runs a half (180 degrees) or entire rotation (360 degrees). The intensity of the reception depends on the exercise and mental automatism, which leads to muscle contractions. This will cause the movement of the rod.

The search for underground water

The diving-rod is probably the oldest extrasensory instrument of mankind. Since the eldest days it is there to search for underground water sources and routes. An expansion is also possible in the field of minerals and ore deposits. In the search for water a methodical way is important. Firstly, you have to divide the area to be searched by imaginary lines and then you have to pace it off gradually. All the time you hold the rod as described earlier and has already set a signal, for example, a certain rotation. If the water vein or the underground source is localized, so the rules can be further refined:

1.) To learn the depth of the water source, every full rotation of the rod corresponds to one depth gauge.

2.) In order to yield the source in cubic meters per second or to determine the water temperature, you can proceed with an analog way.

Part VI
UFOs and ALIENS

Ancient Alien Evidence

Whether or not aliens exist there can be no doubt that mankind has been fascinated with them since ancient times.

Whether or not aliens exist there can be no doubt that mankind has been fascinated with them since ancient times. Historians and archeologists have found many representations of alien looking beings all over the world. Not only do we find evidence of the existence of aliens in ancient artwork, but we also find clues in the stories, legends and lore of the ancients that points to the reality of aliens interacting with humanity.

Here is a stone engraving that was created by the ancient Egyptians. The head covering worn by the two main figures suggests an unusual head shape. In fact the smaller figures in this engraving do have elongated heads.

In the center you can see what appears to be a moon, or star with 19 lines either going toward or away from it. Does this represent the flights of space craft to and from the stars?

Here we have a graphic depiction from ancient Samaria which shows a god flying a ship. Look closely at the image above. Do you see a pilot sitting back in a cockpit amid an instrument control panel? Keep in mind that the artist would probably have had a difficult time fully understanding what was being represented.

Here we have a rock painting from ancient Australia. The figures in the painting are known as 'Vondjina' a god of creation. Notice the large eyes and the classic alien looking head as well as the thing which covers their heads. Was this a depiction of how the artist understood the gods, or aliens, to look?

Alien Evidence in Religious Art?

Why would painters who are representing significant religious themes include strange flying crafts in their paintings? Why hasn't the public in general noticed these supposed anomalies?

We have seen that there is a lot of evidence supporting an alien interaction with humans in ancient writings and artwork. When we take a look at some of the paintings and artwork from the religious painters of 650 to 150 or more years ago we also see a lot of evidence of an alien influence.

Why would painters who are representing significant religious themes include strange flying crafts in their paintings? Why hasn't the public in general noticed these supposed anomalies?

Perhaps we can find further evidence to prove the existence of aliens in the religious artwork of the past.

The Crucifixion with UFOs

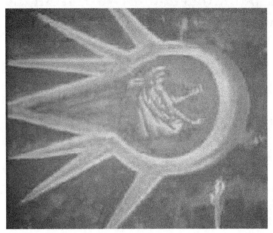

Here is a painting that is titled "The Crucifixion". This fresco was created in the year 1350 and is currently displayed over the altar of the Visoki Decani Monastery in Kosovo. In this painting you will notice two very strange elements in the upper right and left corners. What could they be?

Below you will see, in the zoom in enlargements, just what is being represented in this 650 year old painting. I am sure that you will be as amazed as I was when I first saw this. These craft need no explanation as you can plainly see the pilot in the fuselage.

The Madonna with Saint Giovannino Showing UFO

Here is another very interesting religious painting which seems to show an alien spacecraft. It is entitled "The Madonna with Saint Giovannino".

This Madonna was painted sometime during the 1400s. The artist's name is not known, but the painting has been credited to the Lippi school.

At first glance you will probably notice a strange shape in the sky above the Madonna's left shoulder. If you were to see the original, full size painting you would see the object clearly.

Looking at the enlargement of that area you can see that there is some sort of flying craft in the sky. You can even see that there is a man and his dog standing there who seem to be looking up at the craft.

The Baptism of Christ with UFO in the Sky

Here we have a painting which was created by Aert De Gelder in 1710; it is titled "The Baptism of Christ". This painting is currently on display at the Fitzwilliam Museum in Cambridge.

Pay particular attention to the flying saucer shaped object which seems to be casting rays of light upon Jesus Christ and John the Baptist.

Why did the artist add such a feature to his painting? Why do we see objects which appear to by UFOs in these old religious paintings?

Alien Abduction ~ Fact or Fear

Probably the most disturbing factor to emerge from the entire UFO phenomena is the recurring idea that these alien visitors are forcibly taking humans aboard their craft and using them as experimental test subjects.

While the cases of Betty and Barney Hill, Whitley Strieber and Travis Walton are by far the most well-known and documented cases where people have claimed alien abduction, the occurrence of humans being temporarily taken by extraterrestrial agencies have turned up throughout the ages. Even the biblical accounts of Enoch and Elijah exhibit many standard aspects of the "abduction" phenomena.

Accepted medical authorities state unequivocally that there is no such thing as "alien abduction" and that anyone who says they have been taken is either mentally unstable or under the influence of psychotic drugs. This attitude does not consider the actual condition of those who claim abduction or their lack of discernible mental illness or record of drug use. It is much like the Air Force's conclusions from Project Blue Book where it was claimed in a contradictory way that UFO's did not exist and that UFO's did not present a threat to national security.

Early reports from around the turn of the twentieth century, most notably from a Colonel Shaw of Lodi, California, reported that at first these "aliens" tried to physically and forcibly take humans. Col. Shaw reported that on November 25, 1896 he and a companion encountered a hovering "airship" and the two beings that emerged attempted to manhandle them into the ship but were fought off. In later years, the method reportedly used to subdue victims took a more frightening aspect in that people began being taken from their beds at night in a state of paralysis. Increasingly, reports of "lost time" periods, which the victim cannot remember the events of hours or even days of their lives, have surfaced and lead one to wonder if some sort of memory manipulation has been utilized.

Despite the several distinct types of "aliens" that have been reported over the centuries, it is usually the thin, large eyed "gray" variety that seems to be the most prominent abductors. It is yet to be figured if they are doing it for themselves or are merely the "workers" for other types as hypnotic regression on many abductees has revealed information that there are often two or three different alien species present in the examining rooms where the victims are taken.

Often those who have reported being victims of these abductions find strange markings and puncture wounds on them after an encounter. Many have later found through x-ray that strange "implants" have been injected under their skin or more often far up into the nasal passages. Of the few of these mysterious small objects that have been removed, the artifacts have been shown to be of an unknown material and function. It has been hypothesized that the devices are "tracking devices" as many reported abductees report they have been done this way many times throughout their lives.

Routinely, those who claim to have been abducted, report that they are subjected to medical examinations and experiments. In a hauntingly familiar way, these examinations sound just like the procedures our earthly scientists use to track, tag and examine wildlife. Do extraterrestrial biologists collect their specimens in much the same way and for similar reasons?

With over one thousand official reports of "alien abductions" on file and the speculation that many more go unreported, do we dare casually laugh off and ridicule the experiences of these people? If an extraterrestrial culture views us as merely the "wildlife" on this planet, what then are our rights within their purposes? Of all the phenomena surrounding potential visitation from an unknown advanced race of beings, this factor should be the most strenuously investigated, not the most actively ridiculed!

The Hill Abduction Story An Interrupted Journey.

The beginnings of one of the most publicized alien abduction stories in the United States occurred on a lonely stretch of US Route 3 in New Hampshire

The time was September 19, 1961. Returning from a vacation, Betty and Barney Hill were expecting to be back at their home in Portsmouth in just a few hours when they first observed a bright point of light in the sky.

At first they thought it might be a meteorite until it maneuvered to a point near the moon and held position there. Speculation then was made that it was one of the new communication satellites that were beginning to be placed in orbit so Betty asked her husband to stop the car and give themselves a better view while also letting their dog have a walk. While Barney took care of business with their pet, Betty used the couple's binoculars in hopes of getting a better view of the object. As she watched, it moved across the face of the moon and she observed it was flashing a number of multicolored lights.

Barney had not been watching and assured her it was just an airplane and they continued homeward. However, the object then seemed to be pacing their vehicle and slowly drawing closer to them. About a mile south of the town of Indian Head the object swooped down in front of the car and Barney stopped in the middle of the road and got out for a closer look. He then took the binoculars and observed the craft which he no longer believed was a commercial aircraft. Focusing in on the object which was now only eighty to a hundred feet from him, he states he saw a number of human-like entities observing him through the ports in the craft's side. Immediately all but one of the figures moved away from the "windows" and a set of appendages began to emerge from the sides, each with a blinking red light on the end and another structure emerged from the bottom.

Barney ran back to the car, fearing an unknown danger, and took off down the road. Betty then peered out and up but could see no stars in the sky as the huge craft seemed to be holding position directly over their speeding vehicle.

There followed what they described as a series of loud buzzing sounds which were strong enough to vibrate the car. They reported that at this time they began to feel lightheaded and in a "dream-like" mental state but were otherwise unaffected by any feared electrical shocks. As they passed through Plymouth there was another series of the buzzing sounds which Barney could not duplicate by the mere maneuvering of his vehicle.

They arrived home at about daylight although it was not until later when asked about it that they realized their four hour journey had in fact taken them seven hours to complete. In all, three hours of time had seemed to have simply disappeared along the way.

At first the Hills did not think about their experience much but did attempt to draw pictures of what they has seen. They both had an overwhelming desire to shower to get "clean" but did not know from what. They tried unsuccessfully to remember a coherent account of the night but realized they only had fragmented memories from the time they experienced the first set of buzzing sounds. They both began to experience fatigue even when just rested.

Two days later, Betty called the Pease Air Force Base to report their sighting. The next day Major Paul Henderson phoned the Hills for more details but, despite their descriptions of the craft they saw, ultimately reported to Project Blue Book that the Hills had merely misidentified the planet Jupiter.

Within two weeks Betty had developed recurring nightmares about the experience which were beginning to affect her daily life as well. After investigating several books at the local library about UFO's, Betty contacted the retired Marine Major Donald Keyhoe who was now a civilian researcher and head of the National Investigations Committee on Aerial Phenomena (NICAP). Major Keyhoe turned the report over to fellow NICAP member Walter Webb who was a Boston based astronomer. On October 21 Mr. Webb conducted an extensive six hour interview with the Hills and determined that something about the encounter had generated a sort of mental "block" that made remembering the events difficult.

Over the next two years the Hills began to talk a bit more about their experience and were interviewed by more of the NICAP members. It was suggested that hypnosis may help retrieve some of the "lost" memories of the event. They were referred to a Dr. Benjamin Simon who conducted a number of hypnosis sessions on the Hills between January and June of 1964. The story that was recovered was detailed but hard for the skeptical hypnotist to believe.

Two years after the events of September 19, 1961, Betty and Barney Hill were set up with an appointment with Doctor Benjamin Simon of Boston. While the meeting was set up for them by members of the UFO investigation group NICAP, they had chosen Dr. Simon precisely because he was a skeptic of the UFO phenomena and it was hoped that the data retrieved would not be considered contaminated by leading questions.

The hypnotic regression sessions lasted from January to June of 1964. In order to avoid having the Hill's statements influence each other, Dr. Simon interviewed each of them separately. He began first with Barney Hill. Mr. Hill's sessions were often punctuated with bouts of rage, tears and fear. The trauma of these sessions was such that Dr. Simon gave Barney post-hypnotic suggestions to not remember them after waking up so as to reduce the possible psychological damage they could cause.

Barney told of running back to his car after his last memory of getting out to look more closely at the object. He tried to drive away but soon felt compelled to leave the road and drive into the surrounding woods where they were joined by three entities with very large eyes that took them into a disk shaped craft. He said they kept looking into his eyes and the thoughts kept pushing in to not be afraid. Barney referred to it as "thought transference as he was unfamiliar with the term telepathy. Once inside the craft, the Hills were separated and Barney described being given a full and rather invasive medical examination.

Betty Hill's sessions were not as traumatic as they revealed much the same information as had been plaguing her for years in recurring dreams of the event. While Barney had reported that the beings conversed in a muttering language he could not understand, Betty recalled that they talked to her in faulty but understandable English. She was told that they needed to separate her and her husband to expedite the examinations.

Betty was also subjected to a thorough medical exam and was given a "pregnancy test" via a needle through her navel. She said the pain was agonizing until the "doctor" placed his hand on her head and the pain vanished. At one point in the process another being entered the room and spoke quickly to her examiner who left the room for a short time. When he returned, he examined Betty's mouth and started pulling on her teeth.

It was finally determined that what had caused the excitement was Barney's dentures.

After the medical examination, Betty stated she began talking to the doctor who had examined her and asked for an artifact of some sort as a remembrance of the event. He gave her a large book filled with strange writing oriented in columns. She had asked them where they were from since she had determined they were not from Earth. The information she was shown marks one of the most unusual aspects of the "abduction".

The examiner showed her what appeared to be a star map which had a number of lines connecting various stars and planets. The lines were explained as showing various commercial trade routes and areas of exploration. When asked if she could identity her own star on the map, Betty admitted that by being unfamiliar with such things she could not. She was then told rather abruptly that if that was so then there was no way they could explain where they were from.

Under hypnosis, Betty recreated the star map to the best of her ability. Over the course of several years various researchers tried to figure out what stars were displayed in the map. The most likely identification was made by an amateur astronomer and school teacher from Ohio. Marjorie Fish had used several three dimensional models of the surrounding space around our star system and ultimately determined that the beings had most likely originated from the double star system of Zeta Reticuli. There have since been many more studies made on the star map drawn by Betty Hill during hypnosis. Even such notable scientists as Carl Sagan and Dr. David Saunders, formerly a statistician for the Condon UFO study, have studied the map and weighed in with their opinions of its accuracy. While there has been no absolutely conclusive proof of the Zeta Reticuli hypothesis, it is still determined to be the best guess.

After having looked at the map, Betty and Barney were reunited and the beings lead them off the ship. An argument developed between the ship's crew and finally Betty's examiner took the book he had given her back. He stated that he did not care that people knew of them but that other members of the crew insisted that the Hills not be allowed to even remember the encounter. They were taken back to their vehicle which was now beside the road although Barney had formerly driven it into the woods. As the started back onto the highway, a white light once more illuminated the road and Barney anxiously cried out "Oh, no, not again!", but the craft was gone and they made their way home, inexplicably not remembering the events of the past few hours.

There is still a raging debate as to the accuracy and effectiveness of hypnosis as a method of recovering lost memories and many will say that the entire tale was a fabrication. That does not explain the strange markings on Barney's leg or the fine pink powder on Betty's skirt. It does not explain why two average people would have such extreme reactions to an unremembered event that they felt they needed help with the anxiety and fright they were feeling. The events described by the Hills under hypnosis are very similar to other reports from people who feel they have been "abducted" and taken aboard alien space craft. If these "aliens" are capable of a form of mental manipulation to make their victims forget, can we do less than attempt to use our own mental manipulation to discover what it is these visitors want with us?

Cash Landrum UFO Incident

The Cash-Landrum is one of the most notorious close-encounter UFO incidents ever reported. During one late December evening, in 1980, a car filled with 3 people was driving home on a narrow country road. Occurring near Huffman, Texas.

In interviews following the incident, the occupants of the car described an elongated diamond-shaped object hovering above a thicket of trees. The object appeared unsteady, and periodically expelled flames from its base. The heat generated from the alleged craft was immense, and was reported intense enough to cause the metal body of the car to become excruciatingly hot to the touch.

Betty Cash, then 51 years old, was a small business owner near Huffman, Texas. Her passenger, Vickie Landrum, was 57 years old and enjoying a night out with her employer and grandson. The narrow country road, only occasionally used by locals, was almost completely blocked by the diamond-shaped craft. Betty allegedly stopped the car only 50 yards from the object, and the three occupants of the car got out getting a better look at the object blocking their path. After less than 5 minutes of staring intently at the object, Vickie and the young man Colby got back into the car, and begged for Betty to do the same. When

Betty tried to open the car door, her hand was severely burned from touching the hot metal of the door handle.

Shortly after getting back into the car, the three astonished onlookers witnessed a number of helicopters swiftly approach the object from all directions. Just as the helicopters managed to fully surround the object, the object rapidly moved behind the cover of the tree line. Betty drove the car further along the road until it joined a major highway, at which point they turned away from the brightly lit craft and its pursuers and drove home. Other motorists and residents of the area also reported seeing the object, though few were close enough to describe the object in detail.

In the hours following the incident, the occupants of the car began experiencing symptoms which seemed to mimic the effects of severe sunburn. Their skin reddened significantly, and blisters and boils began to erupt from their hands, arms, and face. Betty, in particular, suffered extreme symptoms, and three days following the incident she was rushed to the hospital, unconscious. Betty Cash, the driver of the car, also began experiencing severe hair loss. Cash's doctor, Dr. Brian McClelland, official described the symptoms as being similar to severe radiation poisoning. There exist photographs of the injuries inflicted by the heat and/or radiation emitted from the unidentified craft, and those photos show both the burns and the extreme hair loss inflicted on the occupants of the car.

The occupants of the car attempted to contact military officials and air traffic control to get more information about the unidentified craft, as well as the military helicopters which were also reported in the area. There has been no official confirmation that the incident occurred, and reports of inadequate radar coverage of the area was reported by the FAA and air traffic control in the Houston area on the night in question. The occupants of the car sued the United States Government for their injuries and suffering, believing that the craft they witnessed was part of a secret military project. The case was dismissed in 1986, owing to the military's unwillingness to admit that such a craft existed in their arsenal. The case was dismissed on the grounds that "no such object was owned, operated, or in the inventory of the U.S. Army, Navy, Air Force or NASA.

The Gorman Dogfight

What occurred in the airspace above the Hector Airfield in Fargo, North Dakota is now one of the classic tales of UFO history.

Following a cross country exercise with the North Dakota Air National Guard, the last thing Lieutenant George F. Gorman expected was a dogfight with an unidentified flying object.

On the night of October 1, 1948, Lieutenant Gorman, a veteran pilot who chose to fly with the Air National Guard following World War II, was flying an F-51 Mustang with a group of other guard pilots on a cross country training exercise. The other pilots landed early in the evening but seizing the opportunity to log more night flying time, Lieutenant Gorman remained in the air until around nine o'clock that night. After circling the football field in Fargo, North Dakota, which was fully lit, Gorman signaled the Hector Field control tower he wished to land.

The tower warned of a Piper Cub plane below him but informed Gorman that his Mustang and the Piper Cub were the only aircraft in the vicinity. At this point Lieutenant Gorman spotted what he first believed were the tail lights of another plane. Contacting the tower, he received a report that he and the Piper Club were the only aircraft on radar. Aborting his plans to land his F-51 Mustang, Lieutenant Gorman pulled within 1,000 yards of the lights to visualize describe an object about six to eight inches in diameter with blinking lights on it.

As he pulled close to the unidentified flying object, Lieutenant Gorman reported the lights stopped blinking and became a steady glow. The UFO also sped up, trying to out run him. As he chased the object, it turned and headed straight for his aircraft. With only about five hundred feet separating them, Lieutenant Gorman dove his plane to avert a collision. The object once again reversed its course and headed toward Lieutenant Gorman. This time he held his course and the object responded by shooting straight upward just before it collided with Gorman's plane. Gorman's pursuit of the UFO ended when his engine stalled at 14,000 feet.

Gorman returned to the Fargo airfield and was said to have been shaken by the events of the evening. His story was corroborated by the two air traffic controllers in the tower, Lloyd D. Jensen and H.E.Johnson, who reported seeing a light such as the one Gorman described. Both the light and the Piper Cub were seen simultaneously by all three men. The pilot of the Piper Cub and his passenger also acknowledged seeing the light in addition to the F-51 Mustang which Gorman flew.

In later describing the incident, Lieutenant Gorman said he felt "there was definite thought behind [the object's] maneuvers." Gorman admitted to losing consciousness temporarily due to the high rate of speed his plan was traveling. Later an Air Force investigation tried to explain away the events as an encounter with a weather balloon or a Canadian jet. When these were ruled out, the Air Force claimed the object's maneuvers were but a reflection of the movement of Gorman's own aircraft.

Whatever happened in the skies above Fargo, North Dakota on the night of October 1, 1948, it is now one of the most famous UFO encounters in history. Labeled the "Gorman Dogfight" in the Air Force's official investigation of UFO sighting, Project Blue Book, it was witnessed by four men in addition to Lieutenant Gorman. Lieutenant Gorman was silenced by the Air Force from further discussing the matter under threat of court martial even though the Air Force continued to investigate UFO sightings.

1964 UFO Landing in Socorro County

One spectacular UFO landing that will never go away is that of the 1964 UFO landing in Socorro County New Mexico that was witnessed by a police officer named Lonnie Zamora. The events leading up to the landing started at 5:45 PM in the month of April. Zamora gave up a chase of a speeding car when he saw an orange, bluish flame in the sky coming from the area of a dynamite shack. He started heading that way and gave the information he had seen to his dispatcher.

What he saw next, would stay with him until the day he died. He was looking at an oval shaped object that was shiny, had no windows and no signs of a door. Zamora was looking at a space ship. He then saw two beings that appeared child size with white overalls. One of the beings jumped as if it was startled when it saw Zamora. What would happen next, it what makes this landing so famous.

He called his dispatcher to report what he was looking at and where he was. Then the oval object sent out a loud roar and bluish flames from the underneath side. It lifted off the ground and head to the southeast. After conducting an investigation, the officers on scene learned that other calls had come in about the bluish flame in the same area at about the same time.

A Public Safety Service worker in Las Vegas analyzed the sandy mixture from the area under the object and determined that it was an organic material that not identifiable. Shortly after the call, Air Force personal showed up and remove all materials and documentation. Two other witnesses described what they saw that night as they were passing through Socorro.

They described the one thing that made it apparent that they had seen the same thing as the officer. They had seen a red marking on the oval shape. They said that it looked like a "Z" and the officer saw the coloring, but could not say what it was.

A report released by Hector Quintanilla, who was the head of the Air Force "Project Blue Book" had this to say:

"There is no doubt that Lonnie Zamora saw an object which left quite an impression on him. There is also no question about Zamora's reliability. He is a serious police officer, a pillar of his church, and a man well versed in recognizing airborne vehicles in his area. He is puzzled by what he saw, and frankly, so are we. This is the best-documented case on record, and still we have been unable, in spite of thorough investigation, to find the vehicle or other stimulus that scared Zamora to the point of panic."

Although this appears to be a cover up by the Air Force, it would not be the first time. Remember Roswell and all the other strange things that happen in the dark of night that are swept under the carpet? This is just one of the first of many cover-ups that could prove or disprove life in outer space.

Missing Persons Never To Be Seen Again

Every year thousands of people go missing never to be seen or heard from again. Where did these people go and why are they not contacting their families to say where they are and if they are okay?

Could they be the victims of an alien abduction? People explain this away by saying that these people are all victims of foul play and have either been kidnapped or murdered. Although this is the easiest way to explain it, who can say for any certainty that these people were not abducted by alien space crafts and kept for studies? Maybe these people were abducted and died in captivity at the hands of another life form.

One can only look back at the famous 1980 UFO case involving two adults and a child in Texas Piney Woods. The trio was driving through the woody area looking for a bingo game on the night of December 29, 1980. Soon after entering the woods, the trio encountered a diamond shaped spacecraft. The UFO would send orange-red flames towards the ground from time to time. Then, they saw so many helicopters coming to the scene. They came from all directions.

One of the women had been out of the car watching this phenomenon and rushed back to the car only to find the door handles so hot that it burned her hand. The women sat and counted the helicopters and were able to count twenty-three of them. Then they headed home to ponder what they had just experienced. Unfortunately, the woman that had been outside the car and burned her hand on the door handle had to go to the hospital where she was diagnosed as a burn patient.

Betty was the woman's name. She was in the hospital for fifteen days during which time she lost her hair and her eyes swelled shut for a week. The boy Colby, seven years old, also had some health issues with his eyes. The second woman, Vicky began to lose her hair as well. These three people were treated for radiation poisoning. Betty was later diagnosed with skin cancer.

No one would admit to having helicopters in the air that night. Further investigation of the road showed signs of damage from the blasts from the sky. The road was quickly repaired to cover up the story. The trio sued the government for medical compensation and lost. Betty died on the eighteenth anniversary of the encounter from health issued related to the encounter.

Were these three people subjects of a terrorist attack by alien beings or was there another explanation for their ailing health, hot burning door handles on the car and severe damage to the road. To date, no one has ever taken responsibility for the helicopters in the area and no one can explain why these three people were exposed to radiation.

Was this just another one of those cover-ups by the government? Where did the helicopters come from and why were they there in the first place? Someone must know something about what these three people saw and experienced.

The Triangle UFOs

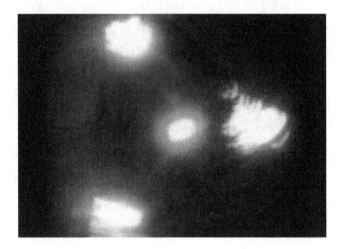

One evening my mate and I were out driving around with a couple of friends when we stopped at the local post office to check our mailbox and pick up any mail we may have had.

At the time we had an older model brown van that we had converted into a small, mobile, living space. We started to leave when we got a phone call on our cell phone from another friend who said they would meet us in front of the post office and lead us out the long and winding roads that led to the group camping area we were all supposed to meet at for a weekend camping trip. While we waited things got really weird.

As we waited for our friend to arrive to lead us all out to the camp site, we felt rather than heard this really odd humming sound. We looked up to see two very large, black, triangle shaped craft hovering not more than a couple or three hundred yards right above our van! Each of them had a bright white light at each of the corners of the craft and one was sitting just slightly higher and forward of the other craft. They were completely silent. The humming 'sound' was more of a sensation we felt throughout our bodies right down to our teeth, but it was at the same time very eerily silent. They just hovered above us. Where they had come from we did not know; they just seem to materialize out of thin air. We sat and observed them, while at the same time they were, presumably, observing us for about 20 minutes.

One of our friends started using the high powered binoculars we had to get a closer look at the craft to see if he could get a better look at any details on these craft. This must have not set well with the pilots of one of these weird craft because almost as soon as our friend raised the binoculars the craft that was sitting slightly higher than the other one changed. First the white lights did a strange convergence towards the center of the this strange flying machine and converged into one single red light and then it shot straight up into the air and disappeared with with incredible speed.

However, the other triangle craft hovered for a few minutes more and then started, gently and silently, drifting forward and away. We all watched it until it suddenly just shot forward so fast that it too disappeared as quickly as a wink.

Shortly after that our other friend showed up to lead us to the camp site. My mate and I and our two friends who had witnessed these weird flying craft told the others of our group about our strange encounter around the campfire that night. We all sat up for most of the night discussing what we had seen and speculated as to what they could be and where did they come from. We have done a fair amount of research on the subject over the years since that warm mid-summer's dusk, and there are still as many speculations and unanswered questions as there were that evening 6 years ago.

Spheres in the Sky

My Mate and I have seen numerous strange flying craft in the skies on many occasions. One memorable time we were spending a couple of days camping on a friend's farm while looking at the clear early evening sky we saw what looked like two bright silver balls hanging in the sky over the area of the local lake which was about 5 miles away from our position. There were odd colored lights glowing around the middle of each of these flying craft. They suddenly started moving in extremely fast maneuvers that nothing either my mate or I had ever seen flying could do. Moving from one side of the sky to the next and back in barely a blink of an eye. Darting up and down, diagonally and any direction it seemed to wish to go. Then suddenly they shot straight upward, flared a bright, fiery orange in the glare of reflected sunlight and were gone in a wink.

The second night of our camp out we once again saw the strange craft except this time while we were watching two more of these large sliver spheres with the softly glowing haze of multicolored light coursing around the equator of these flying spheres when we saw a third one join them and it looked as though it had just phased into being instantly. We watch them go high into the atmosphere until they glowed with the reflected light of the setting sun and then they hung there for a while just glowing like three small bright mobile stars. Then, just as suddenly as the third one had appeared when it joined it's compatriots, all three of them just disappeared.

Over the years we have seen more of what appeared to be these flying spheres. What they are or who may be piloting these craft is anyone's guess. Serenely beautiful, but still unsettling, it certainly would seem that these craft were built with a technology still far more advanced than anything humanity may have developed thus far. Judging by the clarity of detail we saw and way they could reflect the sunlight from the altitude they would have had to have been and us still be able to see them pretty well, told my mate and I that these things were quite large in size. Could it be that the tales told of beings who came to earth in strange flying craft by ancient civilizations such as Sumer are true? Are these ancient people returning? Did they ever leave? Many people believe that the Annunaki, as the Sumerians called them, are still very much among us and those that left many ages ago are returning. In light of many archaeological findings made in the last century this line of thought may not be entirely as unlikely as many would think.

Whatever the case may be, it is clear that something strange is happening in the skies over our little blue-green planet. Whether we have visitors from another planet, another dimension, or that something possibly even more sinister is going on is still a big mystery. Perhaps one thing seems pretty certain to my mate and me though, and that is the fact that it is we as a species are not alone in this universe.

The UFO In Los Angeles In 1942

Searchlights and Anti-aircraft Guns Comb Sky During Alarm

What happened in Los Angeles in 1942 changed the way people would think about UFO's. Hundreds of people saw the space ship just hovering over the city.

The military went so far as to shoot light beams up in the sky and lit up the space ship so it was more visible to everyone. If this was an UFO, why do the government and the military deny that there are UFO's in the sky? If there is so much evidence about the Los Angeles UFO, why is there so much controversy about the sights? How could hundreds of people be wrong about what they saw?

No it was not Japanese fighter planes, it was a huge space ship as it was called then. The space was in the sky hovering the 37th Brigade was going to stop at nothing to take it down. Every attempt to bring down the hovering craft was unsuccessful. Spent shells were the only thing falling from the sky. People could not be on the streets because falling shells could have hit them. The space ship was said to have been sitting there without being affected by the blasting. Then the space ship moved into a different area where there were more lights.

The large craft hovered over the MGM Studios. Once it settled over Culver City, someone was able to get an amazing photo of the craft.

Then it moved over to Long Beach and soon disappeared. Where did the space ship go? How could it just disappear so quickly without anyone seeing it go? Could the space ship move faster than light? All these questions soon became the questions everyone needed answers to. All the people that saw the space ship agreed on one thing. It was huge and had an orange glow color.

Why is it then that any sightings since then have been explained away as an air balloon, a flash in the sky or a plane of some type? Why does the military continue to avoid the discussion about UFO's? The picture that was taken does not show anything other than a craft of some type unknown to us. It shows a picture of something mysterious in the sky. In 1942, there were no available programs to distort or change the way a picture looks. Then we have to assume that this was indeed a UFO and the picture is authentic.

UFO sightings have been happening for many years. We have to consider that aliens and UFO's have been around since the beginning of time. One can only wonder what else is out there is space. Is there another form of life that could be more advanced than we are? How many different life forms could there be in space? More UFO sightings will continue, but until someone else has the pictures that provide real proof that aliens and space ships exist, people will continue to be skeptical and deny that there are any other forms of life other than us.

UFO Sightings

UFO sightings are reported everyday, and while most end up being identified, there are some that never are. Here is some information on five of the most recent UFO reports.

On November 7, 2008, a UFO was just spotted over Bristol in England. The incident was recorded on camera phones of a young citizen named Shellie Williams and her mother. The two witnessed a UFO shooting out "red beams" toward the ground.

On November 4, 2008, an image emerged that was taken in downtown Entre Rios, Argentina. A tourist claims to have witnessed a "strange object" emerging between the two crosses on the St. Anthony of Padua Cathedral domes.

In October, two men in Austin, TX believe they saw a UFO flying above. Carl Lancaster claims he saw some lights, one red and two white, zigzagging in the sky. Doug McCullough, the other gentlemen, claims he was able to record the incident on his video camera. Officials from Austin International Airport claim they have no reports of any strange, flying options that particular night of the incident.

November 3, 2008, another UFO was caught on camera over the town of Filton in England. Paul Matthews, a taxi driver, witnessed the strange object around 2:00 that afternoon. He claims to have seen a hovering, "disc-shaped object" that swiftly disappeared. The Bristol Evening Post wants any other witnesses of the incident to get in contact with them. Denis Plunkett from the British Flying Saucer Bureau, believes this sighting was legitimate.

Late October was when a "Star of Bethlehem" UFO was seen over England. Witness Linda Szabo, from Kingston Avenue, claims to have watched it for eight minutes before it finally disappeared. She describes the strange craft that she saw as "almost like the star of Bethlehem that you see on Christmas cards". She didn't think it resembled a plane or anything similar at all. Whatever it was, it disappeared shortly before sunrise. Unfortunately, she Ms. Szabo didn't have her phone camera at the time and wasn't able to capture any pictures.

The Unsolved Mystery of Area 51

Supposedly, pictures have been taken inside depicting dead or living aliens. Area 51 is a military base that has been a unsolved mystery for years. Is there a UFO on the base? Are there aliens being held captive on the base?

Why did the government deny any existence of Area 51? Could it be that there are toxic chemicals on the grounds? Why is the base so heavily guarded? More questions arise every day about the existence of Area 51. People want to know what is so important on the base that has been kept secret for so many years. Are there really pictures that have been smuggled out of the base? If so, why are these pictures not showing up anywhere?

Supposedly, pictures have been taken inside depicting dead or living aliens. They have shown a spacecraft that looks like a futuristic design. If these blurry pictures or videos are the real thing, why does the government still deny any of these accusations? Was there a spacecraft captured with aliens onboard? Is it possible that the government has something planned for the aliens? Are they trying to learn about them? Are they killing them to see what they are composed of? The more one thinks about Area 51, the more questions become known.

Here is what is known about area 51. In April of 1955, Groom Lake was a site to test the U-2. In July of that year, the first U-2 was shipped and Area 51 was completed. In June of 1958, more than thirty-eight hundred acres where used to make a perimeter around the area for security measures. In November of the same year, the A-12 was received at Area 51. The airspace restriction was expanded in January of 1962. The population of the base rose above eighteen hundred in 1965.

The prototype F117 was shipped to Area 51 in 1977 and in 1981, the first production of the F117 was taken to Area 51. Then we know that in 1984 the perimeter of the base was expanded by another eighty-nine hundred acres. Then in 1988, a satellite from the Soviet Union has pictures of Area 51 that were released to publications including "Popular Science." Whiteside peak and Freedom Ridge were taken away from public access in 1995.

It would seem that the base is being used for military operations that are beneficial to the United States welfare against war and invasion. If this is true, then why are there so many reports and pictures that depict something different about Area 51? Why so much security for the F117 and the U-2? Was there some type of toxic chemical being made on the base? The government said that what is going on by Grooms Lake is classified and would not comment any further.

Is there something not human living on the base? Why is there so much security? Why did they keep increasing the security perimeter around Area 51? What is hiding in Area 51? Can it hurt the citizens of the United States or can it help us?

Did Extraterrestrials Visit Earth Long Ago?

There are some who believe that extraterrestrials have visited our planet long, long ago. Some believe that Earth is currently being visited by alien beings.

Then there are those who go one step further and suggest that the origins of humankind lie in the hidden agenda of those extraterrestrials. Claims have been made that aliens seeded our planet and played a key role in the development of religion and government. Whether you believe in such claims or not it certainly makes interesting reading as well as providing food for thought.

This article we will take a look at one of the major proponents of the ancient astronaut theory. Zecharia Sitchin is a scholar and author with extensive knowledge of ancient Hebrew, Sumerian and other languages. Sitchin proposed the ancient astronaut theory in his first book, The 12th Planet, as well as in subsequent books that have come to be known as The Earth Chronicles. Sitchin bases much of his proposed theory on the interpretation of ancient Sumerian texts and biblical passages that may seem to support his ideas.

According to Sitchin's interpretation another planet in the far reaches of our solar system referred to as Nibiru collided with a planet known as Tiamat. One half of Tiamat became what we now refer to as the asteroid belt whereas the remaining half formed Earth. Planet Nibiru supposedly travels a long elliptical orbit that brings it into the inner solar system every 3,600 years. Zecharia Sitchin goes on to explain that an alien race from the planet Nibiru called the Annunaki came to earth to mine raw materials particularly gold. The work was long and tedious which led them to genetically engineer laborers. Such intriguing information leads to more questions than it does answers.

Were humans genetically engineered? Were the biblical angels what we now refer to as aliens? Are the mythological tales of gods and goddesses actually a history of encounters with extraterrestrials? Were the biblical miracles actually advanced forms of technology? Will 2012 be the year that Nibiru makes its next 3,600 year orbit bringing it into our inner solar system once more?

Although he does have some supporters Zecharia Sitchin has been ridiculed by others in scientific circles. His interpretation of Sumerian texts has been called misleading and his theories have been referred to as flawed. I have read all of Mr. Sitchin's books and have found them to be intriguing to say the least. Although there is no sound scientific evidence to prove his theories there are many artifacts, cave drawings and monuments that remain puzzling to this day.

The Giza pyramids, the Nazca lines and Stonehenge to name just a few remain testaments to a mysterious past. There are artifacts and cave drawings from around the world that seem to depict humanoid beings wearing what appear to be spacesuits. Other artifacts and crude drawings depict what seem to be flying discs or other aircraft. Even certain biblical passages could be interpreted in like manner. Ezekiel described a flying object that had an appearance of a wheel within a wheel. Enoch was taken up to the heavens by a whirlwind. There is also mention of encounters with angels in the Bible. Jacob wrestles with an angel. Angels appeared to Abraham, Sarah and others throughout the Bible.

Angels destroyed the corrupt cities of Sodom and Gomorrah. Were these angels what we would now call aliens?

We may never know the answers to such controversial questions. Then again, perhaps someday we will find that there is more to our origins, our planet and our solar system than we ever imagined. No matter what our beliefs may be it doesn't hurt to keep an open mind since there may be a grain of truth in even the most bizarre or controversial theory.

Part VII
MYSTERIOUS EVENTS

Unexplained Phenomena of Crop Circles

The term, crop circle, or circles, was coined by a paranormal researcher by the name of Colin Andrews to describe the strange circles and complex geometries. He had started researching that were showing up in fields of wheat, barley, rye, corn, soy beans and other crops. While many of these "circles" have been proven to be hoaxes, there are quite a few that defy rational explanation.

There are numerous theories that have been given to explain the crop circles of unknown origin, and these theories range from the id basic idea that all of these crop circles are purely man-made hoaxes to them being messages from extraterrestrial beings from other worlds. It is notable that when the crop circles have been made by human hands, the plants themselves are damaged. Stalks are broken, seed heads crushed, and the damaged plants die. In the cases where the particular "circle" cannot be explained away so easily, the plants have merely laid over and no damage has been done to the plants themselves. The plants in the stricken area continue to grow and ripen, none of the stalks are broken nor the seed heads crushed. Another odd anomaly to these particular types of crop circles is that the genetic structure of the plants themselves have been altered. This does not happen with the crop circles that have proven to be the work of pranksters.

One of the earliest known instances of crop circles appearing is image in a 17th-century English woodcut called the "Mowing-Devil". The wood cut has the classic devil-with-a-scythe image making, or cutting, an oval design in a field of oats. The pamphlet containing the image says that the farmer saw an area of his crop looking as if it were on fire during the night and in the morning an oval pattern had mysteriously appeared in the very same area of the field.

In 1966, in the small town of Tully, Queensland, Australia, one of the most famous accounts of a UFO, and the possible link to crop circles, happened. A farmer was working in the sugarcane field on his farm and swore that he saw a saucer-shaped craft fly 30 or 40 feet above a swamp and then fly away at extreme high speed. The farmer decided to investigate the area where he thought the saucer had been hovering and he found the water reeds intricately woven going in a clockwise pattern. It is also reported that the woven reeds could support the weight of 10 fully grown men.

The crop circle phenomenon became a very hot topic during the late 1980s, after the newspapers and other news media started to report the appearance of crop circles in the towns of Hampshire and Wiltshire in Britain, and the appearance of crop circles were reported in Penrith, Australia and the state of Minnesota in America. No less than 12,000 genuine crop circles have been discovered all across the world. In countries like the former Soviet Union, the UK, Japan, and the U.S. and Canada, this strange phenomenon continues to appear and baffle anyone who observes it.

In a wheat field in Monroe County, Tennessee, a pattern ranging about 150 feet in diameter with the wheat crop laid down in counterclockwise circles was discovered on May 14, 2007. Captain Bryan Graves, of the local sheriff's department discovered it while flying by on aerial patrol.

One of the most fascinating aspects of the crop circle phenomenon is that while many of the pranksters and hoaxers have been caught red-handed, there are many who have witnessed in broad daylight the appearance of strange silver orbs hovering over a field and then literally disappear from sight. A crop circle is always the result of these odd appearances. The designs have gone from the simplistic circles to very complex forms such as fractals, and even multi-dimensional forms and designs given in what are called the "sacred geometries".

Could it be that inter-dimensional, extraterrestrial beings are trying to communicate with humanity? If so, what is the message, or messages, they are trying to send? The mystery continues.

Silbury Hill Crop Circles

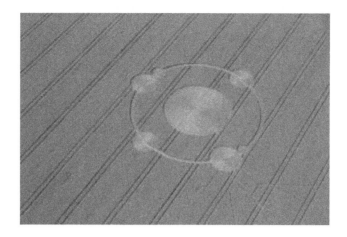

Crop circles first appeared in England several decades ago. Experts believe that most of the crop circles that have appeared around England and other places in the world were simply attractive looking hoaxes that provided a bit of harmless fun at the time. 80 percent of crop circles can be conclusively proven to be man-made, but believers in the crop circle phenomena point out that 20% of the crop circles that appear worldwide cannot be explained as hoax.

A new type of crop circle has appeared as the year 2012 approaches. If these crop circles are messages of mysterious visitors, they may be reminding humanity that the end of the world is near. If they are made by human hands, it may simply be that someone is using Mayan symbols to continue the hoax. Compounding the issue was that the circle appeared close to one of the oldest man-made monuments in England.

The Mayan headdress symbol might be interesting, but it is probably not linked to the end of the Mayan Calendar or any Mayan prophecy at all. Crop circles have appeared in England long before the Mayan calendar craze started, and are more likely to be authentic than other forms of crop circles that appear elsewhere in the world.

Researchers have found little evidence that crop circles that appear near Neolithic sites are man-made formations. The Mayan crop circle formation that appeared in 2009 was the second Mayan-themed circle to use Mayan themes. The first Mayan influenced crop circle appeared in 2004.

The genuine crop circles require the plants to be bent without heated and cooled at the base without breaking. Investigators often find metallic shavings at the site as well. When a crop cycle is a hoax, this does not occur and the plants do not continue to grow after they have been bent. There are as many theories on how crop circles get formed as there are experts on the patterns themselves. Some link the crop circles to UFO activity; other people point out that the formations are likely man-made formations that no one else has figured out how to duplicate.
Crop formation enthusiasts believe that the newest patterns may be to remind people that the Mayan calendar ends on December 21, 2012. The sudden end of the calendar has caused many to believe that a cataclysm is approaching. The History channel ran a special with scientists who took a more measured approach. The galactic alignment predicted will occur on that date. Astronomers say that people who expect the world to end should prepare to be disappointed, because the galactic alignment occurs every year on December 21. If the world has ended on any previous alignment, no one has noticed it so far.

Crop circles will remain popular in the public imagination. Even if the most elaborate ones that appear near the Neolithic sites in England do not come from some out-of-this-world or long forgotten ancient visitor, people will still marvel at the shapes. Nevertheless, if a researcher ever traces crop circles to human activity, they will forever lose the sense of mysteriousness and wonder that people associate with them.

Barbury Castle Crop Circles

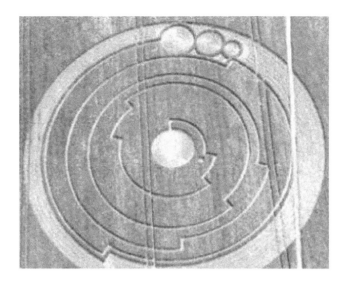

Since the 1970's, strange things began appearing in farmer's fields. They would awake to find crops had been laid down in vast unusual patterns. The phenomenon was not confined to one area as it was occurring all over the world. Some believed the deed was done by pranksters (in fact some did admit to making some of the patterns), others believed the designs were left by aliens, and some attributed them to ghosts or other spiritual forces. Barbury Castle in England has been the site of some of these famous crop circles.

The patterns started as simple circles in the 70's, became more pictorial in the 80's, were complex geometrical displays in the 90's and by the turn of the century the circles depicted what is thought by some to be binary number codes. Extensive research over the years proves that not all the anomalies are the work of vandals. Strange microwave, radiation and iron deposits have been found in the soil and plants within the shapes.

While scientists replicate these findings, they cannot explain for certainty what made them. The intricacy of many of the designs could not have been made without someone somewhere having seen what transpired, as it is estimated an army of people would need to be onsite for the massive detailed compositions.

In the last couple of years, individuals caught strange occurrences on still photographs and videos providing a clue. The evidence shows small spherical objects sweeping along the tops of crops in broad daylight. The path where the orbs travel would immediately lay down the crops. What these flying objects are no one knows but there is evidence of their existence. No one can say for sure that these balls are guilty for the all crop circles.

Many speculate the crop circle's meanings. Most agree that there are mathematical inferences in the designs. The Barbury Castle tetrahedron pattern found in 1991 has a number of theorists interpreting possible definitions. Some believe the geometrical patterns correlate with Euclid's mathematical theorems, which in turn correspond with Pythagoras's musical theory. The theory uses a multiplication and division table that is the basis of scales used in Western music. However, it is not apparent that a definitive melody has been deciphered.

Others believe the circles are merely a signpost for the extraterrestrials. Speculations by some believe that the circles represent various forms of energy. The way in which the energy circulates demonstrates this is in fact a diagram for a spacecraft. Another group of people believe it is a symbol of Divine Order. Still another group interprets the design as a warning that a cataclysmic event will occur to balance the physical and spiritual worlds.

In 1997, two more designs appeared on the property. One was called the 6 Moons Formation and the other the Tree of Life. Theorists believe the dual swirling hexagons represent a cultic symbol while some believe the Tree of Life is an ancient geometric figure mentioned in the Kabballah and only known to rabbis.

Two more patterns emerged in 1999. Aerial views depict what appears to be a Menorah complete with flames and the utensils used to tend the flames. The other design has two circled outer layers with three interlaced crescent shapes in the middle. Asian visitors claim this symbol is synonymous with what is known in their language as the woman/goddess. As recently as 2008, another image was carved into a Barbury field. This image is reminiscent of the one from 1991. The lone image of the ratchet circle first appeared as part of the now famous tetrahedron pattern. Some believe this circle by itself represents a path man must travel.

Ethereal Doubles

Today, the word "Doppelganger" has become an overall conception by which an encounter with the ethereal double is obviously described. There are a number of phenomena which do not correspond to the strict "double walker" definition - even if they are similar.

The phenomenon of the Doppelganger respectively the ethereal double of a person has been confirmed by many people. But what are they and what signification do they have?

In the esoterically sense a Doppelganger is the immaterial ethereal opposite of a person that appears suddenly, often in moments of danger. Generally, the one from whom this copy derives is not aware of it.

The American Gordon Barrows had also an encounter with his ethereal double in 1947. After a drive of 18 hours through the most deserted and most inhospitable desert regions of the US federal state Wyoming, Barrows ran the risk of falling asleep at the steering-wheel because of exhaustion. Short after Laramie he caught sight of a hitchhiker and he instinctively went slow. But when Barrows lowered the window to offer the stranger a ride, he got a shock: The hitchhiker seemed to be his copy.

To Barrows' relief, the stranger offered to drive so that Barrows could sleep a little.

When he awoke some hours later, the car was parked on the road side while his silent fellow-traveller sat motionless behind the steering-wheel. Barrows just found the time to thank the stranger before this one left the car and disappeared wordless in the desert. While Barrows continued his travel refreshed, he was thinking about that mysterious encounter which he could not explain.

However, Gordon Barrows is no individual case. In the past, people have reported again and again about their fascinating and also uncanny encounters with their own or as well a strange Doppelganger. Nevertheless, a highly evident similarity has nothing in common with the extraordinary experiences with their ethereal double, made by Gordon Barrows and numerous other people.

Psychologists define Doppelganger as apparitions of a living person that correspond to the real height of the person concerned. These apparitions are usually transparent, mostly monochrome, and sometimes also visible in pale colours. They imitate the movements of their physical counterpart as if they were his reflexions. This kind of Doppelganger appears mostly at dusk or late at night – but represents not the entire person. Also people who are very stressed or who are totally exhausted have often encounters with Doppelgangers. This connection cannot be explained scientifically up to now.

The earliest recorded incident with a "Doppelganger" dates back to the fourth pre-Christian century. Aristoteles, the Greek philosopher, told of a man who could not go for a walk without meeting his "Doppelganger". The belief in a Doppelganger is not new. It can be traced back to ancient Persia and is still disseminated in old and modern cultures.

Today, the word "Doppelganger" has become an overall conception by which an encounter with the ethereal double is obviously described.

There are a number of phenomena which do not correspond to the strict "double walker" definition - even if they are similar.

Another form of ethereal Doppelgangers is known under the designation "Vardoger" or "Forerunner". This phenomenon differs from the Doppelganger in so far that the ethereal double of the person concerned hurries on ahead already weeks of a possible departure.

As authentically stated by witnesses they could not only see the Doppelganger of another person but could also talk to him while the person concerned was at another place.

Some scientists believe that such phenomena could be the result of thought projections, e.g. of a strong wish which is projected by means of will-power. This happens when the body is subject to extreme emotional or physical stress and that cause visions of the person concerned to appear in front of relatives or beloved people.

Even if there exists a lot of world-wide reports on such cases, this phenomenon is far from being clearly defined. The imagination that all ethereal Doppelgangers are the projection of a single conscience contradicts to the experience of a multiple sighting, made by Reverend W. Mountford together with some friends in the US federal state Massachusetts.

Mountford stayed at friends who expected a visit of relatives on that day. The whole group went outdoors to have a look if the guests were already arriving. To their astonishment they observed how the expected couple approached the house in a Buggy – but they passed by without noticing the waiting people. A little later, the Buggy approached again the house. This time the people in the car waved friendly to the waiting group.

Scientists have several explanations for it. It could be imaginable that one of the waiting people projected a picture of the approaching Buggy.

The Buggy with all its passengers could also be a manifestation because of a group hallucination.

A related phenomenon is called bilocation. This occurs when one person appears at two places simultaneously. To the most renowned "normal" cases of this kind belongs Emilie Sagee, a French teacher in the 19th century whose astral body was sighted at different spots all her life.

Sceptics argue that such sightings are confusions and outgrowths of an eccentric phantasy. This cannot be cleared for the time being. But one day science might perhaps be able to prove the existence of an ethereal double.

The Haunted Busby Chair

For over 300 years, mystery and speculation has surrounded the famous Busby Stoop Chair. Thomas Busby was the original owner of what is now known as the Busby Stoop Inn, which is located in Kirby Wiske, a small village near the town of Thirsk, in North Yorkshire. The death of Busby has been popularly associated with a number of fatalities that occurred later in history, mostly because of the chair itself.

In the year 1702, Busby had a meeting with his father-in-law, Daniel Auty (some historians use the spelling 'Awety'), with whom he had become a partner in petty crime. After a heated argument, Busby returned to the pub to find Auty sitting in his favorite chair. According to the story, Busby, whose reputation as a drunkard was well known throughout the community, ordered Auty to leave, and after a while, went and found him at what was then called Danotty Hall. Here, police say that Busby murdered Auty with a hammer and hid the body in the woods.

The authorities soon located Auty's remains and arrested Busby at the pub. The story goes that as he was being led away to the gallows, Busby screamed out curses to anyone who should ever sit in his chair. Being in a drunken stupor at the time, it is very unlikely that Busby drew much attention to his ranting, although they were documented by several witnesses. Some accounts reported that Busby shouted to onlookers that anyone who sat in his chair would die a horrible death, just as he was about to do. Busby was led across the street and hanged in a makeshift gallows, where his remains were displayed for days afterwards.

Since that time, many people have reported seeing the ghost of Thomas Busby, at or near the hangman's gibbet, with a noose around his neck. But it is the curse of his favorite chair that has become the subject of both folklore and mystical intrigue. There are verified accounts of a good number of people who sat in Busby's "haunted" chair in the years that followed, and meeting with sudden death soon afterwards.

In the late 1800's, a chimney sweep and his friend were sitting in the pub, and the sweep, who apparently had occupied the Busby Stoop Chair, was found dead the next morning, on a gatepost next to the old hangman gibbet.

Later, a certain Mr. Earnshaw, who for a time was landlord of the inn, overheard two RAF pilots talking about the famous chair, and witnessed them take turns sitting in it. On that same day, both pilots were killed when their car struck a tree. There are accounts of several motorcyclists and bicyclists who, after stopping at the inn for a drink, were later involved in fatal collisions with automobiles.

One man who sat in the Busby Stoop Chair died of a massive heart attack the following night. A hitchhiker, after spending time at the pub for refreshment, and who presumably occupied the famous chair, was struck and killed by an automobile two days later. The inn itself was becoming more and more famous as these stories became widely circulated, and most folks agreed that it was either the most amazing of coincidences, or an example of actual cursed enchantment.

The pub was later owned by a brewery, and in the 1970's the landlord asked that the chair be removed from the premises. It is now found in the

Thirsk Museum and it is, of course, now protected from occupancy. No one has sat in the famous "haunted" Busby Stoop Chair since 1978. And naturally, the Busby Stoop Inn is a favorite stop for inquisitive ghost hunters and curious tourists.

The Theory of Earth-Expansion

But in what way the Earth grows after all? Surely by prehistorical comets and meteorite impacts but there exists also another assumption: Neutrinos! These are smallest, uncharged particles that fly through the universe and even through us.

In the field of geology still exists a scientific theory that is ignored by the majority of geologists. But it is unintelligible for any mainstream people because it can explain a lot of open questions concerning the origin of the Earth: The Theory of Earth-Expansion.

The German polar explorer, Alfred Wegener, propounded the Theory of Continental Drift which then was extended to Plate Tectonics. He stated that all continents are well matched like a puzzle and concluded that once a super-continent "Pangea" existed which later broke asunder. But already in Wegener's lifetime, Ott Christoph Hilgenberg wrote his Theory of Earth-Expansion. Hilgenberg placed the super-continent on a much smaller terrestrial globe and found out that it fully encompassed this smaller planet. Hence he concluded that the Earth once was much smaller and slowly broke asunder because of the growth of Earth-mass.

Science has stated that the rotation of our Earth slackens. Furthermore, our Earth does not rotate continually but the rotary speed varies. But one day is defined by the revolution speed of the Earth in 1900. Thus, the atomic clock of the Federal Physical Institute in Brunswick -which clocks the universal time – has to be regularly adapted to the apparent time. This happens every 18 months by means of a leap second.

In compliance with the Conservation of Angular Momentum Theorem a slowdown of Earth-rotation is accompanied by a mass increase and thus a growth of the Earth. According to Professor Konstantin Meyl – field physicist and expert in neutrino research – the actual slowdown of the Earth-rotation by 0,7 seconds each year results in a growth of the Earth's circumference by 19 centimetres.

The NASA has created a geophysical world map by means of satellite data. At first sight it shows a "bursting Earth". In the Pacific, the Earth's crust yearly spreads apart by 15 centimetres, in the Atlantic by 3 to 4 centimetres.

This is supported by the geologist Professor K.-H. Jacob, Chair of deposit research and Study of raw materials at the Technical University, Berlin. He can explain this argumentation by geological fissures and their sediments. Here field physics meets geology!

100 Million years ago, the dinosaurs populated the Earth. Giant saurian which could partly move very fast. But in consideration of today' gravitation it is to question how a Tyrannosaurus Rex that weighed tons could accomplish this. Assuming that the Earth-mass is much lower, the gravitation is also lesser – so an enormous growth is forwarded. The impact of the Yucatan-comet 65 million years ago could have been indeed the initiator of the then beginning Plate Tectonics.

But in what way the Earth grows after all? Surely by prehistorical comets and meteorite impacts but there exists also another assumption: Neutrinos! These are smallest, uncharged particles that fly through the universe and even through us. Due to the vast open and empty spaces in nuclear physics this causes no problem. Some scientists hold the opinion that these small particles are absorbed by the Earth and also the other planets and this causes the slowly increase of mass. This is not proved up to now but could be a logical reasonable explanation.

Moreover, there exists a considerable correlation between the pole drift and the great deluge. This could be the reason why "Atlantis" disappeared under the ice of Antarctica.
By the way, this thought was already pursued by Albert Einstein.

Centralia, PA The Mouth Of Hell

Practically from the time we are born, we develop a picture in our minds of the American dream. In general, to achieve that dream, we find the ideal job, get married, buy a home, and start a family. We live our lives from day to day with the hope of building a bright future, now imagine that everything that you have worked so hard to accomplish went literally up in smoke. as tragic as this may sound, in 1962 the town of Centralia, located in Columbia County Pennsylvania, had that nightmare become a reality, but on a much larger scale. An abandoned strip mine was accidently set on fire, igniting a nearby vein of anthracite coal. From water and fly ash, to back filling and drilling, every idea tempted to put out the fire would have the same results. It would flair up again in a different location making it impossible to control.

Our government showed little concern in extinguishing the flames until 1981, when a 12 year old boy had a sink hole swallow him right out from under his feet, while playing in his own back yard. Fortunately for him, he was not alone at the time and was rescued by a visiting cousin. In 1983, a research study done by engineers, showed that the only way to put out the fire for good is to excavate and dig up the entire vein. At a cost of 600 million dollars, the federal government chose to relocate the villagers at a much lower cost. Many people felt that this was merely a ploy to acquire mineral rights for the coal. They decided to take their chances in court and fight the decision, but to no avail. The Commonwealth of Pennsylvania claimed eminent domain, condemning house after house, stating that it was due to toxic gases, sink holes and the eminent danger that exists. Not only did the residents have the government to deal with, but the post office revoked their zip code as well.

47 years and 40 million dollars later, there are only 9 buildings left with 8 people remaining, in a town that was once the home of over 2000 people. It is hard to say whether or not the many attempts to put out the fire would have been more successful, had the government gotten involved sooner, but if you ask any of the former residents. They would surely have appreciated it if somebody would have at least tried.

Anthracite is one of the most pure types of coal in existence. Because of this, it burns very hot making it the perfect source for the steel industry. The study also revealed that because of that reason, the fire could spread to 3700 acres and could stay ignited for 250 years or more.

Appropriately nicknamed the mouth of hell, Centralia virtually is no more. Route 61 is now detoured through the neighboring town of Ashland. What is to become of the towns and villages that surround Centralia? Will they too suffer the same fate? Will Route 61 once again be rerouted through another town because Ashland is in the path of destruction? Is it not worth millions to dig up a vein of coal that has a value of billions to save these communities? Maybe the fears of the residents were right, maybe it is about obtaining mineral rights after all. Only time will tell.

Queen of Crime Novel missed for 11 Days

Agatha Christie was the most successful criminal author of all time. Her stories about Hercule Poirot and Miss Marple have thrilled millions of readers for more than fifty years and some of her ingenious cases confused even her shrewdest admirers. But with her death in January 1976 she left a real life secret behind that was so amazing as if she had thought it out herself.

In December 1927 – when she was already a celebrated criminal author – Agatha Christie disappeared for nearly two weeks. The headlines of the papers announced the most sensational theories to a breathless circle of readers. Suicide, abduction, murder. The police was looking for any clues why she had disappeared – but in vain.

Agatha Christie was born in September 1890 as daughter of a wealthy American who lived with his English wife in Torquay, Devon. The family lived in luxurious means and Agatha received only few regular classes. But the house was full of books and her mother encouraged her to read.

In 1914 she married Colonel Archibald Christie and while her husband had been abroad with the army, she served as a nurse. She continued her studies as a pharmacist. During this time, she acquired her detailed knowledge in medicine, drugs and poisons which came in so very handy when she became a criminal author.

She wrote her first detective novel when she recovered from an illness and since 1926 she had had literary success. This probably rattled her husband who turned to another woman and confessed this love affair to his wife.

This information – which followed the death of her mother – drove her into desperation. And in the bitter-cold night on Friday, 3rd December, she put on a green cardigan, a grey woollen jacket and a velvet hat, stuffed some pound notes in her purse, got into her two-seated Morris and drove away in the night.

Early next morning the car was found empty at the foot of a hill near Newlands Corner, scarcely half a mile away from her twelve-bedroom-house in Berkshire. The car stood on a narrow beaten field-path. Its front tires towered above the edge of a fourty meters deep lime-pit. The brakes were loosened, the gear lever was put in neutral and the ignition was turned on. In the car some garments were found, among others a fur coat.

On the following Monday the police proclaimed her disappearance und the papers printed it in the headlines. Hundreds of policemen and thousands of volunteers scoured the region.
The preferred theory was that the famous author would have committed suicide. But where was her corpse?

In the meantime at about four hundred kilometers away in Harrogate, Yorkshire, an attractive red-haired woman ingratiated herself with her fellow-guests in the Hydro Hotel. Her name – so she said – was Theresa Neele and she came from South Africa. But the head waiter of the hotel was sure that this friendly guest had a suspicious similarity with the missing author and he contacted the police.

Two years later, Colonel Christie and Agatha got divorced and he was now free to marry Miss Neele. In 1930 Agatha married the archaeologist Sir Max Mallowan and travelled a lot with him. Some of the exotic places that they both visited became plot in some of her novels.

In the course of time the recollection of the author's disappearance faded. In her auto-biography she only indicated that had had a nervous breakdown. But is this the real explanation of what had happened many years before? When she had lost her memory from where was the clothes she wore at the Hydro Hotel and the money she had spent?

Had she in that December night the intention to kill herself and then – as her car did not crashed into the lime-pit – decided to go away for a while to think things over very calmly? When it was like this, why did not she tell the truth to the police?

Was the accident some sort of tactics to cause the pity of her unfaithful husband and to regain him? Was it a complicated trial to clear up the affair of her husband? Or was perhaps everything only a plan to punish the infidelity of her husband? Supposing the suicide attempt were successful. Then the police would have investigated and would have found in Colonel Christie's affair with Miss Neele a sufficient motive to get rid of her. Perhaps this is somewhat far-fetched but not more than some of Mrs. Christie's mysterious novel intrigues.

Most of the people who could have helped to shed some light into the case are dead now. Miss Neele died in 1958 and Colonel Christie in 1962.

In the course of the years, Agatha Christie wrote more than eighty novels, had been more often translated than William Shakespeare and reached an edition of three hundred million books. Despite this renown she remained an isolated mysterious woman. And she refused till her death to care for the solution of her most mysterious crime story – the one of her own disappearance a half century ago.

The Donnie Decker Story

Donnie Decker was named the Rain Boy in 1983. He was a visitor at his friends Jennie and Bob Keefer's house when he went into t a trance like state. After that, the ceiling started dripping water and some sort of mist was apparent within the room. Because Jennie and Bob had no clue what was causing the dripping water, they called on the landlord who was dumbfounded by what he was seeing because there was no logical reason why this was happening.

Not knowing what to do or what was causing this problem, the friends called police. Police officers Wolpert and Baujan arrived and were also dumbfounded by what was happening. The officers in turn call their chief who arrived at the house and was anger by what was happening and ordered them to never speak of this again to anyone. He left the house and denied anything had happened in the house.

Don was at a restaurant with some other friends sitting at a table when rain started pouring down on their heads. The restaurant owner ordered Donnie out of the establishment and told Don that he was possessed and needed an exorcism.

Don later returned to Jennie and Bob's house with his restaurant friends where he was met with anger from his friends. They were blaming Don for the strange happenings when Don's body started levitating off the floor and then thrown across the kitchen where he lay unconscious. Officers were called again. The officers arrived at the house with another officer John Rundle. It was Rundle that wanted to see if Decker was demonized.

Rundle placed a bag over Don's head and put things in Don's hands while they were behind his back. He did this to see if there would be any reaction to each item, which included a crucifix. His hands suffered burns when the crucifix was placed in his hands. Don again levitated and was thrown across the room where he lay unconscious with what appeared to be claw marks about his neck.

Altogether, six people had seen what had happened when Don was in the room and they told the story to the public. Don was later jailed for some reason and in his cell, rain started pouring down. Inmates were angered over being in the same jail cell with Decker. It was then that Decker told the jailer on duty that he could control when it rained and where it would happen. Decker made it rain on the officer while he was at his desk. The officer was then afraid.

A pastor by the name of William Blackburn was called into help Decker. The pastor started reading scripture after the dripping started and a mist filed the air. A raunchy smell filled the cell and the pastor kept praying. Soon, it was over when Decker's countenance changed.

Unsolved Mysteries crew was sent to tape and interview the people involved. After finishing, they were shocked to find puddles of water on each of their hotel room's floors and no other guest but the crew had the water problem. No one knew where the water came from nor did they want to know. Is it possible that a man can make it rain in one area and if so, what is processing him to do so.

The Count of Saint Germain
The man who knows everything
and never dies!

Who was the Count of Saint Germain? Is he immortal or even a time traveler? Apart from him, probably nobody even knows it. The fact is, however, that he often astonished his listeners when he described inventions, which were still unknown in the 18th Century - the railroad and the steamboat. How did he know it?

The Count of Saint Germain is designated as a famous adventurer of the 18th century, who was known throughout Europe as "the miracle man". Nothing definite is known of his parentage, and his death is shrouded in darkness. Voltaire, a cynic who was not easily impressed, characterized him – face to face with Frederick the Great – as "the man who knows everything and never dies!"

According to witnesses, he had lived for at least two hundred years, while hardly changed his appearance.

The count turned up suddenly from nowhere. All his life he was surrounded by intrigue and rumors of magical powers. He should have had more than eighty pseudonyms, and also the name of Saint Germain was probably not his real one.

He first appeared in 1710, which was testified by the composer Jean-Philip Rameau and the young Countess of Geordie, who described him as a forty to forty-five year old man. As for the next two decades, almost nothing is known except that he was a close confidant of Madame de Pompadour and had a great influence in Freemason lodges and other secret societies of that time.

Between 1737 and 1742, Saint Germain stayed at the court of the Shah of Persia, where he acquired probably a part of his vast knowledge about diamonds. In 1743, he appeared at the court of King Louis XV, and was famous for his great wealth and his alchemical skills. He himself claimed to have found the philosopher's stone and produce diamonds, as well as having traveled to the Himalayas and had found the people who "know everything".

In addition, he added that "one must have studied in the Pyramids, as I have done it" to trace his secret. He also said that he had traveled through space. "A very long time I flew through space. I saw globes, the world revolved around me and at my feet." On another occasion he said:" I traveled through time and found myself unconsciously in distant countries. "

The count was assessed a visionary - he told of inventions from the future. It is further claimed that he could make himself invisible in front of witnesses and appeared suddenly whenever and wherever he wanted.

In 1744, the count was jailed for espionage in England but was released after interrogation. 1745 and 1746 he lived at the Viennese court like a prince and was "witty and highly gifted." He was not only described as being very rich, but spoke in addition to several European and Arab, Oriental and classical languages, and was an excellent violin and piano player. Moreover, he was a vegetarian and only drank wine occasionally.

Between 1747 and 1760 he attained the height of his fame at the court of Louis XV., in front of whom he enlarged or increased diamonds. There they gave him a laboratory for his alchemical experiments. The Countess of Geordie - then at the age of seventy years – was very surprised that Saint Germain still looked like when they met fifty years ago.

From 1762 to about 1773 in all Europe reports were published on his scientific and political career: "An extraordinary man, who could turn iron into a metal that for the work of the goldsmith's at least is as good and beautiful as gold."

In Venice, he had a factory with one hundred workers. The company was engaged in the manufacture of linen which looked like silk.

Between 1774 and 1784, after the death of Louis XV., he warned Louis XVI. and Marie Antoinette in vain of a "giant conspiracy" on which he had become aware by his insight into Freemasonry and Illuminati circles.

After that, he mostly lived in Germany. There, he was said to have committed with his pupil and patron, Prince Charles of Hesse-Kassel, in Freemasonry, Rosicrucians and Knights Templar circles.

At the court of Charles of Hesse-Kassel, the count admitted for the first time to grow old. On 27 February 1784 he allegedly should have died suddenly in the arms of two maids, whereby the funeral is said to have taken place on 02 March 1784, which is also registered as such in the church registers of Eckernförde. When, however, days later, his coffin was opened again, it was empty!

Then followed his appearance – confirmed by many witnesses - at a large gathering of occultists on 15 February 1785 in Wilhelmsbad - including Freemasons, Illuminati and necromancers, at which the different views of the lodges should have to be clarified. He appeared there in company with the famous Italian adventurer and alchemist Cagliostro, the Viennese physician Franz Mesmer, who also is the founder of the "animalistic healing magnetism" (Mesmerism) and the French writer and philosopher Louis Claude Saint Martin.

In 1788, he lived mostly in France again and warned the nobles of the impending revolution. But again he was not taken seriously. In 1789, he then traveled to Sweden to King Gustav III. to protect him against a possible disease.

He seemed to have taught the people with whom he associated about the inner meaning of life, and - because he foresaw the impending revolution - have consoled them with the prospect of the subtle world - the afterlife.

To Marie Antoinette he predicted the day and the hour of her death in 1793. The queen herself has testified that the Count appeared with his soul's body (astral body) in her cell and erected her soul by giving her the certainty of the glorious life in the other world, which gave her the noble dignity when mounting the guillotine.

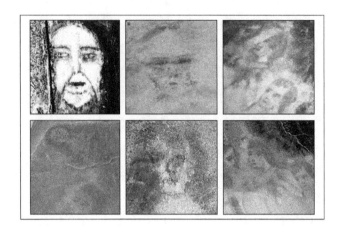

Portraits appeared in a mysterious way on a kitchen floor in Spain. They changed or faded by the time, attracted thousands of visitors and fooled psychologists and scientists.

In the morning of 23rd August 1971, a housewife in the southern Spanish village Belmez de la Moraleda entered her kitchen and stated with fright that overnight a face had been painted on the floor. It was neither a ghost nor a hallucination: The housewife, a simple country-woman named Maria Gomez Pereira, could only assume that a paranormal phenomenon had happened in her house. The news spread quickly and soon everybody in the village had heard of the mysterious event and penetrated the house in the Calle Rodriguez Acosta to see the face. It was similar to an expressionist portrait and the traits of the face stood out very naturalistic in their colouring from the concrete floor.

Finally, the Pereira family tried to remove this extraordinary phenomenon that disturbed their rather peaceful and quite life and decided to destroy the mysterious "painting". Six days after it had appeared, Miguel Pereira hoed up the kitchen floor and filled it up with fresh concrete.

Nothing happened for approximately one week. Then, on 8th September, Maria Pereira entered her kitchen to notice once again the mysterious similarity to a human face that began to manifest exactly at the same place in the concrete of the floor. This time, the outlines of a male face stood up even more clearly.

Now it was impossible to keep the masses of the curious in check. Every day, people queued up in front of the house to see the "face from the other world". It stayed some weeks on the floor; and then – although it did not disappear – the traits changed slowly like it would age or would go through some process of decay.

The Belmez mayor recognized the importance of the faces and decided that second one should not be destroyed but should be preserved like a valuable work of art. On 2nd November 1971, a huge mass of people witnessed how the picture was cut out of the floor, framed behind glass and hung up at the wall beside the chimney.

Afterwards the floor of the kitchen was dug up to confirm if there had been something hidden that could have explained the mysterious appearance of the two faces. In a depth of around 270 meters the diggers found a number of human bones. This discovery satisfied e.g. the spiritists who were interested in the faces of Belmez because it corresponds to spiritistic persuation that a restless ghost haunts the place where he was buried or where he is active as a poltergeist. But for the inhabitants of Belmez, the discovery was not so much of a surprise because they knew that the houses in the Calle Rodriguez Acosta were built at the spot of a former cemetery.

Two weeks after the kitchen floor was dug up, a third face appeared near the place where the first two had been discovered and after another two weeks a fourth one. The first had undoubtedly female traits. But not less mysterious, smaller faces appeared around the fourth one a little later. At last there were up to 18 faces that could be found. On 9th April 1972, professor Argumosa, who was engaged in this case with enthusiasm, had followed the manifestation of a face over a longer period. The gradual appearance of at first unconnected lines on the tile-plastered part of the floor that connected by the time more and more to an impressive and attractive "painting". It was photographed several times, but at the end of the day it was again already disappeared.

Later, the parapsychologist Hand Bender was invited to help at the researches. After questioning the witnesses on-site, he came to the conclusion that the faces were really of paranormal origin. He also remarked another aspect: The faces had a different effect on the observers. One face that appeared one person as a young man was held by another one for an old man. The faces withstood the trials to be removed by detergents. They seemed to develop and to decay according to a strange self-legality.

Bender undertook an experiment to document the origin of the faces under experimental conditions with a procedure that failed when applied by Argumosa. At first, he and his team photographed the kitchen floor in its normal condition and then covered it completely with a thick plastic awning. With that it should be made sure that none of the still arising pictures would be produced by someone on the outside. However, water gathered under the awning and the Pereira family decided to remove it before other faces became visible. The "haunted house", however, became a place of pilgrimage for interested occultists from Spain, France, England and Germany which interpreted it differently as demonically or holy. They also brought tape recorders with them to record séances with the "ghosts" they presumed still in the house. On some recordings loud cries, the noise of many voices talking at the same time and the weeping of people could be heard. Perhaps, something very serious had happened in the house in Belmez centuries ago – probably in connection with the cemetery underneath.

But until now, there could not be found a fully satisfying solution: Also chemists who examined the concrete had not been able to explain the appearance of the faces out of this.

Moving Coffins of Barbados

The first of the Chase family to be laid to rest in the tomb was Mrs. Thomasina Goddard in the year 1807.

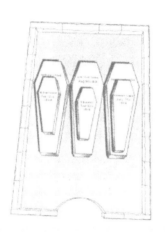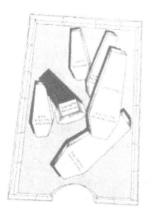

In a West Indies cemetery stands the vault of the Chase family and it would seem that up until the patriarch, Thomas Chase, died it had been the peaceful resting place for the members of the family that had passed on prior to his demise.

Thomas Chase, it seems, was one of the most hated men on the island. One can only assume he was an intensely unpleasant person, even towards his family. When the time came to put Mr. Chase into his final resting place in or about the year 1813 or 1814, and the ground keepers opened the door to the crypt, all the coffins had moved from their original positions. This bizarre occurrence continued to happen for some years. Many of the local people reported actually hearing the coffins moving around inside the completely sealed tomb.

The first of the Chase family to be laid to rest in the tomb was Mrs. Thomasina Goddard in the year 1807. In the very next year two year old Mary Ann Chase was laid to rest in 1808. Then another child, Dorcas Chase, was also put into the vault in 1812. Everything was peaceful and without incident until Thomas Chase was to be placed inside. When the crypt was opened to place his mortal remains inside, the other coffins had moved themselves from their places.

The funeral party was quite angry to find the coffins in disarray and, at first, thought grave robbers to be responsible for the disrespectful act. However, the group soon abandoned this train of thought as nothing was missing from the coffins, nor had anything of value been put in the coffins to begin with. Most importantly, the door to the burial site was a huge stone that had been cemented into place and the seal had not been broken since the last burial. In order to open it, the seal on the huge slab of stone had to be broken with hammers and chisels. The stone was so big that it took at least four men to move it. Unsettled and unnerved, the townspeople placed the body of Thomas Chase inside and resealed the vault. Thomas' coffin was a 240 lb. lead coffin, so everyone figured that it was a pretty near impossible feat to drag the extremely heavy coffin around until it busted open and spilled anything of value out onto the floor.

In 1816 eleven year old Charles Brewster Ames died and once again it was time to open the tomb. When the tomb was opened the coffins had once again moved from their proper places. The lead coffin of Thomas Chase looked as though it had been tossed around like a rag doll. The crypt, once again, had still been completely sealed and, again, it bore no signs of tampering or forced entry.

Just 52 days later, another member of the family Chase was needing burial in the crypt. As expected, a rather large crowd had gathered for this particular funeral, and they weren't disappointed. Once again the cement-sealed door was closely examined before being opening, and once again there were no signs of forced entry or tampering. Again the coffins had been thrown about. The only difference this time was that the first coffin, the coffin of Mrs. Goddard, also the only one made of wood - had been badly damaged. A minister was called in to view the scene, but he could give no new insight into the disturbances. Once again the vault was sealed.

In 1819 another family member required burial. Once again the now infamous vault was opened with all the same results - except this time the wooden coffin found damaged the last time the crypt was opened had not been moved even a centimeter. The governor of the island had had enough of these mysterious, disturbing events and ordered his own investigation. Of course, nothing was found. This time the governor had sand scattered on the floor of the crypt to catch the footprints and movements of anyone who may have gained entry. The governor put his own seal on the tomb in the wet cement, and then the vault was ordered sealed until another of the family Chase needed interment. But the governor did not wait that long.

Less than a year later he ordered the crypt opened in front of him and several other friends and heads of government. The seal was, of course, completely intact upon inspection, but the coffins were still scattered. Some of them had even been turned upside down and standing on their "heads", and the heaviest of the lot was found lying halfway up the steps leading to the door. The sand showed no footprints or any sign of water leakage. The governor ordered the coffins to be moved to a new burial site, and the crypt was left empty and open. It remains empty to this very day.

Anastasia: From Wealth To Misery

Did the only survivor of the Russian czar family live inconspicuous in an American university city? In the meantime, the court documents comprise nearly 8,000 pages, but concerning Anastasia's identity they have come to no decision. Anna became more than 80 years old and lived as wife of Dr. John Manahan in a safe environment. The question, if she was the real Anastasia, stays further a historical mystery.

The nurses of the mental hospital in Dalldorf, one of the biggest psychiatric clinics in Berlin, felt deep sympathy with the unidentified young woman who had been brought there in February 1920, six weeks after her suicide trial in the Landwehr-Canal.

The plunge caused her already very weak lungs to bleed. She was chronic anaemic and showed distinct symptoms that she had suffered from rough violence some time ago: Above her right ear was a trough in her skull like when a bullet had hit the bone. Her jaw was injured, some teeth were knocked out, some of them were loose. The top and span of one foot had three-cornered scars which derived from a sharp object. The officers, who questioned the blue-eyed, dark-haired woman during her two years' stay at Dalldorf, were convinced that she was a Russian refugee and that she was silent because she feared repatriation. Some of the nurses could have shed more light on the dark secret of this woman, for although the patient spoke German fluently, she murmured in Russian language during her sleep from time to time. Some of them she confided to be grand duchess Anastasia who should have been shot together with her father and all family members in the summer of 1918.

But it was a fellow-patient who informed the outer world of a possible member of the Romanow-family. Clara Peuthert, who had lived in Moskow before the Revolution, was dismissed from Dalldorf in March 1922. Soon afterwards she told to a former White-Russian officer that she believed to have recognized grand duchess Tatjana, Anastasia's elder sister, among the patients of the mental hospital. Evidently she had not spoken with the patient who called herself Anastasia. After this conversation, a former police officer from the Russian Poland, Baron Arthur von Kleist, visited the mysterious woman. In July 1922, Baron von Kleist had spread the news and "Anastasia" got into the light of publicity. However, it has to be mentioned that the woman, who later was called Anna Manahan, stated her identity as a Romanow privately but she never tried to convince the whole world of it.

One of the many people to which belong also members of the Romanow clan, who visited Anastasia was Tatjana Botkin, the daughter of the czar's family doctor who presumably died together with the family. Tatjana Botkin had in mind to unmask the "impostor". But instead of she recognized the nameless woman despite her emaciated outer appearance immediately as Anastasia. After some research a strong resistance from the part of the German relatives of the czarina was stated. It was evidently that "they" feared something and were very troubled as if the investigation could bring something embarrassing or even dangerous. In 1928, Anastasia went as a guest of princess Xenia Georgiewna, one second-degree cousin of Anastasia, to New York. Here, she changed her name into Anna Anderson to avoid the rush of the press. In 1931, she went back to Germany and then made friendship with a cousin of the Romanows and stayed during the next 13 years relatively peaceful as guest at different European courts.

During the Second World War Anna Anderson was fixed in the Sovjet Union. Certainly this was an event similar to a nightmare when she was certainly the person she pretended to be. After the war she became more and more eccentric. She settled as a hermit together with an elder woman in a house in the Black Forest which had been bought for her, surrounded by some cats and four wild wolf-hounds.

Later the court of appeal in Berlin dismissed the petition for her legal recognition that was handed in by her attorneys. From 1957 till 1970, that case was nearly continually tried by the German courts. It is stated by documents, that King George V. Suppressed a British plan to rescue his cousin Nikolaus. Presumably he was afraid to endanger his own position when engaging himself for the czar. In 1953, Anna Anderson was justified by a statement of a very authentic source, the German Crown Princess Cecile, daughter-in-law of the German emperor.

In the meantime, the court documents comprise nearly 8,000 pages, but concerning Anastasia's identity they have come to no decision. Anna became more than 80 years old and lived as wife of Dr. John Manahan in a safe environment.

The question, if she was the real Anastasia, stays further a historical mystery.

What is a Mega-Tsunami

A mega-tsunami is a frightening concept. Unfortunately, it is a real possibility, and has even occurred a few times within the past 200,000 years. They could also happen again in the future, and some experts even believe we're currently sitting on a time-bomb. A mega-tsunami is basically a tsunami that has a wave height of hundreds or even thousands of feet!

Normally, a tsunami that is generated at sea has only a small wave height of a foot or so above the normal sea surface while offshore. They also have a long wavelength of many, many miles. However, the height and length of the normal tsunami waves are usually unnoticeable until it gets close to land, whereupon the height increases drastically as the base of the tsunami pushes the water column on top of it upwards.

Mega-tsunamis, however, are defined as actually BEGINNING with high waves. All accounts of mega-tsunamis in history originated extremely close to shore, or in narrow inlets or lakes where water had no other options for dispersal. A number of things can cause a mega-tsunami, including giant landslides, islands collapsing, underwater earthquakes causing giant landslides, and asteroid impacts.

No boat, building, or village could survive being hit by a mega-tsunami. Some evidence points to at least eleven of them occurring in the last

200,000 years, some of which were caused by islands collapsing in the Canary and Hawaiian Islands, as well as an earthquake in Alaska.

In fact, the largest tsunami recorded in recent history was in Lituya Bay, Alaska on July 9, 1958. It was caused by an earthquake at the Fairweather Fault, which loosened about 30 million cubic meters (or 40 million cubic yards) of rock. These rocks plunged down from an altitude of 3,000 feet down into the water. Obviously, the impact generated a local mega-tsunami that crashed against the shoreline.

The wave, upon reaching shore, was an estimated 1,720 feet high! There were three fishing boats out on the water that day. One boat was destroyed and those on board perished. The other two boats rose up with the water; and those on board miraculously survived.

Will a mega-tsunami happen in the future? Some experts believe that there are a few places on earth, such as the Cumbre Veija Volcano (Canary Islands), might erupt, sending a giant mass of rock into the sea. Indeed, there are some who believe that this volcano (along with others throughout the world) is long overdue for an eruption. An immense tsunami will thus be unleashed, and will fan out all across the Atlantic Ocean at speeds of up to 500 MPH (800 KMPH)!

The other Canary Islands and the Wes Saharan shore would be destroyed the most. The Caribbean and Florida would be hit by waves of up to 50 meters (164 feet) waves. Brazil, Britain, France, Spain, and Portugal would also be affected by high waves. At its worst, this type of mega-tsunami would destroy everything in Boston, Miami, and New York. Even skyscrapers would be swept away is if they weren't there.

If something ever like this were to happen, there's nothing anyone could do to stop it. A huge asteroid could even crash into the sea, causing a mega-tsunami. Time will tell if the "worst case scenario" ever happens. Even if scientists are able to accurately predict when something is going to happen, will the nearby civilizations (millions of people) be able to evacuate before the mega-tsunami hits land? What if the lands are spared and the devastation isn't that bad? Is that a risk the governments of the world and millions of people are going to take?

The Mysterious Gelatinous Blobs

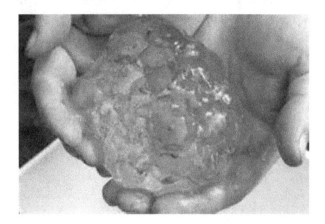

A small community in Washington is used to having rain, but on August 7, 1994, they had more than rain. The community only has a population of 665 people and it seemed that everyone became ill after the gelatinous blobs hit the ground.

It was raining blobs of goo and every one seen it. Were all these people wrong with what they saw? Did they experience gem welfare? Where did this gelatin goo come from? Since everyone in the small community of Oakville became ill with severe flu like symptoms, one only imagine what was in the blobs that fell to earth that day.

Twenty square miles of blobs. The community started becoming sick and no one knew why. One resident explained that his entire family got sick. Then everyone started hearing that everyone was getting sick. The "flu" lasted anywhere from seven week up to three months. The people of Oakville had no idea what was causing the sickness nor did they know what the gelatin blobs were or where they came from other than the sky. News of the torrential rains of blobs soon spread around the country. A police office was the first one to report something strange about the rains.

His windshield was all gooey and the wipers were making it all worst. The officer pulled into a gas station to wash his windows and then saw what was raining down on their little community. The officer said it felt like he had Jell-O or something like that in his hand. When the rains ended the next morning, one resident stepped out of her house to find these gelatin blobs everywhere. Some residents thought it might be left over hail, but that was not the case. What was the gooey substance that fell from the sky?

On the way to a hospital, one resident grabbed a sample of the blob because her mother had gotten sick shortly after going outside to see the blobs. The startling results of the tests on the blob is what shocked technicians. The blobs had white blood cells, human cells that is, but no one could identify the blob. The blob was sent to the State Department of Health in Washington for more testing. One technician found that the sample had two types of bacteria, one of which was known to be found in the human digestive system. What was this blob?

Six times over a three-week period, residents had blob rains. Animals died and people kept getting sick. Was this something that was dropped from a plane? Was the blob an animal nucleus cell as was thought by Microbiologist Time Davis of Amtest Labs? The Air Force denied any knowledge of the blobs. What do you think? Could it be a substance that was made by the military to use against other countries? Did they make it and need to test it on humans to see if it would work? The question stills remains, where did the blobs come from if the military denies knowledge.

Kaspar Hauser

The Mystery of a Strange Foundling – Who was Kaspar Hauser, who killed him and why was he killed?

Everything began on Whit Monday, 26th May 1828, at the Unschlittplatz in Nuremberg. There - at approximately 4 p.m. – a young man (later his age was assessed at 15 to 17) staggered into the arms of two journeymen. The two shoemaker journeymen thought that they had to deal with a drunkard and tried to draw information from the young man to bring him home. He only repeated one sentence: "I want to become a good horseman like my father has been." So the both considered on how the stranger could be helped. Finally he extracted an envelope and the both journeymen brought him to the mentioned address where the cavalry captain von Wessenig lived.

Sir von Wessenig arranged that the young lad was immediately taken to the police station. During an interrogation they tried to find out his name and further details. But the young man only uttered unintelligible sounds and wordings. Only when a police officer gave him a pen in his hand he wrote with difficulty, but nevertheless legible: "Kaspar Hauser".

It was determined to put the stranger under arrest in Castle Nuremberg so that he was able to sleep it off there. On the following days, they always tried to find more details of Kasper Hauser in conversations and interrogations, but except the already known sentence that he wanted to become a horseman, there was nothing to get out of him. After three months in prison, Kasper Hauser was handed over to high school professor Georg Friedrich Daumer so that he could care for the education and development of the foundling. In the house of Daumer Kaspar Hauser was well and he learned reading and writing very quickly, showed great interest in his environment and because of his enormous musical talent he took great pleasure in painting and drawing as well as playing the piano.

His positive development came to an abrupt end on 17th October 1829: A stranger attacked Kasper Hauser in Daumer's house and wounded him seriously but not perilous. This first assassination had been reason enough to remove Hauser from Daumer's domicile and to bring him to a safer place. In January 1830, Kasper moved in the house of the merchant and town council Biberach. Nearly half a year later, he was received in the house of his official guardian, Baron Gottlieb von Tucher. On 29th November 1831, he once again needed to pack his few things and at the bidding of his new guardian, Lord Stanhope, he had to move to Ansbach. Here he lived in the house of court president Anselm von Feuerbach until 10th December and later on stayed in the domicile of teacher Meyer. Feuerbach occupied Hauser at the court of appeal – opposite to Meyer's domicile – as a clerk of the court.

Kaspar Hauser accustomed himself well to Ansbach, even when his relation to teacher Meyer could be described as extremely strained. On 20th May 1833, Kaspar Hauser confirmed in the Schwanenritterkapelle (Swan-Knight Chapel) and in this year he also began to develop the first tender feeling for the daughter of the government president, Lila von

Stichaner. On 14th December 1833 a stranger lured him in the court garden because he wanted to find out something about Hauser's origin. Kaspar Hauser went alone to the court garden on that gloomy December Saturday and the stranger stabbed him down with a cut aimed at his breast. As a consequence of this severe wound, he died three days later, on 17th December 1833 at 10 p.m. in the domicile of teacher Meyer. Again three days later, on 20th December 1833, he was buried at the town cemetery with great sympathy of the population.

The question that has been moving the minds till today is: Who was Kaspar Hauser? From where did he come? Where was he before his appearance in Nuremberg? Essentially, there are two great camps in Kaspar Hauser- research. One camp says that he was a swindler and impostor who duped the whole world until nowadays. The others are convinced that Kaspar Hauser was the first-born son of the grand duke Karl of Baden and Stephanie Beauharnais.

Also the genetic investigations in 1996 could not present a final clarification of Kaspar Hauser's real origin. From that time on, it is only stated that the blood on Kaspar Hauser's clothing he wore on the day of his assassination has no conformity with the descendants of the sisters of the hereditary prince for whom Kaspar Hauser is taken.

In 2002, scientists of the Forensic Institute in Münster carried out another genetic analysis. They used six specimens of dead tissue materials (i.e. hair) and found out that their genetic code is not identical with the blood derived from Kaspar Hauser's pants. In comparison with it, the genetic conformity with the female descendants of Stephanie de Beauharnais is relatively high. A final scientific opinion is still overdue.

But what is the truth? Many questions will have to be clarified now: Why was the House of Baden so afraid of the foundling and why could the story of a foundling disturbing the balance of the European nobility so easily? Why was a spy appointed and why was the young man kept a prisoner? Why were three murderous attempts committed? It stays still obscure who the foundling was and by whom he was killed.

Hallucinations Or
Unexplained Mysterious People

In 1935, Rudolf Lake in Kenya would appear to be a paradise with its quiet lake sounds and nothing is heard but birds, but what lurks on the Island of Envaitenet may surprise you.

The meaning of the name of the island stands for "no return." No one lives on the island anymore. The island is considered cursed and no one will venture near it. It all started back many years before 1935 when islanders stopped coming to the mainland to trade their goods. Concerned as to why they were not coming to trade, two men took a boat ride to the island and what they saw scared them.

They saw no people, nor movement of any kind. All they saw were burnt out fires with decaying fish by them. They quickly left the island never to return again. In fact, no one has ever stepped foot on the island until two members of the Vivian Fush expedition decided to explore the island in 1935. Bill Dayson and Martin Sheflis when to the island of no return. True to its name, the scientist never returned. After fifteen days, no one came back from the island. A rescue team was sent to the island in search of the two men.

Unfortunately, no one was found. There was no sign of the men even being on the island. A plane was called to survey the island from above and nothing was found except for birds. The locals then told Vivian about what had happened to the islanders that once lived on the island. They said that the people vanished and have never been seen again.

Then there is the mysterious disappearing boy. He vanished in front of his family and returned to the same spot a couple of days later. Did they hallucinate his disappearance or is this another strange disappearance with a happy ending? Where did the boy go? Why is it that he could not tell them anything? Is there a force that is more powerful than anything else we know? How is it that people see a person disappear and reappear?

Who are these mysterious disappearing people and how did they vanish? One can only believe what they see, but what about seeing something so bizarre that you think you are losing your mind. Is there something taking people and keeping them for specimens. Because we hear about UFOs and unusual happenings, we have to believe that anything can be possible.

The mystery surrounding the disappearance of the people on the island and the two scientists may never be answered since anyone that goes to the island and stays, disappears and is never heard from again. How will we ever know what happens to people when they mysteriously disappear? We can only rely on years of research to answer these questions. Who as the answers if scientists do not even know what to think?

What would we find out if someone ever came back? Would we understand or would we choose not to believe?

Men In Black Mysteries

For most of the twentieth century, people have reported encounters with beings that have become known as the Men in Black.

Unlike the characters played by Will Smith and Tommy Lee Jones in the hit movies of the same name, these Men in Black do not appear to be of human origins. Men in Black, also known as MIBs, are associated with encounters with UFOs. Some individuals who have claimed to have seen or had a very up close experience with a UFO, or have claimed to have been abducted by extraterrestrial beings, have reported having been visited sometime later by these Men in Black. There have been various reports of MIB visits, mostly in America, but occasionally in several countries of Europe, areas of Australia and a few countries in South Africa.

MIBs are most often reported as having been dressed in black suits with white shirts, black ties, black dress shoes that have odd thick soles, black fedora type hats and wearing dark sunglasses, even at night. These strangers are also always reported as having threatened the people they visit to discourage the individuals from telling anyone about their experiences. Their skin is extremely pale white and faces are expressionless with thin lips; although some of the earliest reports say these "men" had swarthy complexions. They seem to move as though they are unused to their bodies--movements reported as being a bit "robotic".

It is widely accepted by many UFO researchers that one of the earliest cases of an MIB visit happened in September of 1953. A fellow by the name of Albert Bender, who lived in Bridgeport Connecticut at the time, and was an avid UFO researcher, reportedly had figured out some of the origins of "flying saucers", and told his ideas to a close friend in a letter he sent to his fellow UFO researcher. In about a week, three "men" dressed all in black, showed up on his doorstep with his letter in their possession. They apparently had a 'little talk' with Mr. Bender, and he became quite ill. Mr. Bender never told anyone what was told to him by these mysterious visitors and promptly gave up doing anymore UFO research.

According to the reports of people who have said they have encountered them, Men in Black always have very detailed information on the person, or persons they contact, as if they have had the particular individual under surveillance for a long time.

Many people have reported that these MIBs appear to be rather confused by the usage of normal everyday items such as basic ink pens, forks, spoons, knives, or even appearing not to understand how to eat food. They also report that these strange visitors will use slang terms from different time periods, such as the 18th and 19th centuries. More recent accounts state that the MIBs claim to be from some sort of government agency that is collecting information on the strange or supernatural phenomenon the particular person has encountered.

In other accounts these Men in Black are trying to suppress information by either by trying to convince the person the experience never happened or even resorting to threats of extreme physical violence when other methods fail. They have been described as behaving in a very secretive and suspicious manner or as being overtly "friendly"-- with creepy, wide, toothy grins and often breaking into weird, inappropriate giggling fits.

Much more often than not, these Men in Black will claim to be from the US Air force, or even the FBI or CIA. People who have encountered the MIBs say they will show some identification, but when the folks try to get verification of the credentials, the "agents" described often do not exist, have been dead for many years, or, if they do exist, they have a different rank and status in the afore mentioned organizations.

It has also been reported that these Men in Black often drive black vintage Buicks, Lincoln town cars, or Cadillacs. When witnesses do manage to get the license plate number of these vehicles and report them, it always comes back as having never been issued or no such license number exists.

Who are these mysterious strangers? Why are they among us? The mystery continues.

Mysteries of the Sliding Rocks

The Racetrack Playa, famous for the mystery of its moving rocks, sits Death Valley National Park. (A playa is the flat bottom of a desert basin that becomes a shallow lake every once in a while.)

In this extremely dry basin is a flat, bone dry lake known as Racetrack Playa. In this dry lake bed are stones, ranging from pebble sized rocks all the way up to boulders weighing over 700 lbs. These rocks, for reasons no one has been able to figure out or explain, move all by themselves across the dusty, cracked surface of the lake bed.

These rocks, which are usually hundreds of yards from any source area, move across this basin leaving tracks in the surface of the dry lake bed. The trails left by these rocks vary in the length, distance and direction. Some of the rock trails show signs of curving gently and slowly in any given direction while other will have made sharp, abrupt turns when changing direction. The majority of the trails seem to go in a south to north direction.

Many of these rocks have traveled distances of over 2 miles with no real discernible points of origin. Some of the rocks seem to have broken off the cliffs at the southern end of the playa, and moved towards the northern end. The nature of these trails have many scientists believing that the rocks' movements indicate that motion happens only when the playa surface is wet, however this has never been proven and many people doubt that the massive boulders in the playa could be moved by the fairly gentle winds that blow rather infrequently across the basin. The tracks left by the smallest rocks usually do not survive the rare rainfalls, while the tracks made by those massive boulders can last for as long as seven years.

Despite years of research and many investigations, no one has ever managed to witness the rocks moving. No one has ever been able to prove any of the numerous theories that have been suggested by many scientists either. Gravity has been long since ruled out of the equation because the rocks are moving ever so slightly uphill due to the fact that the northern end of the playa is a just few centimeters higher than the southern end of the playa.

When this strange and unique phenomenon was first discovered by white settlers around 1900, some educated observers had the idea that natural magnetic forces were the reason behind the movement of the rocks. In the late 20th and early 21st century, a few scientists believe they may have solved the mystery of the moving rocks of Racetrack Playa. They believe the movement occurs when one of the rare rains wets down the lake bed just enough to make a slick, sticky mud, and then a good strong wind which can get up to around 70 miles per hour on occasion, blows the rocks around. However, this theory does not explain how the very heavy boulders can move around due to the fact it would take a much stronger wind to move these huge rocks--nor, that in spite of long hours of patient observation during these rare wet times, no one has ever been able to observe the rocks moving.

So, what is the real reason behind the mysterious moving rocks of Racetrack Playa? Who knows? It may forever remain one of the wonderful, enduring mysteries of our world.

Marfa Lights

The Ghost lights of Marfa are still just as strange and mysterious as they were when they were first seen 126 years ago by the early settlers and the cowboys who drove their cattle herds into the Marfa area in 1883. When Robert Ellison came to Marfa in 1883 to drop off some of his cattle before driving more of the herd further on west, he never expected anything out of the ordinary was going to happen.

On his second night camping just outside of Paisano Pass, he saw some odd looking lights off in the distance. Ellison's first thought was that these lights could be the signal fires from a roving band of Apache warriors, and decided to investigate. Ellison saddled up and rode all over the countryside looking for the source of the mysterious lights. He found no Apaches, no fires, and no explanation for the lights. Many of the other settlers in the area told him that they had also seen the lights on many occasions and they too had never been able to identify their source.

The strange, unexplainable became known as the Marfa Lights because they always show up near the small town of Marfa, Texas. The town of Marfa has been a little ranching community that sits on the Chihuahuan desert plateau area of west Texas. Due to the now famous Marfa Lights, this small community that is surrounded by beautiful mountains now can add tourism to the list as a means of local community income.

Anyone who has seen the Marfa Lights says they range from 1 foot to 10 feet in size. They look like balls of reddish-orange light and have been reported with the ability to vary their size and move at very high speeds. There are plenty of documented photographs and video footage that show these unexplained lights in action.
There has never been a report of the Marfa Lights ever causing harm to anyone and there is a tale of these lights having helped save a man who got lost in a blizzard by keeping him warm and guiding him safely to his home.

The Marfa lights have appeared in various ways to folks. Sometimes splitting into multiple colored balls, or appearing to jump up and down. Anyone who has seen the lights will say that they will glow as gently as a candle or be as bright as a megawatt flood light. They have been observed to blink off and on like Christmas tree lights and have been known to follow people on occasion. There has never been a daytime sighting of the Marfa lights--which would seem to make it purely nighttime phenomenon.

There have been countless attempts by various scientists to explain this strange phenomenon, all to no avail. This is partly due to the fact that surround terrain is extremely treacherous and that the land is where these lights seem to dwell is private property. Over the years the ranch owners have become quite reluctant to allow any more people on their property and getting permission has become a bit more difficult due to the high amount of people requesting access.

What are these strange and mysterious lights? Where do they come from and where do they go?

Mysteries of Cannibalism

As one can see, the practice of cannibalism has been around since probably Mankind appeared on this blue ball we call Earth. The beginnings of cannibalism is shrouded in the mists of time and more than likely we will never find out its origins nor understand why some species, including humans, eat their own kind.

Many anthropologists speculate that cannibalism began in the very earliest beginnings of known human history, probably even before any records of human history were ever made, and grew with man's unending need to appease whatever gods were worshipped, to survive famine and stave off starvation, or any of a number of other theories that have been presented by various and sundry scientists. Archaeological evidence seems to show that cannibalism has been practiced at least as far back as the Neolithic Period and Bronze Age in the areas that eventually became known as Europe and North and South America.

In a book called Once Were Cannibals, the author Tim White stated that there was evidence found in Croatia that seemed to show that the indigenous Neanderthal tribes of the age practiced cannibalism. Many bones of Neanderthals discovered during an archaeological excavation apparently showed some evidence that this particular tribe of Neanderthals ate the brains of others of their kind. In Cannibalism and Archeology, the author gives some of the criteria archaeologists use to identify evidence of cannibalism from human remains found.

These "earmarks" include skulls showing hammering to expose the brain, severe facial mutilation, burnt or boiled bones, dismemberment, cut marks, bone breakage made by hammer stones, etc. Even though not all of the criteria was met when studying the bones archaeologists discovered in Croatia, main of the most crucial "earmarks" pointing to the practice of cannibalism were present, including crushed skulls and bones, fire damage showing evidence that these bodies had been roasted over a fire and skulls hammered open in order to remove the brain.

With the incredible wealth of archaeological and anthropological evidence that has been discovered in the countries of Africa, Australia, North and South America, the Middle East, and other parts of the world, all the evidence suggests the common frequency of cannibalistic practices is not nearly as uncommon as many people would think. The ideas and reasons behind the rather common practice of cannibalism vary from culture to culture, as well as being purely depended upon the type of situations that lead people to resort to cannibalism. This being said, there appears to be several types of cannibalism that are more prevalent in particular areas of the world and types that are dependent on certain situations.

In many parts of the world, anthropologists have discovered that many cannibalistic tribes have usually incorporated many different forms of cannibalism into their way of life. It is not at all uncommon for one particular culture or tribe to practice a mixture of ritualistic, endocannibalism and exocannibalism, as well as resorting to cannibalism for survival and what is known as epicurean/nutritional cannibalism, which is basically the consumption of human flesh purely for the taste or nutritional value.

As one can see, the practice of cannibalism has been around since probably Mankind appeared on this blue ball we call Earth, but the reasons behind it are still a mystery. A great many psychologists, psychiatrists, and other scientists have long sought for answers, and will continue to look for answers, behind the Mysteries of Cannibalism.

The Little Ice Age and The Year Without Summer

The Little Ice Age was a period of time when the climate cooled down considerably in many parts of the world, especially around the North Atlantic. There is some disagreement as to when exactly the Little Ice Age started, but most records indicate that the North Atlantic began cooling down a bit in the mid thirteenth century. The Little Ice Age apparently marked the end of the Medieval Warm Period. The Little Ice Age lasted for many centuries, and the temperatures began warming up again in the 1850's. There is also some suggestion that perhaps current global warming represents the world officially coming out of the Little Ice Age and entering into a new Warm Period.

Many strange events occurred during the Little Ice Age, especially in the year 1816 — The Year without a summer. The summer of 1816 brought severe cold and even snow storms to New England and eastern Canada. Crops were frozen, many people died, livestock died, and even birds froze in mid-flight and fell to the earth. There were even icy rivers and ponds found as far south as Pennsylvania. Why!? It is generally believed by experts that prior to the summer of 1816; there was an increase of volcanic eruptions, including a large eruption from Mount Tambora, which caused a large amount of volcanic dust to accumulate into the upper atmosphere. This obviously caused less heat from the sun to penetrate through the atmosphere.

The Year without a summer did have a positive impact on culture and art. Mary Shelley, for instance, ended up writing Frankenstein while she was trapped indoors that summer. She, John William Polidori, and their friends decided to have a writing contest. Lord Byron, inspired by the weather that summer, ended up writing his 1816 poem, Darkness. A man named Joseph Smith moved his family from Vermont to New York after dealing with crop failures, and ended up participating in a series of events that led up to the founding of the Church of Jesus Christ of Latter-Day Saints as well as the publication of the Book of Mormon.

Although it's believed by most mainstream scientists that the Little Ice Age ended around 1850, there are some who believe we're still recovering from it, and that global warming is not man-made. This theory is refuted by mainstream scientists claiming that while the Little Ice Age was mainly an epidemic in the North Atlantic, global warming—as the name suggests---is a worldwide problem
Could this happen again?

What happened at Hanging Rock?

In the evening, four of them had disappeared; three of them were never seen again. As swallowed by the earth - St. Valentine's Day in the year 1900 granted brilliant sunshine to the village of Woodend near Melbourne (Australia). On this day, the Applegate College usually undertook a school excursion in the nearer surrounding of the village. In the early morning, a group of schoolgirls with their teachers set out for a picnic to one of the famous outing places.

St. Valentine's Day in the year 1900 granted brilliant sunshine to the village of Woodend near Melbourne (Australia). On this day, the Applegate College usually undertook a school excursion in the nearer surrounding of the village. In the early morning, a group of schoolgirls with their teachers set out for a picnic to one of the famous outing places. In the evening, four of them had disappeared; three of them were never seen again.

According to the report, a group of schoolgirls with their teachers drove out for a picnic at Hanging Rock. This geological rock group of rocks and monoliths is several million years old and of volcanic origin. Around the turn of the century, it was a famous outing place.

The excursion group consisted of 19 girls, most of them were over 10 years old. They were accompanied by their two teachers, Diane de Poitiers and Greta McCraw. At Saturday morning, the group set out to a 7 kilometers far place. They ate there and dozed under the trees and rocks. Another picnic group camped a bit farther away. It consisted of the former colonel Fitzhubert, his wife, her nephew and the groom Albert Crundall.

At around 3 o'clock in the afternoon, three of the elder schoolgirls asked the French teacher for allowance to explore the rock.

The girls Irma Leopold, Marion Quade and Miranda X., all at the age of 17, had been known as reasonable and responsible. When they started, it was stated that the only two available watches within the group had stopped at noon. Finally, the 14 year old Edith Horton accompanied the other three girls as well.

The girls withdrew from the picnic area and disappeared out of sight at 3.30 p.m. The Fitzhubert family saw them passing by. The groom whistled after them and the nephew attempted to follow them what he gave up later on. The others dozed off at the picnic area. At 4.30 p.m., when the protégées were gathered again, the French teacher discovered that Miss McCraw was missing also. It was supposed that she followed the girls. The Fitzhuberts had already left at that time. A search had been organized. A trace of trampled farns leaded to the south side of the rock. But later, the beaten path was lost.

At 5.30 p.m., suddenly Edith Horton came staggering out of the thicket at the south-west side of the rock. She cried hysterically, but could not say what had happened. Of Miranda, Irma, Marion and Miss McCraw every trace was missing. The missing people were reported to the police. On the next day, a Sunday, started a huge systematical search.

In the meantime, Edith Horton had been examined by the physician from Woodend, Dr. MacKenzie. She suffered from a slight concussion of the brain. Her body was covered by several scratches and swellings, but no other injuries could be stated. Later on, in a questioning it came to her mind that she had met Miss McCraw on her way back and had seen how she ran towards the rock. The always so correct teacher was half stripped off her clothes and had not heeded Edith's calls. The police employed now a native scout and a bloodhound. Applied to Miss McCraw's scent, the hound followed a trace up the rock and on half height he stood for some minutes on a round platform, growling and with coat standing at end.

The police gave up the search. The nephew of the Fitzhuberts decided to spend a night alone on the rock. On the next day, Michael Fitzhubert was found undercooled, with sprained ankle and a hasty written note. He must have found something.

The search was taken up again and unexpectedly, Irma Leopold was found. She was unconscious, had several effusions of blood and smaller cuts on the head. Her fingernails were broken and torn, but there were no other injuries. When she woke up, she could not remember anything. Miranda, Marion and Miss McCraw had been never seen again. As a consequence, the schoolgirls were taken from Applegate College which had to be closed afterwards. A few months later, Mrs. Appleyard, the director, drove to the Hanging Rock. Her body was found underneath a ledge.

The mystery of Hanging Rock has produced endless speculations. One theory says that the girls had been abducted by an alien space-ship. Certainly, the rock is conspicuous enough to serve as an intergalactical flight mark. The presence of an UFO could also explain why the watches stood still. When she remembered to have met Miss McCraw, Edith Horton said, that a mysterious pink cloud was visible.

Another theory says that the girls were slipping into some kind of time travel and came out in the past or the future. This assumption refers strongly to the pink cloud. Christian Doppler and Albert Einstein assume that an object that withdraws at a very high speed will be perceived with a "red shifting", a distortion of the light spectrum. The cloud could point to Miss McCraw, disappearing in a time travel.

Further hypotheses proceed from a parallel universe, into which the girls had fallen. Or that they had been spirited away by the native forces of the rock.

So what really happened on that long passed Valentine's Day? By the way, there exist no proves that the event actually has happened.

The Unexplained Mysteries of Dark Matter

Nobody knows what exactly the Dark Matter is! However now, scientists might be able to have a clue what they need to do or where they need to look, if they wanted to conduct a research on it. It is invisible and you cannot identify its presence in the universe. However, researchers know that it's there, as you cannot find appropriate regular matter, in the form of stars, planets, dust and gas, for holding galaxies and the clusters of galaxy together. Some type of invisible (unseen) material, which can be dubbed as dark matter, has to be there that is making them glued to one another.

So How Will You Find Something That Is Not Visible To Your Senses? A new computer imitation of the evolution of galaxy (similar to our Milky Way) is suggesting that it might is possible for observing high-energy gamma rays, which are given off by these dark matters.

Simon White, who is the Director of Max Planck Institute for Astrophysics, has said, 'The calculations brought about by the computer imitation finally has allowed us to come to a conclusion what the Dark Matter distribution can look like, when it is in vicinity of the Sun. There, we might have a chance to detect it.'

White is a member of the International Virgo Consortium. This consortium of Durham University is a team of scientists, which also include cosmologists. The findings of this consortium have been given in details the November 6 2008 issue of 'Nature'.

Previous studies on the issue have given an indication that Dark Matter played a crucial role in the galaxy formation. According to the studies, it was also revealed that this mystery material still continues to hang around in halos surrounding galaxies.

The new computer simulation observed how dark matter halos could have evolved and behaved. The halo of virtual galaxy grew through series of violent mergers and collisions in between smaller clumps of dark matter, which emerged from Big Bang Theory (Theoretical beginning of our Universe).

The computer simulation revealed that gamma-rays, which are produced when particles had collisions in areas having high density of dark matter, could be easily detected when they were present in areas of Milky Way that was close to the Sun.

Carlos Frank, who is the director of the Institute for Computational Cosmology of Durham University, feels that 'Search for this dark matter has been dominating cosmology for several decades now and its high time that we should do something concrete in this regard'.

Scientists researching in Durham University and other top institutions have figured out that Fermi Telescope of NASA should search in this area of the galaxy. It is the only available instrument in the Universe that can discover the signature glow of this dark matter.

Let us see, how long does it take for the top scientists in the world to uncover this truth and how much in depth they can go!

The Knights Templar Curse and Friday the 13ᵗʰ

After the crusades, they came back to France and England and worked as "bankers" of sorts. And then, for whatever reason(s), they were eventually accused of being heretics and executed.
The Knights Templar has always been surrounded by mystery. The only facts that we can gather about them were that they were Christian Knights who escorted pilgrims to the Holy Land and fought in the crusades.

It has been believed that the day the Pope and the King ordered them to be arrested was October 13th, 1307—a Friday. After their arrest, they were all brutally tortured and forced to "confess" such sins as: spitting on the Cross, worshipping "false gods", worshipping the "devil", homosexuality, and sodomy. Considering they were being tortured, they most likely just stated anything in order to for the torture to stop.

One by one they were killed, and seven years later, in the year 1314, the Grand Master of the Knights Templar himself, Jacques de Molay was finally executed. According to legend, his last words on Earth before burning to death consisted of a curse. He allegedly cried out to the Pope, Clement V, and King Philip IV, telling them that they both "will die themselves within a year." They did. Pope Clement V died just one month later and King Philip IV met his fate seven months after that.

As for the real reason or reasons why the Knights Templar was executed, nobody knows for sure. It would appear that King Philip IV didn't like them earning so much wealth and land from being bankers, and felt that their greed was getting out of control. It's possible that he didn't like all of the power and influence that they had obtained. He himself was even owed them money. Perhaps he put pressure on the Pope to accuse them of heresy. The Pope himself could have felt anger toward them for losing control of Jerusalem during the Crusades.

Of course there are some theories that the Knights Templar had a very important secret that they were trying to hide, and that there were much deeper conspiracies involved. It has been theorized that they perhaps found long lost, secret knowledge that would shake the foundations of Christianity. They were trying to protect and preserve the knowledge of this secret so that they Pope couldn't have it destroyed.

Even after Grand Master Jacques de Moly burned at the stake, some believe that the Knights Templar continued to live on in secret. In Scotland, for instance, is believed by some that Robert the Bruce was a Knights Templar member, and that they existed in secret in other European countries as well. Some still believe that the Knights Templar live on today, and that they are still protecting some sort of secret knowledge and/or treasure.

Is Planet X Really on Its Way Here?

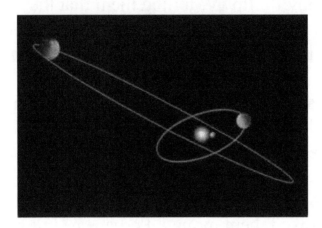

The ancient Babylonians believed Nibiru to be associated with their god Marduk. Nibiru was believed to be a "celestial body" that is usually identified as Jupiter—although there are some who believe Nibiru to be the mysterious "Planet X." The word itself is translated to "Planet of the crossing," and there are those who believe that it crossed here from another Solar System before finally stabilizing itself. It allegedly came here from beyond Pluto. Of course mainstream scientists dismiss such claims as "pseudoscience" and "woo," but there are still those who believe in the legends of Nibiru.

According to Zecharia Sitchin, author of the book The Twelfth Planet, Nibiru's orbit is "highly elliptical," which causes it to go from beyond the orbit of Pluto to as near as the asteroid belt between the orbits of Mars and Jupiter. According to Sitchin, Nibiru completes one orbit cycle every 3,600 years, and it supposedly disrupts the asteroid belt and causes a lot of trouble. Whenever it comes close enough to Earth, it unleashes chaos in every sense of the word — volcano eruptions, tsunamis, vast flooding, hurricanes, pole shifting—you name it. There are many who believe Nibiru is once again heading this way.

So why can't we see it? It's theorized that Nibiru's current position in space cannot be seen from us here on Earth. If the ancients truly believed in it, they must have been able to physically see it at some point. Unfortunately it would appear that by the time they saw it, it was close enough to bring destruction. Humans did exist and flourish 3,600 years ago, so we can only assume we'll survive the catastrophe this time as well, right? But if Nibiru is truly as unstable as some believe, what if it comes closer to us this time or crashes into us completely!?

When it comes down to it, there really isn't evidence of Nibiru or any such "rouge planet" existing at all. The ancient Sumerians did have cryptic writings about their god Marduk and his "collision" with Tiamet — which is said to have been their name for Earth, but what does that have to do with an invisible, rouge planet bringing along the apocalypse in current times? Isn't there sufficient evidence that the ancients simply referred to Jupiter as Nibiru?

Whether you believe that there is sufficient evidence of Nibiru and that it's heading this way or not, the myths and tales surrounding it are very intriguing. Even if there really is a Planet X that is heading this way, there isn't anything we could do about it. While it's nice to speculate and debate, in the end there's nothing we could ever do to stop such a large object from heading this way. There are other large objects such as asteroids that are more likely to destroy us, but there's no use worrying about any of it. While it's perhaps scary to think that someday this world could be destroyed forever, it will happen sooner or later.

The Unexplained Mysteries of Cattle Mutilations

The cattle mutilation mystery is gruesome, strange, and sad. Thousands of cattle have been found strangely mutilated in many places over the years, especially North America. Not only are the poor cows mutilated, but all of their blood is found drained and their organs have been removed from their bodies. There have been many instances when their reproductive organs have been surgically removed.

If their brutal murders aren't strange enough, there is no evidence of anybody ever being there when it happens! No footprints can be found anywhere near the dead cattle, and sometimes there is even evidence that the cattle could have been taken elsewhere and killed and then later brought back to the area they're discovered. As with most strange, modern day anomalies, there are also UFO and Men in Black sightings that take place around those areas where the mutilated cows are found.

Of course when the phenomenon first began in 1973, the killings were blamed on "satanic cults." Over the decades thousands of poor cows have been mutilated and many more theories have surfaced as to what could be the cause, ranging from strange government chemical testing to extraterrestrials. There has also been speculation that it could even be the work of vampires!

As with all strange, paranormal mysteries, there are skeptics. Skeptics believe that the cows probably died ordinary deaths and blame the strangeness surrounding the deaths on mass paranoia and delusion. Even if the cattle were, for instance, killed by other animals, why would all of their blood be gone? And why would other animals take the time to take out specific organs?

Unfortunately, we may never know the answers to these questions. The most likely theory for believers is that extraterrestrial could somehow be involved because of all UFO and black helicopter sightings around the times the mutilations take place. The only thing that we all know for certain though, is that 10,000 innocent cattle have been brutally mutilated for no logical reason(s) during the last 35 years.

Astronomers vs. Astrologers

What We Are Talking about Laymen says that astronomers are professional sky watchers. However, they are more than mere sky watchers. As scientists, they analyze the movement and make-up of the satellites, stars and planets in relation to the sun. They record changes in form, shape, position and movement.

It is understandable that their work is mathematical and scientific which is the opposite of the astrologer. The astrologer predicts future events by interpreting the astronomer's records of the elements of the skies and applying them to present and future events on earth. Simply put, astrology is both an art and a science of life cycles. Astrologers use predictive charts to forecast your future by studying planets and signs of the zodiac.

Astrologers study patterns and relationships between the planets in motion, our birth chart and the interaction of known elements. Since astronomers have discovered new planets near and beyond Pluto, the art and science of astrology is being turned on its ear.

Astrology is believed to be a product of the modern era. However, it had formerly been challenged by Hellenistic skeptics, church authorities and the medieval Muslim astronomers. The study of astrology is one method that can be used to explore our inner self, various relationships and our space in this universe.

About those Charts

Astrology and its branches involve the study of movements and positions of celestial bodies and the possible influence of them on human affairs. The end product of these studies is a horoscope or an astrological chart. Charts are prepared by astrologers based on exact moments and exact places on earth. There are several studies that show people will use selective thinking to interpret any chart in a favorable light fitting preconceived notions about themselves.

What is a birth chart and why is it important? A birth chart is your actual astrological chart based upon the minute of your birth, not the day of your birth. The astrologer will weigh the elements in the chart and determine which behaviors will be stronger and which will be weaker. Although not a crystal ball, many astrologers believe that a birth chart rendering a successful reading should be attributed to intuition or some psychic ability. The truth is that astrology can appear to be scientific at times, based on rules and regulations. Others say it is clearly an art, dependent on the astrologer's creative reading of the chart.

Stars, Planets, Horoscopes and Your Future

Horoscopes are a form of sun-sign astrology. This is the astrology that forms the basis for newspaper horoscopes. A horoscope is a prepared forecast based on the twelve signs of the zodiac. Horoscopes are hand drawn. There is no known computer model that will prepare a horoscope correctly. Simple math and geometry are the only calculations performed when casting a horoscope. They help to determine the apparent position of heavenly bodies on a certain date and time based on tables drawn by astronomers.

The horoscope is divided into twelve unique celestial houses governing different areas of life. Using cosmic shortcuts, some deep meanings can be extracted from the symbols in your horoscope thus making the cast horoscope easier to interpret. Two people with the same horoscope cannot be expected to grow up identically. Astrology does not acknowledge experience and free choice.

Being born on the same day as someone else, or even on the same day of the same year, does not make your horoscope the same. Supernatural powers are not needed to cast a horoscope. Most of it is done according to precise astronomical and mathematical principles. Many years of study still render different opinions among astrologers about the casting of a horoscope and the interpretation of results. A horoscope can be cast and read by different astrologers on the same day and get different predictions, interpretations, or suggestions.

A thorough exploration of your horoscope might be a profound experience in personal validation and self-awareness. Much like the manual of a car, the horoscope reading shows the potential you could achieve when standing at the starting line.

Twelve Signs of the Zodiac

Most people know about their astrological "sign," which is one of the 12 constellations of the zodiac. This is sun-sign astrology, the astrology that are found in the daily newspapers. Astrologers check the sign to see which planet was in the sign at the time of birth.

In astrological terms, the movements of the planets are interpreted for significance as they transit through space and through sun signs. Astrologers note these constellations and attached a particular significance to them. Over time, a system was developed that focused on twelve signs of the zodiac (Aries, Taurus, Gemini, Cancer, Leo, Virgo, Libra, Scorpio, Sagittarius, Capricorn, Aquarius, and Pisces). Each is based on one of the twelve constellations that are considered particularly important.

Actually, there should be 13 signs, not just 12. Thirty days is the correct time interval between the emergences of each sign. Adhering to this time interval would mean an enhancement of a 13th sign presently remaining on the sidelines, Ophiuchus.

Many claims made about signs and personalities are vague and could apply to a wide range of people as well as many different signs. Even professional astrologers, most of whom have only disdain for sun sign astrology, claim only a percent of a chance in making correct horoscope readings.

Today's astrologers have not become any more effective at predicting specific and/or significant events. This problem is to be expected when the entire human population is divided into a simplistic system of only 12 categories. Astronomers maintain that there is nothing wrong with studying predictive powers of astrological signs. They point out that the problem lies in concluding that astrological signs actually HAVE predictive powers.

About those Charts Astrology and its branches involve the study of movements and positions of celestial bodies and the possible influence of them on human affairs. The end product of these studies is a horoscope or an astrological chart. Charts are prepared by astrologers based on exact moments and exact places on earth. There are several studies that show people will use selective thinking to interpret any chart in a favorable light fitting preconceived notions about themselves.

What is a birth chart and why is it important? A birth chart is your actual astrological chart based upon the minute of your birth, not the day of your birth. The astrologer will weigh the elements in the chart and determine which behaviors will be stronger and which will be weaker. Although not a crystal ball, many astrologers believe that a birth chart rendering a successful reading should be attributed to intuition or some psychic ability. The truth is that astrology can appear to be scientific at times, based on rules and regulations. Others say it is clearly an art, dependent on the astrologer's creative reading of the chart.

Stars, Planets, Horoscopes and Your Future

Horoscopes are a form of sun-sign astrology. This is the astrology that forms the basis for newspaper horoscopes. A horoscope is a prepared forecast based on the twelve signs of the zodiac. Horoscopes are hand drawn. There is no known computer model that will prepare a horoscope correctly. Simple math and geometry are the only calculations performed when casting a horoscope. They help to determine the apparent position of heavenly bodies on a certain date and time based on tables drawn by astronomers.

The horoscope is divided into twelve unique celestial houses governing different areas of life. Using cosmic shortcuts, some deep meanings can be extracted from the symbols in your horoscope thus making the cast horoscope easier to interpret. Two people with the same horoscope cannot be expected to grow up identically. Astrology does not acknowledge experience and free choice. Being born on the same day as someone else, or even on the same day of the same year, does not make your horoscope the same. Supernatural powers are not needed to cast a horoscope. Most of it is done according to precise astronomical and mathematical principles. Many years of study still render different opinions among astrologers about the casting of a horoscope and the interpretation of results. A horoscope can be cast and read by different astrologers on the same day and get different predictions, interpretations, or suggestions. A thorough exploration of your horoscope might be a profound experience in personal validation and self-awareness. Much like the manual of a car, the horoscope reading shows the potential you could achieve when standing at the starting line.

Twelve Signs of the Zodiac Most people know about their astrological "sign," which is one of the 12 constellations of the zodiac. This is sun-sign astrology, the astrology that are found in the daily newspapers. Astrologers check the sign to see which planet was in the sign at the time of birth. In astrological terms, the movements of the planets are interpreted for significance as they transit through space and through sun signs.

Astrologers note these constellations and attached a particular significance to them. Over time, a system was developed that focused on twelve signs of the zodiac (Aries, Taurus, Gemini, Cancer, Leo, Virgo, Libra, Scorpio, Sagittarius, Capricorn, Aquarius, and Pisces). Each is based on one of the twelve constellations that are considered particularly important. Actually, there should be 13 signs, not just 12. Thirty days is the correct time interval between the emergences of each sign. Adhering to this time interval would mean an enhancement of a 13th sign presently remaining on the sidelines, Ophiuchus.

Many claims made about signs and personalities are vague and could apply to a wide range of people as well as many different signs. Even professional astrologers, most of whom have only disdain for sun sign astrology, claim only a percent of a chance in making correct horoscope readings. Today's astrologers have not become any more effective at predicting specific and/or significant events. This problem is to be expected when the entire human population is divided into a simplistic system of only 12 categories. Astronomers maintain that there is nothing wrong with studying predictive powers of astrological signs. They point out that the problem lies in concluding that astrological signs actually HAVE predictive powers.

The Unexplained Mysteries Of The Miracles Of Lourdes

The unsolved mystery of the miracles of Lourdes has been known for hundreds of years. The story starts when a fourteen-year-old girl saw the Virgin Mary appear to her eighteen times. The girl was given a message by the aspiration. She was told to tell everyone to pray and do penance for the conversion of the world. The girl's story was investigated for four years before the church approved the devotion to Our Lady of Lourdes. This is one of the most famous shines in the world. Thousands of cures have come forth when people visit the shine. Is this truly a location and shine that can magically cure people?

Doctors who are non-believers as well as believers have all tested the cures through examinations. A movie was even made about event. It is said that spiritual and moral cures are more powerful than physical cures. Many have said that they visited Lourdes with prejudices and have left with their souls and minds suddenly cleared. There are two incredible stories pertaining to the Lourdes that make you wonder about the power of the shine. The stories are unbelievable, but the one is told to be very true and authentic.

The first story is about Gabriel Gargam. He was a devoted Catholic and had promise of becoming a very intuitive student. At the age of fifteen, he lost his faith in God. Gabriel went to work at the post office. In 1899, a horrific train accident left Gabriel paralyzed from the waist down. He lay in a hospital bed unable to take care of himself and dropped his weight to a mere seventy-eight pounds. He was watched twenty-four hours a day. Gabriel was to live this way until his aunt insisted he go to Lourdes. Before the accident, Gabriel had not been to church for fifteen years.

Taking Gabriel to Lourdes required taking him on a train that caused loss of consciousness and almost canceled the trip. The trip was still made to Lourdes. Gabriel received Holy Communion and had confession with no change. He was then taken to the miracle pool and placed into the waters. Nothing happened. They thought he had died and were taking him back to the hotel with his faced covered when he suddenly sat up. He then announced in his strong voice that no one had heard for years that he wanted to get up.

Six doctors examined Gabriel and could not find out what had cured him. He was no longer paralyzed or within inches of death. He was walking around and healthy as the day he was born. He went on to help other invalids that came to Lourdes. He was cured and only God knew for sure how this happened. He had no faith, but still this miracle gave him back life. Was this a real miracle? Is it possible that there is a spiritual connection at the Lourdes? Stories would have one believe that anyone can be cured at the Lourdes.

The Unsolved Mystery Of Jeannie Saffin

Jean Saffin sat at her kitchen table eating with her father when her body burst into flames. Was this a case of deliberate torching or is her father correct when he said that he saw a bright light out of the corner of his eye and looked to see his daughter on fire. Spontaneous Human Combustion has been documented, but others have not seen it until Jennie's father witnessed this phenomenal sight.

In 1982, September 15th, Jennie and her father were seated for dinner at the kitchen table. Jennie Saffin was 61 years old when she suddenly burst into flames mainly around the hands and face. Her father rushed to help her and tried to extinguish the flames by dousing her with water from the kitchen sink. Jennie died at the hospital eight days later of severe burns to her body. Her father had severe burns on his hands from trying to help his daughter.

Investigators at the scene could not find any evidence to the contrary of what Jennie's father had said. The room did not have any signs of burning or charring. The only charring was on Jennie Safin's body. Investigators were dumbfound and confused as to what happened to Jennie that cool day in London England. How was this possible that a woman sitting at her kitchen table suddenly burst into flames? Why did she remain calm as her father stated? Investigators needed answers.

Investigators looked at every angle and still had no answer as to why this woman burst into flames. Nothing around her was burnt. How was it possible for this woman to burn so severely and not leave behind any other signs of a fire? Investigators looked at the death scientifically and came away with more questions. Did Jennie Saffin drink alcoholic beverages? Did she have a poor diet that could have caused a chemical reaction in the body? Did she have flammable body fat? Was her 82-year-old father telling the truth?

Today the death of Jennie Saffin is still an unsolved mystery that leaves one to believe that she did indeed become a statistic of Spontaneous Human Combustion. Other people have been linked to this phenomenal occurrence as early as 1957 when Anne Martin aged 68, was found burnt so severely, no one could identify her. Anne was from Pennsylvania. Does age have something to do with this occurrence?

The fire did not touch newspapers found just a couple of feet from Anne's body. No evidence of a fire was seen anywhere in the house except on Anne's body. Investigators in this case were as mystified as everyone who has heard about this rare and unusual happening. Who or what is responsible for Anne and Jennie bursting into flames. Is there a higher source involved? Is this type of death beyond our control?

You be the judge. How is it possible that two people with nothing more in common than possibly a close age range and gender, just burst into flames and not burn anything else? Why did Anne Martin's shoes not burn? Investigators are stumped as to why Jennie and Anne are dead from fire.

The Shroud of Turin

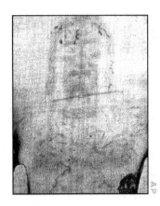

During the mid-1350's pilgrims by the thousands flocked to Lirey, France, to catch a rare glimpse of what was believed by many to be the sacred burial cloth of Jesus Christ. Pilgrims were convinced that the adored object of worship was authentic because the linen bore a faintly visible front and posterior image of a crucified and tortured man resembling a medieval representation of Jesus. The famed knight Geoffroy de Charny owned the famous linen cloth, which he proudly exhibited at the local church, Our Lady of Lirey.

Although Geoffroy's shroud was accepted as genuine by most, some were highly skeptical of its origin and validity. One of the earlier and more vocal skeptics of the shrouds authenticity was a man named Pierre dArcis, the Bishop of Troyes. Based on evidence collected during an investigation initially launched by the previous bishop Henri de Portiers and then taken up by his successor dArcis, there was reason for them to believe that the shroud was a fake.

In a letter to the Pope written in 1389, dArcis stated that Geoffroy falsely and deceitfully... procured for his church a certain cloth which had been cunningly painted, and pretended that it was the actual shroud in which our Savior Jesus Christ was enfolded in the tomb. It was suggested that the shroud was the centerpiece of an elaborate marketing campaign launched by Geoffroy, and intended to drive up the sales of accompanying souvenirs he sold to the masses for a substantial profit. According to dArcis, the shroud was the work of human skill, and the identity of the person who forged the shroud had been established, although his name was never mentioned.

The allegations were the first known mention of fraud concerning the shroud. At the time it was written Geoffroy had already been dead for thirty-three years. The reason dArcis pursued the matter well after the knights death was because by the 1380's the shroud was being exhibited for profit by Geoffroy's son, who bore the same name.

According to Joe Nickell's book, *Inquest on the Shroud of Turin,* Geoffroy II went to great lengths to circumvent dArcis in an attempt to get consent to display the shroud. Nickell wrote that Geoffroy II deliberately went over the bishop's head by appealing to the cardinal for permission, which was eventually granted. Moreover, he reported that Geoffroy II downplayed his claims made at earlier exhibitions that the shroud was authentic.

Despite dArcis appeals to King Charles VI of France and Pope Clement VII, Geoffroy II was granted permission to exhibit the shroud. However, the pope instituted restrictions that included prohibiting Geoffroy II from displaying the shroud as a holy relic. He decreed that every time it was displayed in public, the exhibitor had to inform onlookers that the shroud was not the actual burial garment of Jesus, and contained only an artistic rendition of his face.

Geoffroy II obeyed the limitations and continued to display the shroud to thousands of pilgrims who congregated to see the mystifying cloth. Following Geoffroy IIs death, it was handed down to his granddaughter, Margaret. She ensured the shrouds place in history by fostering rumors that the shroud was indeed genuine. Most believed that, although the church never recognized the cloth as sacred.

Margaret de Charny

During the early part of the 15th century, Margaret asked the canons of Lirey for permission to remove the shroud from the church so that she could relocate it to Montfort castle, where she and her second husband Humbert of Villersexel, the Count of La Roche, both resided. According to historical accounts, Margaret feared the shroud was under threat by the ongoing war and thought it better to keep it near her. After all, it was a family heirloom, once owned by her grandfather and she believed she had a right to protect it.

The church eventually gave permission for Margaret to take possession of the shroud, which she did in 1418. Margaret's husband ensured the church that the cloth would be immediately returned once the threat had passed. Although the shroud was initially kept at the castle, it was eventually moved to St. Hippolyte and housed at the chapel des Buessarts, located on the banks of the Doubs River. According to Ian Wilsons *The Blood and the Shroud,* the cloth was displayed annually in the Pre du Seigneur meadow near the river, which attracted a small cult of shroud worshippers.

In 1438, Margaret's husband, Count Humbert, was killed in battle. Five years after his death, at the end of the war, Margaret failed to fulfill the promise her husband had made to the church in Lirey concerning the return of the shroud. Nickell wrote that Margaret instead took the cloth on tour, holding exhibitions in the diocese of Liege in Belgium, and as far as Geneva, Switzerland.

Some historians have said that Margaret fostered rumors that the shroud was authentic so she could better profit from the exhibitions. Other historians rebuffed the claim, arguing that historical evidence indicates she was upfront about the cloth not being authentic, but merely a representation of Jesus Christ. Regardless of whether she marketed the shroud as the real thing or not, she earned a substantial amount of money from her tour and gained the attention of some in the upper class, including the Duke and Duchess of Savoy.

On several occasions, Duke Louis I and his wife Duchess Anne showed an intense interest in the cloth. In 1453 they offered to buy it. Margaret eventually accepted their offer, and was given a castle near Lyon, France, and a substantial amount of money. The Lirey canons were so enraged when they learned that Margaret had sold the shroud that they threatened to excommunicate her unless she returned the cloth or paid them compensation.

In 1460, Margaret died without ever fulfilling her obligation to the church. Following her death, the Lirey church made a last attempt to collect the money, this time from the Savoy family who were in possession of the shroud. According to an article by Ian Wilson, *Highlights of the Undisputed History,* the duke agreed to pay the church compensation in the form of an annual rent in exchange for keeping the shroud.

However, it lasted only as long as the duke. By the time he died in 1465 and passed the shroud down to his son, Duke Amadeus IX, the annual rent to the church had ceased. Most of the money meant for the Lirey church likely went instead into the building of a magnificent chapel specifically intended to house the shroud.

After all, the shrouds popularity had grown significantly. Not only did most people accept it as authentic, but many believed it had magical properties, a rumor instigated by the Savoy family. The shroud was now unofficially considered to be a holy relic, a view that would hold for centuries.

A Most Cherished Relic

After being taken on tour and exhibited throughout Europe for more than 150 years, the shroud was given a new and semi-permanent home in 1502. The Savoy family had built the Sainte Chapelle at Chambery, specially constructed to house the sacred relic. Initially, the cloth was displayed on the high altar within the chapel. It was eventually relocated to an altar at the rear of the chapel and enclosed behind iron bars for security.

Approximately four years after the shroud was placed in its new home, the chapel was officially renamed the Sainte Chapelle of the Holy Shroud. The renaming was a momentous occasion that attracted royalty and dignitaries of the time. However, the highlight of the event was not just the chapel, which was decorated in an ornate fashion befitting the relic, but the holy shroud itself.

In fact, the shroud was so revered that European kings and queens requested private exhibitions to view what was believed to be one of the most venerated objects in Christendom. Moreover, the shroud was often brought out and displayed during royal weddings and funerals. It was likely used to sanctify the event, which usually lead to increased public approval.

With the exception of special events and tours, the shroud remained in the chapel for more than three decades, safe from the ravages of war and plundering armies. However, it was not secure from the threat of fire. In 1532 a blaze broke out in the chapel. Members of the church rushed to save it from almost certain destruction, risking their lives in the process.

The shroud escaped ruin, suffering only a burn stain left by molten silver that dropped onto it from the melted chest in which it lay. According to Harry Goves book, *Relic, Icon or Hoax: Carbon Dating the Turin Shroud,* nuns repaired the damage by sewing 16 patches onto the damaged area to strengthen the cloth.

The Relic on Tour

Over the next 100 years, the cloth spent less and less time at the Sainte Chapelle of the Holy Shroud. It was frequently taken on tour throughout Europe and exhibited to worshipers who believed the image on the cloth was of divine origin. The shroud spent a great deal of time being displayed throughout Italy, where there was great demand for it.

Between 1537 and 1561, the shroud was moved to various safe houses, convents and churches in the country, including Vercelli, Italy, and Nice, France, to prevent it from being plundered by French invading troops. Eventually, in 1561 the shroud was returned to the Sainte Chapelle of the Holy Shroud in Chambery and kept concealed within an iron box, except when it was displayed for special occasions. However, the shroud did not remain at the chapel for long.

In 1578, duke Emanuel Philibert of Savoy, who was at the time in possession of the shroud, decided to move the relic permanently to Turin. Nickell wrote that the duke made the transfer because Turin made a far more suitable capital for the expanded Savoy realm than Chambery. According to an article written by John Booker Feister, *Shroud of Turin: The Mystery Remains,* the saintly Cardinal Charles Borromeo walked from Milan to Turin that same year to venerate the shroud. Apparently, the cardinal was so moved by the holy image that he actually wept at the sight of it.

The shroud continued to be displayed to worshippers for many decades. Crowds at the exhibition sometimes swelled to tens of thousands of enthusiastic pilgrims and locals. Wilson wrote that during an exhibition in 1647, some of the enormous crowd died of suffocation. Such massive turnouts were more the norm than the exception at the exhibitions. It appeared that time did nothing to diminish the growing faith in the Holy Shroud.

In 1694, the shroud was placed in its permanent home at the Cathedral of St. John the Baptist in Turin. According to Gove, the shroud was, stored in an ornate silver chest inside a wooden box behind a metal grill with three locks that was located within a black marble chapel at the rear of the cathedral. There it would remain for centuries. It would only be taken out and displayed several times each century, usually for special events such as marriages, coronations and private showings to VIPs.

The shroud gained unprecedented attention two centuries later, in 1898, following a public exhibition. That year marked the reemergence of the debate into the authenticity of the shroud, which occupied scholars, historians, religious bodies and scientists for more than 100 years.

The Astounding Photograph

The last exhibition of the shroud during the 19th century was held over an eight-day period in Turin during May 1898. At the time of the exposition, the King Umberto I of Italy, who had inherited the shroud from his forefathers, granted permission for an amateur photographer named Secondo Pia to take pictures of his holy heirloom. After several attempts and failures, Pia managed to successfully photograph the shroud. He had made two exposures, which he developed in his darkroom, shortly after they had been shot.

According to Nickell, Pia was so surprised by the results that, he almost dropped the plate that was used in developing the photograph. During the developing process, Pia realized that the negative photographic plate revealed an almost 3-D-like image that was much clearer and lifelike than what was actually visible on the shroud itself. Thus, the negative plate exposed details of the image on the shroud that were difficult to see with the naked eye.

Shroud, negative

The negative print caught the attention of scientists around the world. They were baffled by the unusual contrasting images and the clarity of the negative print compared to its positive form. Intriguingly, the photograph launched the first modern scientific investigation into the origin and structural makeup of the shroud and the image it bore. It also launched a debate that would pit some of the world's leading experts against one another in an attempt to determine the shrouds authenticity.

Two years after the exhibition, the shroud came under its harshest criticism since the 14th century. According to a scholarly French priest named Cyr Ulysse Chevalier, who was an expert on the Middle Ages and the author of several renowned books, the shroud was undoubtedly fake. His conclusions were based on documented evidence that he was able to amass over a period of years.

Chevalier assembled an impressive collection of 50 documents believed to be the first ever known concerning the existence of the shroud. Many of the documents were contracts, receipts, decrees, reports and letters written by such people as the Bishop dArcis, Pope Clement VII and members of the de Charny family. Chevalier learned of the first investigation launched by Bishop Henri de Poitiers and other theologians who discredited the shroud as a fake in the early 14th century. He also discovered that Poitiers successor, Bishop dArcis, continued the investigation, finding further verification that the shroud was a fraud.

The most impressive evidence he discovered was a document by dArcis that claimed that the shroud artist had been found and actually confessed to painting the image onto the cloth.

Unfortunately, the name of the apparent forger was never revealed, a fact that later led to the story being discredited by believers. Many asked, if the forger existed, why had they not revealed his name? Others believe that the document speaks for itself, supporting the theory that the shroud is merely a representation of a man resembling what some believe to be Christ and nothing more.

The debate over the origin and authenticity of the shroud steadily increased over the years. Many scientific investigations were carried out to get to the heart of the matter. Moreover, many scientific papers were written on the subject relating to the different theories concerning the structural make-up and image on the shroud. Most scientists took one of three prominent views; they either believed that the shroud was a divine creation or that the image was man made or that it was a natural phenomenon. The Shroud of Turin was without a doubt a mystery that challenged faith, science and understanding, one that rekindled mans inquisitive nature in a search for an explanation.

Early Theories

Over the subsequent one hundred years, there was a rash of scientists who were eager to understand how the negative-like image of the crucified man appeared on the cloth. There had been no evidence of such a negative-like image in existence that matched that on the shroud. In an attempt to understand how it could have been produced, scientists tested many of their assumptions hoping that the results would provide some clue into the origin of the shroud. However, the testing of the theories and their results were more problematic than initially expected. In fact, the investigations raised more questions than they did answers, further facilitating the mystery surrounding the shroud.

Vignon, a French biologist wrote a paper in 1902 entitled *The Shroud of Christ*, which was presented to the French Academy of Sciences in support of the shrouds authenticity. Vignon wrote in the paper that he believed the image on the shroud was produced by a combination of body vapors and spices that were used to anoint the body during burial, which fermented, vaporized than projected an image onto the shroud.

Vignon pointed to the Bible to support his theory, saying that there were passages that clearly stated that Jesus body was anointed with an aloe, myrrh and olive oil. He believed that the aloe and oil were combined with natural ammonia-like vapors emanating from the body of Jesus. He suggested that the vapors emanating from the body caused a reaction that produced a chemical-like burn on the cloth in the image of Christ.

Vignon began to experiment to see if his hypothesis was correct. He had many attempts and failures at trying to recreate the negative image that he observed on the shroud. However, he did manage to achieve somewhat successful results, which produced stains similar to those seen on the shroud. He did this by soaking a cloth in oil, myrrh and aloes and exposing the cloth to a plaster mold doused in ammonia to see if the image of the cast transferred to the cloth.

Although there were stains visible on the cloth, in some ways similar to the Shroud of Turin, they were by no means clear images. Moreover, no matter how hard he tried he could not achieve the distinct lines that were apparent on the shroud that produced an almost picture perfect image of a man. Unfortunately for Vignon, many treated his theory with skepticism because he was unable to produce believable results. Many decades later, Vignon's theory would be totally discounted when under modern scientific examination, no evidence of any spices; aloes or oil could be found on the shroud.

Some investigators believed that the anatomical details of the image on the shroud were undoubtedly correct, believing that it gave weight to the authenticity of the shroud being a true and divine depiction of Christ.

One such investigator was a French anatomist and zoologist named Yves Delage, who happened to have paired up with Vignon in search of answers to their anatomical theories pertaining to the shroud image. The men determined that the image of the man could not have been an artistic representation because it was anatomically too accurate.

However, many scientists refuted the theory, stating that the image was anything but anatomically correct. In fact, measurements taken of the image of the shroud man found that many of the features were overly exaggerated, not symmetrical or highly abnormal. Some of the questioned features included the face and head that appeared to be too small and detached from the rest of the body, the arms were significantly uneven in length, there appeared to be no thumbs visible on the hands of the image and the hair appeared unnatural, almost drawn in certain areas.

Although some believed these inaccuracies merely made the image more lifelike being that we are not perfect, others believed that the figure was anatomically impossible. Intriguingly, many of the investigations made in the early part of the century were conducted without scientists or investigators being allowed to directly view the shroud. They had to work from photos or copies of the image.

Another highly investigated feature of the shroud was the pattern of blood. Because it was not allowed for the better part of the 20th century to conduct experiments on samples of the shroud, the major question revolved around whether the blood flowed in a natural pattern. One of the first investigators to tackle this problem was French surgeon and archeologist named Pierre Barbet.

Upon viewing the shroud at close inspection in 1933, Barbet noticed that the reddish bloodstains appeared more visible and stood out from the rest of the shroud. The color of the blood raised the first suspicious eyebrows concerning the shrouds authenticity. Instead of turning a dark brown color like aged blood normally does, the blood remained red.

Moreover, Nickell stated that the blood appeared picture-like as if paint or real blood had been deliberately and artfully placed on the shroud.

Interestingly, Barbet also noticed that some of the blood stains flowed in unusual, almost unnatural directions on the arms. However, he realized that the stains were consistent with ones arms being outstretched and then lowered, much like someone's arms who had been crucified and then let down. If the blood flow was an artist's representation, it was masterfully conceived and skillfully carried out. Yet, many believe that this fact only supports the theory that the image on the shroud is real and that of Christ. Whether it was real blood or not would remain a mystery until the later part of the 20th century.

Historical and Religious-Based Theories

For hundreds of years, there has been much speculation concerning the actual age of the cloth and whether it coincided with historical and biblical accounts. Scholars, religious bodies, historians and sindonologists (linen experts) concentrated on the Jewish burial of Jesus and early representations of Christ in an attempt to gain further insight. These areas have been of interest because understanding how Jesus was buried and how he had been historically represented provided valuable insight into the identity of the man in the shroud image, its date and origin.

One of the main arguments made by skeptics concerning the Turin Shrouds alleged holiness is that there is no mention of its existence, or at least the existence of one with the image of Christ, in the entirety of the New Testament. Many skeptics believe that if the shroud was indeed genuine, then it would have been mentioned in the Bible. Supporters of the shrouds authenticity claim that just because it wasn't mentioned in the Bible doesn't mean that it did not exist.

Another view that had been argued amongst shroud advocates and skeptics was the way in which Jesus was buried. According to the John 19:40 Jesus body was wound in linen clothes with the spices, as the manner of the Jews is to bury. Skeptics refer to the Bible when they refute the authenticity of the shroud because it is clearly stated that Jesus was wrapped in clothes in the plural not *a cloth* as the shroud depicts, being that an entire image is represented. Moreover, it is suggested that spices were used in preparing Jesus for burial, yet there was no evidence of spices on the Shroud of Turin during analysis in the latter part of the 20th century.

However, according to an article by Orthodox America titled *The Shroud of Turin: A Mystery Across the Ages,* it could have been that the Turin Shroud was merely a preliminary burial cloth to be replaced when full absolutions and anointings could be completed. Furthermore, the article suggested that because Jesus was prepared for burial in great haste there is even more likelihood that the preliminary burial cloth was used, at least until proper burial rites could have been observed, which involved the traditional use of a separate face cloth and body cloth. Although this could have been a possibility, there is no evidence in the Bible that suggested there was ever a preliminary shroud. Therefore, the argument remains unsubstantiated.

Another point brought forth by shroud advocates is that the weave of the cloth indicated the shroud was undoubtedly from the Middle East. Thus, further supporting their argument that the shroud was possibly from the area where Jesus once lived. Yet, skeptics claim that there is no precise way to determine in what exact region the cloth came from. Therefore, although the cloth could have originated in Jerusalem, it is just as likely that it came from some other Middle Eastern country. Moreover, they claimed that even if the shroud was from Jerusalem, the pattern of the weave was indicative of those used at a much later date, possibly from the Middle Ages and not from the era in which Jesus lived. If that were the case, it would explain why there had been no mention of a shroud with the image of Christ before that time.

If the shroud is from a later date, the entire theory of it being the burial cloth of Jesus must be entirely dismissed. There are those who believe that the mere image represented on the cloth is testimony to it having been produced centuries after the crucifixion of Christ. Most skeptics agree that although the man in the shroud was likely a representation of Jesus, it was one that was probably from the Middle Ages. Nickell further supported this theory when he stated that the depiction of Christ on the shroud was, merely characteristic of medieval Gothic art and quite unlike the earliest known representations of him from the third century, which depicted Christ as young, beardless and with cropped hair. Years later scientific tests would support the theory of the shroud being a product of the Middle Ages, a fact that forever changed the way in which many viewed the relic.

On Closer Inspection

On November 24, 1973, the exiled King Umberto, who owned the famous shroud, granted permission to Cardinal Pelligrino to allow a small group of eleven people to examine the relic on close inspection and gather samples for testing. However, there were strict orders that the entire examination remain secret. Moreover, Umberto decided that any of the findings were to be withheld from the public until the time was deemed suitable to reveal the results.

During the inspection of the cloth, Professor Gilbert Raes of the Ghent Institute of Textile Technology was allowed to collect two samples from the shroud to be examined under an electronic microscope. Another member of the secret commission, Swiss forensic criminologist Max Frei was granted permission to collect pollen samples from the cloth for later inspection. Their examinations would reveal important information concerning the make-up and possible origin of the cloth.

According to Gove, the samples taken by Raes showed that there were trace amounts of Egyptian cotton present in the make-up of the shroud. Wilson stated that the samples taken from Frei were found to have traces of pollen from plants indigenous to Israel and Turkey, suggesting that the shroud must have been exposed to the air in these countries.

Incredibly, Frei stated that there was a real possibility that the shroud originated from the time of Christ. However, Gove suggested that it was highly unlikely such information could be obtained from pollen samples. It would take much more sophisticated equipment to date the shroud. Other than Freis remarkable claim, nothing else of great significance was revealed concerning the cloth and all of the results were kept secret for approximately three years.

In the fall of 1978, a group of scientists formed a team whose main goal was to gather scientific data and perform experiments on the Turin Shroud. The undertaking would later be popularly referred to as STURP or the Shroud of Turin Research Project, Inc. Scientists working on STURP would eventually make history by performing the most detailed investigation ever conducted in the shrouds history.

Some of the members of STURP, including a group of 24 scientists from the United States, Switzerland and Italy, gathered together in Turin's Royal Palace in October 1978 to perform a five-day uninterrupted examination of the shroud that had mystified the world for so long. During the investigation the shroud was photographed extensively, x-rayed, unstitched for closer examination and vacuumed for dust and pollen samples. After 120 hours of gathering samples and inspecting the cloth with great scrutiny, the shroud was returned to its place behind the altar in the chapel.

That same year, world-renowned micro analyst and member of the STURP team, Walter McCrone began examinations on approximately thirty-two particle and fiber samples taken from various portions of the shroud. He studied the samples microscopically and came upon a startling conclusion. More than half of the samples taken from the shroud, including those from the areas of the body and where there was allegedly blood, were found to have a significant amount of pigment made up of iron oxide and tempera. Thus, McCrone's discovery suggested that the image was the work of an artist and likely not the work of divine intervention.

The news of the discovery sent ripples of panic through many of the STURP members whose analysis was still ongoing. McCrone claimed that, anybody who is emotionally wrapped up in the shroud should start to consider the possibility that he better relax his emotions. Wilson stated that some of STURP's members disagreed with McCrone's research methods and his conclusion, which eventually led to a rift between him and the team. In fact, not long after his discovery, he was allegedly dismissed from the project.

In 1980, the first scientific articles related to STURP's 1978 investigation were published in academic journals. According to Gove, the majority of the articles concluded that the evidence was against its being a painting. In fact, several of the STURP scientists confirmed that the samples analyzed by McCrone actually tested positive for blood.

Some shroud advocates believe this is proof enough that the cloth was indeed the genuine article and the burial shroud of Jesus. However, skeptics believed that the artist may have actually used a mixture of blood and pigment in order to achieve a more realistic effect. Regardless, the fact there was pigment and blood led many to further question its authenticity. It wasn't until the 1980's that more sophisticated techniques would lend greater insight into the age of the shroud and put to rest many of the arguments relating to its genuineness.

Revealing the Truth of the Shroud

Although STURP can be credited for gathering the largest quantity of data on the shroud, three independent laboratories were credited for gathering information concerning the age of the cloth. In April 1988, the three labs, one from Oxford University in England, one from the University of Arizona in the United States, and one from the Swiss Federal Institute of Technology in Zurich were given the first chance ever to test the shroud using radiocarbon dating techniques. The results of the tests stunned the world.

The three labs were permitted to obtain samples taken from the shroud, with the intention of conducting three separate and independent analyses. On October 13, 1988, the results from the three laboratories were revealed to the public. To the shock of many, the shroud was said to be dated from between 1260 and 1350 A.D. Newspaper headlines around the world branded the shroud a forgery and declared that the Catholic Church has accepted the results.

However, not everyone agreed with the results of the carbon dating tests. According to some scientists and shroud advocates, the reliability of carbon dating is not absolute, especially if there has been a chance of contamination of the samples. In an article written by Daniel Porter titled "The Resurrection Problem and the Shroud of Turin," it was suggested that the exactitude of the tests were questionable, that the samples were likely contaminated due to their having been handled by so many people over the centuries and that the samples taken from the shroud were believed to have come from patches likely sewed onto the shroud by the Savoy family.

Regardless of whatever facts are uncovered, many will continue to believe what they want concerning the authenticity of the shroud. Amazingly, no one has yet been able to successfully explain how the unique 3-D negative-like image on the shroud was constructed. In actuality that remains the biggest mystery.

3-D image of Shroud

To date, the shroud, which was bequeathed to the Catholic Church in 1983 following the death of King Umberto II, remains in its chapel in Turin. 1997 marked an eventful year for the shroud, when it was rescued once again from a fire in the cathedral. Luckily, the shroud sustained no damages.

No pigments, paints, dyes or stains have been found on the fibrils. X-ray, fluorescence and microchemistry on the fibrils preclude the possibility of paint being used as a method for creating the image. Ultra Violet and infrared evaluation confirm these studies. Computer image enhancement and analysis by a device known as a VP-8 image analyzer show that the image has unique, three-dimensional information encoded in it. Microchemical evaluation has indicated no evidence of any spices, oils, or any biochemicals known to be produced by the body in life or in death. It is clear that there has been a direct contact of the Shroud with a body, which explains certain features such as scourge marks, as well as the blood. However, while this type of contact might explain some of the features of the torso, it is totally incapable of explaining the image of the face with the high resolution that has been amply demonstrated by photography.

The basic problem from a scientific point of view is that some explanations which might be tenable from a chemical point of view, are precluded by physics. Contrariwise, certain physical explanations which may be attractive are completely precluded by the chemistry. For an adequate explanation for the image of the Shroud, one must have an explanation which is scientifically sound, from a physical, chemical, biological and medical viewpoint. At the present, this type of solution does not appear to be obtainable by the best efforts of the members of the Shroud Team. Furthermore, experiments in physics and chemistry with old linen have failed to reproduce adequately the phenomenon presented by the Shroud of Turin. The scientific concensus is that the image was produced by something which resulted in oxidation, dehydration and conjugation of the polysaccharide structure of the microfibrils of the linen itself. Such changes can be duplicated in the laboratory by certain chemical and physical processes. A similar type of change in linen can be obtained by sulfuric acid or heat. However, there are no chemical or physical methods known which can account for the

411

totality of the image, nor can any combination of physical, chemical, biological or medical circumstances explain the image adequately.

Thus, the answer to the question of how the image was produced or what produced the image remains, now, as it has in the past, a mystery.

We can conclude for now that the Shroud image is that of a real human form of a scourged, crucified man. It is not the product of an artist. The blood stains are composed of hemoglobin and also give a positive test for serum albumin. The image is an ongoing mystery and until further chemical studies are made, perhaps by this group of scientists, or perhaps by some scientists in the future, the problem remains unsolved.

A Startling Revelation

Based on recent studies of the shroud and previous examinations of it during the five-day scientific investigation in 1978, Dr. Raymond Rogers, a former member of the Shroud of Turin Research Project (STURP) and a retired physical chemist believed that the techniques used to date the artifact were flawed, Bijal P. Trivedi reported in April 2004 for the National Geographic Channel. Rogers recommended that there be a new scientific investigation, using more advanced technology and better samples to date the shroud. Carbon dating in 1988 dated the cloth to medieval times, thus discrediting the theory that it was Jesus burial cloth. However, Rogers alleged that there was a chance that it was actually much older.

Thus, Rogers conducted a new experiment to date the shroud, which he hoped would disprove the premise that it was from medieval times. In December 2003, Rogers received radiocarbon thread samples taken from the Turin shroud, which he closely scrutinized. He made a surprising discovery, which he published in a January 2005 article in the *Thermochimica Acta.*

Rogers found that the sample used in the 1988 investigation did indeed date to medieval times but the threads examined were from a patch, likely sewed on by nuns sometime around 1260 to 1390, in an effort to restore the shroud after it was damaged by fire. In fact, the rest of the shroud proved to be much older. According to a January 2005 Associated Press article, Rogers said he analyzed the amount of vanillin, a chemical compound that is present in linen from the flax fibers used to weave it, which is known to slowly disappear from the fiber over time at a calculated rate. The samples he studied had hardly any vanillin on them, indicating that the shroud was between 1,300-3,000 years old rather than around 700 years old as previously purported.

Rogers was further quoted in the article saying, The chemistry says it was a real shroud, the blood spots on it are real blood, and the technology that was used to make that piece of cloth was exactly what Pliny the Elder reported fort his time." Pliny the Elder was an ancient Roman scientist and author who lived between 23 and 79 AD. Based on Rogers's research and historical data, the shroud has been accurately dated to around the time of Christ. The discovery rekindled the age-old debate of whether the shroud was or was not the actual burial cloth used to wrap Jesus body. Chances are we will never know.

In June-July 2002, a major restoration of the Shroud of Turin was undertaken by its owners. All thirty of the patches sewn into the cloth in 1534 by the Poor Clare nuns to repair the damage caused by the 1532 fire were removed. This allows the first unrestricted view of the actual holes burned into the cloth by the fire. It appears that some of the most seriously charred areas surrounding the burn holes were also removed during the restoration, most likely to allow the Shroud to be properly resewn to the new backing cloth. The original backing cloth (known as the Holland Cloth) that was added at the same time as the patches was also removed and replaced with a new, lighter colored cloth, which can now be seen through the burn holes. Although the creases and wrinkles that had been previously evident on the Shroud are not visible in this photograph, I am assured by those who have seen the restored cloth that they are in fact, still there. These are critical because they can help determine how the cloth was folded over the centuries and constitute an important clue for historians.

Shroud of Turin (Dorsal Image) Reference Photographs

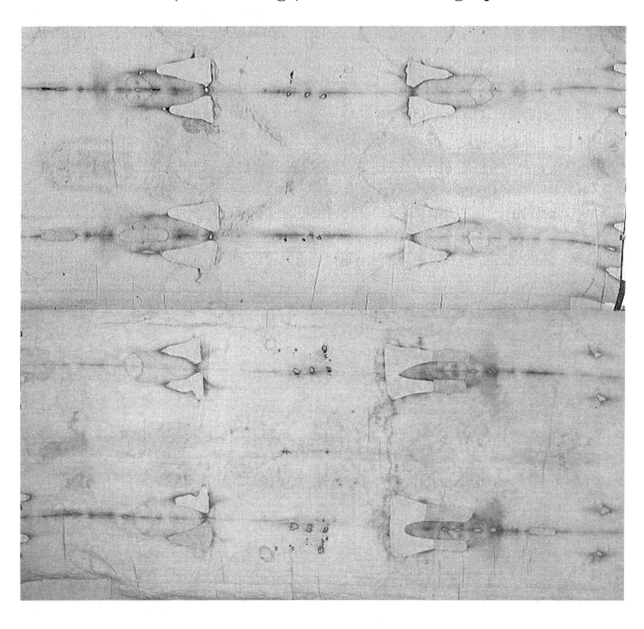

The image on the Shroud of Turin is very subtle. The closer you get, the less distinct it becomes. One of the best ways to look at the Shroud image is on a photographic negative. There, the light and dark values are reversed and the image appears more realistic and natural.

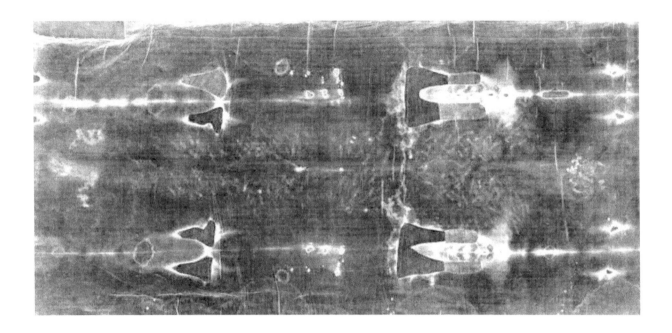

The Answers as to the origin of the shroud is still a mystery. To some it may be the burial cloth of Jesus, to others just a hoax. But no matter what it is, it is still a mystery that cannot be 100% explained.

In Closing

While it is the paranormal community's goal at large to turn all reported instances into the paranormal, it is *my personal hope* this simply will never be. While there are many answers yet to be discovered, I feel some things exist and happen simply because they can. Some things just shouldn't be too closely examined. As the old saying goes, *"Do not meddle in the affair of dragons, for you are crunchy and good with ketchup."*

What then shall we as a whole leave to mystery? I haven't quite figured that one out yet, but I do know that the world will become a very sad place when the last of life's mysteries are solved and there is nothing left to explore.